TIME CAPSULE

By Serafino Bianchi

Third Edition: April 2012

ISBN 978-0578033310
Printed in the United States of America
10 9 8 7 6 5 4 3 2

INTRODUCTION

I am a native Italian immigrated here to the US in the early 1960s. My early education was in Italy, but my high school and university studies were done in the US. I hold a degree in Civil Engineering from the University of Illinois; I am licensed in the state of California where I also hold a Real Estate Brokers' license.

I have always been interested in archeology and geology and how ancient civilizations achieved and subsequently lost knowledge. Our recorded history points to a cycle. We have records of great civilizations such as the Greeks, Romans, and Egyptians. These civilizations held knowledge that was later lost due to wars, barbarian takeovers and natural events. The period we call "the dark ages" was merely 1,000 + years ago.

The renaissance was the beginning of a new knowledge cycle and much of what was known 3,000 years earlier, had to be re-discovered.

If in our very short history we can actually account for these knowledge cycles, then, since the earth is billions of years old, we can postulate that there have been countless cycles where ancient advanced civilizations lived and died thousands or even millions of years ago, never to be discovered due of the vast time span that destroyed any possible evidence of their existence; thus my idea of an ancient civilization and the discovery of a time capsule.

I believe this concept to be unique and original and I hope you will enjoy reading it as much as I enjoyed writing it.

I would like to thank all of the people that have helped me and encouraged me to finish this project.

Serafino Bianchi

CHAPTER

ONE

The young geologist ducked under the wing of the small aircraft. Wind whipped and tugged at his golden blonde hair until it stood on end. Dry sand pelted at his bare face, arms, and legs. The roar of the wind made his ears ache. He looked at the older man who sat huddled in a lawn chair, his head buried in his hands. The geologist leaned down and wrapped him in a protective embrace. He would do anything to shield the man who had become like a father to him.

"What the hell's going on?" the man asked.

"I don't know," the geologist answered, "but it should be over soon." He turned his head to the left, in the direction of the noise, but a wall of sand blinded him. He squeezed his eyes tight and turned away. "Don't try to look at it," he yelled to the man he held wrapped in his arms. "Protect your eyes."

The airplane's wing offered little cover, but there was nowhere else to go. Nothing but miles of blistering sand stretched in every direction. And with the intensity of the wind pressure, there was no way they'd get the aircraft's door open. Waiting out the maelstrom was all they could do.

Where had the pilot gone?

The geologist blinked his eyes open. Tiny dry granules ripped at his corneas so that hot tears streamed down his face. He looked to the right, but there was no sign of humanity. Had the young pilot made it safely inside the airplane before the onslaught had started?

The raging storm of noise and sand went on mercilessly. The geologist's skin felt as if it were being licked by searing flames. His head pounded from the thumping tumult.

Who was doing this . . . and why?

In an instant, the thumping grew faster . . . and then faster again . . . until it turned into a deafening whir. The younger man thought his head might explode with the pressure. The older man groaned.

And then the sound started to move away, and the intense pain on his skin, the burning like a hundred thousand bee stings, finally subsided. Grains of sand fell from the air and landed at their feet. The two men remained still, huddled together like frightened children.

Within a few minutes the air was motionless and the desert was silent once again. The geologist slowly stood up, intense pain shooting across every inch of his ravaged skin. He brushed the stinging tears from his cheeks, tried to open his eyes, but squeezed them shut again. Leaning forward, he placed his hands on his knees and let the tears fall, allowing nature's liquid to rinse away the grit. He blinked a few times and, at last, could keep his eyes open for more than a few seconds. Holding up his hand to shield the blazing sun, he looked off in the distance. An indistinguishable aircraft, barely a dot in the distance, vanished over the horizon.

"Are you all right?" He asked the older man.

"Yes, I think so." The man hacked a few times and spat a mouthful of red sand back to the earth. "What the hell was that?"

"I think it was a helicopter."

"A helicopter? It felt like a damned cyclone," the man sputtered. "Who? . . .What? . . ."

"I have no idea."

The geologist walked away from the craft and stood at the precipice of a gaping hole in the sand that was about the radius of large helicopter blades. He gazed into the chasm and then out into the distance to the place where the craft had vanished over the horizon. Someone was very interested in what they were doing, and he was going to find out who . . . and why the hell they had found it necessary to sandblast a couple of innocent men in the middle of the desert.

He turned to walk back to the craft when a glint of light at the bottom of the hole caught his eye. He peered closer and spotted a small half-exposed metal object. He glanced over his should at the older man who was still sitting in the lawn chair attempting to brush the offensive sand from his profusely sweating skin.

The geologist stepped over the edge and slid down into the newly formed abyss until he reached the spot where the object lay. It was no longer in direct sunlight, but still glistened like a flawless diamond. The strange greenish gold orb almost glowed, as if someone had spent hours polishing it to perfection.

The young man knelt down and blew the sand from the shimmering metal until the entire object was exposed. He reached for it, but hesitated and pulled his hand away. What could the strange piece of metal possibly be? How had it gotten there? It was like nothing he'd ever seen in his geology classes.

It was foreign . . . alien.

He drew a deep breath. Whatever it was, there was no way he was leaving it behind to be once again swallowed up by the harsh Saharan desert. His hand trembled as he reached out. He picked up the object and turned it over in his hand. It was a perfectly shaped orb that gleamed on all sides.

He dropped it into his palm and, in an instant, a tingling sensation ran up his arm, into his neck, and rushed through his head. He threw the object to the ground, stepped back, and shook his hand as if he'd been burned. "What the hell," he murmured.

"What's going on?" the older man called.

The words seemed to rattle around in his brain. His lips moved, but he couldn't form a cohesive sentence. What had he been asked? He couldn't remember. He held his hands to his head and blinked his eyes, yet his mind wouldn't clear.

"Is something wrong?"

The words made some sense now. He could remember.

"Nothing's wrong . . . nothing at all," he called over his shoulder.

The tingling had lasted only a moment, but his brain seemed to be shrouded in a dense fog. He looked back at the object.

Now he for sure wasn't leaving it behind.

The scientist in him had to know what it was and the archeologist in him needed to know who had left it in the middle of the desert and why. He gave the object a quick poke with his index finger.

Nothing.

He poked at it again, this time letting his touch linger a moment longer. Still, nothing happened. Tucking his hand behind his t-shirt, he lifted the object through the cloth and then stood up. He maneuvered the thing into position and let it drop into the pocket of his khaki shorts.

No tingling. No head rush. Nothing.

He took a deep breath and climbed out of the hole.

"How are you doing?" he asked the older man as he approached the aircraft.

"I'm fine," the man answered, and then his mouth fell open. "What's wrong with your eyes?"

"What do you mean?"

"They look strange," the elder leaned forward and gazed into the young geologists eyes. "Your pupils, they're enormous?"

"Must be from the sand . . . the irritation," he mumbled.

"I don't see—"

The pilot popped open the airplane's door and came down the steps looking as fresh as when he'd picked them up that morning. "What's going on?"

The older man looked to the pilot. "I was just noticing—"

"Nothing," the geologist said.

"Sorry I couldn't get you fellows inside the plane in time," the pilot said, his voice sincere. "Are you both okay?"

"Yeah, we're okay," the younger man answered. "I'm just wondering who the hell just sandblasted us."

"Oh, that," the pilot said. "That would have been the Egyptian Department of Antiquity."

The geologist's heart slammed into his ribcage. He held his palm over the lump in his pocket and swallowed hard. Something extraordinary was going on in this godforsaken patch of desert, and he was determined to find out what it was.

CHAPTER

TWO

A warm May sun warmed Ralph Spencer's shoulders as he made his way across Harvard's sprawling campus. It was the end of a grueling academic year. Summer was near and he had yet to find the job of his dreams. He had enjoyed his time at Harvard, but he was now ready to contribute to the world.

In a few days he would interview with Calpetro; the giant oil conglomerate based in San Francisco that had operations all over the world. If only they would see how perfect he was for one of their international positions. Sure, his passion was archeology, but that degree could mean only professional starvation. Geology on the other hand gave him financial security. And what was to stop him from searching for ancient civilizations while drilling for oil? There was a lot of money in oil exploration, especially for a talented geologist. If he got the job at Calpetro, he could travel to the birthplace of humanity. Who was to say he couldn't participate in archeological digs along the way? Maybe he'd even make enough money to fund his own dig one day.

A tingle ran down his spine. Nothing got him more juiced than the idea of uncovering the mysteries of mankind. With two post-graduate degrees and an outstanding GPA, there was no one better qualified for the geology position at Calpetro. But with the economy in such disarray and most major corporations cutting costs in every department, he might have to fight for the job. He drew a deep breath and rolled his shoulders back. He would land that Calpetro job. He had to.

Spencer pulled his jacket around his neck to fend off the early morning San Francisco breeze. In a few hours the sun would break through the fog and it would be another glorious California day. He'd always dreamed of living in the city by the bay and now he had his chance. He'd had enough of the freezing Virginia winters, which was no better than the bitter cold he'd endured while attending college in New York and Massachusetts. He approached the Calpetro building with a smile. The structure was a glassy black affair that soared above the buildings around it.

A few minutes later a tall man with silver hair strode across the marble Calpetro lobby. "You must be Mr. Spencer." He shook Spencer's hand with a firm grip. "I'm John Fortica.

"Yes." He matched the man's grip. "I'm Ralph Spencer. Pleasure to meet you."

Fortica leaned back and stared at Spencer through piercing blue eyes. "I'm due at a site in Indonesia," he said, "but I stayed on an extra day to conduct your interview myself. Your credentials are impressive."

"Thank you." Spencer's face warmed. A top Calpetro exec had gone out of his way just to interview him. Did it mean the job was in the bag? Probably not, but maybe all he'd have to do was not blow it.

Fortica led Spencer to a small but elegant conference room with a round mahogany table, six executive chairs, and a magnificent view of the San Francisco Bay. There was nothing cheap about Calpetro. But then why should there be when they'd posted a seventeen billion net profit the previous year?

"Please sit down Mr. Spencer and tell me why you want to join our firm?" Fortica said with a tone of sincere curiosity. He gazed at Spencer with that same piercing intensity.

The guy was good. He must have had a lot of interviewing experience. To obtain the position Spencer coveted, he would have to be flawless in his persuasion. "Calpetro is the best in the business. I've done extensive research on every oil firm in the world," he said, "Calpetro has me intrigued. Yours is the only oil firm I know that will assign a geologist rather than a project engineer to a major drilling project. I think that's smart. But then, I am a geologist . . ." He chuckled. Fortica didn't seem to get the joke. It was as if he was in a stare down with Spencer. What was going on behind those intense blue eyes? Whatever it was, Spencer wasn't about to let it make him squirm. "Anyway," Spencer added, "my dream is to head up a major drilling operation. The idea of making new discoveries has always excited me."

"Which explains the archeology degree," Fortica said.

He broke into a smile. "Yeah, I suppose so." Spencer's mind raced ahead. How many digs could he fund with the money earned running a drilling operation? "Moving to San Francisco would be a great perk too. I could definitely live with the warm climate and gorgeous countryside."

Fortica's eyes shifted from Spencer to the spectacular view of the Golden Gate Bridge. His eyes then glazed over for a moment, as if he were checking some internal data stream. He finally turned back to Spencer and gave him a broad smile. "Oh, yes," he said, "I can understand that. I was born and raised here and wouldn't live anywhere else. Tell me about your research at Harvard . . ."

Fortica seemed to relax as he asked, and Spencer answered, dozens of questions. Once the staid executive got past interview mode, he chatted cheerfully with Spencer for more than an hour. He was a likable man with a singular devotion to the conglomerate that employed him.

Spencer exited the Calpetro building with lightness in his step. He loosened his blue and gold necktie then bounded down the stairs two at a time. Fortica was impressed, he was sure of it. He'd told Spencer that he would hear from the firm in a week or two. "If you are selected, you'll be flown back to San Francisco for a briefing and final details on the position," he'd said.

That night Spencer lay in his hotel room bed staring at the shadows on the ceiling. All he could think about was the job, San Francisco, and the possibility of a new life in California.

Early the next day he called Paul Seiber, his best friend from undergrad school who had moved to San Francisco two years earlier and made a small fortune in the microchip business. "I might be moving to the Bay Area," he said.

"You mean permanently?" Paul asked.

"Yep, although I may have to travel for my new job . . . at Calpetro," he announced with a laugh."

"No shit? Calpetro?"

"Well," Spencer said, "I haven't been offered the job yet, but I feel pretty damn good about yesterday's interview."

Two weeks later Spencer sat in his tiny Massachusetts apartment, half-packed boxes at his feet. What would he do if the Calpetro job didn't come through? He'd been so certain that he'd be hired, he hadn't made any contingency plans. Yet here he was, two weeks had gone by, and he still didn't have an answer. No one had better credentials than he did. Calpetro would be crazy not to hire him. Why hadn't they called?

When the telephone rang the next day, Spencer jumped out of his chair, knocking a cup of hot coffee onto his laptop keyboard. "Damn!"

He grabbed the cordless and punched the green button. "Hello?"

"Mr. Ralph Spencer?"

A lump formed in his throat. It was the call he'd been waiting for; he knew it. "Yes," he said.

"This is Deb Fisher calling from Calpetro headquarters. I'm Mr. Fortica's assistant. Your flight to San Francisco is at nine on Monday the twenty-fourth. We've arranged a room for you at the Fisherman's Wharf Marriott. Your briefing will be at two the next day. Is this all acceptable?"

Spencer gazed around the room at the worn gold sofa, scuffed coffee table, and twenty-five year old console television, all of which he'd lugged from one forgettable college apartment to the next for the last eight years. In that moment he made up his mind. If he landed the Calpetro job, he'd leave it all behind and start fresh in San Francisco. He smiled. "Yes, completely acceptable."

He had promised to meet Paul at Ghirardelli Cafe for a cappuccino. The evening was calm and clear. An assortment of sailboats dotted the San Francisco Bay and a puff of white fog hovered over the Golden Gate Bridge. From Spencer's vantage point high up on one of San Francisco's famous hilltops, it was a spectacular sight. He had always imagined the sea as a turbulent predator, its huge waves ready to swallow any sailboat without a moments notice. But today the bay was as smooth as an oil slick and the faraway sailboats slid peacefully through the water. He sighed and let the calm of it all wash over him. He could get used to this new sense of freedom. It was a freedom inspired by nature and guided by the skill of man; it fit him like a well-worn suit.

"Spencer, my man."

He would have known his friend's familiar voice anywhere. After all, they had been roommates at Cornell for three years during his undergrad stint. He turned around and Paul engulfed him in a bear hug.

"Long time no see," Paul said. "How was the flight? And the job, did you get the job?"

"I'm due for a briefing this afternoon. I'm pretty sure it's in the bag."

"Congrats, my man," Paul smiled and shook his head. "You look great. Getting out in the real world must agree with you."

"Yeah, college has been a long stretch, but I think it was all worth it . . . I mean, Calpetro . . . can you believe it?"

"Yeah, man," Paul said with a wide grin. "I really can."

Spencer gazed out over the Bay. "God, it's beautiful here. Have you ever seen so many sailboats at one time?" He turned to Paul. "Do they have rules of the road out there?"

Paul shrugged. "I'm not a sailor, I just appreciate the view." He gave Spencer's shoulder a double slap, "Welcome to California, man, it's great to have you here."

Spencer gave his friend a quick embrace. "You, too," he said. "You know, I've heard this city saves Calpetro millions in salary and benefits. Once prospective employees see this view, they're hooked for life."

Paul nodded and smiled. "Probably true. I know I'm hooked."

Spencer and Paul chatted over cappuccinos at the Ghirardelli Cafe and then strolled the city streets heading nowhere but taking in all the sites and sounds. Even the smell of the city, a combination of the pervasive salty fog and humanity, seemed to carry with it an exotic quality. When they parted ways, Spencer walked to the Calpetro building to meet the man who he was sure would be his new boss.

Like the main lobby, the thirty-fifth floor of Calpetro headquarters was all marble and deep-colored wood. A steady flow of people walked back and forth along the long carpeted hallway that led to the various executive offices. Within minutes a cheerful secretary guided him to the office of the man in charge of worldwide drilling explorations. His monstrous office was covered with mahogany paneling and decorated with colorful geological maps from all over the globe.

William McPearson was a legend at Calpetro. Spencer had read an article in Time about how McPearson had headed up the discovery of the largest oil deposit in South Africa. The fact that this powerful man would now be guiding his career gave him a chill. Would he measure up to McPearson's expectations?

McPearson came into the room and smiled at Spencer. He wasn't what Spencer had expected. The man's large belly hung over his belt and his movement across the room was closer to a waddle than a walk. He had a jolly countenance and well-lined eyes that sparkled when he smiled. Put him in a red suit and beard, and he'd have made a great Santa Claus.

McPearson picked up a file with Spencer's name on it. "John was impressed with you, Mr. Spencer, and I can see why. Let's see . . . dual doctoral from Harvard, undergrad at Cornell . . . geology and Archeology."

Spencer's face warmed and he ran his finger under the collar of his shirt. "I think the two sciences go hand in hand," he said.

"Indeed they do." McPearson gave the file another glance then threw it on the desk. He dropped his large frame into the executive chair behind his cluttered desk and motioned for Spencer to sit. "We know you have the desire to head a drilling operation someday," he said. "We here at Calpetro pride ourselves on taking worthwhile risks. We believe that you, Mr. Spencer, are a worthwhile risk. I'm authorized to offer you a position here in my department as a lead geologist."

McPearson slid a piece of paper across the desk. Spencer all but gasped when his eyes landed on the dollar figure at the bottom of the page. The salary being offered was nearly double what he'd hoped for and far more than he'd been willing to accept. McPearson handed him a second sheet of paper that outlined an extensive bonus package. His head began to swim. It was all happening so fast and the offer was beyond his wildest dreams.

"We would like you to report here for work July first. Is this an acceptable arrangement?" McPearson asked.

"Yes, sir," he said as a warmth of excitement and relief washed over him.

After spending a good part of the afternoon with his new boss answering dozens of questions about himself, his family, and his background, McPearson stood up and shook his hand. "I like to get to know my people," McPearson said. "Let me show you around and introduce you to some of the other department heads."

Spencer stood up and smiled. He had made it. He was now a part of the inner circle of one of the world's most prestigious oil companies.

McPearson smiled his infectious smile and clapped Spencer on the back. "I'm looking forward to working with you, Spencer. I'll have my secretary put everything in writing. It'll be ready for you by the end of the day. Enjoy California and we'll see you on July first."

Spencer admired the Napa Valley countryside out of the winery's huge picture window. Paul had insisted on showing him some of his favorite sites in the Bay Area. The winery was already on his favorites list. He tipped his half-full wine glass toward Paul. "This is my last glass," he said with a chuckle. "I came to enjoy the scenery, not get sloshed." He let his gaze fall on the golden hillside in the distance. "This countryside is more beautiful than I imagined."

Paul stretched his legs and interlaced his hands behind his head. "Yeah," he said with a sigh, "we're pretty damn lucky to live here."

Spencer took a sip of the ruby liquid in his glass and savored its rich, smooth flavor. "By the way, can I get you to help me find an apartment near my office. I want a short commute and you know the area a helluva lot better than I do."

"Sure. I know of a great complex near Fisherman's Wharf. It'd be perfect for you. I think it's a five-minute walk to Calpetro."

Spencer settled into the California lifestyle with ease. He reported for his first day of work with a golden tan and a smile. He was assigned an office at the far end of the long hallway with a center window overlooking the bay. The office had apparently belonged to George Bellici, one of Calpetro's senior partners. Bellici had died suddenly of a heart attack. Spencer heard the story from virtually everyone at the firm within his first week. Apparently, he had some big shoes to fill.

McPearson's Research and Development department consisted of twelve geologists, half dozen assistants, seventeen soil engineers, and forty-two reconnaissance technicians, not to mention the secretarial staff.

"You got lucky, Mr. Spencer. This is the only office available. I hope you can live with it." McPearson chuckled at his own joke and shuffled over to the window.

Live with it? He'd never even dreamed of such a luxurious office.

"You'll be taking over some of Bellici's work," McPearson added. "This used to be his office until he died last month. It was a real loss to the firm."

"I was sorry to hear about Bellici's passing. Thank you for this opportunity. I'll do my best."

McPearson gazed at him, his brow furrowed. "I believe you will, Mr. Spencer, I believe you will." He walked to the doorway and turned back. "The gang here calls me Bill, I hope you'll do the same. We'll get together later, once you've had a chance to settle in."

"Sounds good," Spencer said, "And everyone calls me Spencer. You can drop the mister."

McPearson nodded and smiled.

A moment later a petite young brunette wearing a pale yellow dress and high-heeled white sandals walked through the door. She held a steno pad in one hand and a pen in the other. "Hi, I'm Sarah Nugent, your secretary," she said with a slight southern twang.

"I take it you're not from around here." Spencer shook her hand and smiled.

"Alabama," she said. "Moved here six years ago with my husband. He's a computer engineer, but we're divorced now . . . I've been trying to lose the accent since I got here. Guess I haven't been too successful, huh?" She said with a shrug. "Anyway, I'm assigned to three geologists here and I can help you with whatever you need. Today I'll be helping you get set up, answer any questions you might have regarding office procedures…stuff like that."

"Well, Sarah, I'm Ralph Spencer, the new geologist."

"I know who you are." She smiled. "Great office by the way. Lucky you."

Spencer smiled and followed her gaze out the window. The Bay glistened in the late morning sunshine and small puffs of fog floated above the water. "Yeah, pretty lucky," he said, turning back to Sarah.

"Bill is a stickler when it comes to procedure." she warned. "He says documentation is the backbone to a successful division. We have to justify all our expenditures carefully since Accounting is convinced that our only purpose is to waste company money."

Apparently even at a progressive company like Calpetro, divisions not producing revenue were looked down upon.

"Who do they think is responsible for the oil finds anyway?" Sarah added. "After all, without R and D there would be no Calpetro."

After a week with Sarah at his side, Spencer was grateful to have her on his team. She was organized, witty, and quick on her feet. Sarah's high energy was contagious, and she had a knack for keeping the department ticking. Her workstation was centrally located, easily accessible, and well organized. A picture of her two young boys was prominently displayed on the corner of her desk for all to see. Being a single mom in the high-priced Bay Area was tough, but that was Sarah, strong and proud. Her knowing gaze often gave Spencer a secure feeling. He wasn't sure why, but she sometimes reminded him of his mother.

Spencer's assignment included the analysis of aerial maps taken by a reconnaissance plane. The aerial data on his first big assignment was taken over North Africa near the southern tip of Egypt. The photo quality was astounding. The pictures were taken the previous November over a period of three weeks when the weather had been exceptionally clear. The reconnaissance material also included several infrared photos taken by the space shuttle. Calpetro had paid handsomely for them, but the cutting-edge technology could make the difference between millions of dollars in profit and thousands of miles of useless sand.

Spencer scanned the infrared mapping. The images made using heat detection would require Spencer's well-trained eye to be deciphered. He would analyze the topographical heat intensity map and chart all the heat sources.

Sarah dropped a large box on his desk. "We have two more boxes of photographs coming."

"Nothing like diving in head first." Spencer laughed. He had a long, tedious job ahead of him. "It's a good thing I love my work."

For the next several weeks Spencer buried himself in his new job. He wanted to make a great impression and spent most of his time at the office. He had neglected to return several calls from Paul. He was too busy to eat, let alone spend long evenings in bars drinking and chasing women. Besides, his work excited him. He didn't need any distractions right now. The touch of mystery, the feeling that he was a detective trying to solve a case, enticed him into the office at all hours. The photographs were like a crime scene; they contained all the answers . . . but where?

Aided by one of the largest databases in the world, Spencer reviewed old photos from other successful sites and compared them to his pictures. Calpetro had an extensive computer system. All previous site pictures were digitized and stored in the computer's memory banks.

Spencer spent each day comparing photos until his eyes could no longer focus. Bill McPearson made regular visits to his office. They chatted and compared ideas over multiple cups of coffee and piles of aerial photographs.

"I'm telling you, Spencer, I worry about our profession sometimes," McPearson said, shaking his head and scowling. "Some people believe the oil's going to run out soon . . . practically any day now."

"I wouldn't worry about that. This country relies on oil reserves. I doubt there's any chance it will run out in our lifetime. Of course," he added, "that's no excuse for not staying up with alternative energy technology."

McPearson stood up, stretched, and yawned. "I suppose you're right."

"Hey, Bill." Spencer typed a security code into his computer. "Before you go, do you have a minute to look at something?"
"Sure, what's up?" McPearson ambled around to Spencer's side of the desk.

The last big oil find for Calpetro was George Bellici's dig three years earlier. McPearson needed a break soon or he'd have the suits breathing down his neck. Spencer had held off on showing him the Egyptian photos until he was sure about what he was looking at. But why not get his boss's point of view now? It was too exciting for him to keep to himself any longer. Besides, McPearson was known for handing out extra large bonuses for the whole floor after a find. Spencer clicked on a large aerial photo of the Sahara Desert. He then dragged an infrared image of the same region and superimposed it over the map.

"How did you do that?" Bill asked, his brow furrowed.

"I had this infrared photo taken by the space shuttle back in July and then loaded it into this new imaging software." He pointed at the thirty-two inch monitor on his desk. "I remapped all of the shading on it and superimposed it over the latest aerial map . . ." Spencer's heart was thudding against his ribcage. "Take a good look at the composite of the two maps," he said to McPearson. "Tell me what you see."

Spencer chewed on a hangnail and his knee bobbed at a rapid pace. McPearson ran his finger over the screen as he zeroed in on areas of interest. When superimposed, the two maps created a three dimensional view of the terrain and the ground below.

"I've never seen such detail," McPearson said finally. "Is this for real?"

"Absolutely. It's the latest in GPS. This map is accurate to within an inch. It came from three different sources." Spencer brushed a tiny speck of dust from the screen. "Aerial photos, space shuttle infrared, and satellite positioning ensures the congruence of the two maps."

"If this is accurate, then there's something . . . unusual . . . here." Bill pointed to a large shaded area that appeared to be far below the surface.

"Glad you concur with my findings," Spencer said, a quiver of excitement in his voice, "I've been looking at that spot for days. The infrared shows a large heat source, yet the aerial map has no evidence of it. When superimposed, we get the results seen here." He circled the shaded area with his finger. "Something's troubling me, though. The shaded area appears to be void. See there?" Spencer ran his finger along barely visible lines in the map. "These contours are too far apart to establish evidence of an oil mass."

McPearson stared at the map, several deep lines furrowing his brow. He scanned the image a second time. "If that's a void . . ." He looked at Spencer with wide eyes. "Why, it must be the largest cave ever discovered at that depth. Christ, it's massive." He ran a finger along the darker image. "It must be at least two hundred miles long by twenty miles wide. Any idea how deep it is?"

"Not yet, I just sent the latest data up to the computer lab for depth analysis. I should have an answer tomorrow."

"I don't know what we're looking at just yet, but there's got to be oil down there, and if there is, we're looking at the largest African deposit ever."

Spencer arrived at his Calpetro office before dawn the next day. It was a Friday and he had promised Paul he would spend the weekend Christmas shopping in Palo Alto.

That afternoon he got the answer he was waiting for. The average depth of the oil mass, if that's what it was, was about two and a half miles. He spent the rest of the day preparing his final report for Bill McPearson, and with Sarah's help, was able to finish before the end of the day.

On his way out of the office that night, he requested a full staff meeting for Monday at nine sharp. By that morning, the word was out that Spencer had called a staff meeting and that he was on the verge of discovering a large oil deposit. The department crackled with excitement when he arrived. The secretaries, assistants, and even the mail clerks were whispering. The news had attracted half dozen execs from operations, along with John Fortica, and McPearson offered them the best seats. The conference room was equipped with the most sophisticated multimedia equipment available, and large computer monitors, strategically placed, allowed for teleconferencing anywhere in the world.

Calpetro demanded the tightest security, especially for the R&D division. If there was a leak about a possible discovery, the result could be disastrous. Competition for oil was fierce and an information breach could break even a well established company like Calpetro. McPearson had requested that only invited parties attend the presentation and anyone without clearance was turned away. Spencer and Sarah arrived with a laptop fully loaded with the aerial maps. He started with a PowerPoint presentation that explained the procedure he had undertaken with the infrared map. He then superimposed the map over the aerial photograph. "As you see here, when the infrared mapping is superimposed precisely over the aerial data, the computer program that I developed shows a three dimensional resolution below grade."

There were a few gasps and murmurs in the room. Clearly his procedure had impressed those who understood its significance.

McPearson wore a pleased, if slightly smug, expression. Spencer's face warmed. In less than a year he had impressed some of the top execs at Calpetro. What more could he ask for? "On Friday our computer lab used sound waves to confirm the depth of this possible deposit at about two and a half miles from the surface." Spencer paused. "I'm optimistic about this discovery, but I still have a number of questions. I'd like to take a closer look."

"What kind of questions, Mr. Spencer?" McPearson asked. He was obviously impressed with Spencer's presentation and struggling to hide his enthusiasm. And why not, this could be one of the company's biggest oil finds.

"Sir, I'd like your permission to go to Africa to see the site for myself. I'm concerned that the infrared shaded area might be a large void and not actual fossil remains. If that were the case, the two hundred-mile long, twenty-mile wide void would be the largest cave ever discovered at that depth. There's no telling what might be down there."

Spencer sat down and McPearson walked to the front of the room. "This discovery must be treated very carefully. I'll implement extra security immediately." McPearson glanced at his superiors and then walked over to where Spencer sat. "I'm impressed with what Mr. Spencer has been able to do since joining this firm, and—"

"Way to go, Spencer," someone called from the back of the room. His team members broke into a round of applause. The back of Spencer's neck warmed. He had never been publicly praised before. He turned around and waved at his peers. Spencer stole a quick glance at the executives in the front row. They were all clapping politely.

McPearson raised his hands. "And, I'm going to give Mr. Spencer my one hundred percent support." He looked at Spencer and smiled. "You'll be on a plane to Africa as soon as possible."

Spencer's heart pounded. He ran his fingers through his hair. He couldn't contain his happy grin, but then again, why should he? His career was moving forward faster than he'd ever dreamed possible. Two junior geologists patted his back. "Congrats, Spencer," said one.

"I'll need to fly over the area with the local reconnaissance crew that took the original shots," Spencer said to McPearson.

McPearson turned off the projector. "No problem. We'll meet at three today to finalize the details."

The Calpetro executives stood up and walked over to Spencer. The first, an Asian man in a navy suit, put out his hand. "Good job, Mr. Spencer, glad to have you on the Calpetro team."

"Thank you, sir." He shook hands with each executive in turn. John Fortica stood back a moment and gave Spencer his sharp, assessing look. The silver-haired man could be a formidable presence when he wanted to be. He stepped forward and offered his hand, a twitch of a smile playing on his lips. "Looks like I made the right decision in hiring you," Fortica said, laying his hand on Spencer's shoulder. "You know that Calpetro's counting on you?" He shook Spencer's hand. "Keep up the good work."

Spencer frowned as he watched Fortica walk out the door. The man's last statement had sounded more like a warning than a compliment. But why?

CHAPTER

THREE

The enormous jet touched down at the Cairo airport. McPearson glanced over at Spencer, who was looking out the window, his green eyes wide like those of a schoolboy. He'd taken an unexpected liking to the tall young man whose earnest optimism had captivated his entire department, he was proud of what Spencer had accomplished in such a short time. He hadn't intended on tagging along to Egypt, but he'd gotten caught up in Spencer's enthusiasm. McPearson, like Spencer, was a workaholic, not because he loved to work, but because he loved the work he did. Even when he wasn't working, he was planning projects or researching future opportunities. He took his first look out the window at Cairo. Waves of heat rose off the tarmac and everything was covered in red sand. Two dark-skinned men waved the jet into the gate. This was Egypt, the cradle of modern civilization, the keeper of mankind's greatest mysteries; it was the ultimate dream for archeologists like Spencer.

A droplet of sweat trickled from McPearson's forehead and slid down his nose. He swatted it away. His enthusiasm for the region was already waning. Desolate, godforsaken, and damn hot, that was his take on Egypt.

Jeff Miller, the young pilot assigned to the aerial reconnaissance of the North African region, greeted McPearson and Spencer as they exited Customs. McPearson had interviewed Jeff a year earlier. He liked the man. He read over Miller's file on the flight over and then shared it with Spencer. Jeff Miller was employed by Calpetro, but had not been in the States for over eight months. His assignment had been exclusively in the Egyptian region. He'd been flying practically every day since his arrival. Jeff was twenty-nine, rugged, intelligent, and careful. He once navigated an emergency landing that had saved the lives of a dozen crewmembers and had since become known as "Steady Miller" among his fellow aviators.

"The reconnaissance plane is at a small airport just outside the city," Jeff said. "We'll go there by car and then I'll take you to the site." By the time they boarded the small reconnaissance plane, McPearson was drenched in sweat. He pulled a handkerchief from his pocket and wiped his face. How could Spencer and Miller both look so damned comfortable? He heaved his weight up the steps, fell into the too-small seat, and then strapped the seatbelt around his waist. Maybe when he got home he'd start that diet the doc had given him.

Jeff handed him and Spencer each a headset. "We'll be able to talk through these," he said.

Jeff climbed into the cockpit. A few minutes later his voice came through the headset. "We are ready for take off, gentleman." The plane raced down the runway and within minutes was soaring above the desert, "Here's your chance to see Egypt from a great vantage point," Jeff said.

Spencer had given Jeff exact coordinates for the dark void on the infrared overlay.

"Can you land there?" Spencer asked, pointing at a long stretch of sand.

"No problem. Here in the desert the only hazards are sand pockets and the wind," Jeff answered.

"Circle over a couple of times first." Spencer said. "I want to take some more aerial photos in this specific zone."

"Are the plane's cameras ready?" McPearson asked.

"Always," Jeff replied.

"Okay, set the elevation at six-thousand feet for the first pass, and then let's take it at four-thousand feet and a final at two-thousand."

"Will do, Mr. Spencer."

"Hey, forget the mister. Everyone call's me Spencer, all right?"

"Sure, Spencer, here we go."

Ten minutes later they were on the ground. Jeff's desert experience had helped him choose a flat area where he could land with relative ease.

McPearson stepped out of the plane. "Hell . . . that's where we've landed. This sun will cook me alive. I mean, stick a fork in me, I'm done."

Spencer and Jeff looked at each other and laughed.

Jeff put his hands on his hips and looked around. There was nothing but sand in every direction. "What the hell do you expect to find here anyway?"

Spencer glanced at McPearson.

Should they tell Jeff the truth? The man did work for Calpetro and, if they decided to dig, he'd be putting in long hours on the project. He nodded to Spencer.

Spencer grinned and turned to Jeff. "We are standing on what we all hope is a very large oil deposit," he said, his face flushed and eyes gleaming. "It might be more than two miles underground, but we know something's there. I'm looking for abnormalities on the surface. If we find them, we've got additional evidence to corroborate our map data. Sometimes pressure builds in the underground location and the only way to release it is for the oil to slowly find its way up and above the surface. I know it's unlikely, considering that, at this point at least, we're estimating the find at two miles, but we have to check."

The breathless words had tumbled out of Spencer's mouth. Damn, the man was wound up about this project. Maybe wound a little too tight?

"I'm also looking for ground movements," Spencer said. "You see, over the centuries, with such a large mass of liquid below, ground motions such as earthquakes can produce surface displacements that are characteristic of a hidden wealth of underground oil."

"Well, Spencer," Jeff replied, with a smile and a clap on the back. "That was way more than I needed to know, but good luck."

Spencer laughed. "Thanks, luck is something we just may need."

McPearson sat down in a folding chair under the plane's wing, the only shade to be found for at least twenty miles. He alternated between sipping water from a canteen and dabbing sweat from his brow. "Godforsaken place," he muttered.

Spencer held a small video cam. Using the satellite positioning system, he scanned the surface over a three-hundred-sixty degree circle. He also took still photos using the same technique. He then used a magnetometer to record the variations in geomagnetic intensity.

"I'm glad you're up to speed on all this new-fangled technology," McPearson said. "I can't keep up. Must be getting close to retirement time."

"Come on, Bill, you'd be bored in a day," Spencer said.

"I think I could manage to find—" A blast of wind slammed into his face and sucked the breath out of his lungs. A thunderous thump, thump, thump pounded at his ears. He dropped his forehead to his knees and held his head in his hands. A moment later the protective warmth of Spencer's body enveloped him.

"What the hell's going on?" McPearson yelled.

"I don't know, but it should be over soon . . . Just don't try to look. Protect your eyes."

McPearson struggled to breathe. His every inhale was laden with dust and sand. How much more of this could he take?

The tumult seemed to last for an hour, but was probably only a few minutes. By the time it ended and he was able to look up, the craft that had stirred the desert into a wild frenzy was vanishing in the distance. Spencer had brushed himself off and gone off to investigate. McPearson didn't expect him to find much. They were in the middle of the most desolate desert on earth. What could be out there? But then again, what were those idiots in the jumbo helicopter trying to prove? All he could do was sit tight, hack up sand, and try to catch his breath. Every attempt to brush the grit from his damp body was futile. He stuffed his handkerchief in his pocket and gave up.

A moment later Spencer walked back toward the aircraft. He seemed shaken and he had the oddest look on his face.

"How are you doing?" Spencer asked.

"I'm fine . . ." McPearson answered. But there was something very not fine about Spencer. "What's wrong with your eyes?"

"What do you mean?"

"They look strange . . . Your pupils, they're enormous."

Spencer mumbled something about the sand and irritation. But no, it was something more.

Jeff poked his head out of the airplane and apologized for not getting them inside in time. "Egyptian Department of Antiquity," Jeff said, "local patrol . . . they're checking up on us to make sure we're not digging without permits."

Spencer stood just a few feet from them, but by the eerie look in his eyes he was clearly a million miles away. Something had happened to him out in the desert, but what?

"The Egyptian government is super protective when it comes to archeology," Jeff said. "They're always patrolling this region to discourage unauthorized digs."

"I'm finished with the photos anyway. Let's get out of here." Spencer said.

McPearson peeled his damp shirt away from his skin. He'd get to the bottom of what had happened to Spencer later, when they were in a nice air-conditioned lounge. "Best news I've heard all day," he said. "Let's go."

Spencer stepped out of the shower and toweled his hair. A hailstorm of fine sand fell to the tiled floor. He dropped the towel and stepped back in the shower, this time washing his hair twice. That damned helicopter had coated him with sand. It had somehow gotten into every conceivable part of his body. The discomfort was worth it, though, to stand on what would possibly be the biggest oil find in decades. He glanced at the glistening object sitting on the bathroom counter. And to find such an unusual artifact was beyond his imagination. He should really turn it over to the Egyptians, but that would put an end to the dig before it ever started. Plus, he wanted to find just what the artifact was for himself.

Later that evening he relaxed at the hotel bar and was joined by Jeff. McPearson had chosen to nap in his air-conditioned room. A group of loud Americans wandered in and straddled the stools at the bar. Jeff gestured to a table on the patio beside the pool. Spencer nodded and picked up his beer. The two men walked out into the night air. It was still warm, but a light breeze stirred the palm fronds above them. Jeff slid into a chair and looked at Spencer with bright eyes and a crooked smile. "So, Spencer, how do you like Egypt?"

"Godawful hot. But I love it. I'm here doing geological work, but my first love is archeology. What better place than Egypt for an archeologist?" He leaned forward and took a sip of his beer. "Jeff, I'll tell you in confidence, I think the zone we surveyed today will qualify for a drilling project . . . a big one."

"Wow, really?" Jeff ran his hand through his hair and desert granules showered onto his lap. "I've given up fighting the sand months ago," he said with a boyish grin.

"I gotcha." Spencer brushed his fingers through his air and sand fell to the table. "And that's after three showers," he laughed, brushing the particles to the floor.

"Have you told McPearson about your findings?" Jeff asked.

"I need to fully analyze today's data, of course, but I'm optimistic that something is down there. I have to be sure before I discuss it with McPearson."

"I'll keep my fingers crossed. There'd be a bonus in it for me, and I could sure use it."

The two men chatted for about an hour. A full moon had risen and was reflected off the still pool water. The bar patio wasn't crowded, but a few people wandered outside trying to cool off in the night air. A tall, dark-haired woman in a long white shirt approached the deep end of the pool. She kicked off her sandals and tucked them under a chaise lounge. She shrugged the shirt off of her tan shoulders and threw it across the chair. She wore a black one-piece bathing suit that showed off her long, sexy legs. She hesitated at the edge of the pool and then took a graceful dive forward, leaving rings of rippling water in her wake. Jeff was rambling on about some late-night television show that featured naked Egyptian women. Spencer ignored him. He watched for the woman to reappear. The water grew still. Where was she? He waited a few more seconds, fighting off the instinct that was telling him something was wrong. She'd been under for at least thirty seconds. He stood up and rushed to the pool's edge, knocking his beer over on the way. The woman was floating face down in the pool. A thin trickle of blood meandered through the water. She must have hit her head on the bottom. He dove in and turned her over, pulling her to the pool's edge. He touched her neck, feeling for a pulse. A tremor, like an electric shock, ran through his body and the hair on the back of his neck stood up. He pulled his hand away.

What the hell?

"Call an ambulance!" he yelled out. "Medical emergency! Is there a doctor here?"

A tall thin man in a cotton shirt and tailored pants rushed to Spencer's side. "I'm a doctor," he said.

He was one of the Americans who had been sitting at the bar for hours. The man stunk of stale liquor. He could only hope he wasn't too smashed to help her.

The doctor began resuscitation and soon the woman was

coughing up pool water. Spencer retreated to his table, his eyes full of concern for the strange, beautiful woman. He tried not to stare as the doctor led her past his table toward the emergency vehicle that had pulled up in front of the bar. As they passed, the woman leaned over and laid her hand on his shoulder. "Thank you," she whispered.

Her fingers were like ice, but there was no shock or tremor and the hair on his neck stayed in place. She looked into his eyes and smiled. Her eyes were black, like deep, dark pools. If he let himself fall into those eyes, he too, might be at risk of drowning.

Early the next morning Spencer was awakened to loud knocking

"Get up. I have a surprise for you."

Still half asleep, Spencer opened the hotel room door. He looked at McPearson through squinted eyes. "Is something the matter?"

"No, Mr. Archeologist. I've got something to show you. So don't just stand there, get dressed. Come on, this is my treat."

After a quick breakfast at the hotel, the pair approached the first taxi from the lineup outside the hotel. "Do you have air conditioning?" McPearson asked the driver.

"Yes, yes, get in," the man answered in a heavy accent.

To the pyramids," McPearson said.

Spencer's jaw fell slack.

"C'mon, don't look so surprised. I think we both deserve a break after yesterday, and we've got the whole day free."

Five minutes into the drive, the air in the car became stifling. McPearson looked as if he'd just come out of a swimming pool. "What about the air conditioning?" Spencer asked the driver.

The man shrugged his shoulders, mumbled something in Egyptian and drove on. "Do you want to go back?" he asked McPearson.

"No, no, let's just roll down the windows." McPearson said with a forced smile.

Spencer preferred the open air anyway. For the first time, he was able to take notice of the Egyptian charm. He even waved to some of the locals as they rode by on camels. McPearson pointed to the great pyramid of Caofes, but signaled for the driver to keep going.

"This is why I studied archeology." Spencer shouted as they

bounced over the pot-holed road. "All my life I dreamed of this day. Here stands one of the greatest mysteries of our world, still unsolved. Many theories have been put forth, but even today with our technology, we are not able to duplicate this magnificent feat."

McPearson nodded with a stiff smile and patted a limp handkerchief to his wet face.

The man looked miserable. "Sure you don't want to turn back?"

"Not for anything," McPearson said.

When they finally stopped, Spencer approached the pyramid and touched it solemnly. He looked at every detail and admired the accomplishments of the ancient Egyptians. McPearson followed him around, but said little.

Particularly impressive was the size of the pyramid and of the individual stones. What logical explanation could there be for how such large granite stones got placed the way they did. Face to face with the actual structure, he was at a complete loss. "Bill, do you see this fit here?" He pointed to the space between two large stones. The joint here is less than one millimeter. It's an engineering feat that has yet to be duplicated."

"Sure is a marvel. I would love to know how those darned Egyptians did it." McPearson said. "And I'd really like to know what happened to you in the desert yesterday." He stared at Spencer with piercing eyes.

"You mean besides getting pelted by a billion grains of sand?" Spencer laughed.

McPearson said nothing, but the concern reflected in his eyes said it all.

"C'mon, Bill, I'm fine. I was just experiencing a little shock, that's all." He turned back to the pyramid. "What's most remarkable to me," he said, changing the subject, "is how the older pyramids are better crafted than the newer ones. Egypt's past is still one of the great unsolved mysteries. I think it holds the key to who we are today."

"I'm going to ask you one more time, and then I'll let it rest . . . Did something happen to you in the desert yesterday?"

How could he lie to the man who had given him this amazing opportunity? But then, what would he say when he didn't even know what had happened? It all seemed like a dream now . . . and he'd touched the object dozens of times since then and nothing has happened. "No, Bill, nothing happened. I was just a little shook up, that's all."

McPearson clapped his shoulder. "Okay, then . . . I'm glad you're okay."

They rode back to the hotel in silence. A deep frown had settled onto McPearson's face. Rivulets of sweat streamed down his cheeks and neck and into his collar. He seemed to have given up on wiping his brow. Why the grim look? Was he still suspicious of what had happened in the desert? Or was he envious of Spencer's hunger for the truth? Did the passion that was surely reflected in Spencer's own eyes make him jealous? Or make him long for the days when he was twenty years younger and fifty pounds lighter and the world was still his to conquer?

Spencer gazed out the window at the desolate landscape and sighed. As it was, McPearson was an important man doing an important job. His schedule and priorities could hardly include a long romp through the mysteries of Egypt.

CHAPTER FOUR

Spencer parted ways with McPearson at the San Francisco airport. McPearson's wife, Marta, was waiting for him in baggage claim when they arrived. The couple offered him a ride, but he couldn't see the point in making them maneuver through downtown traffic at rush hour.

He climbed into the back seat of a cab and pulled out his cell phone. The line rang a few times before Paul picked up.

"Spencer, my man, you're back," Paul said. "So how did you find Egypt? Was it all you'd hoped for?"

"And more," he said. "I finally saw the pyramids. They were more amazing than I'd imagined. Definitely the highlight of my trip." He hesitated for a moment. "I need your opinion on something. I want to convince my boss to authorize a drilling operation. The results of my on-ground tests were inconclusive, but I'm convinced that we'll find something down there."

"Wow, you've been with Calpetro less than six months and you may have found an oil strike?"

"Yeah. My problem is not so much getting Calpetro to drill, it's convincing them that I'm the right guy to head the operation."

"You mean you want to be stuck in Egypt for the next year?"

"I'm willing to do whatever it takes. You know how I feel about archeology. This is one chance I can't pass up."

"Then I say go for it. I know you can do it. Hell, with your smarts, they'd be fools not to give you the assignment."

"Thanks, buddy, I knew I could count on you to inflate my ego," he laughed. Oh, something else happened while I was there . . ." Spencer was about to tell Paul about the dark-haired woman at the pool. A vision of her sun-tanned, swimsuit clad body flashed through his mind and his heart skipped a beat. No, that was a story to be told in person. "Never mind," he said. "I'll tell you about it later."

Spencer walked into his department mentally rehearsing every argument he'd come up with over the weekend. He had expected to suffer from jetlag, but instead had been too excited about the possibility of an oil find—or something even more exciting—to sleep.

"Mr. McPearson said he wants to see you as soon as you get in," Sarah said with a smile. "He's sure in a good mood. Y'all must've had a good trip."

Spencer went to his office and set his briefcase on the desk. He walked to the window and gazed out at the swirling fog. This was his chance, maybe the only one he'd get. He took a deep breath and turned to the door. It was now or never.

He tucked his hands in his pockets and casually walked down the hall. As he walked past Sarah's station, she smiled and winked.

What was that all about?

He tapped on McPearson's door. "Good morning, Bill," he said.

"Spencer, come in, have a seat." McPearson waved in the general direction of the chair opposite his desk. "Any jetlag?" he asked.

"Not really. How about you?"

"Slept like a baby the last two nights," He laid his hands on a neat stack of folders on his desk. "There's nothing like sleeping with the windows open on a cool San Francisco night." Bill sighed. "Yep, I sure am glad to be out of that damnable Egyptian heat."

"Glad to hear you slept well," Spencer said with a smile.

McPearson leaned forward and looked Spencer in the eye. "I think you know you've proven yourself to be a valuable team member in a very short time here."

Spencer nodded.

"You've done impressive research on this project and I'm convinced that this will be a successful dig."

"Bill, I—"

McPearson raised his hand. "I know you're going to ask me if you can head the drilling operation . . ."

Spencer's heart sank. How could he deny him now, after all the work he'd done? "But I—"

McPearson raised his hand again. "And that's why I've already decided to let you head up this project. Congratulations."

Spencer opened his mouth but no words came out. "Wow," he said finally, "I don't know what to say."

"You don't have to say a thing, I know you've been itching for this for months, and I know you'll do a great job. Now listen, it'll take our legal department about six weeks to get permits from the Egyptian government. I think Jeff made it pretty clear how tough Egypt is when it comes to excavation projects, especially near their precious archeological sites. We do, however, have a good working relationship with them and should get our permits without too much delay."

"I guess oil talks," Spencer said.

"Better than cash." McPearson said with a laugh. "You'll need to prepare all the details of the operation so I can get the budget approved by the suits upstairs. It won't be a problem, just have Sarah help you. She has our approved list of vendors for that region. Have her set up the necessary accounts. You'll also need to contact our liaison in Egypt to work out the details of getting local help. Sarah knows the contact." Spencer stared at his boss with wide eyes. The reality of what he was hearing had him frozen in place.

"Well, get going," McPearson said, handing him the stack of folders, "I know you're dying to."

"Right," Spencer said, "I'll get started right away." He stood and headed for the door, then turned back. "Thanks, Bill, I won't disappoint you."

"I'm not worried about that."

He walked back to his office in daze. Sarah jumped up and grabbed her steno pad. "Okay, so he told you, right? When can we get started?"

"You mean you already knew?"

"Of course," she followed him into his office and took the stack of folders from him. "I've already contacted Antonio Casenza, he's Calpetro's legal counsel in Egypt."

"Yes, I've heard of him."

"I worked with him on one of George Bellici's digs. He's a real shark. Anyway, McPearson probably told you it would take six weeks to get the permits, but don't you worry, Mr. Casenza will get them in half that time." She sat down across from him and opened the first folder. “Now, here’s who I recommend for supplies . . .”

How did Calpetro ever function before Sarah Nugent came along to keep everyone in line?

Twelve days later Spencer arrived in Cairo. He checked into the hotel after midnight, lugged his suitcases to his room, and fell into bed. Jeff Miller was waiting for him in the lobby the next morning. The pair discussed the drilling operation over breakfast.

“The drilling team will be ready to start work on Monday,” Jeff said as the waitress approached.

Spencer flipped over his mug. “Coffee, and keep it coming,” he said to the waitress. Starting on Monday would be just fine. It would give him the weekend to catch up on much-needed sleep. He’d have the weekend to sleep, relax, and prepare for the long project he had in front of him.

Jeff looked up as a small man with round glasses perched low on his nose approached. A sporty straw hat barely camouflaged the man’s baldness, and his suit was an Armani that fit him to perfection but looked out of place in the Egyptian heat.

“Spencer,” Jeff said, “Let me introduce you to Antonio Casenza, legal counsel for the Calpetro European Operations and the man in charge of getting permits from our good friends at the Egyptian government office.”

Antonio looked Spencer up and down. “So you’re the wonder kid McPearson put in charge of drilling, huh?”

“I guess that would be me.” Spencer shook the man’s moist hand.

So, Giuseppe,” Antonio said to Jeff with a smirk. “You still flying in circles these days? I heard you got another desert sandblasting.”

“Yeah, no big deal.” Jeff looked to Spencer with pleading eyes and then back to Antonio. “So where are we with the permits?”

“Hey, I’m a Casenza! We get things done.”

Jeff turned to Spencer and rolled his eyes. Clearly he was not a fan. Spencer had heard a lot about Antonio in the last few weeks and had read his Calpetro file on the flight over. The man was known for his efficiency and for his skills of persuasion. Born in Italy, he spoke fluent Italian. He had grown up in Boston and earned his corporate law degree at UC Hastings College of Law in San Francisco. Calpetro had snatched him up fresh out of school, totally impressed by his brilliance and his inability to accept failure. Spencer had heard about him and knew this was a man he wanted on his side.

"We're ready to proceed on Monday, Mr. Casenza." Spencer smiled.

"Call me Antonio, please."

"Okay, everyone just calls me Spencer . . . Antonio, I want to thank you for your fine work. I'm impressed with how quickly you got our permits."

Sarah had been right, it had taken Antonio twelve days to obtain what headquarters had said would take six weeks.

"I'm glad that I could help. McPearson seems to think you can move mountains, so you just get to work on your drilling and let me worry about keeping the spies off your back"

"Spies?"

Antonio chuckled. "Egypt is a strange land. You will be watched like a hawk by the government. Any drilling in this region is looked at as an excavation and any excavation will be monitored by Egypt's Department of Antiquity…monitored closely."

Spencer looked at Antonio with raised eyebrows.

"Not to worry," Antonio said. "Egypt is a hotbed of archeological finds, it's the basis of the tourist business here. They're just protecting their assets." Antonio tucked an unfiltered cigarette between his lips and lit it. "Antiquity is what brings tourists to Egypt, not the slums of Cairo. Illegal digs can get you a long prison sentence and every now and again it will get you dead."

"I understand," Spencer took a sip of coffee and gave Antonio a quick assessing look. "Since you've taken care of our permit, we have nothing to worry about then?"

"Not a thing. Just do your job and don't piss them off."

"How could I piss them off?"

"By not informing them of your progress and findings on a regular basis. I'll see that you have the forms you need to submit weekly."

"You're shitting me. I have to fill out government forms every week?"

Antonio blew a cloud of smoke over their heads. "If you want to keep drilling you do."

That night Spencer and Jeff went to the bar for a cold beer before calling it a night. "It'll be a short night," Spencer said. "I'm exhausted. This jetlag's wiped me out."

"No problem," Jeff said.

He saw her in the back corner of the bar, flipping the pages of an oversized book. Waves of dark brown hair fell to her shoulders, obscuring her face. She wore khaki shorts that showed off her slender brown legs. She tapped a pencil on the table. He couldn't see her face, but it was the woman from the pool; he was sure of it.

She looked up and their eyes locked. Had she sensed that he'd been watching her? She nodded and gave him a full smile then looked back at her book. Spencer had never seen eyes quite like hers, large and round, with the richness of dark chocolate. Her teeth had flashed white against her dark skin. "Do you know the woman at the corner table? He asked Jeff"

Jeff gazed in the woman's direction and his brow furrowed. She had tucked her hair behind her ear, but she continued to read her book and the pencil was tap, tap, tapping on the table.

"Yeah, I've seen her here a few times over the last few weeks. She's a graduate student from Cornell working on her thesis. If she is who I think she is, her name's Roula, or something like that, and she's some kind of whiz in hieroglyphics." Jeff glanced in the woman's direction and ducked his head. "Heads up, dude, she's coming our way."

"Hi, I'm Roula," she said looking at Spencer. "I never got to thank you properly."

Jeff looked from Roula to Spencer and back again. "You know

each other?" he asked, and then recognition washed over his face. "You're the lady from the pool."

Her face flushed, "Yeah, I suppose I am."

"He saved my life." Roula said, nodding toward Spencer, her voice husky. "The least I can do is buy you a drink, uh . . .?"

"I'm Ralph Spencer, but people just call me Spencer."

"Then maybe I'll just call you Ralph," she said with a laugh. Jeff kicked Spencer's foot and cleared his throat.

"Oh, and this is Jeff Miller, he's a pilot."

"How do you do, Jeff Miller," she said. "May I sit?"

"Of course." Spencer stood and pulled out the chair.

"Wow, such gentlemanly charm," she said.

Roula sat down at the table and crossed her arms in front of her. Her fingers were long and graceful, and her oval nails were trimmed and unpolished. Her white shirt was rolled up at the sleeves and open at the throat to reveal her slender neck. She wore a light dusting of eye shadow and a touch of gloss on her lips. She was the most beautiful woman he'd ever seen.

"And what is it you do, Ralph Spencer?"

"I'm a geologist with Calpetro. We're here on a drilling exploration about twenty miles south of Cairo."

"Ah, I see," she said with a polite smile. "So about that drink, another cold beer?"

"You don't have to do that," Spencer replied, blushing. "Please, I want to." Roula gestured to the waitress for a second round. "I'm rather embarrassed about my little bump on the head. I swim all the time . . . I was thinking about something else, and . . ." Her face reddened and she gazed around the room as if searching for the words. "Anyway," she said, looking back at Spencer, "I'm a student at Cornell. I'm working on my doctoral thesis."

"Wow, small world," Spencer said. "I did my undergrad at Cornell. Too bad I never ran into you there."

"I did most of my work here in Egypt. I'm majoring in hieroglyphics and the field is about as narrow as you can get." She measured about a half inch with her thumb and forefinger. "I mean narrow," she said with a laugh. "I've studied every place on earth that offers a hieroglyphics program first hand. I've been in Egypt four years."

"Sounds fascinating," Spencer said. "I love archeology, but I never had any training in hieroglyphics."

Jeff rolled his eyes. "Spencer's being modest." He gave Spencer a nudge with his elbow. "He has a doctorate degree in archeology from Harvard."

"Really?" Roula looked at Spencer, her brown eyes wide. "Impressive," she said.

Spencer made a mental note to thank Jeff later.

Roula leaned forward and put her slender hand on Spencer's arm. Her eyes darkened into black orbs. "Thanks for everything, Ralph, I really mean it."

Spencer swallowed. The touch of her hand gave him a rush, but not the electrical shock kind he'd experienced at the swimming pool. "You're welcome."

"So, my name's Roula Grazulis. It's Greek, but I grew up in New York." She shrugged. "Tell me, what's a geologist drilling in Egypt doing with a degree in archeology anyway?" She tipped her head inquisitively.

"Well, geology pays my bills, but archeology is my passion. I'm working on a simple drilling exploration, but I'd much rather spend my time in a pyramid than in that damned desert."

Roula pulled her chair closer to Spencer and took a sip of her beer.

Jeff stood up, his half-empty beer mug in his hand. "I've gotta get going."

"I'm sorry, Jeff," Roula said. "You don't have to go."

"No worries, I've got an early morning." Jeff drank down the last of his beer and pushed in his chair. "You two have a good night."

Spencer spent the next hour telling Roula about the site, his scanning techniques, and the firm's curiosity about what's in that twenty-mile span. She listened with genuine interest and interjected with questions from time to time. Her interest in his work was a pleasant surprise. There was no denying that there was chemistry between them, and that would make up for all the luxuries of home he'd been missing.

"Would you like to come over and view the site some time, Roula?" Her name seemed to roll off his tongue, as though he'd been saying it all his life. Maybe he was pushing his luck, but he wanted to see her again and she had seemed curious.

"That'd be nice." Roula said with a smile. "I'll check my schedule. My classes and research keep me pretty busy, but I'll let you know."

Jeff yawned and stretched. "Well, I guess I'll call it a night," he said with a wink at Spencer.

"Goodnight, Jeff," Roula said, "It was a pleasure meeting you."

"You, too." He turned to Spencer. "See you tomorrow."

Spencer let his gaze fall on Roula once again. She was smiling at him, and it was the kind of inviting smile every man wanted to see on a beautiful woman's face. "Okay, Roula, now it's your turn . . . tell me all about hieroglyphics."

They talked until the bar was empty and the waitress told them it was time to lock up. The pair walked out of the lounge hand in hand, like lovers on a leisurely stroll. If it were up to Spencer, he would have frozen his life right there, with his fingers wrapped around this lovely woman's hand.

CHAPTER FIVE

Drilling started right on time Monday morning. It was a warm January day. The plan was to drill a six-inch diameter hole some fifteen thousand feet inside the Egyptian desert. Core samples would be taken at intervals of a thousand feet for the first ten thousand feet and then increased to every five hundred feet until they reached the projected level.

The months of drilling dragged on. The cores were all the same with no sign of anything interesting. Every day Spencer had to ship the core samples to headquarters for a full analysis, along with the drudgery of clearing customs. The bureaucratic hassles seemed endless.

Spencer checked every new core sample before shipping it to the US. He would ask opinions from the team soil engineer, and each day the answer was the same. "Looks like your everyday standard dirt," Matt would often say.

Matt Garrett was a local contractor working for Calpetro. He was in charge of the drilling team. Matt was loyal to a fault to his employer, and his knowledge of the local culture had been indispensible. He knew who was capable of handling certain jobs and who was certain trouble. Matt was approaching forty and his dark complexion and sun-dried skin gave him a rugged, angular look. He was a big man and had a spark in his eye that charmed just about everyone who met him. He had a reputation for being fair but strict. No one dared cross him. A native of Boston, he had spent seven years in Africa following a nasty divorce. His wife had had an involved affair while he was conducting a drilling project in Mexico. Here he had kept mostly to himself. He sometimes seemed to wear the pain of his divorce like a weight jacket. He put all his energy into learning the players in Egypt and at Calpetro. Spring was near, but Spencer would never have known it from the weather. The sun radiated off the desert like a dry sauna on full blast. One blistering day seemed to melt into the next.

To his dismay, he had not seen Roula again since their night together at the bar. For the first two weeks he had fully expected to hear from her each day. By the third week doubt had replaced his optimism and a week later, on a Saturday afternoon, he went to the hotel and inquired about her. She had checked out a few days after their meeting and left no forwarding information.

How could he have been so wrong about her? She had felt the chemistry between them; he was certain of it. What had gone wrong? He could put her out of his mind during the day, but the long nights in his hotel room were filled with thoughts of Roula. He had replayed their evening together dozens of times, but there was no explanation for her sudden disappearance. Why hadn't she at least said goodbye?

Jeff introduced Spencer to a local hangout and the two of them spent many of their free evenings there. The place was frequented by Americans and especially by university students, which suited Spencer just fine. Having other academics around made him feel at home. Here Spencer could unwind, have a cold beer with fellow archeologists, and engage in endless debates about the origin of the great pyramids.

Early in April, Matt arrived at Spencer's office with the day's core sample. Spencer sighed, silently preparing himself for another dull examination; they had done this hundreds of times.

"Spencer this one is from thirteen-thousand seven-hundred feet, sample 137A. Let's check for porosity and water content and do a stress test."

"We really need to get some results soon," Spencer said. "We'll reach our final projected depth in the next few days, and we're still coming up empty."

Matt placed the core sample on the laboratory's working table and removed some of the soil for testing. His face seemed to light up. "Hey, Spencer, look at this! Maybe we've got something here."

Spencer looked at the soil extracted from the core. There were a few chunks of what appeared to be stainless steel, but with an unusual greenish color. Spencer's hand went instinctively to the familiar lump in his pocket. He had taken to carrying the strange object with him everywhere. He still had no idea what it was, but he'd come to think of it as a strange sort of good luck charm. The piece of metal he was looking at had the same greenish gold color as the item in his pocket. "Did you guys break the drill bit?"

"Absolutely not," Matt answered. "Look at the core sample, it's intact."

"This is strange." Spencer used a tweezers to extract a tiny piece of the metal. It was round, smooth, and not at all splintered the way metal would be from drilling.

"What's the matter," Matt asked, his eyes wide.

"Nothing." Better to not say anything until they studied the fragment a little further. "Let's check our drill tip. When did you get this sample?"

"At 11:15 this morning. The drill tip hasn't been used yet."

Spencer looked at his watch. It was 12:23. "Let's get over there before the crew resumes drilling. We need to be certain about this."

Removing the drill tip for examination would set back the daily drilling, but it had to be done. Spencer had the tip taken to his office lab for examination.

"Like I told you," Matt said, "it's perfect." He turned the bit over and tilted it from side to side. "No dents or chips anywhere."

"What the hell did we find in that core then?" Spencer stared at the drill bit. None of this was making sense. They were looking for evidence of oil, not rare metals. Let's get a core every twenty-five feet from now on. This could get interesting."

Late the next morning Matt came in with core sample 137B. Spencer's stomach was in knots. He'd been able to eat only a few bites of his breakfast that morning. He would handle the retrieval of this soil sample himself.

"Holy shit!" Matt shouted. "There it is, another fragment of that strange material. What do you make of it?"

Spencer's heart thudded against his ribcage as he held the sample up for closer inspection. He would never find out what was in his pocket, or in this core sample, without help. "I think we'll have to send this with special instructions to our lab in San Francisco. They'll figure it out."

That night Spencer couldn't sleep. His mind was spinning, searching for explanations for the strange material he'd found in the sand, and then again some two and a half miles under the Sahara desert, and for the electrical shock that he'd felt when touching the object. Had he only imagined it?

The next morning McPearson sounded as if he might have a heart attack right there on the phone. "Spencer, my boy, you're not playing a joke on us are you? Those two damned core samples are driving us crazy. The round fragments were found throughout both core samples, and no one in the lab seems to be able to classify them."

"I suppose they might be artificial," Spencer offered, "but I'm not convinced. I mean, how would they get there?"

"Our DC office has the best lab contacts in the country for that type of analysis. If we want answers, we'll have to get them involved in this."

Spencer sighed. He toyed with the round piece of metal in his pocket. This didn't sound good. The fewer people involved, the better. "I didn't know we had a lab in DC. Who are you referring to?"

"Well, unfortunately it will have to be done by our . . . er . . . outside consultants." Not to worry, McPearson said, "They're the best."

There had to be a better way, but no alternative was coming to mind. "All right, let me know as soon as you hear anything. I've got a strong feeling those fragments are artificial. Has Calpetro drilled here before?"

"No, never, and as far as we know, no one else has either. We've had the drilling rights to that land for the last thirty years."

Waiting to hear from headquarters had kept Spencer's stomach queasy. He had warned both Matt and Jeff to keep things under wraps until they knew more. It was the middle of the night when the phone rang. "Did you get the results from Washington?" He said, not even bothering to ask who was calling.

"Catch the first flight home," McPearson said, "we need to see you in a hurry."

Wasn't this the wrong time for him to leave the site? What if the Egyptian inspectors showed up? "Uh . . . well . . ."

"There's no other choice. We've got a briefing set for nine on Friday and I want you here. Set up strict security on this. It's need-to-know only. See you Friday."

"Wait, Bill, what do I tell the crew?"

"Tell them your aunt died. Tell them your house fell in the ocean. Tell them whatever you want, but keep this find quiet."

Spencer had never seen San Francisco in April. The cool breeze was a welcome relief after the hot Sahara sun. Sarah greeted him with her usual cheerfulness. "It's so nice to have you back, we've missed you around here!"

"Yeah, it feels good to be back. Has Bill told you anything? What's with all this rush and secrecy?"

"I think Mr. McPearson's lost his mind over this. I've never seen him so agitated and elusive."

Spencer narrowed his eyes. "So you don't know anything?"

"Nope. I'm in the dark on this one, I swear."

Spencer approached the main conference room. A security guard was posted at the door. Now that was a new one.

"I need to see your ID badge sir."

Spencer held out the ID that hung around his neck. The guard analyzed the badge, looked at Spencer, and then reassessed the badge. The man had either been told to use maximum security or he took his job way too seriously. "Please sign here." The guard handed Spencer a clipboard and pointed at a handwritten X next to his name. He then peered closely at Spencer's handwriting and compared it to the signature on the badge. He frowned at the clipboard as if he suspected Spencer of wrongdoing or was disappointed that he didn't find any. "Okay, you're cleared by McPearson."

"I should hope so," Spencer said as he brushed past the abhorrent guard.

The conference room was almost empty. McPearson came across the room and greeted him with a warm handshake. The Asian man from operations, the senior vice president above McPearson, and two men dressed like they just walked off the set of Men in Black sat around a table. No sign of John Fortica. The MIB were probably the outside consultants McPearson had mentioned over the phone. They didn't look like scientists, or engineers for that matter. Could these be the men who performed the tests on the soil cores?

One of the MIB stood up. "Gentlemen, we are here on behalf of the US government."

All of Spencer's blood seemed to rush to his head. "What the hell?"

McPearson laid his hand and Spencer's arm and nodded for the Fed to continue.

Our lab tested the abnormalities discovered in your core samples 137A and B. We are here to ensure that these results maintain the highest level of security and to enforce any breach of same." The first Fed sat down and the second stood up.

"Unfortunately, we are not at liberty to discuss the test results. We are only here to ensure that this project receives the highest level of security."

"That's bullshit, those samples belong to Calpetro and—"

"Spencer, please," McPearson said. "Let the man finish.

As agreed by your top management and CIA headquarters, you will be the only people from your firm allowed access to the project. After our briefing, those of you who will continue to work on this project . . ." He looked Spencer in the eye, "That is, those of you who are cooperative, will be requested to report to CIA headquarters in Washington for details on the results of our lab tests."

What was this, some kind of spy novel? "Why all the secrecy?" he asked in the calmest voice he could muster.

"As I said, details will be provided in Washington." The other Fed stood up and both men gathered their files and walked out of the conference room.

Spencer and McPearson made their way out of the down the hall. "In twenty-three years with Calpetro I've never had to go through anything like this." McPearson whispered.

"But—"

"I know as much as you do." McPearson's face had gone pale and his hands were shaking.

"Are you all right?"

"Sure, I'll be fine. Guess I'm just getting too old for this kind of thing."

"Exactly what kind of thing are we talking about?"

McPearson shrugged and continued to walk down the hall in silence.

"Maybe it's from aliens." Spencer laughed.

McPearson gazed up at him without saying a word.

Spencer had been to Washington DC only once for a grade school field trip. Soon he would be on his way to Langley—CIA headquarters. What the CIA had to do with any of this was a mystery—a mystery he, Ralph Spencer, was going to unravel. What did they think those fragments were anyway?

He could already see himself swaggering into the CIA building with his shoulders back. And why the hell shouldn't he? This was his big adventure—the one he'd dreamed about since the first time he'd watched Indiana Jones as a kid—he was going to enjoy it.

McPearson held up his arms and allowed the armed guard to search him. Spencer followed the same routine. The guard nodded and escorted the two men to the main conference room. Tom Detton, who introduced himself as head of research operations, greeted them. He was a tall, nondescript man with brown hair, brown eyes, and a crumpled brown suit. No one would have guessed him CIA by his appearance. A computer geek? Yes, but not CIA. He showed McPearson to his seat and then gestured for Spencer to sit across the table.

A woman dressed in a navy business suit entered with a tray and placed steaming mugs of coffee in front of each of them. Detton thanked her and signaled for the meeting to begin. McPearson watched Tom Detton closely. The agent's face had hardly moved, as if it were fixed in stone.

"Gentlemen, you have been well briefed concerning the delicacy and security of this project. What I am about to tell you is considered highly classified and must remain within these walls. Ralph Spencer . . ." Detton looked Spencer in the eye, obviously holding his gaze long enough to make Spencer uncomfortable. "Your exploratory drilling has unearthed an unusual material. The core samples, 137A and B, submitted by Calpetro . . ." He looked at McPearson, "which I assume were not tampered with in any way . . ."

"Absolutely not. We at Calpetro have very strict procedures to ensure that core samples are kept intact." He stopped and took a breath. Good God, he sounded like a high school kid at his first debate. He cleared his throat and lowered his voice. "We are required to perform a preliminary field analysis from the upper one fourth of the core and ship the rest to headquarters for full testing."

"Well then, as you are all aware, our CIA lab ran extensive tests on the two core samples. What we found has stumped even our most skeptical scientists. The strange fragments found in both core samples are of artificial origin, and," Detton's voice lowered, "they are of an unidentified material."

"What do you mean unidentified?" Spencer asked.

Detton ignored him. "This strange material has been tested for various stresses and it's harder than diamond. It has a stress capacity of ten thousand times that of stainless steel and yet it possesses a specific gravity lower than aluminum. What we have here is a material so sophisticated that whoever developed it had abilities far beyond today's technology."

"Are you telling us that what we found is alien?" McPearson asked.

Detton sighed as if an errant child had interrupted him. "Like I said, the material is unidentified. We have nothing to match its characteristics. We believe the substance was buried for many centuries, maybe millennia."

McPearson shifted in his chair and glanced at Spencer, whose jaw was hanging slack. Detton was dead serious. This was no joke.

"So what you're saying is the substance is alien," he said.

"No," Detton's stone-face reddened. "What I'm saying is that the department wants to know what's down there and is prepared to take over the operation. Our plan is to drill a large mine shaft to the final depth."

McPearson stood up and slammed his fists on the table. "Over my dead body," he shouted. "Calpetro owns that dig. We've had the right to the site for over thirty years. It could be the biggest oil find we've had in decades. We're not about to just hand it over to the CIA." A second agent entered the room and stood directly behind him.

"What's this?" he demanded, "Some kind of threat?"

"Please, Bill," Detton gestured for him to sit. "We understand that Calpetro has a big stake in this," His voice was smooth as glass, "what I meant is that we would like to assist in this operation."

He looked at the agent behind him and then turned to Detton. No way was he backing down now. Detton nodded at the agent and the man walked backward to the doorway and then slipped out of the room.

"Bill, please have a seat." Detton's ingratiating smile looked as if it might crack his granite face. "This may be the single most important discovery in the history of mankind, or it may be nothing. The sophistication of this material could imply that . . . someone, at some time, possessed weapons of sophistication that, if in the wrong hands, could put our national security in danger.

"And you're basing all this on a few chunks of unidentified metal?" Spencer asked.

"In the interest of national security, the CIA will pursue this mission. Of course, we'll require full cooperation from Calpetro." He turned to face Spencer. "You have the right expertise for this project, but this is a very delicate situation that will remain classified. We've already done a complete background check on you—"

It was Spencer's turn to stand. "You've done what?"

Detton raised his hand. "This would be easier if you gentleman would stay seated and let me finish," he said. "Ralph—"

Spencer sat down and leaned into the table toward Detton. "Please, just call me Spencer," he said in an icy tone.

"All right, Spencer. We had to know that we could trust you with the security of our country. Surely you understand that."

He couldn't let this go any further. "Mr. Detton," McPearson said, “I can assure you that no one is better suited to manage this dig. If you consider our firm incapable of handling the scope of this project, then you underestimate Calpetro. With the proper guidance, we will be as qualified as anyone to keep this project classified. We already have strict security measures to ensure that no one else knows about our digs.”

“I’m sure that’s true, Bill, and that’s why we’re having this . . .exploratory . . . meeting.” Detton took a long sip of his coffee and sighed before he continued. “Surely you’re aware that we have the authority to take over this project without involving Calpetro at all.” “I’m aware of your jurisdictional powers, Mr. Detton, but I would reconsider that threat. Without our cooperation, you could spend decades in that desert and never find what you’re looking for.” McPearson turned to Spencer. “Isn’t that right?”

Spencer put his hand to his mouth, coughed once, and then cleared his throat. Was he stifling a smile? “Bill is absolutely correct,” Spencer said, his tone serious. “We have full documentation of the core sample’s location as well as the drill site location. Without our cooperation, you’d be looking for a needle in a very large, not to mention hot and sandy, haystack.”

Detton stood up, red faced, and paced the room. His gaze was intent on the floor and his brow was furrowed. He was clearly trying to figure out whether or not what they said was true and if he had any way around them. He stopped, walked over to Spencer and McPearson, looked at the men one at a time and then sat down. “You realize that if I allow your company to proceed with this project, you must report to me directly. The Department will supervise the entire operation and will have full control, is that clear?”

“Certainly, but I’m afraid that if your department insists on supervising and controlling the project, Calpetro will have to insist that you also pay for it.”

Detton leaned back in his chair, crossed his arms, and nodded. “The project will be funded by the US government.”

Score for Calpetro’s stockholders. He’d be a hero for this win for sure.

Detton continued, "This mission is considered classified and requires the highest level of secrecy. You will be given a complete briefing of our internal procedures, equipment, satellite monitoring, and field assistance."

The meeting had, for the most part, gone his way. Spencer couldn't have played it better if he'd tried. No doubt, it could have been a whole lot worse. Now he just needed to be sure Calpetro had competent staff supervising and directing the project. This was his chance to make all of his demands.

"Of course Mr. Spencer will continue to be in charge of the project. I can assure you that he is a brilliant and capable geologist. It's thanks to him that we're here today."

"Fine," Detton said in a dismissive tone. "I am not here to dispute Mr. Spencer's capabilities, but Steve Sullivan will run things for us. Mr. Spencer will report directly to him."

"As I said, we have already checked out the Calpetro personnel vital to this project. You and Mr. Spencer are cleared. The Department will provide Spencer with a satellite hookup and you'll have access to our latest monitoring systems. Bill, Calpetro will have to acquire permits for the mining operation from the Egyptian Department of Antiquity."

"Wait a minute," he said, "We're not talking about a six-inch dig anymore. How can I explain a mining shaft the size of this office? What kind of oil am I looking for?"

"We've already thought that through," Detton said.

Of course they had.

"You'll tell them that you think there's gold at that depth and the only way to confirm it is to widen the dig so that the men and equipment can get in there and find out. If you need proof, the department will provide you with the necessities."

For a man with such a nondescript countenance, Detton had guided the meeting his way in a determined and authoritative manner. It was obvious he had known that he needed Calpetro's help all along.

Clearly, this CIA agent believed in his own capabilities and knew he'd been assigned a mission that required his full attention – the stakes were too high.

For Spencer the next few days were an eye opening experience. He was exposed to intricate yet mysterious procedures and technology, including some of the secret inner workings of the CIA. Tom Detton familiarized Spencer with the latest technological advancements in satellite communication and mining, and he briefed him on the inner workings of the Egyptian government. Tom introduced Spencer to Steve Sullivan, a thirty-year-old computer genius. Steve was to oversee the project for the CIA.

"Since Egypt falls within the Middle East hotbed, we've installed a geodesic orbit satellite for that region, so we are able to monitor any land activity twenty-fours hours a day," Steve said. "Here, let me show you." He turned to a giant screen on the wall and flipped on the satellite transponder. The screen came to life with the clarity of a high definition television. With a few minor adjustments, Steve focused the camera on the coordinates of the great pyramid at Giza.

"Here, look." He pointed at the screen. "Under ideal conditions, I am able to zoom in and can read a license plate on a car if I want to." Spencer's jaw fell. The great pyramid was as clear as if he were flying over it with a small plane.

Steve manipulated the controls to show Spencer different views and positions. He zoomed in on some tourists. "Watch this. I'm zooming in on that woman to the left of the screen. The computer will automatically enhance the image . . . just a few seconds . . .there see it?" "Wow," a tingle ran down his spine. "I can see the Nike logo on her shirt."

"Yeah, now watch what happens when I go infrared."

The woman turned into a blurry red heat-generated image.

"So this is useful at night?"

"With our infrared high resolution, we can detect things at night almost as well as in broad daylight."

Spence rolled over, punched his fist into the pillow, and laid his head in the hole. The clock on the dresser read 2:18 a.m. He'd been lying there for hours replaying everything he'd seen and heard over the last few days. Big Brother was watching in a more terrifying way than he'd ever imagined. He'd have to watch his step as the mystery of the dig unfolded. He was safe as long as he was necessary for the project, but what would happen to him after the CIA found what they wanted? And what if what they found was in fact a security threat? Make no mistake, in the eyes of the CIA, Ralph Spencer was replaceable.

The next day he received his project ID with a level five clearance. Steve explained that his clearance was specifically for this project and any other access would be restricted. His ID was exactly the same as the one he carried for Calpetro with the exception of the small number five printed in the lower right corner. The card was also coded for the operation of special equipment, communication encryption, and satellite links. He was now a first class spy working for the CIA. In the light of day, his trepidation from the night before seemed like a dream.

His briefing on the inner workings of the Egyptian government was boring compared to the previous few days spent with Steve. He would let Antonio Casenza handle this part of the assignment anyway. Antonio could get just about anything from the Egyptians. Still, he had to go through the training. There was no getting out of it.

For the next two weeks, Spencer made preparations for the biggest adventure of his life. He was about to embark upon the largest secret drilling project ever undertaken. Steve Sullivan kept close tabs on Spencer to the point of making him nervous.

"We're on the same team," he said to Steve one day.

"I have strict orders to ensure this project's secrecy, Spencer. You are a civilian; a damned good geologist, but a civilian nevertheless. You're just not used to this level of security."

"I'll be fine Steve, but I'll need to see my friend Paul on the West Coast before I leave or he'll be suspicious. He knows about the dig and that I've been in DC."

"Okay, but tell him nothing."

"Don't worry. He knows that I'm doing exploratory drilling, but that's all. I'll give him the same story we're giving the Egyptians."

"Good." Steve placed his hand on Spencer's shoulder and squeezed. "As long as you keep this project under wraps as ordered, you'll be just fine." He smiled and gave Spencer a quick pat on the back.

Was he being given friendly advice or a warning? Probably the latter. "Of course," he smiled back at Steve. "I'm aware of the delicacy of this project."

The following Saturday morning Spencer waited for Paul at Peet's Coffee Shop in Palo Alto. Just because he couldn't tell Paul the truth didn't mean he couldn't ask for his help.

Paul had barely sat down when he started asking questions. "Do you think you guys will hit it big in Egypt?"

"We're still at a low level of drilling. We ran into all kinds of problems at ten-thousand feet."

"Like what?"

"Like an underground river for one. It's flowing pretty hard. Our drilling will have to be stopped until a special casing can be designed to handle the problem."

"Wow, an underground river in the desert. How strange."

"It's not so strange really. There's underground water all over the planet."

"It all sounds pretty fascinating, but I wouldn't give up my gravy job at Intellisoft to go digging around in a desert." Paul went to the counter to pick up his latte and walked back to their table. When he returned, his face was flush and his eyes wide. "We're working on a new program that'll blow your socks off. It's very hush-hush, but I know I can trust you."

A pang of guilt hit Spencer in the gut. As much as he wanted to, this was one secret he couldn't tell Paul.

"We're working on a new software program that'll revolutionize virtual reality." Paul said. "Our program involves actual stimulation to the human brain to create a virtual sensation so real that it'll be impossible to distinguish it from a real event."

"No way," Spencer said, "that's way beyond anything out there?"

"I know. It's all built into the device. You wear it over your eyes and its built in program stimulates the optic nerve, the ears, and nose. Basically all the sense organs are stimulated, and it sends all of these stimulants to the brain, fooling it into believing in the unreal."

"Has it been tested yet?"

"We are finishing up our logic systems now. The next step will be mounting the chip inside the virtual reality glasses and then doing our compulsory testing. It'll probably be years before it's released."

"It sounds great, can I try it?"

"Sure." Paul laughed. "Just get in line." Paul pulled the lid off his coffee and sipped at the creamy foam. He looked over his cup at Spencer with a sparkle in his eye. "This'll be the hottest technology since the PC, you'll see."

Spencer had something even bigger on his mind, but at the moment it had to remain with him. If nothing else, the meeting with the CIA and the following weeks spent with Steve had proved that he needed to make some alternate plans in case things got hot in Egypt. He was aware that between Egypt's Department of Antiquity and the CIA, he could end up in a situation calling for a quick change of scenery.

"Paul," I was wondering if you could do something for me while I'm in Egypt."

"Sure, if I can. What do you need?"

"I'll need to tell you something in confidence, okay?"

"Of course."

Egypt's Department of Antiquities has more power than I realized. I've heard stories that they employ spies to monitor the activities of digs and drillings. For Egypt, any destruction of ancient finds translates to money lost in the tourism business and any loss in tourism flips them out. Remember when I went to Africa the first time to look at the region?"

"Yeah."

"We were followed by the Egyptians, our every move monitored. They can be very . . . persuasive . . ."

Paul frowned. "You're worrying me—"

"No, don't worry. It's probably no big deal. I just need to be sure."

"Okay, so what do you have in mind?" Paul asked.

"This may make you think I'm being paranoid, but when I'm in Egypt, I want you to discreetly find me a new apartment, possibly near the San Jose airport. It's got to be completely secret. Tell no one and set it up under a fake name. Leave all of my things in my present apartment. Whatever I don't take to Egypt can stay where it is."

"Okay, that's easy, but I'd really like to know what's going on? Are you safe over there? It's not like you to be paranoid."

"It's probably nothing, but I don't want to take a chance. Rent some furniture for the new place too, or if you can find a furnished apartment, even better."

"You mean you're going to pay rent on both places?"

"Yeah, but I'm going to charge one of them off on my expense account." He'd have plenty of discretionary money from the CIA, but he couldn't tell Paul that.

"I'll give you my e-mail address. When you have the apartment ready, just leave me a coded note. Say there's a new cafe in San Jose, that you hear it's great, and that we must try it when I get back. Get it?"

"Got it." Paul scrutinized Spencer while sipping at his coffee. "You're into something deep, I can tell," he said, his eyes shining. "Whatever it is, I hope you're having fun."

"More than you can imagine," Spencer said. "Once you've got the apartment, put the address with the key in an envelope and leave it with the concierge at the San Jose Marriott. Write on it, 'please hold for Mr. R. Spencer.' Let me know all the costs and use the cafe idea as a decoy."

"I'll take care of it."

"Great, and remember this is just between the two of us. No one else can know."

Spencer was taking all the precautions he could. Who knew what the CIA would do if things went against their plans.

Paul looked at his friend, concern in his eyes. "You're not in any real danger Spencer, are you?"

"I don't think so, but I like to have my bases covered."

Paul spent the rest of the hour reminiscing about how much fun they'd had at Cornell pulling crazy fraternity stunts. He seemed to relax and was enjoying the idea of participating in a clever covert operation.

The two men stood to leave. Spencer walked to the counter, threw a twenty-dollar bill in the tip jar, and winked at the blonde barista. She smiled and winked back. He didn't think she'd overheard any of their conversation, but it couldn't hurt to make sure she remembered his generosity.

Outdoors in the bright California sun, Spencer pulled his friend into a tight hug and patted his back. "Can't thank you enough," he said.

"My pleasure, I'll take care of everything. Just relax while you're in Egypt. Maybe you'll meet some sexy Egyptian women to keep your mind off your paranoia," he said.

Spencer's chest tightened. He hadn't thought of Roula since finding the unusual fragments. Where had she gone? "Yeah, maybe," he said.

"When do you need everything ready?"

"Do it the minute I leave for Africa," Spencer answered. "No one will be suspicious."

"You got it."

CHAPTER

SIX

The plane made its final descent over the Cairo airport. The early morning sun colored the sky a brilliant red. How many past generations had seen this sight? Early May in Egypt was pretty much the same as January. He hadn't thought it could be any hotter, but it was. He'd be far too busy to let the weather bother him. He sighed and watched the desert sky as the plane taxied down the runway. Africa had never looked so beautiful.

"Mr. Spencer! How was your stay in San Francisco?" Antonio Casenza came at him across the tiled airport floor, looking like he belonged on Wall Street and not in the blazing Egyptian desert.

"Hello, Antonio. Am I that important already?" Spencer joked. "I got the order right from McPearson. He wanted me to fill you in on our permit situation right away."

McPearson had told Tom Detton that Antonio was key to the project's success. After the CIA had completed it's background check on Antonio, something Detton had demanded and that had made McPearson's face look like an overripe tomato, Spencer had received permission to brief Antonio on the project.

"Antonio, we need to talk about something important . . . somewhere secure."

"Yeah, sure," Antonio said. "I'll take you to the hotel. After you've had a chance to rest a bit, call me and I'll pick you up."

Later that day Antonio slipped in his black Mercedes into the chaotic Cairo traffic and took Spencer to a large, modern home in an affluent part of Cairo. "Welcome to my home," Antonio said.

The pair sat under an umbrella on the verandah sipping iced tea served by a tawny Egyptian maid while Spencer explained the situation to an incredulous Antonio.

"Mamma mia! You're planning on digging a two-and-a-half mile mineshaft . . . in secret? "

"Yes, with your help and the help of the CIA."

"I'll tell you right now, it's going to be impossible to keep this from the Egyptian government."

"I know. We're going to tell them that we discovered precious metal. It's not really a lie. We think that what we've found is some kind of metal, and it sure is precious."

"The CIA has a plan. If the inspector's get too suspicious, they'll supply us with samples of gold to offer them. Calpetro will promise a large percentage of the gold find to Egypt. We think they'll jump at the chance. What do you think?"

"Very risky. If they find out that this is all a front, they'll shut us down faster than you can up-link to the CIA and tell them about it."

"Detton thinks they won't shut us down as long as they see gold coming their way."

"Okay, so that explains why we're digging a large mine shaft. How long do you think it will take to drill a mine to the eighteen thousand foot level? You'll need some damn accurate data to give me a heads up and still have the lead time to remove whatever you find before the Egyptians see it."

"I don't know yet. I need to find out what equipment is available. We've been authorized to work three shifts a day, so I estimate an average of eighty feet daily. For a seven day work week without interruptions, that translates to about a year."

"In that case, I'd ask the Egyptians for double that time, two years at least."

Antonio rocked back in his chair and took a sip of his tea. He gazed at Spencer with dark, unreadable eyes. "So who's going to keep the inspectors quiet?"

"You are, Antonio. We're counting on your expertise."

"Ah, so that's why I've been brought in on this." Antonio chuckled. "I should've known." He sighed and pushed his glasses back up the bridge of his nose. "Calpetro will need new contracts with Egypt. Part of the contract is the assurance that the project will be kept secret. For them, the downside will be obvious. Gold can make people crazy, and the last thing they need is an Egyptian gold rush."

"That's what the CIA is banking on," Spencer said. "Egypt's losses would be huge if thousands of gold-diggers showed up in the Valley of the Pyramids."

"Whoever came up with this idea is pretty damn smart."

"I can't take the credit. It was the CIA's idea. We'll be able to dig our shaft without any interference from Egypt." Spencer swirled the ice cubes in his empty tea glass. The CIA had come up with a great plan, but too much depended on how well Antonio could manage the Egyptian gatekeepers. What other option was there? He'd have to stay on top of Antonio's actions if this was going to work. The maid refilled their glasses and disappeared into the house. He tilted his head toward Antonio, who was staring into the distance over the reading glasses that once again looked ready to slide off his nose. The man rubbed his bald head absently and his face was more pinched than usual.

"Antonio," Spencer said, breaking the silence. "I have full confidence in you. I know you'll make a great presentation to the Egyptians and get us the necessary contracts and permits."

Antonio gave him a strange, crooked smile, and a light came into his eyes. He seemed to be imagining the political intrigue and strategizing that this deception would require. "I think this is going to be a fun one," Antonio said, his smile broadening.

"You know what, Antonio," Spencer said. "I'm glad you're on my side."

When Spencer arrived back at his hotel there were a half a dozen messages awaiting him. One in particular made his stomach tighten. It was from Steve Sullivan, the CIA operative in charge. Steve was on his way to see Spencer to do a preliminary inspection of the site. The constant CIA monitoring was going to be a pain in the ass. He had to gain Steve's trust if he was to get any freedom here. He'd have to keep reassuring Steve that he was on board with the CIA and be sure to run this project to the strictest CIA imposed standards.

At least until they found what they were looking for.

Steve had left instructions to meet him at the US military base near Cairo at nine a.m. the next day. At nine sharp a large C130 transport plane taxied to a stop. Steve emerged waving to Spencer and signaling him over.

"Spencer, over here. Just wait till you see what I got you." He was grinning like a big kid.

Maybe managing Steve would be easier than he'd thought. He walked over to where Steve stood. "What do you mean, you got me something?"

"Look."

The back of the C130 opened and the crew unloaded a large vehicle.

"A motor home?" Spencer asked.

"No, not a motor home… a CIA state of the art FOU"

"A what?"

"A CIA Field Operation Unit"

Spencer walked over to the vehicle and peered in the driver's side window. "What does it do exactly?"

"This unit was designed to spec for this operation. It has equipment for communicating with headquarters over secured channels. You'll have full access to our local tracking devices over this region." Steve walked the length of the vehicle, sliding his hand along its side the way one pets a beloved animal. The guy had to be the biggest gadget geek Spencer had ever met.

Steve stopped by the side door and fondled the handle. "I think I told you before, we have a geodesic orbit satellite in this region. You'll have twenty-four hour visual communication with headquarters. Our lab will be at your disposal. If you run into any problems, we are ready to jump in."

Spencer gave Steve his most charming smile. He didn't want the CIA jumping in the middle of anything, but for right now he needed to play along. "This is cool, what else is on board beside satellite hook ups?"

Steve's eyes lit up as if Spencer had finally asked the question he'd been waiting for. "Come see for yourself. You'll be amazed."

Spencer climbed inside and gasped. The unit was obscenely luxurious. It contained all the modern conveniences from a microwave oven to a subzero refrigerator. He opened a few cupboards and the frig. He found the kitchen stocked with enough food to last for months. Along one wall stood a massive entertainment center flanked by a handsome desk with a state-of-the-art computer. He sunk into the microfiber sofa and then stood and moved to the matching recliner. He then walked to the back of the rig where he found an elegantly appointed bedroom and full bath. Damn, it was good to be the government.

"The entire unit is bulletproof and the generator is powered by batteries that are a top secret design, only used by the military." Steve's words tumbled out, like a kid whose brain was working faster than his mouth. "The batteries have a guaranteed life of six to eight months, even if you run the unit daily for twenty-four hours a day. The unit will recharge the battery packs whenever you're driving, with the power alternating between two independent battery systems. Come here, let me show you something." Steve took Spencer outside and opened a storage compartment hidden within the vehicle's design. This is where a spare battery set is stored in the unit for emergencies." He popped open a few more compartments. This is all for your gear." His eyes lit up as he opened the last compartment. "Here's a reverse osmosis system for drinking water and a sewer waste system that's separate from, but circulating through, the reverse osmosis."

"This is beyond anything I expected," Spencer said. "I wonder what a rig like this costs—"

"That's a question you never ask." Steve laughed. "With this unit you could live in the desert totally self sufficient for eight months."

"Great, I'll turn into a monk."

Steve laughed and clapped him on the back. "You'll love this unit at the job site. It'll be your home away from home. We can even up-link your favorite TV shows."

"Doubt I'll have much time for that."

Steve sat down at the desk and pulled out the keyboard. He clicked a key and the monitor lit up, the CIA emblem filling the screen. "The security in this rig is unparalleled. Watch this . . ." He typed in a few codes. "This'll blow you away." The screen switched to a detailed map of the airport and surrounding area. A tiny curser flashed on their current position. This unit is equipped with a satellite positioning system so you'll always know your exact position." He typed another code. "You can also activate perimeter scanners that detect any intrusion up to a hundred feet from the unit." The screen shifted and now looked like an advanced radar system. The unit is equipped with infrared detection and jamming so that at night you can be made virtually invisible." Steve looked up at Spencer, an expectant look on his face.

Spencer uncrossed his arms and leaned in to get a better view of the screen. "Wow, man," he said, "this is better than Star Trek."

"No shit," Steve said. "The unit is waterproof too, and it'll navigate in water."

"I don't think we'll have to worry about that out here," Spencer said.

"Yeah, right," Steve said with a frown. "But," his face brightened, "it's also hermetically sealed to protect you from a chemical gas attack. You have an emergency air supply system that's good for ten days. As a defense system, the unit is equipped with state of the art weapons, including laser guided missile capabilities. We could take out a satellite in space with this baby if we had too."

Spencer shuddered. What did the CIA think they were getting into here? "I sure hope we won't need any of that," he said.

"We at the Department cover all the possibilities," Steve said, with a reassuring tone. "We live in a hostile world. It's my job to be prepared for anything. You will most likely never need to know about the weapons system on this unit, but they are there just in case." Steve went on to explain the many features of the computer system and the incredible capacity it had. Spencer was assigned an e-mail address and with his level five clearance, he had full access to the encrypted CIA computer system.

"Spencer, I also got you a personal vehicle that you will use to drive the daily commute to and from the site." With that, Steve ordered the men to unload the four-wheel drive jeep. "This jeep" he said, "is loaded with special equipment also. You can up-link to our satellite from here." He pointed to the GPS screen inside the vehicle. Oh, and you can up-link from your laptop computer anywhere on the planet." Spencer put his hands on his hips and sighed. If this was the technology the CIA was willing to tell him about, who knew what kinds of advanced systems they might have that were classified beyond his clearance. He let his gaze slide from the jeep to the FOU and back again, and his mouth went dry.

Steve opened the door of the jeep and waved Spencer into the driver's seat. "We have a few more surprises for you, Spencer, but we can cover the rest over lunch. Let's go to the hotel, I'm starving."

While Steve gulped down a super-sized burger and plateful of fries, he covered some of the daily procedures that he expected Spencer to follow. Spencer was to provide a full report on each day's progress and any unusual findings. Steve would be at headquarters monitoring daily activities and helping in any phase of the project, as needed. "Believe me, if you need computer assistance or any other service, I'll be there for you."

That was what he was afraid of.

When Spencer arrived at the site, the shiny FOU was in place. He'd never seen so much equipment and material or so many men for a single project. Matt Garrett was there, busily giving directions to his crew while Spencer went over the final details of the actual drilling site. Steve had personally located the unit in a strategic spot overlooking the entire site, yet far enough away to reduce the deafening sounds of the heavy equipment. Representatives from the Egyptian government attended the opening ceremonies and congratulated Antonio and Spencer on finding the site.

Antonio had drafted a bulletproof agreement. The Department of Antiquity was aware of the need for secrecy and the immediate area was surrounded with a perimeter fence that would keep it off limits to locals. Antonio had negotiated a twenty-four hour guard at the main gate as well as a patrol along the perimeter fence. The media had been kept in the dark. As far as they were concerned, this was just another oil drilling site and not worthy of coverage. Since ecologically this site had minimum impact, the media had no interest in covering the story anyway.

During the first few weeks, work proceeded without interruption, and Spencer's life fell into a daily routine. The project involved the drilling of two parallel mine shafts; the main shaft and the air and emergency shaft. Approximately fifty feet separated the two to ensure ground stability. Both shafts were to be concrete lined for added stability. A depth of fifteen to twenty thousand feet had never been attempted before on land, only in ocean drilling. Logistically, this was a monumental project requiring a special dumping site for all excavated fill and a concrete site for the pouring of the lining. Special support bracing along the wall of the shaft was designated every fifty feet. These braces doubled as support and as a guide for the main elevator. A man-lift was to be installed in the airshaft. This lift operates as an open elevator with a running vertical belt on one side. Every twelve feet a platform would be installed for a man to stand on while holding onto specially designed straps. This lift would be used for quick evacuations if needed. Both the main elevator and the man-lift would be powered by separate generator systems as back up. In order to work at night, massive lighting systems were installed at the digging area and around the immediate surroundings. Trucks carried the excavated fill to a nearby dump area and massive concrete pumps continually filled the newly created wall cavities. In order to expedite the project, quick-setting cement was used to solidify the outer walls so that the vertical excavation could proceed uninterrupted.

Since the abrupt departure to the US to meet with the CIA, Spencer had been working non-stop. He was in desperate need of some down time. Jeff Miller had asked Spencer to join him for drinks a few times, but he'd always turned him down. When Jeff approached him with the idea this time, Spencer took him up on it.

They went to the usual hangout that was filled with university students, the place where he had met Roula. Her beautiful Greek face filled his mind and his stomach tightened.

And then she was there.

Roula, sitting in the farthest corner of the bar as if she'd never been away, her face buried in a book, and her dark hair shining under the dim bar lights. She was even more beautiful than he'd remembered. He made his way over to her, determined to tell her so.

"Hi, Roula."

She took off her glasses and looked up. Her dark eyes brightened and she smiled. "Ralph," she said, "oh my god, it's great to see you."

"Really?" he said. "I thought maybe you never wanted to see me again."

"Oh, gosh . . . I'm sorry I never called. I had to go back to the States . . . suddenly. My aunt was in an accident and summoned me to her bedside."

"I'm sorry, how is she?"

"Uh, she died."

"Are you okay?"

"I am now."

"I've thought about you a lot. I was sorry when you didn't call."

"I've been thinking about you too. I never got to see your drilling project. I'm really sorry—"

"You've already apologized. It's okay, really."

"If you forgive me, then are you still willing to show me the site? She flashed her pretty white teeth at him and her eyes deepened a few shades.

The look on her face was enough to knock a man off his feet. Damn, the woman was gorgeous. But how the hell was he going to get her into a classified project. There had to be a way. He'd just have to figure it out. He placed his hand on his chest and bowed. "I would be honored to give you a special tour."

"It sounds fascinating, and thank you for forgiving me."

"Okay then. Give me a few days to make my office presentable and I'll be your host."

"You don't need to clean your office for me. I understand African dust. I live in it daily."

He needed to buy time to prepare for her visit. She might ask questions that he couldn't answer. He also needed to figure out a way around Steve. Refusing her the tour now would look bad and could jeopardize whatever their relationship might become. He tucked his hands in his pockets and shrugged. "I just need a little time to get settled and organize my crew. I want to make a good impression when you visit. After all, I should look like I know what I'm doing, I am the boss."

"So you're in charge, huh? Impressive." She tore a sheet of paper from her notebook and scribbled her number on it. After folding the paper in two, she handed it to him between two long fingers. "This time, I'll wait for your call."

Spencer typed his personal password, ZEBRA@WORK, onto the slim keyboard and the monitor screen flickered to life. Beneath the CIA logo the word OPERALI appeared on the screen. OPERALI was the CIA's code word for the mining project. Steve had told him that it stood for "Operation Alien," but insisted they'd come up with it as a joke and that no one at the CIA really believed the substance to be from outer space.

He keyed in another code and a few moments later Steve's smiling face appeared on the monitor.

"Hey Spencer, what gives?"

"I need some guidance . . ." warmth crept up his back and into his neck. The situation was awkward, but he had to get Steve's blessings. "I met this girl—"

"You need my advice about a girl? I'm probably not the best guy for that kind of help."

Spencer's face turned hot. "No, nothing like that. I met her while drilling at the site a few months ago, you know, before all hell broke loose. I really like her. Anyway, she wants to visit me at the site . . . and now everything's classified . . ."

Steve grinned. "Okay, so who is she?"

"She's a Cornell graduate doing a thesis on hieroglyphics."

"Hmm." Steve scratched the stubble on his chin. "It could be tricky given the nature of the project. Although, creating secrecy among your friends might cause unwanted curiosity. That'd be worse than if we treated this as a normal project."

He ran his fingers through his hair and sighed. "Listen, I'll check her out and get back to you, but I'm not making any promises." He grabbed a pen and notepad out of his desk drawer. "Now give me all the details on her."

Spencer told Steve the little he knew about Roula and then fell asleep watching television. He had been working an average of sixteen hours a day and this was the first day since he had arrived back in Egypt that he had forced himself to relax. He woke up two hours later to Steve calling his name from the laptop monitor.

"Listen, Spencer, we checked out your friend."

"That was fast."

"Yeah, that's a very interesting woman you're courting there. She's a real brain in hieroglyphics. Actually, she's considered an expert in the translation of several as yet unknown writings found in Southern Israel. She's also received several large scholarships from the Egyptian Department of Antiquity." Steve rubbed his cheek stubble and sighed. "That worries me."

"Why?" Spencer asked, yawning sleepily.

"Because money often has strings."

"What kind of strings?"

"Let's just say that Egypt could ask for favors in return."

"You mean that she could be doing dirty work for Egypt?"

"It's possible. We have no evidence of any such activities, but we need to be cautious."

"I don't know this girl all that well, but I can't imagine her being bought by anyone." An image of Roula filled his mind and his lips twitched." What do you suggest?"

"I want to help you out here, I really do, but I'm not sure . . ." Steve took a couple of swigs from a Diet Coke then leaned back with his hands behind his head. "I suppose that if we keep things simple—" "She thinks we're only drilling for oil," Spencer offered. "She has no idea how an oil operation should look . . . and the mining shafts could be explained as procedural."

"I suppose, we just have to be careful," Steve said, his face brightening. "I have an idea, tell her the site has a huge deposit that will last far into the next century. Then tell her the oil has a high viscosity so it has to be extracted differently. That'll explain why we need broader access to the deposit, to properly get at all the oil."

"Do you think she'll buy it?"

"Don't see why not, she's studying hieroglyphics, not mining."

"Cool," Spencer said, with a nod. "Thanks for not pulling the plug on me. I really like this girl."

"Spencer, my boy, I can see why. She's wicked beautiful!"

"Have you seen her?" Spencer asked, his brow raised.

"Naw, I have pictures of her in the file," Steve grinned, a dark look in his eyes. "I told you we were thorough."

"Right." Spencer nearly choked on the fake laugh he offered Steve. "There's no doubt you guys are good at your jobs."

Spencer clicked the off icon and the connection ceased. He stared at the screen for a long moment. Roula could visit his project, which would give him a chance to spend several hours with her. That was the good news. But would she believe his story? And what about the CIA's intrusion into her life? She'd be livid if she knew the CIA had investigated her, or that Steve had gotten off looking at her photos. His stomach wrenched. It was all because of him, because he'd wanted to impress her. And what about Steve's concerns about her ties to the Egyptians? It was hard to imagine Roula being bullied by anyone. Yet the Egyptian government was damned ruthless. And Roula had mysteriously disappeared for several weeks. He'd have bought the sick aunt routine without question, except it was the very same lie he'd planned on using when he had to go back to the US unexpectedly. He stood up and shook himself. His imagination was taking him places he had no desire to go. Was he being paranoid? Maybe. But he had a helluva lot to be paranoid about.

Roula arrived at the site in a sparkling gold tank top, tight denim shorts, and with a beautiful smile on her full lips. "So tell me all about your big project," she said.

His eyes were locked on her long, slender legs. God, how he'd love to run his hand along one of those beautifully sculpted thighs? His fingers tingled. He could only hope that one day he'd have the chance to touch her thighs and so much more.

"Spencer?"

"Huh . . . what?"

"I asked you to tell me about your project . . . and take a look at this site trailer. Very impressive. Calpetro must have money to burn if it can equip your field office like this."

"Yeah," he said, his face warming. "I guess they like me. I was told that this is standard equipment for an operation in such a harsh climate, but it's definitely state of the art."

"Well good for you. Cornell let's me fend for myself. I'm lucky to get a tent at my field site."

"A tent in the Egyptian desert doesn't sound like much fun." Although he wouldn't mind seeing how much fun the two of them could make in that tent.

"More fun if you were my sheik." She made a clicking sound out of the corner and her mouth and winked.

"Cute."

They both laughed and then fell into an awkward silence. "So anyway," he said finally, "this project has potential for being one of the largest oil deposits ever found. I was approved for a twenty-four hours a day, seven days a week work schedule… a tent just wouldn't do."

"Oh, Ralph," she said, laying her hand on his chest. "You don't have to explain yourself to me. I'm teasing you. I love your home away from home. I just hope that I can come by once in awhile. I really enjoy your company."

Now that was what he wanted to hear. "I enjoy your company too," he said. "Of course you're welcome anytime." Just how he'd get her into the classified site another time he didn't know. He'd have to worry about that later. "Now, let me give you a tour of this place." He handed her a yellow hard hat. "Here, you'll have to wear this." He took her hand and walked her over to the mine. "These monstrous machines over here are specially designed for digging the mine shaft. The excess dirt will be transported to a local dump site," he said pointing to three large trucks. "And over there," he pointed, "we make fast-setting concrete fo r the shaft's outer lining."

"I don't get it," she said, her dark eyes gazing into his. "I thought you drilled for oil. Why the mine?"

"This site is unusual. Our exploratory drilling showed that the viscosity of the oil is so dense here it would be impossible to pump the oil out of the ground. So, Calpetro decided to gain full access through a mine. It's worth it for such a rich deposit. "

Her gaze swept over the concrete plant, monstrous dump trucks, the FOU, and mine. "It doesn't seem very cost effective. It looks more like your mining for gold."

Damn, the woman was perceptive.

"Or something just as valuable," he said with a shrug. "As big as this find is, we could cover most of our fuel needs for the next century. This deposit is way too large to leave to chance. It could balance the oil reserve from the Arab nations and keep our fuel at the pumps affordable for a long time to come."

"What happens if most of the cars in the next century are electric," she asked with an elbow to his rib, "then what?"

"Good point. Calpetro projects that by 2040 seventy-five percent of all vehicles on earth will be electric, at which point the bulk of this oil will be refined for jet fuel. The viscosity is perfect for that use." She looked up at him, the light of curiosity shining in her dark eyes.

He touched the small of her back and steered her toward the mine's entrance. "Let me show you the progress we've made," He should have known that with her sharp mind she would have lots of questions. The problem was that sooner or later he was bound to run out of clever fabrications.

CHAPTER

SEVEN

The mineshaft was at ten thousand feet when the crew hit water. All work was halted." Matt Garrett, the chief in charge of drilling sat in the FOU across from Spencer explaining the situation.

Spencer got up and ran his hands through his hair. He'd been only half listening, letting his mind replay his time with Roula. "So, we finally hit that underground river, huh?"

"Yeah, that's what I've been telling you." Matt watched him through squinting eyes. "We have water everywhere. I've halted all excavation until we resolve this. Any suggestions?"

He sat at the computer station and turned on the screen. "According to our sonar mappings and the latest electromagnetic readings." He tapped in a few codes and the screen shifted to a full view of the site. "This underground river makes a sharp right turn approximately three hundred feet down stream. See it here?" he said pointing at a snakelike image on the screen. "We will need to re-route the underground channel diagonally and block the flow at our mine shaft location."

"Sounds good. I'll have the crew start drilling a channel to intercept the river down stream."

"Be careful, underground rivers have very high turbulence. The constriction

of the rocks could create high pressure surges that can be pretty damned dangerous."

"Don't worry boss, we'll take all the right precautions."

The next morning Spencer watched his crew make a horizontal bore that was to re-route the raging river away from the mine area so that excavation could resume to lower levels. By noon the rumble in his stomach reminded him that he hadn't eaten all day. He gave Matt a few instructions and then walked back to the FOU.

"Steve," Spencer said to the monitor. "We have a serious delay caused by the underground river I told you about. I checked it out myself. The current is raging in some spots. It could be dangerous for the crew."

"Shit," Steve hung his head for a moment. He looked up, worry lines creasing the corners of his eyes. "What do you want me to do?"

"What's the matter?"

"Nothing."

"Come on, you look worried. What's up?"

Steve stared through the screen for a moment and then seemed to make up his mind. "There are some powerful people watching this project. They're getting antsy." He shook his head. "I'm not looking forward to reporting a delay to the higher ups."

"I told you it might happen—"

"I know, I know. Don't worry, I'll handle it." He smiled, but even through the screen his face appeared drawn and anemic.

"I have a plan that should have us back on track in a few weeks. The only possible delay is if we encounter hard material while drilling."

"What's the plan?"

"We are going to re-route the river."

Steve rubbed his smooth cheek. "What are we talking about for the size of the bypass?"

"To make this work, based on hydraulics calculations, we need a tunnel with a cross sectional area of two-hundred twenty-five square feet, that makes about a fifteen by fifteen foot opening."

"Must be quite a river."

"It is. I mapped the river down stream and it makes a sharp right turn at about three hundred feet. With luck we could have this river re-routed in a week."

"Let's hope we're lucky," Steve said.

"I'll keep you up to date on our progress. We could encounter problems, so let's stay in close communication."

"Let's hook up the satellite feed so we can monitor your actions . . . uh . . . progress full time."

Steve provided the satellite system so Spencer could mount cameras underground and the actual live work would be beamed directly to CIA headquarters. So far, Spencer had only used the set up a few times to show Washington and Calpetro the site. It was too soon for full time live hook up. It was supposed to be reserved for later when they closed in on the objective. Steve's slip about monitoring his actions had his nerves on edge. They didn't trust him. What would it hurt to cooperate at this point? "No problem. I'll set up the live feed so you guys can keep abreast of the situation as it unfolds." He leaned forward and offered Steve what he hoped was his most earnest look. "Thanks, Steve, I can use all the help I can get on this one."

Steve flicked off the monitor and rolled his chair backwards toward his workstation. He lifted a handful of pages from the printer. It was Spencer's schematic of the tunnel. The new section of mine was to begin above the river and then slant down in front of it. The final connection would have to be the last operation after they reached the other end. Spencer had worked out a plan where a series of vertical holes would be drilled from above the slanted tunnel toward the raging river. The diversion of the water to the new tunnel would be painfully slow. The final phase would require blocking the river's present course so that the drilling of the main shaft could resume while the water rushed down the new path.

Steve stayed glued to his monitor while everyone around him worked on special contingencies should the tunnel give way to rushing water. At a pace that felt like that of a slug, the men and machinery created a new tunnel.

Extra bright lights were used for the cameras. For hours each day he stared at the screen until his eyes burned so much that an occasional hot tear ran down his face. If anyone could accomplish this task, Spencer was the one to do it. He'd come to trust Spencer over the months they had worked together. The man was young, but he was damn talented and key to the success of the operation. Tom Detton was right to leave Calpetro's staff in charge of the field details and Steve had, on occasion, told Spencer so. There would be time enough for him to take over the operation and remove all civilians, Spencer included. It wouldn't be long now until the most important find in centuries was in his hands.

Spencer had only been asleep for three hours when his cell

phone rang. He sat up with a start and reached toward the incessant noise on his nightstand only to knock the telephone to the floor. "What now?" he grumbled. He switched on the light and grabbled the telephone from the floor. "Hello?"

"Mr. Spencer, is that you?"

"Matt?" Yes, you woke me up." That should have been obvious. "What's going on?"

"Please come down right away. There's something we need to show you."

Spencer looked at his clock on the dresser. It was 3:25 am. "This can't wait 'til morning?"

"No sir, I think you should come now."

"I'll be right there." He flipped the phone shut, not even bothering to say goodbye. It had taken him until midnight to update his report to the CIA on his plans for the river divergence. With squinting eyes, he walked to the bathroom to splash cold water on his face. He slipped on a pair of khaki shorts and pulled a white t-shirt over his head. When he arrived at the tunnel, Matt was waiting for him at the entrance.

"This had better be important," he said. " I just went to sleep. Did we hit water?"

"Come with me," Matt turned and headed into the mine. You need to see this . . . or better yet, hear it."

At the end of the tunnel the lights for the cameras were blinding. Spencer stopped and waited for his eyes to adjust. The ground rumbled beneath his feet and a muddled roar filled his ears.

"It's the river." Spencer shouted.

"It sure is!"

"Then all we have to do is drill down to the water."

Matt's face fell into a deep frown. "If we open this up, won't the water fill the tunnel and trap all of us in it?" Matt was visibly shaken.

"No. The water is flowing below and away from us. Opening up the tunnel by drilling a large cavity on the floor will only expose the water. We should be okay, all we'll see is rushing water going by."

Matt tucked his thumbs into his belt loop and gazed around the tunnel. "Are you sure?"

Matt's concern was justified. It was only right for him to fear for his crew. Several of the men had already complained of the potential danger. Spencer clapped Matt on the back. "I understand why you're worried," he said. "Down here, nothing is a hundred percent certain. It's a dangerous mission. I'll talk with Steve before we proceed. Once he's aware of the situation we'll get moving." Spencer turned to the camera and asked for Steve Sullivan. The small monitor that was propped on the side of the scaffolds lit up. There was some commotion on the screen, as if people were scuffling about, and then an agent, who looked about seventeen, came into view.

"Steve's out for a few hours," the young man said in a sharp tone.

"Fine, ask him to call me when he gets back." Spencer walked away before the rude agent could respond. He didn't have time for bad-mannered boys. Steve's absence was actually a relief. It would give him a little time to think. "Let's take a forty-five minute break. Get some fresh air everyone. I'll see you back here at 5:30 sharp."

The crew seemed happy for the break from the tension. The men could be heard muttering their concerns as they made their way out of the tunnel. Spencer turned to Matt, whose face had turned ashen. "Jesus, it's so much louder when no one else is down here. Sounds like a torrent."

"It probably is," Spencer said.

"I have to admit, this project is starting to get to me," Matt turned his worried eyes on Spencer. "I'm not a brave guy when it comes to taking chances like this."

"No one is going to take any chances, Matt. We mapped this underground river in advance. We knew it was here and are prepared to handle the situation scientifically and safely." Spencer spoke in the most reassuring voice he could muster. "The trick is to get the water to go where we want it to go instead of where it wants to go."

"Okay, so how do we do it?"

"I think we should drill a small exploratory hole to the water level, send a probe down with a camera, and take a peak at the river from that view." I'll need to ask Steve for a special camera." He turned his back on the dark eye of the camera. "I'm sure he can get it," he added dryly.

Matt nodded. "Let's take some precautions, though. I think we should have a tap ready to screw the opening shut should water suddenly rush up the probe opening."

"Great idea. We'll install a small vent hole in the middle to determine the water pressure.

"Okay." Matt shivered despite the heat. "Let's get out of here for now."

By the time the pair reached the surface, Matt's face had returned to its normal ruddy shade and the worry lines from his brow had vanished. Spencer understood. He also felt relieved whenever he reached the surface.

The morning light was glowing over the eastern horizon and Spencer stopped and stared. The Egyptian desert may be one of the harshest places on earth, but it was also one of the most breathtaking.

Matt took a few steps toward his jeep and then stopped and turned back to Spencer. "I really need some time off . . . I know this isn't a good time but—"

"No, no, you're right. You deserve a little time away from this place. I need to go over everything with Steve anyway, and that special camera will take a while to get here. Would two days do it?"

Matt grinned. "Thanks, Spencer. See you in a couple of days. Page me if you need me sooner."

"You got it."

Spencer walked back to the FOU. He dropped into the ergonomic chair and flipped on the monitor. The top of Steve's blonde head filled the big screen.

"Hi, Steve," Spencer said.

Steve looked up, his face as cheerful as ever. He was wearing a polo shirt and looked well rested and relaxed. At least someone was getting a little shut-eye.

"We're at water level," Spencer said. His voice sounded tired and gravelly even to him. Who cared? He was too tired to hide his exhaustion.

"You okay?"

"Yeah, just tired. I need a camera to get a look at the river."

Steve grinned. "I have the perfect device. The camera is mounted on a small flexible wire with a built in high intensity light. The entire device is less than the circumference of your thumb. The camera has the capability of remote operation so you can pivot its position up to three hundred sixty degrees."

"When can I have it?" Spencer asked, his voice now anxious.

"I'll ship it immediately. It should be in your hands by six tomorrow your time."

"Great, thanks."

"Hey Spencer, make sure that we are linked at all times. I want to see this myself."

"Of course." He flipped the monitor's off switch and the screen went dark. "Asshole," he muttered.

The constant surveillance of the CIA was beginning to get under his skin. He had heard too many CIA horror stories, enough that their involvement kept his stomach in knots. Antonio was even more distrustful of the CIA. He had warned Spencer that they couldn't be trusted. Antonio had said that the CIA was just a form of legitimate Mafia. "Those idiots have absolute power over secret operations," Antonio had said. "They decide what information is withheld from the public and private sectors. All of this power is justified in the interest of national security." Antonio had spat out the last sentence. "With those two words, all actions taken by the CIA are justifiable, including murder."

Of course the CIA would never call it murder. To them it would simply be the elimination of a problem, a nuisance. Damn, this job had turned him into one distrustful individual. He rocked back and folded his hands across his chest. He thought about all the people involved in the project. Who could he trust? Certainly not Tom Detton or Steve Sullivan. Confiding anything to the Department of Antiquity would be certain disaster. And what about the other players? Matt Garrett and Jeff Miller had proven indispensable to the project and had become welcome friends. But how would they react if an alien ship were ensconced within the cave? Or what if it's something more dangerous and sinister? What about Antonio Casenza, or even McPearson for that matter? How will they respond to whatever is in that cave? Would greed or the desire for self-importance cloud their judgment?

And what of Roula?

He sighed as an image of her beautiful face and smoky eyes filled his mind. Would his feelings for her get in the way if there was, in fact, a threat to national security?

The truth was, he could trust only himself. He had already told Paul Seiber too much, but he could control that. In the future, he would share only the minimum information required. He would formulate an alternate plan, strictly for his protection. He turned on the computer and downloaded his e-mail. The cryptic message from Paul was there—his secret apartment was ready. Paul had taken care of all the details and everything was in place as planned. This gave Spencer great comfort. If things got sticky, he would have a secret place where he could escape. He would expand his plan to formulate a full disappearance if necessary.

A day and half later they were ready to deal with the river.

"Matt, I hope you relaxed the last couple of days because we're going to get a good look at that rushing water today."

"I'm ready. Did you get the camera?"

"Came in two hours ago. Let's go check it out."

A crewmember walked over from the field shop carrying a steel pipe with a threaded cap. Spencer examined the pipe and fittings. "Looks like exactly what I specified," he said to the man with a smile.

A crew of a half dozen men followed Spencer and Matt into the tunnel. "Let's drill right there," Spencer said, pointing to an X he had marked in the sand. They could have drilled just about anywhere.

Marking the X had been his way of creating an air of confidence—an emotion he didn't really feel.

The drill advanced slowly as the threaded pipe plunged farther and farther in. Suddenly, water rushed out from the vent hole.

Spencer stood to the side with Matt who held the camera cradled in his arm like a baby. A man moved closer to get a look. "Let's stay clear of the drilling machine," Spencer said.

With a loud swoosh water spouted from the vent hole and hit the top of the gigantic tunnel. "Stop!" Spencer yelled.

"I told you I didn't like this idea, Spencer," Matt yelped. "Do you think the pipe will hold?"

Spencer ignored him.

"Pull back three inches at a time." Spencer yelled to the drill operator while watching the vent hole at the top of the pipe. "Three more inches, very slowly now."

"Spencer, what are you doing? If you pull the pipe out we'll be deluged." Matt edged away, his face white with fear. "You two," he said to two men who were standing back watching. "Get out of here."

"No one needs to go anywhere," Spencer said. "The drilling machine advanced a little too far and hit water, that's all. If we back out the pipe slowly and stop at the roof of the river, the water should stop."

The pair looked at each other with wide eyes but didn't move.

"Two more inches." The waterspout sputtered and dropped a few feet. "There, see? It's stopping."

The men backed the drill out a few more inches and the spout diminished to a gurgling bubble.

"How'd you know that would work?" Matt asked.

Spencer shrugged. "We didn't know when the machine penetrated the rock because the thread advances evenly even after the bottom is out. Backing out let the water flow freely again." He pointed to the camera in Matt's hands. "That probe camera will tell us how much room we have."

"Congratulations, Spencer," Steve's voice echoed through the tunnel. "It looks like you'll be able to divert this water without a problem. Good job."

Spencer turned and looked at the small monitor propped in the tunnel. He'd almost forgotten that Big Brother was watching. "Let's see," he said, an edge of irritation in his voice.

Spencer installed the small camera down the center of the pipe. As it reached bottom, he adjusted the remote control until it was turned ninety degrees. A crisp picture of rushing water appeared on the screen. Spencer turned the camera toward the ceiling.

"Steve, can you see that?"

"Yes, clearly. It looks like you have room to open your tunnel right above this cavity without any danger of water flooding the tunnel."

"I agree. Quite a gadget, this camera." Spencer counted the graduated markings on the pipe. "I read about nine inches of space. What do you figure the horizontal distance to be, Steve?"

"The camera has built in sonar. Just rotate it to the horizontal position and activate the SR button. It should give you a reading in feet on the small instrument screen."

Spencer manipulated the camera according to Steve's instructions. "Yep," he said with a smile. "We're in business." He glanced up at Matt who was shaking his head and smiling, a look of relief apparent on his face. Matt seemed incapable of hiding his emotions. He should never become a poker player. "I want a hole here that's sixteen feet in diameter." He turned to the crewmen, "And don't take your eyes off that water. It can still be unpredictable. I don't want anyone hurt."

"Great job, Spencer," Steve said.

Spencer waved in the general direction of the monitor without looking up. "Matt, let's go work on the other end." He lowered his voice. "That's a bit trickier."

Spencer had worked out the design weeks earlier. They would drill down from the slanted tunnel side to the water below and then build a concrete wall in front of the opening, sealing the new tunnel to the ceiling. The concrete wall would prevent the water from flowing into the tunnel area just above the underground river near the mine-shaft. Spencer had ordered twelve steel plates. When these were all in place, the last step would be to create concrete forms and slide them in pre-drilled slots down to the bottom of the river. Each plate was massive, and when placed in the slot, would restrict the flow of water downstream and re-direct the water in the man-made tunnel.

One by one, all twelve plates were placed in position. Water rushed into the sealed opening behind the concrete barrier, into the newly built tunnel, and down the sixteen-foot diameter opening at the other end. All that was left now was to pour a new concrete wall. Matt's face once again reflected relief when the concrete had set and the water flow stopped completely. They had done it. Spencer celebrated the occasion by buying the entire crew a round of beer. Now the real work could continue. It had taken them exactly nine days to divert the underground river.

Back in the FOU the light on his e-mail icon blinked in the darkness. A message from Antonio was waiting. Antonio Casenza warned Spencer of an inspection from the Department of Antiquity. They had heard the news about the underground river and wanted all work stopped until their field team assessed the situation. Spencer had briefly met some of the inspectors during the opening ceremonies. Surprisingly, the government of Egypt had kept out of the picture since then. Spencer had heard stories of projects being held up for months, but in this case it hadn't happened. At least, not yet. Would this be the beginning? He picked up the phone and dialed Antonio's private line. "I just read your e-mail Antonio. I've already finished the water diversion, now what?"

"You're finished already? They've sure got you hopping in that mine hole!"

"Tell me about it." Spencer said, not bothering to hide his irritation.

"I just received word of the inspection. They usually give me more warning."

"How do I handle it?"

"Just show them the work and tell them as little as possible, just that the diversion was minimal, created no disruption to the ecological balance, and nothing was found that would pertain to the realm of antiquity."

"Are you joking?"

"No. What else could you do? You worked efficiently and the problem was resolved without consequence. That's the truth and it's all you need to tell them."

Early the next morning Spencer stood at the tunnel entrance surrounded by four Egyptian inspectors from the Department of Antiquity. Three of the men seemed nervous. Their black eyes darted about the site, taking in the men and equipment. They looked like hungry pigeons waiting for breadcrumbs. The fourth man was an altogether different sort. He was a barrel-chested man with a thick mustache and course black hair. Fifty pounds lighter and he'd have been a dead ringer for Omar Sharif. His hands were large and his fingers were puffed up like sausages. He held an ornate cane in his right hand, which he seemed to use more as a prop than for support.

"My name is Mohammad Aiel Abdul," the man said. "I am the chief inspector for the Department of Antiquity."

The Egyptian's words came out in short puffs. He either had trouble pronouncing the English words or he was too fat to breathe properly, Spencer couldn't tell which.

"We received notice from Mr. Casenza that an underground river has flooded your mine shaft," Abdul said. "As you may know, we are here for an inspection. You must cease all work until further notice from us."

He may call himself the chief inspector for the Department of Antiquity, but Spencer knew better. The man's real job was to spy on unauthorized excavation sites. His task was to recover precious artifacts from these sites and turn them over to the department. This trick gave the Egyptian museums an abundance of artifacts at no cost, and provided additional revenue from the heavy fines imposed on the culprits.

"Mr. Abdul, I'm afraid Mr. Casenza was in error. The river never flooded the mine. It simply prevented us from proceeding with the work. It was a minor problem and it has already been resolved. I'll be glad to show you."

Why had Antonio told the Egyptians about the river? He would need to have a talk with Antonio later.

The elevator gave a slight jolt as it reached the ten thousand foot level. The three inspectors, who had been silent so far, clung to the bars as if they were plummeting to the ground. Spencer's lips twitched into a smile. He stopped the elevator and signaled the group to exit. The three men took in their surroundings and then looked up, their mouths agape, and their hardhats sliding back on their heads. He really couldn't blame the young inspectors for their nervousness. They had surely never been this far underground before.

Spencer escorted the group along the mammoth tunnel above the river to the newly built concrete barriers. Abdul's pace was slow and when he walked his body swung from side to side. He favored his left side. He was probably only fifty, but he acted much older.

"Now, here below our feet, at approximately one and a half meters, rushes an underground river," Spencer said, sounding like a tour guide. "Its path intersected our mine shaft and so it became necessary for us to divert the water around our shaft and reconnect the river downstream. This is exactly what has been done."

"Do you mean to tell me Mr. Spencer, that you have diverted water without our permission?"

"Well, yes. I wasn't aware that dealing with this type of common problem during deep underground excavations required your approval. We found no sign of ancient ruins, and I assure you no artifact was affected by this water redirection. We simply dug a new tunnel diagonal to the river and intersected the water downstream. We then sealed off this tunnel here," he pointed to the concrete wall, "so that when the water rushed in, it flowed down the tunnel and into the existing river at the other end. We then blocked the river right here below your feet and the flow was diverted."

"Mr. Spencer," Abdul sputtered. "I'm sure you are a very clever man, but our department has not been given the opportunity to provide input. The government of Egypt needs to make a determination regarding this water. As you know, water is very scarce in the Sahara, this new source might be important to the welfare of Egypt. We will need samples to analyze."

Spencer gave a surreptitious glance in the direction of the CIA cameras. The camera lights had been shut off and the cameras themselves were now hidden by dark shadows. Steve had ordered that Spencer take every precaution to make sure the inspectors knew nothing of the CIA's involvement. Even though Steve couldn't see what was happening, he was surely listening.

"Of course, we will provide whatever you need. I can save you some time, though. Calpetro did an extensive analysis last week. This water is highly toxic, non-potable, and very hot—about ninety-three degrees. I can have the results for you when we get back in my office." Spencer used his most polite voice. He wanted to prevent any further delays and this was certainly an unnecessary one.

"Mr. Spencer, we will take your results and check them against our own. Now, please send in a crew to extract five gallons of water."

Spencer radioed Matt and asked him to drill a small hole into the new concrete wall to siphon out five gallons. Ten minutes later the inspectors left carrying jugs filled with the noxious water. Mohamed Aiel Abdul returned to the site two days later. He paced furiously back and forth in Spencer's office, his cane prodding at various objects as if to let something out from underneath.

"Mr. Spencer, your weekly reports to our department have been very lacking. I received the one pertaining to the underground river just yesterday." Mohamed's voice was rising with every word. "May I remind you that as part of our contractual agreement you are to provide us with complete and detailed reports on a weekly basis," he shouted. "If not for Mr. Casenza's efforts, this project would be shut down indefinitely."

"Mr. Abdul, need I remind you what is at stake here for your country?" He moved close to Abdul and lowered his voice to a whisper. "We are doing our best to keep this project's true objective a secret. Egypt will realize a tremendous profit in gold if we succeed."

Abdul grunted.

" In the meantime, I promise you I will be more diligent in the future with my reports."

Abdul signaled for his assistant to hand him the water report. "Mr. Spencer, we concur with your findings. The water is toxic. Our department, however, is very concerned with this project and has placed it under my direct supervision. I can tell you that periodic inspections will take place in the future."

"That will be just fine, Mr. Abdul. Now do we have your permission to proceed with the mine shaft?"

Abdul handed a signed release to Spencer and left. There was no doubt that from now on the Department of Antiquity would be watching with greater intensity. The real reason for all this digging was still hidden at the bottom of the mine. Who knew what he'd find there? Now he had to worry about the CIA and Abdul. The trick would be to stay one step ahead of these treacherous people.

"Antonio, I could kill you!" Spencer yelled into the receiver.

"Oh, so you met Mr. Abdul. I did you a big favor Spencer, believe me. I know that character well and if he had found out about the water from an outside source, you would be drinking at the local hang out for months."

"Why?"

"Well, let's just say that the prick would shut the project down cold."

"He says he's going to inspect us regularly now. Should I worry?"

"Not at this point. Abdul's an ornery old bastard, but he's manageable."

"I guess you don't like him much?'

"Let's say I detest him, but I can get around him. He's like a pesky insect that I have learned to live with."

"Thanks for the advice. I called to yell at you and I end up thanking you. I keep forgetting that nothing gets by a Casenza."

Spencer contacted Steve and filled him in on the details of Abdul's inspection. As expected, Steve had heard almost everything. Steve promised to do a little background check on the chief inspector. "Everybody's got a little dirty laundry lying around," Steve said. "And Abdul strikes me as the kind of guy who's got dirtier laundry than most."

Spencer disconnected with Steve and called into his voicemail. Roula had left two messages and she sounded anxious. Now that the digging was back on course, he'd be able to dedicate more time to his favorite person. He dialed her number.

"Ralph," Roula sighed, her voice rich with concern. "I heard about the underground river. I was worried."

"Oh? Don't worry. It's all over. We diverted the water and things are back to normal . . . How did you hear about it?"

"I, uh . . . oh, everyone's talking about it."

"Really?"

I've missed you, Ralph." Her voice had turned husky. "I have some free time tomorrow, want me to come over?"

"I'd love that. I've missed you, too. Why don't you come by around nine in the morning and I'll make you breakfast."

"You've got a date," she said. "See you then."

Roula arrived the next morning looking even lovelier than he remembered. How she managed to look so cool and comfortable in 102-degree heat was beyond him. They sat huddled at the small table in the FOU eating pancakes and eggs. "You're a good cook," she said. "These pancakes are fantastic."

"I can cook a pretty mean breakfast, but that's about it," he said, looking into her eyes. "Didn't you wonder why I didn't invite you for dinner?"

"No," she nudged him fondly, "I thought you were just anxious to see me."

They nibbled on the pancakes and eggs and Roula told him all about her latest hieroglyphic translation project. "It's one of the most challenging I've ever encountered," she said.

He took her slender hand in his. "Sounds fascinating," he said, and he meant it. Besides her physical beauty, Roula's intelligence and her passion for her work were what had drawn him to her in the first place.

She dropped her fork onto her plate. "Full," she said, patting her flat stomach. "So now that the danger's past, can I see the underground river?"

"Well, you could, except that I had it sealed off."

Her shoulders dropped. "Oh," she said.

"But if you like, I can show you the tunnel that we dug to get above the water."

Her eyes lit up. "Cool. I've never been so deep in the earth. There's something . . . exhilarating . . . about it."

He laughed. "Not for me. I've been down there nearly every day for months now. It's not really my idea of fun."

Her bottom lip poked out forming the most enchanting pout he'd ever seen.

"But I suppose it is cooler down there," he said, his throat suddenly tight.

She ran her tongue along her lips seductively. "Cool is good."

"Yeah," he said, "very good."

CHAPTER

EIGHT

The crew had been working around the clock and all the heavy equipment was already well below the tunnel. Roula and Spencer found it deserted and very dark. The only light was coming from the main shaft some thirty feet behind them. "We pump air down the auxiliary shaft and the convection system cools the entire shaft," he said.

"That's interesting." She took his hand and drew him toward her.

Her eyes were like black opals bathed in moonlight. The warmth of her body sent a ripple of heat through his body. He wrapped his arm around her shoulders and led her to the concrete barrier. "Put your ear against the cement," he said.

"Oh my god, I hear it . . . I can hear the water rushing by. It sounds like the roar of the ocean in a shell. This is so impressive. I'm proud to know you. You're not only a geologist and an Archeologist, but also an engineer."

"I had a lot of help."

She turned to face him and pulled his arms around her. She closed her eyes, leaned in, and pressed a tender kiss against his lips. The warmth of her touch combined with the cool darkness of the tunnel enflamed him. He pulled her tighter and kissed her deeply. She seemed to melt into his arms and for a moment nothing in the world existed but the two of them. They were wrapped in their own little cocoon fifteen thousand feet below ground. He had dreamed of kissing her, but he hadn't expected her passion to flair here, now, in a cold, dark tunnel.

They rode back to the surface without speaking a single word, as if by mutual understanding their time together in the tunnel had been sacred.

Time at the dig passed too slowly when Roula wasn't around. He'd spend every minute with her if he could, but his demanding schedule allowed for only short dates a few times a week. Every time he saw her, his heart skipped a beat. Whenever they had to part, his chest constricted. Life before Roula seemed dim and empty.

The dig was progressing quickly, even with the daily crises and problems to resolve. With a twenty-four crew there were no slowdowns. The crew was now at nearly seventeen thousand feet and had reached a thick layer of old lava rock. Sonar revealed a huge cavity directly below them. The crew was jubilant. The bottom was near. Mr. Abdul kept his promise and his inspectors had become regular visitors. They would come at least once a week, spending most of their time above ground making sure that the soil excavated from the shaft was properly disposed of. To them the dirt coming out was more important than examining what was at the bottom of the mine, or so they said. Considering their reaction to being so far underground, a more likely explanation was that they didn't want to take their chances on a second trip into the darkness of the inner earth. Besides, what could possibly be disturbed seventeen thousand feet below the surface?

The CIA had kept a close watch on Spencer's progress and insisted on daily monitoring of the excavation via satellite. Their constant presence in the mine was an annoyance he'd rather be without. For now, though, he had to be as cooperative as possible. Attention to the proper arrangement of the cameras had become a hassle that he and the crew resented. Too often a crewmember would accidentally trip the wires and the connection would be lost, leaving the agents in Washington in the dark. Despite the inconvenience, Spencer enjoyed those moments. It felt good to occasionally have a little power over the watchful eye of the CIA. There were enough hints of their true intentions that he had come to mistrust their every move. He had formulated an alternate plan to deal with a hostile CIA once he reached the bottom of the mine. Whatever was down there needed protecting. Would he share the find with Roula? He wanted to, but every time he'd start to tell her about the unusual substance they'd found, something stopped him. Roula still had an air of mystery about her and he couldn't quite shake the doubts he had about her. It was true; Roula had become his passion. She was a wonderful diversion from the daily stresses of the mammoth project that had taken over his life. She often insisted on meeting him while he was working at the site, which made concentrating on his work a real challenge. She was surprisingly fascinated by the complexity of the project—always asking questions and wanting to know the details of various operations.

"Spencer do you have a minute?" Matt Garrett stood in the doorway of the FOU, a ball cap clenched in his rough hands.

"Sure, what's up?"

"I'm not sure how to tell you this . . ." Matt gestured to the chair across from Spencer.

"Sure, sit down."

Matt edged his way into the seat and looked around the interior of the FOU. "This thing is so cool," he said.

Matt had been inside the FOU at least a hundred times. He was stalling.

"Why don't you just tell me what's going on," Spencer said.

"Uh, okay. Well, you see . . ."

Spencer leaned forward and perched his elbows on his knees. "Go on."

"Yesterday, while you were, you know, meeting with the Egyptian inspectors at the cement site, I saw Roula at the bottom of the shaft on one of the scaffolds."

"Oh, I know, she's fascinated with this site."

"Well, sir, there's more. I saw her messing with the up-link cable. She didn't know I was watching."

"What are you talking about?" Spencer asked, his defenses up.

"Look, you're the boss, and I know you really care about this woman. I'm sure there's a logical explanation . . . I just think it might be better for everyone if she didn't have access to the shaft without an escort. I mean, not only are we working on a classified project, but it could be dangerous for her."

Matt's attempt at avoiding offending Spencer only succeeded in getting his hackles up. He broke into a sweat, his neck burned, and his mouth had gone dry. He brushed aside his own doubts about Roula. "I'm sure she wasn't doing anything inappropriate."

"Oh, I'm sure," Matt agreed. "It was just a small incident that

I thought you'd want to address before something . . . unpleasant happened."

"I'll talk to her. Thanks for coming to me.

Matt stood, placed the rumpled ball cap on his head, and jumped out of the FOU, ignoring the steps. "See ya later."

"Uh, Matt? Wait a second," Spencer said.

Matt poked his head back in the doorway.

"What was Roula doing with the up-link cable?"

"I looked at the connections after she left. Couldn't see anything wrong with it. I have no idea."

Spencer smiled and nodded. "I'll talk to her. Thanks again."

"Sure thing."

Spencer's stomach tightened into a knot. What had Roula been up to? What was this obsession she had with the project? She was a hieroglyphics expert. Why would an oil dig, even one this extensive, hold any fascination for her? He picked up his cell phone and dialed her number.

"Hi there. I have some free time today. Can I take you to lunch?" Spencer asked, trying to be nonchalant.

"Lunch would be great. I came by yesterday, but I couldn't find you."

"Oh, yeah, well I was on a supply run for part of the day. Pick you up at twelve."

He took her to their favorite Italian restaurant on the outskirts of Cairo. He held out her chair for her and she slid into the seat gracefully. She looked lovely in a ruffled blue tank top that showed off the mounds of her full breasts. Damn, why'd the woman have to be such a mystery?

"So I finished deciphering the—"

"Why didn't you tell me that you came by the site yesterday, Roula?"

She sat back in her chair and raised her eyebrows. "What are you talking about? I just told you on the phone—"

"I know, it's just that I like being with you and would have enjoyed seeing you yesterday."

She leaned forward and placed her chin in her hand. "So what's the problem? You barely said a word on the drive here, and now you're acting as if I've done something wrong. I don't get it."

"There's nothing to get," he said with a shrug. "I just wanted to see you."

Roula sat back and crossed her arms, her brown eyes boring into his. A confrontation with Roula was the last thing he wanted, but he had to find out what she had been doing in the mine. "Matt saw you at the bottom of the shaft . . . he was concerned for your safety, that's all."

"If he saw me alone and was so concerned, why didn't he say something?"

"He said that he tried to catch up with you, but you had already headed back up the elevator."

"I see."

The waiter arrived to take their order. "We haven't had time to look at the menu yet," Roula said, never taking her eyes off Spencer. The waiter nodded politely and walked away.

"I was surprised to see a TV monitor at the bottom of the mine," Roula said. What's it for?"

"Oh, nothing really." Spencer ran his fingers through his hair and gazed around the restaurant. When he looked back at Roula her eyes were wide and her jaw was slack. How had she so deftly turned the tables on him? "Calpetro owns a satellite link in this region so headquarters can monitor our progress. They are actually very helpful when we encounter drilling or excavation problems. They just jump right in and help resolve the situation." When had he become such a smooth liar?

Roula said nothing, but her gaze was relentless, although those lovely liquid brown irises had softened a little.

"Here's the deal," he said. "Since my bosses can see what goes on at the bottom of the mine, let me escort you next time. It could mean my job."

She smiled and reached her hands across the table. "Of course. I just went down looking for you. The TV was a surprise that made me stop and look."

"I guess I forgot to mention it to you. It's really no big deal." He looked down at his menu. "So what do you think you're going to order?" He wanted off the subject and quick.

At the office Steve had left him an urgent e-mail. Spencer punched in his password and the screen came alive.

"Hi Steve. Here I am."

"Spencer, thanks for the quick reply. We have a situation that needs your immediate attention. Our computer model of the soil strata and the electromagnetic instrumentation at the bottom of the mineshaft are suggesting a large void at approximately eighteen thousand feet.

"That means we're getting near the bottom."

"The problem is your last core sample. It's almost entirely dense lava rock. Our model suggests a thickness in the range of eight hundred to eleven hundred feet."

"Wow, what do you want me to do?" He had known about the lava since earlier that morning when the crew had reached that level. He had learned, though, that it was easier to let Steve do the talking. The more Steve thought he was in control the better.

"This morning Mr. Detton gave us a directive that must be followed to the letter. He wants the mine off limits to all non-essential personnel. That means no visitors and no one without our authorization gets down that mine. Is this clear?"

"Of course," Spencer said, biting back what he really wanted to say. "What about the inspectors, what do I tell them?"

"You'll need to create a diversion. We want no one down there. What do you anticipate in terms of the time needed to penetrate the lava rock?" Steve asked, his voice anxious.

"If your calculations are correct on the thickness, I'll be able to give you an estimate once we reach the lava layer and determine the rate of excavation. Right now, it's impossible to guess." He knew exactly how long it would take, but he needed to buy time for himself before the entire CIA team converged on the project.

Antonio Casenza was always well dressed no matter what the occasion or the weather. Antonio was also always pleased to see Spencer.

"Spencer, my boy," Antonio said, always the charmer, "Nice of you to visit, come in." He led Spencer through his plush living room and out onto the patio. He nodded to the maid, who bent down and flipped a switch. There was a sputter and then a cool mist filled the air. Antonio signaled for Spencer to have a seat. The maid disappeared into the house.

"Thanks. Antonio. Thanks for seeing me. I need to discuss something rather, uh, delicate with you." Spencer swallowed hard. He trusted Antonio, but still hesitated to tell him too much. "We've reached the lava layer. That means we're nearly at the depth level where we first detected the strange material."

"Great job." So what's the problem?"

"Steve just called and he has orders to seal up the area tighter than a drum. Frankly, the CIA worries me. I know that once we reach the area in question, we'll no longer be needed. They'll take full control of the project and we'll never know what's down there. You yourself told me not to trust them. What do we do?"

Antonio lit a long, thin cigarette and blew a puff of smoke into the mist. "We buy time. How long did you tell Steve it would take to reach bottom?"

"I didn't. I told him that we haven't yet reached the lava layer and that I had no way of telling how fast we could excavate through it. It was a lie, we reached the area this morning."

Antonio tapped his cigarette on the ashtray. "Hmm," he said. "What do you think it will take to get through?"

"Not much. Based on my calculations, we'll be there in less than three days. The lava is much softer at lower levels. I've kept the core samples here so Steve has no idea yet."

"You're a rascal, Spencer. I'm glad to hear that you aren't trusting them."

"You told me not to, remember?"

"Of course." Antonio gave Spencer an approving smile. "You do know that this could get us in very serious trouble," he added.

"Yeah, I know, but I think the alternative is a lot more dangerous."

Antonio nodded in agreement. "I admire your courage, Spencer," he said.

Coming from a man who seemed to know no fear, that was quite a compliment.

"We should be able to stall the CIA at least two weeks," Spencer said, sounding more confident than he felt. He had spent hours going over the latest lava samples, but there were dozens of ways things could go terribly wrong.

"Good." Antonio crushed out his cigarette. "Let's find out what's really down there and evaluate the situation then. This could all be for nothing."

Or the archeological find of the century.

The maid returned with a tray and two glasses of iced tea. Antonio thanked her with a kind smile. Spencer had been only a child when he lost his father. Over the last few months Antonio had unexpectedly become a sort of father figure to him.

"How are you going to handle the live feed?" Antonio asked.

"We've had glitches before. I'll simply shut it down at the appropriate time."

"You'll have to be careful with that. Don't give them any reason to get suspicious."

"I'm sure I'll come up with something. I've got Steve thinking he's in full control. He trusts me."

"I have great confidence in you, Spencer. I'm sure you'll manage just fine."

Spencer sipped his tea and gazed out at the desert through the mist. The misters were a shameful waste of water, but he had to admit it made the desert heat bearable. "What should I tell McPearson? He has standing plane reservations. He wants to be here the minute we reach the area containing the alien material"

"I say treat him the same as the CIA. If you don't, someone will get suspicious. Time is our best ally right now, let's take advantage of it."

Four days later Spencer swung open the door of the FOU. Matt was sitting in the recliner, his face flushed and beaming. "Good morning, Mr. Spencer," he said with a big grin.

"You got through, didn't you? You hit the void?" Spencer's heart started racing.

"We did boss, less than an hour ago." Matt was clearly excited to be the one to break the news. After all, they had been waiting for this day through sixteen months of non-stop grueling work.

"Who else knows about this?"

"You and me and the first shift crew. They're still waiting at the bottom for instructions from you."

"Great. Let's get down there and survey the area first. No word of this to anyone Matt, clear?" Spencer took Matt by the shoulders and looked him in the eye. "Are we clear?" He had only a small space of time before word would leak out to the CIA. It was time to put his plan in motion.

"Hey Spencer, I'm on your side, remember?" Matt had expressed his fondness toward Spencer before. He would have done anything for him. And both men were suspicious of the CIA and the Egyptian Department of Antiquity.

Spencer kept stride with Matt until an unsettling thought hit him. His stomach tightened. Had Washington seen the crew reach the void? He stopped and grabbed Matt by the arm. "Matt, is the feed on?"

"No, I cut the it two hours ago," Matt smiled. "When the first equipment broke through the lava rock, I pulled the plug." Matt said, hesitation in his voice.

"You did the right thing."

Matt placed his hands on his hips, took a deep breath, and

looked off in the distance.

"You look worried," Spencer said. "What's bothering you?"

"Well, when I disconnected the main feed at the bottom of the shaft something strange happened."

"What?"

"I was trying to cut the feed so that it would look like an accident, but I noticed a strange loop in the wires. I followed the lead from the monitor . . ."

"And?"

"I think it's not ours."

"What do you mean?"

"I think we've got someone out there watching every move we make, and I don't mean the CIA."

"Shit." Spencer took a few long strides toward the mine. "We've got to get down there."

Matt rushed ahead and stepped in front of him. He looked Spencer in the eye. "I know how much you care for Roula, but I saw her at that very spot, you know, the day she wandered down the mine alone." Matt stepped back. He'd said what he had to say.

"Come on, you think Roula's a spy?"

"All I'm telling you is what I saw."

"I already asked Roula about it. She said she was just looking for me and happened upon the monitor. She was just trying to figure out what it was for."

Matt continued to gaze at Spencer, doubt reflected in his eyes. "Maybe it's all a coincidence . . . But it must have occurred to you, too."

"Well, it did. But like I said—"

"Okay, forget it." Matt stepped out of Spencer's path. "The only sure thing is that someone is spying on us and we had better find out who it is."

"Abdul would be my first guess." Spencer's face flushed with anger. "Sneaky old bastard."

As they approached the mine, Matt signaled to the two men at the entry to open the gate. "We'd better hurry," Spencer called. He was the first in the elevator and he had a video camera ready. "Actually, Matt," he said, "this can work to our advantage. We'll tell the CIA about the breach. They'll insist that we keep the feed off. This will give us precious time to examine the cavity."

Matt smiled. "You're always a step ahead, boss."

He didn't feel a step ahead. In fact, his head was spinning. Was Roula up to something? And if so, what?

CHAPTER

NINE

At the bottom of the shaft Spencer congratulated the crew and gave them the rest of the day off. He explained to them the importance of keeping everything quiet until he had a chance to survey the entire cavity. Matt assured Spencer that the crew could be trusted. Equipped with his video camera, Spencer led Matt deep into the mammoth cavity.

"Damn, this cave is huge," Matt said. "What do you think happened here?"

Spencer walked in a circle. The sheer magnitude of the cave was overwhelming. "This cavity was formed a long time ago by a huge volcanic eruption." Spencer replied. From the flow characteristics of the lava, the cavity was formed in a very short time, sealing everything in it. This type of volcanic upheaval would have to date back hundreds of thousands of years."

"There's no oil here, Spencer."

"I know."

Matt raised his eyebrows. "You mean—"

Spencer nodded. "What we saw on the aerial reconnaissance was the resonance of this huge cave. There's something more important than oil somewhere in this cave. We're going to find the source of that alien material."

Matt's face shone with anticipation. "The eruption would have closed off all life as it existed and preserved the site in its original state."

"That's right." Spencer bent down and rubbed his hand across the smooth lava surface. "Do you realize that we're the first humans to walk on this soil." He stroked the ground as if it were a beloved pet. "It's been undisturbed for hundreds of thousands of years." Spencer turned on the video camera to document this incredible moment in his life. The cave seemed to extend for miles and the ceiling varied from twenty feet to several hundred feet in height. The ground was hard and the lava rock was slick. It made walking treacherous. Spencer and Matt moved forward slowly, trying to locate the position of the exploratory drilling that had hit the alien material. The mineshaft had been drilled approximately two hundred feet from the original drill site. This was done as a precaution since no one knew what was at the bottom. He didn't want to take any chances while excavating the large mine shaft. He adjusted the overhead lights to shine farther into the cave. A strange silvery object appeared in the distance. Frantic, he hurried forward until he was about a hundred feet away.

He dropped to his knees, the video camera falling into his lap. "Jesus Christ . . ."

Matt came up behind him and stopped at his side. "What the hell . . .?

The two men stayed that way for a long moment, as if frozen in time. There were no words to describe what they were seeing.

"It sure as hell ain't natural." Matt said finally.

Directly in front of them was a huge geometrical object partially buried in the lava rock.

"My God! It's incredible," Matt said. "But what the hell is it?"

The object in front of them was of enormous proportions. It appeared to be perfectly geometrical and was in the shape of two pyramids joined together at their bases.

"They're pyramids," Matt said, stating the obvious. "They look like they were made by a . . . a . . ."

"Giant spider," Spencer finished the sentence for him.

"Yeah, it's like a gigantic pyramid made of spider webs." Matt took the camera from Spencer's unmoving hands and turned it on. "I don't know what I was expecting," he said, "but it sure as hell wasn't this."

The entire outer shape of the object was composed of stiff parallel wires approximately thirty inches apart with perfect connections at each intersection. The wires were of a strange metallic composition that resembled gold. In the center of the two pyramids was a cigar shaped object. It was so smooth it shimmered, and it projected outward from where the wires formed the pyramids. The connected pyramids spanned a distance of well over a hundred feet. One of the pyramids was partially embedded in the hard lava floor with the cigar shape center lying horizontally within the web of wires.

"This is why we're here." Spencer whispered, awestruck. "This is the discovery that will change the world forever." Spencer stood up and brushed the dust off his knees. "Whatever this thing is, it has been here for a very long time." He took the camera from Matt and filmed his approach toward the object. His mind wandered to a distant past left undiscovered until today. He approached the object with caution.

"This thing must be over a hundred feet tall!" Matt exclaimed. "I wonder how far it's embedded in the lava." Matt had gone pale, a look of awe and astonishment on his face.

Spencer ignored Matt's comments. He had to make sure he documented the discovery in a scientifically acceptable form. The entire world needed to know about this, and they had to believe his findings. Nothing could be left to chance. Even with scientific accuracy, it would be difficult to convince anyone that this wasn't a scene right out of a science fiction novel. Even now, looking at it with his own eyes, could he really believe what he was seeing?

"Spencer, look at this!" Matt called. He had walked behind the object and crawled through the wires. He stood at the base of the cigar shaped capsule. "It looks like some kind of entryway. Maybe we'll get lucky and find a way to get into this thing." Matt ran his hands across the smooth surface. "It's a door, but there's no lever or handle to get in."

Spencer carefully made his way over to Matt without stopping the camera. "Shine your light here," he said, pointing at a panel.

What is it?" Matt asked.

"Looks like some kind of writing . . . very strange . . . I've never seen it before."

Spencer looked over the camera. "It looks like hieroglyphics," he said, "but damned if I can read it!" Spencer sighed and looked through the video viewfinder as if it would somehow give him a clearer picture.

"Oh, yeah, I think it is hieroglyphics. I've seen that type of writing before," Matt said.

The inner capsule was made of an unusual gold-green material. The light from the video camera reflected off its shiny surface.

"Matt," Spencer said, speaking as much for himself and the camera as for Matt.

"This object is perfectly preserved. When the cavity formed, it must have happened in an instant, sealing everything inside."

Matt let out a nervous laugh. "Do you think this is a spaceship from some other planet that crashed here?"

"Before we can make that determination, we'll need to get inside. I can't see how this contraption could fly." Spencer sighed again, puzzled.

"For now we need to secure this area and create a diversion for the CIA and whoever else is spying on us. Let's get back and figure out a way to open the capsule's door."

"Right. What do we tell the crew?"

"Assemble only your most trusted men and let me talk to them. We'll have to tell them the truth. It's the only way they'll help us."

Spencer's mind filled with an image of Roula. He needed her more than ever now. She was the only person he knew who had a shot at deciphering the writing near the door, but could she be their spy? Why would she do such a thing? None of it made sense.

Spencer stopped just before they reached the entrance and turned to Matt. "We have to blow up the mine shaft."

"What?" Matt stared at Spencer, his jaw slack.

If the CIA found out what was down there, they'd remove him from the project in an instant and take over. If that happened, the discovery would be lost to humanity forever. "This discovery is too big," he said to Matt. "If word gets out, we're history."

"If we blow up the shaft, how will we get back in?"

"I have a plan. Let's meet back here in two hours. Remember, get only the most trusted men from the crew that was here when we broke through. Tell them to meet me at the mine shaft opening at one sharp."

Roula Grazulis padded across the cool tile floor and opened the door. Ralph Spencer stood in her doorway, a deep frown on his face. A chill ran down her spine. "Spencer, what happened? Is something wrong?"

"Yes, something is very wrong. Can I come in?"

Spencer's voice was cold and his green eyes had an icy glaze. Whatever was on his mind, it wasn't good. "Of course," she said in a vain attempt at sounding breezy, "Come in." She ran her fingers through her hair and then twisted it into a knot. It was a nervous habit she'd had since childhood and had never been able to break. There'd been a quaver in her voice? Had Spencer heard it? There was only one thing to do. She pulled him close and pressed her body into his. She tilted her head back and moved to kiss him. Spencer gently pushed her away and told her to sit down. He sat across from her but said nothing. He seemed to be searching for the right words. Whatever he had to say, she had the feeling it was going to be painful.

"Roula, I want you to know that I have fallen in love with you."

A flood of relief washed over her. "Oh, Ralph—"

He held up his "And that's why what I'm about to ask you is very hard for me." Roula reached out to take his hand and then stopped. Her own hands were trembling. It would do no good for him to see how nervous she was.

"We've discovered a breach of security in the mine. Someone is monitoring our satellite transmission. Matt found evidence of a tap into our feed on one of the monitors."

"Why would anyone do that? It's just an oil dig, right?"

Spencer ignored her question. "The tap was on the line Matt saw you looking at."

"Are you suggesting I tapped it?" She jumped to her feet, strode across the room, running her fingers through her hair, and then walked back to where Spencer sat.

"Did you? " Spencer asked, his eyes narrowed.

"I thought we'd already discussed this." Roula stepped away from him and looked at the floor. She opened and closed her mouth several times, but said nothing. What could she possibly say that would convince him of her innocence?

"Did you?" Spencer repeated gently.

He stood and gently lifted her chin toward him. The gesture melted her heart. Her eyes filled with tears. "It wasn't me," she said, "But I know who it was."

Abdul?" Spencer asked.

"Yes, how did you know?"

"Who else?"

" Mr. Abdul came to my apartment and demanded that I place the tap. He somehow knew that we'd met and that I could gain your trust and get access to the mine. He must have had someone spying on us." She spoke through gritted teeth. "That night at the bar . . . someone must have been watching." She took a step back, crossed her arms, and shook her head as if trying to clear the thought from her head. "Abdul made it very apparent that if I didn't cooperate, I would be on the next plane to New York and my work in Egypt would be over for good. That's why I left for a while. By the time I got back, it seemed as though Abdul had forgotten about me. I know I should have told you, but I was afraid of what Abdul might do."

"Well, if you didn't set the feed, who did?

"He must have found someone else."

Tears were flowing down her cheeks. She needed to pull it together. She needed Spencer to believe her. "The Department of Antiquity gave me a full scholarship for my PhD . . . I didn't want to blow that, and I thought that if I told you . . . well, I thought Abdul might make good on his threat." She searched Spencer's eyes, but couldn't get a read on his thoughts. The man could sure shut off his emotions when he wanted to. He had found something in that mine, and she would find out what it was. What more could she say to convince him? " I'm so sorry that I didn't tell you. It was selfish of me, but . . ."

"But what?"

"Well, my career . . . my life's work . . . it was all on the line."

"I understand," Spencer wiped the tears from her cheeks.

"I wanted to tell you so many times. I'm glad that it's finally out. I am so sorry for hurting you, and for disappearing the way I did. I hope you can forgive me."

"Roula, I need your help."

"Anything."

"You might not say that when you find out what I need. Are you willing to risk your job and your future to help me?"

"Yes," Roula said, looking fully into his eyes. "I will do it for us . . . because I've fallen in love with you, too." She leaned in to kiss him and this time he didn't push her away. His lips pressed into hers and he wrapped her in his arms. Her body stopped trembling as she relaxed and allowed his body to melt against her.

He pulled away and groaned. "I so want this, but now is not the time," he said. "I've got too much to tell you." He took her hands and sat her down. "If this is going to work, you need to tell me all you know about the Department of Antiquity and what they know."

Spencer held Roula's hands as waves of relief washed over him. She hadn't set the tap. She was innocent. And she had willingly revealed Abdul's duplicity. Best of all, she had admitted that she loved him. It was music to his ears. He believed her. But even if he hadn't, he had little choice but to trust her. He needed her to decipher those hieroglyphics. They would be a great team together. He pulled her to him and held her close. They were secure, for now, in one another's arms.

Roula was the first to break the embrace. She looked into his eyes with an earnestness he'd never seen before. "The department of Antiquity has suspected that something strange was happening with this project from the beginning, Abdul wanted me to find out what you were really up to. They checked into your background and knew about your archeology degree. Abdul believes that Calpetro has a secret plan involving an archeological discovery. He wanted me to find out what that plan was . . . but I refused . . . Her voice trailed off and she appeared to be lost in thought. "They're still in the dark about what you're looking for and . . ." She paused. "So am I."

Roula had stopped trembling and her words seemed sincere. He wanted to tell her everything, but he had to do it carefully. He was still in shock over what they'd found, he didn't want to overwhelm her. "We have a contract with Egypt. Calpetro told them that we might have found gold under the desert. We told them to keep this operation secret to avert a local gold rush. Since we are in a sensitive archeological region, a gold rush here could destroy any remaining archeological finds or even the well known existing sites."

"Wow, is that true? I was never told anything about that." She seemed genuinely surprised by the news.

"Well, sort-of." Spencer looked down. The truth had to be explained to her. He needed her to decipher the inscription on the door of the capsule. What was holding him back? He wanted desperately to trust her, but could he?

Spencer led her to the door. "Let's take a walk. What I'm about to tell you needs to be told where no one could possibly hear us."

Her dark eyes grew wide, but she said nothing. He held her hand as they strolled into the streets of Cairo. They walked to one of their favorite spots in the park. He gave her a long, passionate kiss. "I can't believe how hard I've fallen for you," he said. "I love you, and I feel as if I've known you always."

She laid her hand on his cheek and smiled. "I feel the same way, and I don't care what Abdul does to me or my visa. All I care about is being with you." Roula kissed him, her eyes focused on his.

He needed her, and God knew he wanted her, but he had to be

able to trust her. His confusion was muddling his brain. Spencer took both her hands in his and kissed them. He took in a deep breath and then let the entire story pour out of him.

Roula's stomach was doing summersaults. "Let me get this straight. You found an alien machine at the bottom of the mine?"

"We don't know if it's alien—"

"What else could it be?"

"We don't know. Matt and I discovered a door, but we've been unable to open it. The inscriptions on the door are some sort of hieroglyphics."

"Who else knows about this?" Roula's voice was gruff and her hands trembled. She was excited and frightened all at the same time. And why shouldn't she be? This was the find of the century and her chance to decipher what may very well be the oldest writing known to man. How could she possibly contain her enthusiasm?

"We pulled the feed as soon as we found the breach. No one knows yet. I'd like to keep it that way, at least until we figure out what we have.

"Oh, my God, the feed . . ." She looked down at her plate. "You killed the entire feed?"

"Yes."

"Good . . . that's good."

"The CIA will be here in the blink of an eye," Spencer said. "If they find out what's really down there, it'll be all over for us. We'll be debriefed."

"Debriefed?"

"Yes. That means the CIA takes over, and we will be removed from the project. To us and the rest of the world, this project will never have existed." Spencer spat the words as if they had tasted bitter to him.

"Our own government would do that?"

"That, and I'm afraid, possibly much more. Antonio's warned me that this is dangerous business, and I believe him. Any non-cooperation would require our immediate . . . elimination."

"Are you serious? They would actually kill us?"

"I don't know that they'd kill us, but I do think they'd go to any length to keep this secret. At the very least, they'd destroy our reputations and our careers . . . you know, make us out to be fringe scientists so no one would believe us."

Her stomach roiled at the thought. This was something right out of a spy novel. Surely the CIA wouldn't destroy an innocent person's career just because he knew about an archeological find. She sighed. "It wouldn't be hard for them to do it, either. No one will believe any of this without hard evidence . . . I mean, I wouldn't believe it if I hadn't heard it from you."

"That's right. So we can't underestimate the CIA. Me, you, and anyone else who might get in their way." He took her chin in his hand. "Anyone with knowledge about this discovery is at risk, and that's why we need to move quickly. Are you still on board? Will you help me?"

Fat tears rolled down her cheeks as she nodded. "Anything," she said with far more confidence than she felt. "Nothing could stop me."

"This isn't a game Roula. It will be very dangerous." A smile spread across his face, "But it'll be a hell of an adventure too, huh?

His excitement was contagious. "Absolutely," she said. "Together we can beat them."

Roula walked alongside Spencer at they approached the dig site. The scene was so surreal, she was tempted to pinch herself to make sure she wasn't dreaming all this. Never in her wildest dreams had she imagined being part of such a crucial find.

Matt stood at the entrance to the mine surrounded by four of his most trusted men. He greeted Spencer and then, spotting Roula behind him, looked at Spencer with a big question in his eyes.

Spencer put his hand up. "Matt," he said. "Roula's here to help us. She told me that the Department of Antiquity was behind the breach—"

"Then what the hell is she doing here? Have you lost your mind?" Matt stuffed his hands in his pockets and shuffled from one foot to the other.

"She didn't set the tap. She refused Abdul. Don't worry, she's with us a hundred percent."

"Matt, I—" Roula said.

Spencer turned to her, the look on his face making her stop

cold. What did he think she was going to say? The trust and concern that she saw in his face was almost more than she could bear.

Spencer looked to the four men. "You've all seen Roula here before. She knows about the real project and she's with us. She'll be deciphering the hieroglyphics, which means we'll get inside. You men have been hand picked to help us with this unprecedented discovery. All of you are aware of the utmost secrecy this project warrants. Our lives depend on it. I must advise you of the danger we all face from this moment forward. If any one of you has concerns or doesn't wish to continue, now is the time to tell me." Spencer paused and looked each man in the eye. No one said a word.

"Great," Spencer said. "Let's find out what that mysterious object is before it's too late."

Spencer led the small group down the mineshaft. Matt placed two of the men as guards at the entrance of the shaft. The other two helped with the cameras and equipment Spencer had assembled.

At the bottom, Roula felt her own jaw drop. The sheer magnitude of the object was beyond belief. "This is magnificent."

Spencer pushed her lower jaw back into place. "It's beyond that, it's the discovery of the millennium. We need to get inside."

The three of them worked their way between the golden wires. It was as if they were entering a giant three-dimensional web. As she got closer to the door markings, her hands began to shake.

"Matt, put the lights here so Roula can see the markings." Spencer stood back with his arms crossed.

Roula stepped closer to the door. Her heart slammed against her chest as she ran her hands along the markings.

"What do you make of it?"

"Incredible! Are you sure we're not dreaming all this?" Her voice sounded shrill even to her own ears as it echoed through the cave.

"I am afraid this is quite real," Spencer said. "Now what do you make of these markings?"

"Hold on," she said with a nervous laugh. "I need to examine them carefully." Roula sat on one of the wires and held a flashlight over the inscriptions. Matt was intent on filming the event as instructed by Spencer.

"Here, see this symbol?" She said.

"Yes." Spencer waited, his eyes shining.

"This is a form of the earliest hieroglyphics known to man, except that here we have such a refined sophistication. I've never seen anything like it. It incorporates some very complex sentence structures. It will take some doing to decode this." She swallowed hard. This discovery was beyond even her considerable imagination.

"How long?" Spencer asked, his voice anxious.

"Since these inscriptions are on this door, it's likely that they pertain to the door and its function." Roula paused, intent on analyzing every symbol.

Spencer alternated between hovering over her shoulder and pacing back and forth. She hadn't answered his question, but she didn't know what to tell him. Deciphering this kind of hieroglyphics would be a slow methodical process. That the decoding of the inscriptions would lead to the opening of the door was the only thing she was sure of. She looked closely at one of the inscriptions. "Of course," she muttered.

Spencer stopped pacing and rushed over to her. Matt followed behind him.

"These are instructions for opening the door." Her fingers searched for something near the bottom of the door. "Here." She looked up at Spencer and then Matt. "Stand back. The door is hermetically sealed. When it opens the air inside will rush out. It'll be very old air and it could be contaminated." She had found a small button on the bottom of the door concealed by a sliding plate that matched perfectly with the outer surface. She pressed in and the door moved upward with a smooth sliding hiss. They all froze. She looked at the two men, both of whom appeared awestruck. This was the biggest discovery in human history. Roula was deafened by the sound of her own heartbeat.

CHAPTER

TEN

Spencer asked Matt to keep on filming as he slowly stepped inside followed by Roula. What awaited them had been kept secret from the world for millennia. Who knew what they would find?

Inside the object everything gleamed like brand new, as if time had stood still, everything preserved by the fast-setting volcanic void and the hermetically sealed door. Things were left exactly as they had been eons ago by whoever had constructed this mechanical marvel.

Matt followed them through the door, the video camera clutched in his hands. "I want to get everything," he said, his voice breathless, "This is for all future generations to see."

"Look here!" Spencer ran his finger along a smooth wall where a row of evenly placed metal boxes stood, each one covered with hieroglyphics.

"What are they?" Matt asked.

"I have no idea." Roula said.

"Here, let me zoom in on them," Matt adjusted the camera's lens.

Roula picked up the first box from the shelf and squinted as she attempted to read the inscriptions. Spencer was surveying the rest of the room, looking for additional clues as to what this strange object might be.

"Oh, my God!" Roula gasped, tears streaming down her face.

"What is it?" Spencer rushed to her side and wrapped his arm around her shoulder.

"I know what this is," she said. "It's astonishing." Her eyes, wide open, searched Spencer's face. Her jaw moved, but no words followed.

"Is it a weapon?" Spencer asked, his voice somber.

"No, not at all." She turned to the camera and held up the box, pointing at the odd lettering. "According to the inscriptions," she continued in an authoritative voice, "these strange little boxes contain recordings from what must have been a very ancient civilization or some other civilization not from this earth." Roula was beaming, her confidence in the assertion she had just made written all over her face.

"This is incredible!" Matt shouted.

Spencer turned to him and held a finger to his lips. Matt's face flushed and he looked back into the camera's lens.

"Are you saying this is some kind of . . . some sort of . . ." He couldn't seem to find the right words.

"Time capsule," Roula said. "Some civilization, at some time, wanted future generations to know who they were." She looked around the capsule. "This is their legacy."

Spencer stared at Roula. His doubt was likely written all over his face, but he couldn't help it. What she was proposing seemed preposterous.

"Do you want to look inside?" she asked.

He opened one of the boxes. Inside lay a small cylinder, perfectly smooth, approximately three inches in diameter and about one and a half inches thick. The cylinder seemed to be made of metal, perfectly solid and yet when looked at under the flashlight as transparent as glass.

"Spencer, these writings are suggesting some type of sequential order," she whispered.

"You mean it's some kind of databank?"

"Yes," she said.

"Jesus, it is a time capsule." He placed the cylinder back in the box that Roula still held. "Spencer's mind was racing. The cylinders had to be historical recordings. But recordings of what? Would they be able to activate the device? If so, what would they find? "Damn," he said shaking his head. "This is a time capsule."

"Yes." Roula laughed. "That's what I told you." Roula held up the cylinder and faced the camera. "I believe these cylinders are here to show us the culture and history of another society," Roula spoke directly into the camera's lens. "These inscriptions," she pointed to the box, "are surely pointing us in that direction." She dropped her authoritative voice. "It could be anything," she said, the words rushing out now. "It could come from this world, some ancient society, or from another, maybe from an advanced, planet."

Spencer walk toward the inner chamber of the capsule. "If these cylinders contain records of an advanced civilization, there must be some device here to play or scan these cylinders. It could work something like a CD player of today."

"Matt, bring the camera around, I want to examine the inner core of this capsule."

Spencer walked toward the center of the capsule where a very ornate door sealed the access to some inner chamber and Matt followed behind him.

"Roula," he called, "can you read this?" Spencer was pointing along a wall full of unusual hieroglyphics. Roula walked over to where Spencer stood, the box holding the cylinder still clutched in her hands. She passed the box to Spencer. "Be careful with it," she said absently.

She ran her hand along the hieroglyphics. After a moment she pulled out a notebook and started scribbling a combination of symbols and words.

Spencer stood behind her and Matt continued to film. The hieroglyphics here appeared far more complex than anything else Roula had encountered; even he could see that. Her brow was furrowed in concentration. He signaled to Matt to stop filming. Roula didn't need any more pressure. She already seemed desperate to figure out the code needed to gain access.

"No," she finally answered, disappointment in her voice. "Matt, please film this entire wall very carefully. I'm going to work on this at home with the aid of my encryption program."

"Hold on." Matt was listening to his earpiece connection with the outside guards.

"Shit. We need to get the hell out of here. Abdul's on his way here…he just called."

"How much time do we have?" Spencer drew in a deep calming breath.

"Less than an hour. What do we do?"

Spencer gazed at Matt's questioning face. There was only one solution. "We'll blast the mine shut."

"What?" Matt said.

"Tell the crew to prepare the explosive. I want to blow this tunnel in twenty minutes. Help me load all these boxes in the elevator. Let's move!"

The three of them stacked all of the boxes inside the elevator. Matt's men had placed enough explosives at the very bottom of the shaft to block off at least the bottom fifty feet of it. Would it be enough?

The small group rode the elevator to the surface in silence. The twenty-minute ride seemed like an eternity. Spencer ushered the group out of the elevator and directed them to the mine entrance. "Set it off now!" he yelled.

There was a muffled rumble deep inside the mine. Spencer sighed in relief. "Matt, bring your crew here and please hurry."

Once the five men were assembled, Spencer shoveled up a pile of dirt and threw it onto the men, several of whom gasped in surprise.

"What the hell is this?" Matt said.

"This will make our accident seem more real." Spencer said, a mischievous smile on his lips. "Thank God no one was hurt."

The crew got in the spirit and started throwing handfuls of the dry desert sand at each other.

"Roula," Spencer said, "You need to get out of here right away." He pressed the small camera into her hand. "If Abdul sees you here, it could put you in grave danger."

"I know."

He pulled her into a tight embrace and kissed her honeysuckle-scented hair. God, he didn't want to let her go. What the hell was he thinking dragging her into this mess? "It'll be fine," he whispered, knowing that it may not be fine at all. "Now go." He released her and watched her run toward the gate. She stopped, turned, and waved. He'd never forget the lost look on her face at that moment. He nodded and waved back. He suddenly didn't give a damn about the discovery that lay buried in the mine. He just wanted to go with her, for the two of them to be alone, in each other's arms, maybe on some quiet island in the Caribbean. But that was impossible. There was no turning back.

"Let's go," he said to Matt. The two men jogged side by side toward the FOU. "Activate the alarm system as soon as you can," Spencer said.

Matt nodded and took the key from Spencer's hand.

A long black sedan pulled up and a moment later and Abdul stepped out. He was surrounded by absolute chaos. Sirens screamed and men were running everywhere.

Perfect.

Spencer stepped out of the FOU and walked to meet him. "What's going on? Abdul demanded.

"This is a very bad time, Mr. Abdul. There's been a serious accident inside the mine. Over fifty feet of the shaft collapsed." Spencer spoke in a stern voice and let himself appear shaken, which wasn't too hard to do given the circumstances.

"What do you mean?" Abdul's eyes reflected his confusion. "Can't you turn off that damned alarm?"

"We'll try, sir." Spencer answered. "Here's what happened . . ."

He headed for the mineshaft at a rapid pace. Abdul walked alongside him, waving his cane in the air and struggling to keep up.

"While excavating this afternoon," Spencer said, "we hit an unstable strata and the shaft suddenly caved in. There was no time to give notice and close off the mine. We were lucky to get all the men to safety without any serious injuries."

Abdul was huffing along beside him. Spencer pointed to the dirt-covered men who were standing near the opening eyeing Abdul suspiciously.

Abdul grabbed Spencer's arm and stopped. "We need to perform our inspection. I had planned on going to the bottom of the mine today."

Spencer yanked his arm free and brushed at his sleeve as though Abdul had soiled it with his touch. "No disrespect, sir, but you'll need to reschedule this inspection. I have to determine the extent of the damage first and ensure that all safety precautions are in place." He needed this disgusting man to go away at least for a few days.

"No." Abdul huffed. "I must inspect the bottom of the mine now, Mr. Spencer. Let's go!" Abdul stamped his foot and headed for the elevator.

Spencer shrugged. He had not choice be to give Abdul what he wanted. He ushered the Egyptian past the dusty men and into the elevator. Thank God he'd had the men hide all the boxes containing the cylinders in an equipment crate. They started the long descent. At about fifteen thousand feet the dust became so thick the men could barely breathe. He wasn't about to stop, not until Abdul told him to turn back.

Abdul started hacking. He pulled a handkerchief from his pocket and held it over his mouth. "I . . . can't . . . breathe," he said.

"For our own safety, we need to turn back," Spencer said, "This is unsafe . . ." he coughed "without the proper equipment." He pulled his t-shirt over his mouth and nose. "If we go any further," he yelled, "we'll run out of air."

Abdul's expression changed from anger to fear. His eyes were red and watering. What more did the man need to be convinced that indeed an accident had blocked the mine.

"Damn," he said finally. "Okay, get me out of here."

They rode the elevator back to the surface without speaking.

By the time they arrived at the top, they were both coughing and tears were streaming from their eyes. Spencer pulled open the grate for the older man. "I will personally call you sir, the minute we have this shaft cleared and safe for your inspection."

Abdul grunted and stormed out of the mine entrance waving his cane before him. He stopped just outside, leaned the cane against his leg, and wiped his face with the handkerchief. "How long?"

"About two weeks." Spencer used his most reassuring voice.

"You have four days."

Spencer sighed in relief as Abdul's car passed the main gate and headed back to Cairo. He met Matt back at the FOU. "How long will it take to clear the mine shaft?"

Matt shrugged. "We'll need to determine the extent of the damage caused by the blast. Since the outer walls are lined in concrete and the shaft is made of lava rock, I would say we could get to the bottom pretty quick."

"How quick?" Spencer asked. He didn't want to get impatient with Matt, but Abdul's timeline had him on edge.

"I would guess forty-eight hours or less."

"Dammit. That'll give us almost no time to get back inside the capsule." Spencer paced the narrow FOU.

"What about the man-lift?" Matt asked.

"The man-lift." Spencer snapped his fingers. "Of course." We can get back down there as soon as Roula has deciphered the hieroglyphics that'll let us into that inner chamber."

"How long do you think that'll take?"

"Knowing Roula, not long. She won't sleep until she's figured it out."

Matt nodded but said nothing. Did he still mistrust Roula? Well, if he did, it didn't matter. Roula was their only hope for getting inside that inner chamber.

"I think we need to make a core shipment to the US today," Spencer said.

"But shouldn't we—"

"We need to get a few of the cylinders to the US. We'll ship them in an empty core sample. It's doubtful customs will find them in there."

"Great idea, boss."

"Remember, not a word of this to anyone. This is between us. I think you know the consequences if word gets out."

"Don't worry," Matt said. "I still can't believe what I saw down there today. You couldn't drag me off this job."

Spencer laughed "Yeah, I hear you. So, for safety's sake, let's ship that package."

The two men stuffed the first four boxes inside an empty cardboard cylinder used for core samples. Spencer packed both ends of the cylinder with actual dirt samples for extra security. Spencer wrote Paul's address on the shipment and used the regular procedures for shipping core samples to Calpetro. Back at the FOU, he sent an e-mail to Paul with coded instructions to personally take the shipment to Spencer's new place near the San Jose airport. He typed "ZEBRA@ WORK" as his personal password onto his laptop and the screen came alive. The CIA "OPERALI" was online. He sent an encrypted e-mail message to Steve.

We have had a breach of security. The Egyptian government is monitoring our satellite transmission. I ordered the feed cut until security is restored, please advise.

We have also had a full collapse of the mineshaft near the bottom. The bottom fifty feet of the shaft is totally blocked by the collapse. Matt estimates forty-eight hours to get back on schedule. It was a close call, but no one was injured. We estimate getting through the hard lava bed in ten days. The shaft walls gave way directly above the lava section. We believe that the collapse was caused by excessive vibration while excavating the strata containing the hard lava. Please do not use landlines or satellite link up for communication. It's too dangerous until we get to the bottom of that unauthorized feed. I will keep you informed as needed.

He signed off and leaned back in his chair. Would his warning keep the CIA off any live transmissions? Only time would tell. He'd have to move fast. They had to get inside that inner chamber before anyone else found out about the capsule.

Spencer tapped on Roula's door then turned the knob. The door was unlocked. Roula was working intently at her computer. She was so intent on decoding the hieroglyphics, she hadn't even heard him come in.

"You look exhausted." Spencer said.

"Tell me about it. I've been working on this since I left."

He hadn't even startled her. "Why was your door unlocked? What if—"

"He's already been here," she said.

"Abdul?"

"Of course.

"I think he came straight here from the site," Roula said, an indignant tone in her voice.

"What happened?"

"He wanted to know why the feed died."

The muscles in Spencer's shoulders tensed. "Why would he think you'd know that?"

She shrugged. "I guess because he knows I'm seeing you."

"What did you say?"

She rolled back in her chair and looked into his eyes for a long moment. "I told him I didn't know anything. That you had called and said there was an accident, but that was all I knew."

"And . . ."

I suggested that the accident had probably cut the communications and that it would take some time to restore."

"Did he buy it?"

"Well, apparently. He told me about going down the shaft with you, which I kind of figured cause he was covered in dust. He seems to believe that some sort of accident happened, so I think he bought it." Roula's words were coming out in a rush.

Spencer stepped closer and took her hands. "What's wrong then?"

"I'm worried . . . about us . . . about everything. This thing is so big and so surreal. I keep thinking about your warning . . . the CIA, Abdul . . . If this gets out, we don't have a chance in hell."

He pulled her to her feet and wrapped his arms around her. She held him close as if she were afraid he might somehow escape her.

"We'll just have to stay ahead of them." He brushed her hair out of her eyes. He needed to keep her calm, make her feel secure. "I have a plan, but first we need to get into the inner chamber."

She released him and sat back down at the computer. "I'm

working on deciphering the inscriptions."

He moved closer to the computer as Roula began typing. Her fingers flew over the keyboard. "This program is the cutting edge of hieroglyphics translation," she said. "Now that I've inputted everything I was able to decipher, I can make an attempt at decoding the entire alphabet. It's definitely ancient. Once we have the basic meaning for each symbol, the computer will scan the writing and automatically translate it." She spoke with confidence. This was her field of expertise and she seemed to be in her element. She knew she was essential to the project and to Spencer's success and it showed.

"How does it work?" Spencer was curious.

"This computer program is similar to high level encryption programs usually used to decode passwords or sophisticated security messages. The program works on probabilities. It experiments with millions of options for any given symbol and it matches them with known translations. It's sort of like finding out the combination of a bank safe, except harder." She laughed.

Spencer smiled at her little joke. They both needed some relief from the stress. "How long will it take to translate this footage?" Spencer pointed at the monitor, which was showing Matt's film of the inner chamber door.

"It should be done by morning." She stood up and stretched. "I've been looking at this screen so long, I can hardly see straight.

He took her hand and led her to the sofa. "Here, sit," he said.

He stood behind her and massaged her shoulders. Her muscles softened under his touch.

She closed her eyes. "Mmmm," she purred, "That feels wonderful."

"We should get some rest," he said with a catch in his throat. He had no desire to return to his hotel, but they both needed a good night's sleep. "We have a very busy day ahead."

She looked up, a mischievous smile on her face. Her hand reached for his. She rose and pulled him toward the bedroom. "You're right, we need rest." She giggled and her fingers fumbled with the buttons on his shirt.

How could he resist? He turned her around and walked her backwards pulling her tank top over her head. They fell together onto the bed. She ran her fingers over his bare chest. He kissed her, tenderly at first, and then with an urgency that nearly overwhelmed him. She slipped off her bra and pressed her bare breasts into his chest. He stopped kissing her for a moment and gazed into her heavy-lidded eyes. "My God, you're beautiful," he said. She smiled and, weaving her hands through his hair, pulled him to her and kissed him in a way he'd never been kissed before. He surrendered to her.

When Spencer awoke, daylight was just breaking. He watched Roula sleep for a few minutes and then forced himself out of bed. He staggered to the kitchen and started coffee brewing. The screen saver was running on the computer, so he clicked the mouse to see if the program was still running. He gasped. On the screen was the full English translation to the inner chamber inscriptions. He read what he saw on the screen out loud. "Historic replicator - remove first -none -first - device left - right - right - left - up - left - pressure - one – none. He stumbled to the bedroom and woke Roula. "The computer," he said, "come and see."

Roula slipped into a silk bathrobe, tied it around her narrow waist, and sat down at the computer.

"What does it mean?" Spencer asked. The translation seemed to need another translation to understand it.

"This is fascinating." Roula's face brightened. "Replicator is a modern word. It implies a device that will reproduce images or recreate past historic events." Roula frowned as she studied the rest of the translation.

"A time capsule would house historic accounts of the time." Spencer said, excitement in his voice. "This replicator could be the device that plays the cylindrical objects."

"That's likely," Roula said.

If they could just figure out how to make it work, what would they find? If the capsule actually contained recorded accounts of some alien world or ancient civilization, it could be anything. Roula's hands hovered over the keyboard. Her hair was tousled, her brow was furrowed, and her lips were turned down in an enticing pout. The urge to kiss her was overpowering, but he'd have to think about those sexy, pouting lips later. "What does the rest mean?" He asked, turning his attention to the strange translation on the screen.

"I don't know. I'll need to think about it. All the visible inscriptions had been translated. The level of accuracy is above ninety-eight percent. I think the answer is inside the capsule itself."

"Let's get back down there right away," he said. "I'll inform Matt."

"Give me a minute to get dressed," Roula slipped out of the robe on the way to the bedroom.

Following her gorgeous brown body was a temptation he could barely resist. Damn, but she was hot. He pulled his telephone out of his pocket and sent Matt a quick coded text message.

"Ralph?" Roula called from the bedroom. "How will we get down? What about the blast?"

"The man-lift. It's in perfect working order." He smiled, pretty sure of what was coming next.

"Wait a minute." She peeked out the bedroom door, her eyes wide. "You mean I'll have to hang on the side of a belt for the eighteen-thousand foot ride down?"

"It's perfectly safe, honest, it's a piece of cake . . . Just don't let go." He chuckled.

She smiled, but her face had gone pale. "How did you keep Abdul away from the lift?"

"Abdul thinks the lift only goes to fifteen-thousand feet. He was told that the balance of the lift was on backorder due to a shortage of parts. We actually built two lifts; the second lift that starts at fifteen thousand feet is only known by Matt, the crew, and me. We built it as a secret escape and a separate access to the cavity."

"Wow, I'm so impressed. You've really thought this out." She came through the door dressed in khaki shorts, a green t-shirt and hiking boots. She looked sexier than ever.

"Let's get down there and open that door," she said with conviction.

Matt had been pacing for more than twenty minutes. Where the hell were they? He was ready to get back in that mine and was prepared to do whatever Spencer asked him to do to keep this find a secret. He had come to care for and respect Ralph Spencer. In equal measure he hated the snooping CIA and that sleazy Abdul. Spencer had asked him to assemble the rig to transport the needed equipment down the man-lift. He had brought two video cameras and the necessary lights.

When the couple arrived, Roula was carrying her laptop computer and extra flashlights. He was still suspicious that she'd been messing with the feed when he saw her in the tunnel, but Spencer trusted her, and they needed her skill with the hieroglyphics if they were ever going to get into the inner chamber.

Spencer instructed the crew to bring extra tools, shovels, and various types of explosives, which were to be used as a last resort to open the inner chamber door. They were only a contingency in case Roula couldn't make sense of the translation. The blast had closed off the entrance immediately adjacent to the main elevator. They would have to dig out a small tunnel by hand to access the cavity area. It would take a second blast to the tunnel when they left the capsule to reseal the area. Spencer had told Matt to pack oxygen masks for the three of them and for the men who would stand guard at the bottom of the shaft.

The man-lift hole was only thirty-six inches in diameter and was equipped with a continuous heavy plastic belt stretched parallel to one side of the hole. The belt was approximately twenty inches wide and was supported by two parallel steel channels anchored on the side of the hole every ten feet. Two steel wires secured the entire length of both ends of the belt. A small steel grate platform protruded out from the belt every ten feet. These platforms ran the entire length of the belt and were to be used in case of a quick evacuation. Each platform had bar grips and an upper steel cage designed to lean against while in motion. Personnel were trained to quickly jump on the rising platform without stopping the lift. This was done during evacuation training and all employees were required to participate.

"I can't jump on that thing while it's moving." Roula said, her eyes wide with fear.

"Sure you can, nothing to it. Just watch the others and do the same thing."

Matt nodded at Roula and smiled. "You can do it," he reassured her. If Spencer had confidence in her, then so did he. He signaled to his men to climb on. He then loaded the equipment and turned on the lift.

"Wait, wait, let me on before you start this contraption." Roula said to Matt, a pleading look in her eyes.

"You need to learn how to jump on," Matt said. "Sorry, but there's no time to train you at the bottom and we need to be ready for all contingencies."

Spencer took her by the shoulders and looked into her eyes. "You can do this."

"Fine, but if I break my legs, you'll both be to blame," she said, looking from Spencer to Matt.

With all the equipment loaded and his trusted crew ahead of him, Matt jumped on the moving lift.

"Okay, Roula, hold onto the grab bar as it comes by and just climb on the platform." Spencer spoke patiently as though guiding a child. "Here comes the bar . . . now grab it, step on quick. I'm right behind on the next platform." Matt and the crew clapped when she maneuvered herself onto the lift. She smiled and waved. Spencer quickly jumped on the next platform above her. The way down seemed to take forever. The lift went considerably slower than the main elevator and they needed to switch lifts at fifteen thousand feet.

"Oh, my God, how do I get off when we reach bottom?" Roula sounded panicked. She seemed to be yelling to anyone who would listen.

"Keep your eyes on the bottom floor markings," Matt called to her.

"You'll be warned at fifty feet to look for the wall markings on the side of the lift," Spencer said. "They're painted in bright red. When you're a couple of feet from the bottom, jump off the lift onto the yellow markings. It's really simple. See now why we wanted you to jump on?"

"Okay, okay, I'm ready." She seemed to have had enough of the lift and wanted off at any cost.

Soon the team was at the bottom of the second lift. Matt looked at his watch. It had taken less than forty minutes. The main opening to the cave was totally covered with dirt as expected. He immediately put the entire team to work. They needed to open a new passage in a very short time. Roula sat alone against the wall, her computer in her lap. She had a look of resolve on her face. She seemed determined to unravel the strange translation.

It took the crew two hours to remove enough dirt for them to pass through and enter the cave. Matt followed Spencer and Roula inside the time capsule for the second time. Strange how the place felt familiar now.

CHAPTER

ELEVEN

"We've been down here for three hours and nothing." Spencer groaned. "If we don't get inside soon, we'll lose this thing to the CIA for good."

Roula had been sitting cross-legged by the inner chamber entrance, her computer on her lap. She looked up at him with sad eyes. "I'm sorry, I'm doing the best I can."

"I know you are," Spencer said. "I'm sorry."

"This isn't getting us anywhere," Matt said. "Let's brainstorm some other ideas about that code. Think the way someone who really wants you to figure this out would think. What would they do to make it easy for some future generation who knows nothing about their language or culture?"

"I've been pondering that very thing for the last two hours." Roula spoke in a monotone as if trying not to disturb her own thoughts. "Based on the data and the translation of the hieroglyphics, I think the code is some sort of combination."

"Like a safe?" Matt asked.

"That sounds logical." Spencer tugged up his khakis at the knees and knelt next to Roula. "If we transpose actual numbers to the strange phrase, we'd get what?" Spencer pulled out a crumpled piece of paper from his pocket and balanced it on his knee. "Let's see . . ." He started to write. "First . . . none . . . first . . . that would be . . . one . . . zero . . .one. Okay, that's a hundred and one. We've got exactly a hundred and one boxes here minus the four we sent to California." Spencer went to the area where they had first found the boxes. "Let's see what's under box one-oh-one?"

"Matt, bring extra light over here, there might be something hidden under where box one-oh-one was."

Roula ran her hand along the shelf. "I think Ralph is right."

"Ralph?" Matt said, smiling at Spencer.

"I think Spencer is right," Roula said. "If that translation is correct, there should be a device here similar to a combination safe. The rest of these instructions could just imply turning in left and right motions and then applying pressure. . . first . . . none . . . that would be ten." She closed her eyes. "Pressure of ten." Her eyes popped open. That's it! But ten what?"

"Pounds? Kilos?" Matt said.

"How likely is it that their math was the same as ours?" Spencer asked.

"Not likely," Roula answered.

"Here!" She exclaimed, "Under this smooth surface . . . I feel bumps.

"Bumps?" Spencer said.

"Yeah, they're jetting in different directions. Let's try the code, left, right, right, left, left, pressure ten."

Roula traced the bumps under the smooth surface with her hand. She used her palm to apply pressure.

"Hey, it's opening," Matt said.

"That's it, Roula, you did it." Spencer pulled her to her feet and planted a kiss on her cheek.

"Let's get inside," Matt said.

Spencer made his way into the inner chamber with video camera in hand. He wanted all the details documented. The room was small and shaped like the inside of a pyramid. The walls were oblique, very smooth, and converged in a point high in the ceiling. In the center of the room there stood a pedestal with a box on it. Spencer slowly opened it and retrieved a small pyramid approximately eight inches wide at the base and twelve inches high. Tiny markings ran all around the base. On all four equal sides were circular holes that converged at the center of the device. It was totally black and so smooth it gleamed. Spencer picked the apparatus up and placed it on the palm of his right hand. He instantly was overcome by a strange vibrating sensation. He looked at the holes puzzled. "I have a feeling that the little cylinders we sent to San Francisco belong in these holes."

"If this is a time capsule, and the cylinders are the actual data," Roula said, "then it stands to reason that this device is the player that shows what they contain."

Roula had come to the conclusion virtually at the same time as

Spencer. It was time to get back to the surface. God only knew what Abdul was up to by now.

"We need to move fast." Spencer said. "Let's make sure that we have everything we need from this chamber then move on."

"We'll have to go to San Francisco to read the cylinders." Spencer said to Roula.

"I know. We'll be gone for at least a week. How do we keep the Egyptians out?"

Spencer put the pyramid decoder back in the box, then slipped off his jacket and wrapped the box in it. How would they keep out the Egyptians? And what about the CIA? Steve wouldn't buy the feed breach story for much longer. There had to be a way to buy the time he and Roula needed to get to San Francisco, view the cylinders, and then get back again. His stomach tightened at the thought of what the cylinders might reveal. It could be anything, and whatever it was, it would revolutionize Archeology, he was certain of that.

"Earth to Spencer." Matt said, breaking his reverie. "What're we gonna do?

"Let's blast another section of the main shaft and the lower man-lift."

Matt didn't question him this time. He turned to his men and gave them instructions for making the blast happen.

They were back at the base of the upper lift when Matt told them to duck and cover. The large explosion shook their feet, knocking Roula off base and to the floor.

"Roula, are you okay?" Spencer yelled over the din.

"Yes, just a bit shaken. That was quite a blast."

"Yeah, I think the entire lower lift is out and the main shaft has collapsed at least another two-hundred feet . . ." Matt grinned. He sounded pleased with himself.

"Let's move quickly and keep what we found to ourselves. No one is to say a word about this." He looked to Matt. "I'm counting on you to keep the crew in line on this."

"Of course," Matt said. "Don't worry about a thing, boss. I'll keep things in order while you and Roula go to the States."

"Thanks, I know I can depend on you." He had no doubt that Matt would stop at nothing to protect the mine shaft from any intrusions.

Spencer shipped the viewer to Paul's address with instructions to take the box to his new apartment along with the other box containing the cylinders. He used the same method as with the cylinders, shipping it inside the core samples to disguise the precious cargo. He then set out to meet with Abdul and explain the new problem. He needed to convince him that the mine would be shut down until new safety procedures were in place and Calpetro headquarters conducted a full inspection. He arrived at Abdul's office armed with Polaroid's and footage of the disaster.

Abdul listened to Spencer's story with a scowl on his face. He yanked the photos out of Spencer's hands and flipped through them. "Mr. Spencer, we must send a team to the site at once and ascertain the damage first hand." The Egyptian's heavy jowls shook as he spoke.

It was exactly the response Spencer had expected from Abdul. Cooperation was the best weapon he had. "Of course Mr. Abdul, what time should I meet your team?"

"We'll see you at the site today at three sharp."

"Fine." Spencer left breathing a sigh of relief. Abdul wasn't happy about the turn of events, but at least he'd bought the story.

The inspection team crawled over the site like a troop of army ants. It looked as though Abdul had brought his entire crew. At the same time, Abdul himself reviewed the safety protocols.

"Mr. Spencer, my men tell me they found evidence of an explosion at the base of the shaft. They found traces of explosive material. You must explain this."

"Of course, Mr. Abdul, I should have mentioned that . . . We had just reached a very hard lava rock layer and decided to use explosives to get through. That's when something went wrong and the shaft caved in." Damn, he was getting good at coming up with lies on the spot. "We had minor injuries, but no fatalities."

"I am ordering the shut down of this project until you can put together a new safety program." Abdul put his shoulders back and raised his chin as of daring Spencer to defy him.

The man couldn't have made Spencer happier if he'd tried. "But, Mr. Abdul—"

Abdul put his hand up, his face turning beet red. "This is not negotiable."

Spencer held up his hands. "Okay, okay, I understand," he said. "I need to go back home to see my family anyway." He shrugged and kicked at the sand under his feet. "I guess we could all use a little break."

Abdul turned on his heel with a huff and walked away without another word to Spencer. His entourage of men followed him to their line of cars. Spencer breathed a sigh of relief as he watched the cars pull away in a cloud of dust. Things were starting to go his way. The mine would be off limits, even to the CIA.

The CIA? Shit.

An army-style Hummer broke through the dust with Steve Sullivan at the wheel. It was the last person Spencer wanted to see. Steve jumped out of the vehicle with two other agents trailing behind him. "Hey, Spencer. You surprised to see me?" He didn't wait for Spencer to answer. "George, Mike," he gestured to the men next to him, "meet the man in charge, Ralph Spencer."

Spencer sucked in a deep breath, trying to slow his pounding heart. He couldn't let Steve see how annoyed he was. "What's with the unannounced visit?"

"After your communication about the possible tap on our project, I rushed right over. We'll take over from here." Steve's lips twitched into a disdainful smiled.

The man clearly thought he'd won, but so what? It would take them more than a week to break through the rubble and by then he and Roula would have already viewed the cylinders. "Fine." He shrugged and kicked the sand the way he'd done with Abdul. "I'm going home for awhile anyway." He turned and took a few steps, then looked back at the men. "Oh, by the way," he snapped his fingers, "I almost forgot, the project was just shut down by the Egyptian Government. We had another accident this morning and the tunnel caved in over two hundred feet. They are demanding a new safety program. It'll take Calpetro a couple of weeks to get that done."

Steve's face fell. He stuffed his hands into his jacket pockets. "Shit, Spencer. What gives?"

Spencer stuck his hands in his pockets, mimicking Steve's actions. "Sorry, dude. We reached the lava rock last night and it was incredibly hard. We wanted to keep to schedule so we tried blasting. It must've been more powerful than we thought cause it collapsed the upper shaft. I guess the concrete wasn't quite hard enough to endure such punishment. Over two hundred feet of the ventilation shaft caved in. It wasn't anyone's fault. There was no way we could have predicted the cave-in."

Steve stood with his legs wide, hands in his pockets, and his jaw slack. The other two agents gazed around the site looking uncomfortable.

Spencer had installed a man-lift along all the ventilation shafts but had kept it a highly guarded secret. He had kept it hidden from the prying eyes of the CIA all these months. If they bought his story now, hopefully they wouldn't go snooping around and find the lift. "I'm sorry, man. We were lucky to escape with only a few minor injuries. It could have been fatal. Abdul, the chief Egyptian inspector just shut down the project."

"Well, we'll just have him re-open it." Steve was not smiling anymore.

"I doubt it, Steve, this guy's a real prick. It's his way or no way. He's placed guards all around the mine. The best solution is to agree with him."

Steve stood stock still, staring at Spencer through squinting eyes. He seemed to be weighing Spencer's words. Was he getting suspicious? Spencer's stomach lurched at the thought. He needed to keep playing it cool. I am going to San Francisco tomorrow," Spencer said.

I'll be reviewing our safety procedures with McPearson. We can probably be back online in about a week."

Steve still said nothing. Was it better to keep talking or just shut up and let Steve think what he would? It probably didn't matter much. There was no way any crew would break through the rubble for at least a week anyway. "Look, we've worked hard here for the last eight months so let's not screw it up now." Was he actually telling the CIA how to run the project?

Steve sighed and nodded to his men. The CIA still needed Spencer's expertise. They had no knowledge on how to proceed. He had made himself and his team indispensable once again, but for how long?

Steve stepped forward and closed the gap between him and Spencer. He clapped Spencer on the shoulder and put out his hand. "It's good to see you, man. I wish it was under better circumstances."

"Me, too."

"I want to take a look around on my own . . . if it's okay with you."

Steve's tone spoke volumes. He wasn't really asking for Spencer's permission. He was flexing his CIA muscle.

"Meet me at the FOU in two hours." With that Steve and company walked back to the Hummer.

Spencer called Roula on a secure line and told her the news. "Will you be ready to go? There's a flight to San Francisco leaving Cairo tonight at eleven."

"I'll be ready."

"Great. Be at the terminal thirty minutes before the flight, but don't speak to me or even come near me. Just board the plane on your own. They will be watching."

"I have a clever disguise. They'll never recognize me," Roula reassured him.

The trip home seemed endless, but with Roula in the seat ahead of him, he was able to relax a little. She was dressed in a beautiful golden sari complete with veil. She could have easily passed for a

Hindu woman. No one at the airport gave her a second glance.

Spencer spent the time on the airplane formulating a plan for keeping their discovery secret and safe from the meddling hands of the CIA. His secret hideaway was going to be very handy.

He stood up, stretched, and headed to the restroom. On the way back he dropped a note into Roula's lap. The note explained his plan to Roula and gave her the address of his new apartment. He told her to meet him at the apartment at nine sharp, but to take a taxi from her hotel and make sure she isn't followed.

When the fasten seatbelt light finally clicked off, Spencer stood and stretched. A warm hand brushed his back. "I'll be there," she whispered. But please, you be careful, too." The softness in her voice made his heart sing.

The concierge at the San Jose Marriott had a line of people at her desk. With the many Silicon Valley conventions going on, the place buzzed with questions and requests from the hotel's guests. Spencer made his way through the crowd and headed straight to the front desk. "Do you have an envelope for a Mr. Ralph Spencer?" he asked a pretty brunette.

"Let me check for you, sir." She searched the entire reception area but found nothing. "I'm sorry, sir, I don't see anything here."

Spencer's hands turned ice cold. What could have gone wrong? Had Paul run into a snag? "Please check again," he said. "A friend has assured me that he left a package here in my name."

The brunette walked over to a colleague, whispered something in his ear, and left the room. Spencer waited for what seemed like an hour. One disaster scenario after another cascaded through his mind.

"Here Mr. Spencer." The woman handed him the package. "Sorry for the delay, but we have been holding this envelope for over eight months. And for a non-guest, well, let's just say it took a little doing to find it. Will you be staying here at the Marriott, sir?"

"Yes, I have reservations for this weekend. In fact, I might have to extend. Will that be a problem?" He'd made the reservation rationalizing that the best decoy would be to be booked at the hotel.

"I believe we will be able to arrange it. Our last convention ends this Saturday with the next group coming on Thursday." She was already pointing him to the receptionist's desk. Spencer registered and went to his room. The secret apartment was near the San Jose airport. He needed to get there well before nine without being followed. He didn't want to take any chances on Roula arriving before he did. He picked up the phone and dialed room service. "Fruit and cheese platter," he said into the phone. "Twenty minutes? Yes, thank you."

Right on time the waiter arrived with an oblong tray filled with assorted fruits, cheeses, and crackers. Spencer's mouth started to water. He hadn't eaten since the plane ride and had barely been able to eat then.

The waiter placed the tray on a table and turned to Spencer with a grim expression as though he half expected to get stiffed on his tip.

"Is this satisfactory? Will there be anything else?"

Spencer pulled a crisp fifty-dollar bill from his wallet and held it a few inches from the waiter's reach. "I need to ask a small favor of you," he said.

"I'll do what I can, sir"

"It's kind of embarrassing," Spencer said while scratching his head. "It's my ex-wife. She's been trying to serve me with papers, and I think she's found out that I'm staying here." He shook his head. You know how it is, man. She's trying to squeeze me for more alimony . . . I need to get out of here through the kitchen or staff entrance. Can you help me?"

"No problem. I hate process servers. They hunt you down like a criminal. My ex-wife did it to me once too." The waiter nabbed the fifty out of Spencer's hand. "Come this way."

Spencer darted out of the back entrance and walked several blocks away from the hotel. He then flagged a taxi. The secret apartment was tucked away in the back corner of the complex. It was perfect. Paul had come through for him on this one. He slid the key into the lock and turned until it clicked open. He flipped on the light and squinted as the room filled with light. A beige sofa sat against the wall with a small coffee table in front if it. A floor lamp stood to the side of the sofa and across the room there was a television that looked like it had been sitting there since the 80s. All of the boxes were stacked in the center of the living room with a note from Paul sitting on top.

Dear Spencer,

If you are reading this, you must be here (ha, ha). I have a set of duplicate keys just as you asked. I could have used this place once or twice with a lady friend, but I kept my word. Here are all your precious boxes. Core samples? Call me when you get a chance. I'd like to see you and catch up.

Paul

P.S. I hope no one is after you."

Spencer smiled. If Paul only knew what was really going on and the danger they were all in . . . and from their own government. It took him less than a minute to check out the rest of the spartan apartment. The kitchen was supplied with a four-piece set of white stoneware, plain silverware, and a few pots and pans. He pulled open the refrigerator door. There was a six-pack of beer on the bottom shelf with a note in Paul's scrawl. Thought you might need this. Enjoy!

The bedroom was also beige and was furnished with a full-size bed and one small dresser. He looked at the bed and saw an image of Roula; she was naked and patting the side of the bed inviting him to join her. Interesting that he didn't care much about missing meals during this crisis, but he damn well could still think about sex. It wasn't totally his fault, though. Roula was just so damned sexy.

He flipped off the bedroom light and headed for the sofa. Remote in hand, he clicked on the television. He flipped through the channels for a few minutes and then shut it off. He had way too much on his mind for the nonsense on television. He pulled his cell phone out of his pocket and dialed Paul. After three rings Paul's voicemail picked up. "Hi Paul, it's me, Spencer. I'm in town. Listen—"

There was a rap on the door. He flipped his cell phone closed and rushed to greet Roula.

She stood in the entryway, a large black roller suitcase at her side. Her eyes were wet and at least half her hair had fallen out of the clip at the back of her head. Her cheeks were flushed and the tension pulsed from her like an animal on the prowl. She'd never looked more ravishing.

Roula wrapped her arms around his neck and pulled him close. "I was so worried about you." She held his face and gave him a long kiss.

He pulled her close and let his lips linger on hers. After a long moment she pulled away and looked into his eyes.

"I'm fine. Honest. Everything is going well so far." He kissed her forehead. "I missed you." He reached into the hall and pulled her suitcase into the room. "C'mon let's settle in."

Roula stood in the center of the living room and turned a full circle. "Nice place," she said with a smile.

"Okay, so it's a little ordinary, but it's safe . . . for now."

The smile disappeared from her face and her beautiful mouth fell into a slight pout. "Are we really in that much danger?" she asked.

Roula, I—"

"Never mind," she said. "I already know the answer." She squared her shoulders and pointed to the suitcase. "You can throw that in the bedroom," she said.

He grabbed the handle and pulled the bag into the bedroom. He hated that he'd put Roula in harm's way. But what alternative did he have? No one else could have deciphered the hieroglyphics the way she had.

"I'm really hungry," she shouted to him from the living room "Can we order in?"

He strode back into the living room. "I'm suddenly starved," he said. "I guess it's because you're here . . . and safe." He brushed a wisp of hair from her cheek. "I've been dying for a good pizza," he said.

"Me, too. That's a great idea. I haven't had pizza since my trip to Italy last December."

"And guess what?"

"What?"

"Paul stocked the frig with beer."

"I think I like Paul," she said with a grin.

While Roula carried the paper plates, empty pizza box, and beer cans into the kitchen, Spencer unpacked some of the cylinders and carefully placed the first three into the viewer's holes. The cylinders fit with such precision, it was like a work of art. Spencer studied the viewer, his hands gliding over every inch of it. He looked for a switch or button to turn it on, but nothing worked. There was no hint of how to make it work.

"Let me take a look," Roula said.

She held up a small magnifying lens with a battery-powered light. He had seen her use the device many times before to illuminate dark areas and to decipher small hieroglyphic markings. She intently studied every facet of the strange device.

"Here, look." She handed the lens to Spencer. "If you look carefully, exactly in the center of each side and about one third up the side from the base, there are small holes. They're perfectly circular and no more than one millimeter wide. See?"

"Yes, I see. They line up perfectly with the converging point of the four holes.

What do you make of them?"

"I haven't got a clue." Roula took back the device. The base had her intrigued. She continued to examine the tiny inscriptions that adorned all four sides. She suddenly jumped. "Oh, my God, these tiny markings on each side of the base, I know what they are." She handed him the magnifier. "Look at them one at a time."

"Holy shit."

"Yeah, they're hieroglyphics." She beamed at him.

"What do they say?"

"I don't recognize these symbols. They're different from those on the door. We'll try the computer program and see if it can translate them." She went into the bedroom and came back with her laptop in hand. "Since these are all brand new markings, the encoding program will have to run for quite a while."

"Well, unless these inscriptions tell us how to turn this contraption on, it will be of very little use to us." She looked up at him with a frown. He hadn't meant to sound so short. Maybe the stress was starting to get to him. God only knew what was going on back in Egypt. Maybe he'd call Matt to find out. No, it would be too risky. He looked from the decoder to the computer screen and back again. If the computer program didn't work, the secrets of this ancient world or alien world or whatever it was might remain forever hidden in that strange time capsule buried deep under the Egyptian desert.

Roula watched the screen for a few moments and then looked up at him with that heavy-lidded gaze that could mean only one thing. "This will have to run all night," she said, her voice husky, "Let's go to bed."

In the comfort of the bedroom, he was free to show Roula how much he cared for her. They stood in the center of the room, slowly undressing one another. He lifted her, naked and warm, and carried her to the bed. Her skin seemed so fair against his arms that were now a deep tan from the African sun. She was light in his arms, no heavier than a feather. He laid her on the bed and then slid his body over hers. The touch of her skin sent waves of pleasure through him. He lowered himself onto her, pressing the hard warmth of his body against her, She sighed and melted into him.

CHAPTER

TWELVE

Spencer was startled awake by the sound of voices coming from the living room. He scrambled out of bed and slipped on a pair of sweat pants and a t-shirt. He bent over Roula and brushed the hair out of her face. "Roula," he whispered. "Wake up."

Her eyes popped open. He put a finger to her lips. "There are voices in the living room."

Fear reflected in her eyes. "Who?"

"Shhh . . . I don't know. Maybe the CIA . . . Abdul. You need to get up quietly and get dressed. Can you do that?"

She nodded and pointed at the pile of clothing she'd left on the floor the night before. Her hands shook as she put on her bra, underpants, slacks, and sweater. She flipped her hair over her shoulder and nodded to Spencer.

He inched the bedroom door open. How could they have found him? He had been so careful. And now there were CIA operatives lurking in his living room, checking out his newfound treasure? Ever so slowly he cracked his bedroom door a bit wider. The voices grew louder, but were still incomprehensible.

"Could Abdul have followed us here?" He whispered to Roula.

"Impossible. I was very careful. I'm sure no one noticed me at the airport," she whispered back, her voice shaking.

"He could have checked the airlines. The man has a broad reach, you know," Spencer whispered. He poked his head around the corner of the bedroom door. "Oh, my God," he said.

"What . . . what is it?"

He swung the door open. "See for yourself," he said. "You're not gonna believe it."

She stepped into the living room and he followed behind her. They had left the pyramid viewer on the coffee table still loaded with one of the cylinders. The morning sun was shining through the window right over the smooth surface of the viewer.

Spencer walked over to the device. "Well, I'll be damned."

"It runs on solar power?" Roula asked.

"Looks like it," Spencer said with a smile. "Never saw that one coming."

"Me either."

Projected onto the living room floor was a three dimensional holographic image of a man dressed in ornate clothing. He spoke in a monotone voice and in a language so unusual it was almost like no language at all. Spencer glanced at Roula. She stood at his side, her jaw slack, watching the image. She appeared to be spellbound, as if fixed to the spot where she stood.

Spencer stepped closer to the figure. The man stopped talking, turned, and looked him in they eye with the most brilliant blue eyes Spencer had ever seen. A chill ran down his spine. For the first time in human history, they were witnessing a recorded account of an ancient or alien world. Roula took a step forward and the man turned to face her. She smiled and embraced Spencer, tears of joy running down her cheeks. "How are we going to communicate with him?"

"I have no idea." The image was a three dimensional figure proportioned to approximately five feet nine inches. It was as if this man from some distant past stood right there in the room with them.

"I can't decipher his language," Roula said. "It's like nothing I've ever heard before." Roula took a walk around the image and he turned to follow her movements. "Maybe we're looking at one of the later cylinders. Maybe we need to look at the very first one for instructions. Whoever left this time capsule was very advanced. Surely they must have recognized the need for exact and easy to understand instructions on how it all works." Roula walked over to the stacked boxes. "Let's find the very first cylinder as outlined in the capsule library. We'll start with that one," she said, pointing.

Roula clearly couldn't wait to try her experiment. Spencer loaded the cylinder they had marked as number one. With a notepad in hand, Roula waited for the character to come to life. The stream of sunlight had shifted away from the pyramid. Spencer moved the coffee table so the pyramid was once again centered in the light. The viewer snapped to life and another image projected into the room. It was a three dimensional image of the inside of the time capsule. A beautiful flaxen-haired woman dressed in a multi-colored robe appeared inside the capsule image. She pointed to the numbered boxes. Her language was similar to that of the previous image. She seemed to be explaining the sequence and contents of each individual cylinder. Between sentences she would turn and look at him or at Roula. Her eyes were the same brilliant jewel-like blue as the man's, yet there was nothing cold about them. They were eyes that reflected the wisdom of ages.

The demonstration appeared so real that for a moment he wasn't sure that he hadn't been transported back inside the time capsule in Egypt. Spencer looked down at Roula's notepad. She had made a lot of scribbles, but none of it made any sense. She dropped the pad on the sofa and went to the kitchen. She poured two glasses of water and carried them back to the living room. She walked past the kitchen table and then froze. She took a step back, set down the glasses, and then tapped the keyboard of her laptop. It immediately came to life. She stared at the screen with wide eyes.

"Spencer, look at this. We have the four sides translated. I think we've hit the Jackpot."

Spencer stepped backwards toward the kitchen table, keeping one eye on the image.

LANGUAGE...FOR...POSITION...TRANSLATION... PALM... FLAT...BASE... AT...."

"I don't get it," he said.

Roula pointed to the computer screen. "If you rearrange these words to make a sentence you get, 'FOR LANGUAGE TRANSLATION POSITION FLAT PALM AT BASE.'"

Spencer stared at the words and then looked to Roula. She had wrapped her arms around herself, but her eyes were glistening with excitement. "Do you know what this means?" she asked.

He looked from the computer screen to the image in his living room. "The device has to be much more than just a viewer. It must have the capability of a very sophisticated computer . . . Does this mean it can translate languages by somehow reading electrical impulses from humans?"

Roula nodded.

"How is that possible? I mean, I'm familiar with the encoding process of my computer program. It's at the cutting edge of encryption. With millions of combinations to process, the programs develop a translation by trial and error. Its data bank contains the unabridged Webster's dictionary in all known languages and with all variations on word meaning."

"I read somewhere that pyramids have unusual powers," Roula muttered. "Some people believe that pyramids can influence your mind."

Spencer ran his fingers through his hair. "I don't know about that," he said. "But we do have some computers today that work through telepathic instructions. It's all very basic though. The programs are written mostly for disabled people who otherwise can't function at all."

Roula stared at the computer screen as if all the answers could be found in the one-sentence translation. "Maybe what we have here is an advanced computer that works on telepathic instruction. Before it can do that, though, it must be able to translate your thoughts into its original language . . . amazing"

If his and Roula's assumptions were correct, Spencer could add them to the quickly growing list of mind-boggling discoveries that this adventure had brought to light.

"I suppose it makes sense." Roula walked over to the image. The woman turned and looked at her, a look of eternal patience in her sapphire eyes. "After all, a human being is like a computer." She seemed to be speaking to the image now. "We retain all input from birth, but are only able to retrieve about ten percent of the stored data. If this machine can read a human mind, it'll take in all of our data." She turned back to Spencer. "Think about it . . . inside each mind lies a dictionary, or rather a memory bank, of all human experience in addition to our own individual memories. We've both been in school for a combined period of over forty years. We should certainly have enough data in our heads for this computer to perform basic translation." Roula turned back to the woman. "That's right, isn't it?" she said.

The woman looked at Roula with an odd expression on her face. What was it? She looked almost . . . proud . . . as if she had somehow followed Roula's train of thought and was pleased that she had figured things out. Spencer shook his head. Was he reading more into this than was there? It all seemed so impossible. "Let's try it." He picked up the device, making sure that the sun was still energizing it, and placed its base flat on his palm. A surge of energy ran along his arm and up to his brain. He was immobilized, unable to move or think. It was as though, for an instant, the strange machine controlled his entire being. Then it stopped. The whole process had taken less than fifteen seconds. He held the pyramid to his chest and fell to his knees.

"Spencer," Roula gasped.

"I'm all right. I don't know what happened. I was totally helpless." He tucked the pyramid under his arm and crawled to the sofa.

"Okay, my turn," Roula said.

"Wait."

"Why, did it hurt?"

"No, but it was strange. I'm just not sure you want to go through that."

"I think I can handle it," she said.

"Maybe we should see the results from my input before we continue." He only wanted to protect her. After all, they had no clue what possible effects this machine could have.

"There's no time for us to research it. We need to provide this machine with as much data as possible. With my background in language translation, I should have unique information not available to you. Here let me have the pyramid."

She took the device to the kitchen table and balanced it on her open palm. Her body shuddered and her eyes glazed over. She must have felt the zap of energy rushing to her brain. A few moments later her eyes closed and she fell limp like a rag doll.

"Roula, Roula, wake up." Spencer shook her shoulder.

Her eyes fluttered open. "What happened?"

"I think you fainted." Spencer pulled her upright. He took her chin in his hand and looked into her eyes. "Your pupils are enormous," he said.

"So are yours," she said with a faint smile.

"Do you feel okay?"

She squared her shoulders and looked from side to side then up and down. "I feel amazing actually."

"Yeah, me too, almost a little too good, like I need to run a marathon."

She stood, twisted her hair into a thick knot, and fastened it in place with the clip she'd worn the night before. "Let's use all this energy to find out what this mechanical marvel can do." She kissed him on the cheek and walked back into the living room.

Warmth spread over his face and down his neck. Amazing what such a small gesture from the woman he loved could do. The cylinder they'd marked number one was still sitting on the coffee table. He placed it inside the pyramid's hole and waited. The machine came to life and the image of the woman again appeared in front of them. This time she stood still and lifeless, like a movie on pause.

Roula held her hand to her forehead and waited. "What's going on?"

"Look," Spencer pointed to the cylinder.

"My God."

The cylinder was spinning at an incredible speed, yet no sound emanated from it. "Maybe it's translating," Spencer uttered with a shrug.

"It must be. What else could it be doing?" She watched intently, waiting for the spinning to stop. Not more than two minutes had passed, when the woman unexpectedly came to life. She looked from Roula to him and smiled. A wave of excitement made Spencer's body quake. He was suddenly a schoolboy again, the boy who would tremble with anticipation when a scientific discovery was at hand. This discovery, though, was far more than he could wrap his mind around. No rational scientist would even believe what he was seeing.

The woman continued to stare at them and smile. Her expression was one of patience and kindness. "Greetings from Phamuria," she said finally. "I am Neflani. I serve our High Counsel as the narrator of the capsule. This library contains a recorded account of our intact history. Your thoughts have delivered us your language. What you are hearing is your own language as translated by the device. I apologize if my speech is uncomfortable for you. Your diction was developed solely from thought contribution. It is possible that you may be having problem understanding."

"Not at all," Roula said as if speaking to a live human being. "We understand you just fine."

Neflani turned to Roula and smiled. Had she understood Roula's words? She certainly seemed to have been conversing with Roula directly.

"On my mark," Neflani continued, "please recite your language's alphabetical signs. You may stop this machine at any time. Simply use voice commands. The command for stopping is 'Stop Narration.' To start simply use the contrary command 'Start Narration.'"

"Stop Narration." Spencer spoke clearly. Immediately the image disappeared. "Holy shit! Are we dreaming all this?"

"It's real, my dear." Roula squealed and wrapped him in hug. "Do you know what we have here? This is unprecedented." She jumped up and down and clapped her hands. "I'm sorry," she said, "I'm just so excited . . . and this thing has me so energized."

"I know what you mean." Spencer laughed. He took her in his arms and waltzed her around the room. "We're the luckiest science geeks on earth!"

He gave her two more turns around the room and then stopped to kiss her. "Lucky in more ways than one," he said.

Her gaze met his. "Yeah, so lucky." She touched her finger to his lips and smiled. "Let's bring back Neflani and find out who these people were."

He kissed her nose and then took her by the hand to the sofa. "Start Narration."

The viewer projected Neflani's image into the room. "Please wait for my mark to recite your language's signs. Three, two, one, mark."

Spencer recited the alphabet slowly and with clear enunciation. Roula squeezed his hand.

"Please wait." Neflani disappeared again and the cylinder started its wild spinning.

The machine appeared to be adjusting the databank on the cylinder based on Spencer's dictation of the alphabet. "Amazing," he said. "We'll have a being from an ancient civilization narrating their society's history with a Virginia accent."

Roula rolled her eyes and smiled. "There might be some of my accent in there too, you know."

Neflani reappeared and turned to face them. "Greetings from Phamuria. I am Neflani. I serve our High Counsel as the narrator of this capsule. This library contains a recorded account of our entire history." She spoke excellent English. Her pronunciation made her sound as if she had lived in the Southeast. Spencer looked at Roula and they both shrugged.

"All of the data delineating the history of our great nation of Phamuria is contained in these one-hundred-and-one polished crystal storage cylinders. If you are able to understand me, then may I offer my congratulations on achieving this great accomplishment. You have used your intuition well. Ralph Spencer and Roula Grazulis, you are privileged to witness the accounts of our existence. Through your willingness to share your biological data with our time capsule master computer, we have accessed your entire combined knowledge and completely translated our data into a format and language that you can understand. My ability to speak and converse at your level of understanding depends solely on the input you provided our master computer, as you would call it. Both of you should be able to fully comprehend what I am about to tell you. Please do not be shocked if you hear personal information about yourselves. Remember that the master computer has all of your data from the time of your birth to this moment."

Neflani stopped talking and gazed at them, a small smile playing on her lips. Was she pausing to give them a chance to regroup and take it all in?

"Based on your present day calendar," Neflani continued, "the geological information provided by Ralph Spencer, along with the historical knowledge of Roula Grazulis, our estimate is that two-hundred-fifty to three-hundred thousand years have elapsed since our nation perished."

Roula put her hand to her mouth and gasped.

"Phamuria was indeed a great nation. Its geographical location was at the very center of all land masses…the land you now call Egypt."

"Stop narration." Spencer needed a minute to think. The implications of what he had just heard were mind-boggling.

"Do you know what this is?" he said to Roula, "This is the greatest discovery in recorded history. These people lived on earth as much as three hundred thousand years ago. Look at what they built."

"I know," she said, confusion reflected in her dark eyes.

"What I'm saying is, this could mean the end of speculation about humanity's origins. My God, it could mean that the theory of evolution is put to bed for good. This is massive!" He stared at the device as if in a trance. "Their technology is so much more advanced than ours. People will kill for these cylinders—"

The thought sent a jolt through him. Bile rose in his throat. He looked over at Roula, his heart aching with concern for her.

She squared her shoulders and her jaw jutted out slightly. The woman was one tough act.

"I want to hear more," she said. "We must know more. Do we have time to listen?" She was practically pleading with him.

He looked at his watch. It was only eleven am and they had been in the country less than twenty-four hours. I have a suspicion that Steve put a tracer on me. The CIA knows we were very close to hitting bottom. I don't know if they totally bought the accident routine at this late stage of the game. The same is true with the Egyptians. Abdul will be watching every move we make."

Roula's eyes filled with tears and her face went pale. "Yes, Abdul," she said absently.

"I'm sorry," Spencer said, "I was just trying to delineate the worst possible scenario. For now I think we're safe. I had Paul pretend to be me and go to my hotel room. I think it will work for a while, at least until the CIA starts wondering why I haven't budged from the room. They're suspicious, but I don't think they know much yet. We're safe here. No one else knows about this place except Paul." He glanced at Roula and nodded. "We do need to learn more about these people from Phamuria. Let's give it a couple more hours."

"Start narration." Roula said loudly. Spencer put his hand over Roula's long fingers and sunk back into the sofa to listen.

Neflani came to life. "My narration will explain our history and our destruction. Our mother Earth is the ultimate judge. It is forever changing, giving birth to and reclaiming great nations. Human beings are simply one of the byproducts of her judgment." Neflani appeared solemn and her voice was sad. Her eyes were damp with tears and her face was expressionless as if she had no hope left in her. "Your minds have been fused with this computer and your knowledge is now available to this machine's central brain processor. The immense capabilities of this machine are beyond your comprehension. With its enormous data and processing capabilities, this machine is able to answer most any question you might have. The computer will simply search for a plausible answer and my voice will provide the audible response. The degree of accuracy will totally depend on the nature of your requests. Empirical requests will have accuracy well above ninety-nine percent. Subjective questions will be tailored in accordance with your existing knowledge and beliefs.

"Now, I must tell you the most important function of this computer. As you see, on the slanted four sides of this pyramid-shaped machine are four circular openings. You already are aware that these openings are for the input medium. As you presently see, my projected holographic image comes from the very first crystal data storage unit. We call this the first dimension. Sequential input from the appropriate crystal data storage unit will result in what we call the fourth dimension. From your present knowledge, you will have trouble comprehending these results, but I will try to explain them in terms that are available to you today. You call this type of existence virtual reality. Your knowledge of virtual reality, however, is primitive and limited. The fourth dimension mode enables the viewer, or viewers, to participate in the time continuum, though without the ability to alter any future outcomes. Viewers interacting in the fourth dimension will not be harmed nor be able to harm anyone. You may now ask questions." Neflani stopped talking and, with a gentle smile, waited for one of them to speak.

Spencer looked to Roula. She sat staring at Neflani, her jaw slack and tears sliding down her cheeks. She, too, was struggling to take it all in. Was this real? Were they awake and not dreaming? There was only one way to find out. "If I am hearing you correctly, Neflani—"

The image turned toward Spencer and smiled, "Yes, Ralph?"

Spencer's jaw moved but no words came out. Was he actually going to be conversing with this hologram? "Well," he muttered, "what I wanted to know is if you are saying that we can actually enter your world through this device?" He spoke to Neflani as if she actually existed right there in his living room. He shivered involuntarily. It was like talking to a ghost.

"Yes. Both of you may wish to experience our world." Neflani explained. "You will see, feel, and experience our culture with the full capacity of all your senses. All communication will be in your language. You will not have the power to change the events of our people's history, nor will you be able to change even minor events. This machine will only transport you into the virtual world created for your experience. To you, all events will appear real. Is this clear?" She waited.

"What you're telling us is that this device acts as a virtual time machine and if we activate the proper sequence of input, we will be transported into your world?" Roula held her head in her hands, as if she didn't believe her ears. She seemed disoriented. And why shouldn't she be? What they were witnessing was beyond anyone's wildest imagination.

"In some ways this is true. The important distinction is that you will be observers with the ability to fully interact with the given environment. However, the system is limited to the historical data contained here. The virtual ambiance therefore interacts solely with our time period as recorded. This machine is not capable of choosing an arbitrary time and space and opening a gate to it. The ability to engage the fourth dimension can only be achieved from the inner chamber of our time capsule. The outer web like material of the capsule provides the exact gravitational and magnetic fields required for the master computer to open the temporal passage. This is very important. Passage is only available within the capsule. You must be in the capsule's inner chamber to enter. You will be returning into your present world in the same location...in the inner chamber of the time capsule.

"I must caution you. Do not allow anyone to remove any of the crystal data storage while you are in our world. If this happens, the temporal passage will immediately shut and you will cease to exist." She paused and stared straight ahead, a grave look on her face.

"Where would we be then? Dead? But how?" Spencer asked.

"You would be lost, Ralph . . . for lack of a better word. As the gate closes, connection with our world ceases. You would be trapped in the continuum. Re-establishing a gate will always result in new coordinates, since time is always changing," Neflani answered.

"How do we get back?" Spencer asked.

"You simply ask to be returned to your time. This command will activate the program in the main computer and a reverse gate will transport you to the very same spot in the time capsule. Your verbal command is: return us to our time." Neflani paused. She seemed to be waiting for their next question.

"What about power for the computer? How long can we stay? Does time elapse while we are in the fourth dimensional mode?" Spencer asked.

"Time lapse is in your real time. Always have an accurate chronometer when entering into the fourth dimension. The solar powered unit, when fully charged, will retain power for twenty-four hours. The master computer is programmed to alert you automatically when the power level reaches the last sixty minutes. Verbal alarms will alert you every fifteen minutes. You must exit the forth dimension prior to system shut down. Failure to do so will result in your non-existence. Manual shutdown or malfunctions are virtually impossible. This would require the total destruction of the main computer. Are we very clear?" Neflani gave them the same grave look she had earlier.

Spencer's mind was racing. They would have to bring all the equipment back to Egypt for the experiment to work. Spencer scooted to the edge of the sofa and tapped his fingers on the coffee table. It was a nervous habit he'd developed in college and had never been able to stop.

"Yes, we are clear." Roula replied. "Your time capsule is far away from here. We won't be able to enter the fourth dimension right now. In the meantime, we would like some background on your world. Can you give us a brief historical account?" Roula had often pondered the origins of the ancient hieroglyphic writings. Perhaps the history of this civilization would answer her questions.

"That is my primary function." Neflani stated matter-of-factly. "As I stated, Phamuria was once a great nation and a beautiful country. I must start with the geological condition of Earth during our time. Spencer, you will appreciate this more. Some three hundred thousand years ago the geological and geographical location of all landmasses were significantly different from today. The Earth was in the middle of yet another ice age. Most of the continents as you know them today were under thousands of feet of ice. Phamuria and parts of a land called Iucania, were the only considerable exceptions. Some small land masses also existed in the land you now call Australia and Micronesia.

"Phamuria and Iucania were separated by a sea now called the Atlantic Ocean. These lands were very fertile and had the ideal climate to sustain life. Our history spanned fifteen thousand years. The facts of our origin were never resolved. Many believed in a creator similar to your beliefs, Ralph. Many others chose to believe in a destiny originating from far away planets colonizing our Earth in order to propagate their species. Our history spanned several cycles of prosperity and hardship ending with the cataclysmic destruction of both nations. We advanced technically and socially over the centuries. At the peak of our civilization, our people numbered well above twelve million. Our great discoveries and technological advances all happened as a result of a long lasting peace between our two nations. The lack of habitable land anywhere on the planet gave us an inner understanding that we could only survive through harmony. Our fertile land gave us an abundance of raw materials and food for our people. Our world was beautiful." Neflani sighed. "Full of life with beautiful streams and lush valleys." Her eyes seemed to mist over as she talked. "Animals roamed the forests and fish were abundant in our lakes and rivers. Over the centuries, we invented flying machines capable of fast travel, harvesting machines for our fields, and building machines used for our great structures. Our religious theorists argued that our origin was the stars and that someday our creators would be back to visit. They were successful in convincing our governing council and our scientists to construct an astronomical beacon that would last for millenniums. I believe that this beacon still exists today. You refer to it as the great pyramid of Giza." She paused for a second.

"Are you telling us that your people built the great pyramid?" Spencer gasped.

"Yes, we built it. It was built on the largest rock formation known to us. Our knowledge of tectonic plate movement along with volcanic and glacial changes dictated the exact location. The great pyramid has its foundation on miles of solid rock. Roula you have done much research into our language base and I am here to tell you that much more data is available underneath the great pyramid. Exactly below the base, at its center, our people constructed a tunnel deep into the existing rock. The tunnel turns several times and it extends well over a mile into the rock. At the end of the tunnel is a large chamber filled with ancient hieroglyphics that explain much of our origin. This chamber was to house the time capsule. It was the desire of the ruling council to place the time capsule you found in this chamber for safekeeping. Unfortunately, Phamuria suffered great cataclysmic events that eventually led to its destruction, and the capsule was buried deep underground before it could be placed in the chamber. I am surprised Ralph, that your people have not yet discovered that tunnel. The entrance to the tunnel is charted on cylinder number thirty-four." Neflani tucked her hands into her sleeves and waited.

"What exactly caused your country's destruction?" Spencer asked.

"It had been calculated by our scientists that a major earthquake was about to strike our land, triggered by the eruption of several large volcanoes. No one really knew the exact time, but our instruments indicated a violent and destructive force capable of annihilating all living things. The Supreme Council ordered an immediate evacuation. In fact, some of our citizens did escape to the far ends of Iucania and some were able to hide in the great pyramid. The pyramid was built to withstand great forces and it proved able to do just that, since it is still standing as I have ascertained from your biological data," Neflani said this with a hint of pride in her voice. "Others used our flying machines to flee to the small lands you now call Australia and Micronesia. The end of both nations came suddenly. I have no access to any of the data detailing the destruction because we all perished. I do have information that I personally inputted on the cylinder the very last day of my own existence. That information is found on cylinder one hundred and one." She paused as if remembering her last actions as a living being.

Roula had listened intently and was looking at Neflani with a strange expression on her face. Was she still numb from the discovery they had made, or was it something else?

"I'm sorry." Roula's face reflected the horror Neflani must have experienced on that dreadful day.

"Thank you, Roula. My people have been dead for three hundred thousand years, but for me it could have been yesterday. You will be the first human beings to witness the calamity we endured." She looked sad as the words left her lips.

How was it that this holographic image could interact with Roula? "You have emotional responses," he said to Neflani, "as though you are real and here with us reliving events. Can you explain?"

"Ah, Ralph," Neflani smiled. "This is a question I would expect from you. There is a logical answer. You see, the master computer has read both your minds, the electrical impulse recorded not only your knowledge and memories, but also your emotional responses. My facial gestures and words are configured by the computer to best respond to your questions including the appropriate emotional outcome."

"This is too much for us to grasp, Neflani. We need to inform my boss about this discovery. We have to figure out a way to protect it. Our world today is very different from yours and if this information got into the wrong hands, it could destroy our nation," Spencer explained.

"Yes, you should inform McPearson, you trust him." Neflani said.

Spencer stared wide-eyed at Neflani. How did she know about McPearson?

"I know all about your world, remember?" Neflani laughed. "I have all of your data and Roula's stored here." She pointed to the master computer.

"Oh yes," Spencer gave her a shy smile. "I'd almost forgotten." Spencer wanted to experience the fourth dimension. He wanted to experience the world as it was that very long time ago. "Stop narration," Spencer ordered. Immediately the image of Neflani disappeared. Spencer removed the proper crystal cylinder and carefully placed it in its box. "This is beginning to make sense Roula. Our ancestors must have been the survivors of the cataclysmic event that destroyed Phamuria and Iucania. Since most people died, nearly all knowledge died with them. As the surviving generation grew old and died, less and less of their knowledge was passed on to their children. Survival became the principal focus. After a few millennia, all was lost. Civilization had to start over." He may have just solved one of the fundamental questions that had plagued the minds of men for the last few centuries. It was too much to think about. He turned to Roula. "We need to get back to Egypt and inside the time capsule as soon as possible."

"Are you going to tell McPearson about this?" Roula asked.

"We need protection from the CIA and Abdul. If word gets out about our discovery, we'll be history. Like Neflani said, I trust McPearson. He'll help us get into the time capsule. I'm sure Steve put a tail on me the minute I stepped off the plane at SFO. Hopefully it's Paul they're watching in my hotel room right now. I told him not to leave the room unless I called him. We're safe for now." He used his most reassuring voice for Roula, but an uneasy feeling had his fingers nervously strumming the coffee table. They had made the greatest discovery of all time. With it came great danger for him and his friends. He picked up the phone and dialed McPearson's private line.

"Spencer, my boy, I was wondering what happened to you. We've been waiting for you to contact us. You haven't run into more trouble, have you?

Spencer opened his mouth but then stopped. Chances were good McPearson's line was bugged.

"No, sir. No other problems. Just the collapse of the main shaft."

"Yes, I heard. Our team will advise you on what to do about that damned collapse. They're working on a plan now."

"Bill, I'd like to have a chance to catch up with you. It feels like I've been gone for a long time. How about meeting me for a cappuccino at Ghirardelli Square . . . say one o'clock?" Spencer glanced at his watch. He'd have about an hour and a half to sneak back to his hotel room and relieve Paul of his duties.

"Love to." McPearson said. "See you there."

Spencer turned to Roula. "Stay here and guard all the equipment. I'll meet with Bill in private and see if he can help us out." He stroked her hand gently. How could he reassure her that everything was going to be all right when he wasn't sure of that at all?

At the hotel, Spencer used the service entrance to the kitchen and looked for the room service waiter who had helped him before. Hopefully the man still hated his ex-wife.

"Psssst."

The waiter turned and smiled. "Hey, man, you still ditchin' your ex?"

"Yeah, I need to get back to my room, quickly and quietly. There's another fifty bucks for you if I can borrow your uniform and deliver myself some lunch."

The waiter laid open his palm and grinned. What did he care? He was on a break soon and fifty bucks was fifty bucks.

"Glad to help." The waiter winked. "I hate those ex-wives."

With a large tray above his head and the confidence of a butler,

Spencer knocked at his hotel room door. "Room service."

"Come in." Paul smiled and waved him through the door.

Spencer set the tray on the coffee table. "Close the door quickly," he said to Paul.

"Good to see you, man. I was going out of my mind wondering where the hell you were. You okay?"

Spencer moved about the room looking in corners and behind furniture. He kept his head tilted low, hiding his face in the shadow of the bellman's cap.

"Listen, man, I'm losing a day's work here . . ." Paul stood with his hands on his hips watching Spencer search the room. "Dude, what're you doing?"

"Nothing."

"Isn't it about time you tell me what's going on?"

Spencer pulled back the curtains and ran his hand along the windowsill.

"I made the phone calls this morning and charged them to your phone card just like you said. Your mother says to tell you hello, but she's worried about you."

The hotel room seemed to be clean. There was no sign of any bugs or cameras. The intrigue was clearly driving Paul crazy, but there was nothing Spencer could do about that now. He had to get to the meeting with McPearson and then back to Roula. "Paul, I can't thank you enough. You're a true friend. I promise I'll explain all of this to you, but right now I'm late for a meeting at the office. I need you to change clothes with me."

"What?"

Spencer looked at his friend with sad eyes. "Please?"

Paul sighed and slipped out of his shirt. They quickly exchanged clothes, and Paul left with the empty tray. Spencer rehearsed in his mind what he would tell McPearson while gobbling down a quarter of the turkey sandwich Paul had left behind. It was the best he could do. He was too nervous to eat. So much was at stake.

CHAPTER

THIRTEEN

Bill McPearson sat in the back corner of Ghirardelli's watching the tourists and waiting for Spencer to arrive. He had a steaming cup of black coffee in front of him and a cappuccino waiting for Spencer. Something was up at the site, something big, he could feel it. He'd been around the block a few times and he'd always been able to sense when a big find was imminent. Spencer obviously had something to discuss with him in private, otherwise why hide out in a coffee shop? But what could it be?

The crowd at the counter parted and Spencer weaved his way to the corner table. Spencer's blonde hair hung in his eyes as if it hadn't been cut in months. His khaki pants were wrinkled, his loafers scuffed, and he wore no socks. His green eyes were the giveaway though; they had a wild, almost feral look to them. McPearson's heart pounded. Oh, yeah, there was a big secret hiding behind those shining eyes.

"Here's your cappuccino, Spencer. I hope it meets your specifications."

Spencer sat across from him and smiled. "Thanks, Bill." He took a sip through the hole in the plastic cover. "It's perfect," he said absently.

McPearson laughed. "Okay, so what gives? I know you better than you may think. You've never asked me out for coffee before."

Spencer glanced around the shop with a wariness that made McPearson's stomach knot up.

Spencer sipped the cappuccino and sighed. "I'm not sure . . ."

Ghirardelli's was situated in the center of the busy square. The tables that dotted the open area along the frontage were all occupied, mostly with tourists, as was every table inside. It was an ideal spot for a clandestine conversation. With all the noise and chaos, there was no way anyone would overhear their words. "You're safe here, my boy. Now tell me what's on your mind."

"You're right, I need to speak with you. But it must be in strict confidence. I trust you, but what I'm about to tell you could put you in danger. Do you want me to continue?"

Spencer looked McPearson in the eye. Was the boy serious?

"For Christ's sake Spencer, I'm in charge of this project. I can take care of myself. I respect you and, in the past year, I've grown to like you. I'm glad you came to me for help, but spill the beans already." McPearson eased forward and wrapped his hands around the hot coffee cup. He never had learned to handle his emotions around people he cared about.

Spencer's eyes brightened as if he'd just made up his mind about something important. "We found it, Bill."

"I knew it! What about the shaft collapse?"

"Just a diversion to protect the capsule."

"Capsule? What capsule?" McPearson moved his large form to the edge of his chair. "What about the oil?"

"We didn't find any oil, and I don't think we will."

The excitement drained from McPearson's body. "No oil? Then what for God's sake?"

Spencer stared at McPearson through his shaggy bangs, his eyes gleaming. "What we found is a time capsule from the distant past. It's over three-hundred thousand years old."

"Holy shit!" McPearson shouted.

A hush fell over the room as people from the surrounding tables turned to stare at the jolly-looking man with the robust curse. He leaned in until he was almost forehead-to-forehead with Spencer. "Holy shit," he said in a much lower voice. "How is that possible? Are you sure?"

"What we found is beyond anything I've ever dreamed of. It's beyond your wildest imagination. The capsule was apparently trapped by an ancient volcanic eruption and has remained buried deep below the surface. We reached it at eighteen thousand feet. It's in the massive cave that has served as its tomb for all these centuries. It's so well preserved, it's like new." The words were pouring out of Spencer now. His tone was one of relief.

"Roula was able to decipher the hieroglyphics and open its main door. Inside, we found crystal cylindrical disks full of data. The history of an ancient land called Phamuria."

"Wait, who?"

"Phamuria."

"No, before that."

"Roula? Oh, I guess you haven't met her. Roula Grazulis. She's a student studying hieroglyphics in Egypt.

McPearson swallowed some coffee. The magnitude of the discovery was starting to settle in. His face had gone pale, he was sure of it. "She was able to translate this ancient language so quickly? How?"

"She's really good." Spencer answered with a gleam in his eye that told more than he'd likely intended.

"It gets better. These crystal cylinders contain data that can be projected by a sophisticated device we found inside the inner chamber of the time capsule. The people that built these devices were advanced beyond anything we have today. The machine acts as a master computer and is powered by solar light. It can scan the human brain's electrical impulses and make use of a hundred percent of its data to translate the information into our language. Roula and I had our brains scanned, and the machine was able to translate all of the data into English."

"That's incredible . . . and more than a little dangerous. Are you both okay?

"Oh, yeah, fine. Our pupils were dilated for a few hours and were felt super energized, but that was about it."

McPearson sat back in his chair and stroked his chin. None of what Spencer was saying seemed plausible. Was this some sick prank the guys had thought up one night at a gin joint? "Are you on the level, Spencer? Cause if this is a joke, you've gone too far."

"No joke, sir. This is a hundred percent on the level. I'd stake my reputation and our good friendship on it." Spencer brushed his hair out of his eyes and looked McPearson in the eye.

The look on his face said it all. He was telling the truth.

"I'm not talking about just a recording of the past. When one of the crystal cylinders was loaded into the master computer, it projected a holographic image into the room. The image was of a woman named Neflani. She appeared in the middle of my living room and proceeded to tell us about her world. Since we had been scanned, her words were all in English. Because of the immense amount of data the computer can process, she was able to converse with us, answering our questions when asked." Spencer paused, shaking his head in disbelief.

"My God, this is beyond monumental. It's the greatest discovery of the human race."

"Better than oil, huh?"

"Way better . . . I'm having a little trouble taking it all in," McPearson said.

"I have more to tell you."

"You're kidding. There's more?"

"The master computer that reads the cylinders has the ability to process four cylinders at once. Neflani, the woman who spoke to us, explained that when all four cylinders are loaded in the proper sequence, the computer creates a sort of virtual reality called the fourth dimension. This can only be achieved inside the time capsule. The capsule creates appropriate magnetic and gravitational fields needed and the master computer creates a temporal gate transporting the viewers into a virtual reality of Phamuria."

"A time machine?" McPearson asked, incredulous.

"Not exactly. According to Neflani, we can participate, experience, and feel as if we're actually in the past, but we can't alter any future outcomes. We can't cause harm or be harmed. It's as if we could interact with the spirits of dead ancestors. All of the conversation will be in our language. The computer has already adjusted by reading our brains. It knows everything we know and more. Most of our memory is suppressed, but that device was able to access a hundred percent of our electrical thought impulses, past and present. There are some dangers. If somehow a cylinder is removed prior to returning to reality, the traveler would be lost forever."

Spencer paused and sipped at his cappuccino. McPearson was now speechless. He stared blankly into his empty cup, unable to comprehend the magnitude of the discovery.

"I'm sure the CIA has a tail on me," Spencer said. "I took great precautions last night to disappear and view the cylinders. I believe we're in grave danger . . . and now you are, too. I'm sorry for that."

"Don't be sorry. You did the right thing coming to me. We'll figure this out."

Spencer nodded but he didn't look convinced.

"Once the CIA figures out what we've got, they'll take over the project and God knows what will happen to it. It's entirely possible that they will do God knows what to us as well. This discovery will alter the world as we know it. The knowledge on those cylinders is incredibly powerful. In the interest of national security, they'll take care of anyone not in compliance with their goals—namely us. Plus, the government will make this so top secret it will be as if it never existed . . . the world will never know. We can't let that happen. We need to outsmart them, before it's too late." Spencer turned and surveyed the crowd, his green eyes slowly scanning the room, the patio area and beyond into the square.

"Where is Roula now?"

"At my apartment with the cylinders and the machine that reads them."

"Is she alone."

"Yeah."

"Okay, the first thing we need to do is hold a meeting at my office. Tom Detton expects you there at three this afternoon."

"Good. I'll brief them about the explosion and the collapse of the main shaft. We need to come up with new safety procedures and convince the CIA that reaching the bottom will require more time." Spencer drank down the last of his cappuccino. "Are you aware that Steve Sullivan is already investigating the site with his team of goons?"

"Yeah, I heard. Tom called me late yesterday. We need to pretend that our main objective is to repair the damaged shaft and continue drilling through the lava rock. Once we set the new safety procedures in place, you'll need to estimate the time required to reach the base of the cavity. All we need to do is add a few days to the estimate in order to complete our objective." McPearson liked the ring of authority in his voice and the surge of energy that a new adventure always gave him. He was, after all, known as a man of bold action. "I'd like to see this discovery for myself. Tonight, after the meeting, can we arrange it?"

Spencer's nod was tentative. "We'll need to be really careful. I have a secret apartment near the San Jose airport. No one knows about it. I arranged it before I left for Africa. My friend Paul took care of the whole thing. We'll have to figure out a clever way to get you there without being followed." Spencer seemed more at ease now that he had shared his secret with someone of McPearson's stature and clout.

Spencer walked into Calpetro's main conference room. McPearson was seated at the far end of the large table and Tom Detton stood at the front of the room, a steaming cup of coffee in his hand, pacing nervously. Spencer walked to the front of the room and offered Detton his hand. "Hello, Tom."

"Mr. Spencer, good to see you." Detton shook his hand and then gestured for him to sit down. "We're all ready for you. Steve will participate via satellite." Detton seemed even more uptight than usual. What was he so jumpy about?

The large monitor on the far wall was already linked with the site and projected Steve's face. The transmitting camera was positioned directly at his chair.

"Hey Spencer. I hope you're staying cool at home. Today was in the low hundreds here." Steve managed an unconvincing smile.

"Hi Steve. I've not had any time to enjoy the weather yet. Have you talked with Abdul?" Spencer's heart started to pound. Had they discovered anything since his departure?

"Oh, yeah. What an ass. I could have come down hard on him, but I didn't want to increase his suspicions about our real purpose for the mine shaft."

Spencer breathed a sigh of relief. Abdul's bullheadedness was actually helping to keep the CIA out of the mine.

"Please give us a full briefing, Spencer," McPearson ordered.

"We have a twofold problem here. Last week, we discovered an illegal tap into our satellite feed. Fortunately, it was of poor quality. Thanks to your sophisticated encryption, whoever planted the device got a fuzzy picture and garbled audio. As a precaution, we immediately pulled the feed. I have a suspicion that the feed is the work of Abdul. Steve, you can back me up on this after your full investigation."

"Who planted the feed?" Tom asked, his voice calmer.

"We're still not sure. Hopefully that's something that Steve will find out soon. The mine employs well over a hundred regular workers and specialty sub-contractors. We could have as many as two hundred people at the site on any given day. Our deal with Egypt requires us to employ their local work force. Abdul could have paid any one of them to do his dirty work."

Detton's eyes narrowed. What the hell was going on inside the man's head? Did the CIA know more than they were letting on? It was impossible to know. All he could do was stick with the story he and McPearson had agreed upon. If the CIA knew more, it would come out sooner or later. "The second problem," he continued, "relates to the explosion that destroyed portions of the main shaft and ventilation shaft. At about the seventeen thousand foot level, we reached a lava stratum. With the use of our ground penetrating radar, we were able to map the upcoming geological features up to a hundred and fifty feet ahead of the face. This allowed the miners to determine the state and structure of the rock. Matt Garrett, our man in charge of the drilling team, is, as you know, an expert in his own right. He was unable to break through this incredibly hard stratum. Hydropower rock drills, impact rippers using hydraulically driven hammers, and other non-explosive devices didn't budge the rock. These devices are the latest in mining technology. Matt thought the only reasonable alternative to keep the project on schedule was blasting, and, frankly, I agreed wit him. We knew it was a risk, but there was really no other option. I'm afraid that the detonation strength required for such hard rock caused the damage to the already built shaft and ventilation shaft." Spencer got up and poured himself a cup of coffee. He'd give Detton and Steve a few minutes to digest what he'd said. He didn't want to say any more than he absolutely had to. At this point he just needed to prove to them that he knew his stuff. The technical language was to make them feel as if the whole thing was over their heads. But had it worked?

"How many feet did we lose?" McPearson asked, already knowing the answer.

"Approximately three hundred to five hundred feet. We can repair this section in less than two weeks. The collapse of the shaft also caused our main water pumps to fail, filling the main shaft with water. This problem will require at least an additional two weeks to correct."

The sump pump in the ventilation shaft was still working. Hopefully Steve had not discovered this fact.

"Of course we need to consider our third obstacle," he continued, "Mr. Abdul, as you are fully aware, has ordered the mine shut down. He has placed guards at the entrances to ensure that absolutely no one will enter until we receive new clearance from his office. This clearance is predicated on a new set of safety procedures ensuring the safety and wellbeing of each worker. We were lucky. Only four people suffered minor injuries . . . two broken legs, a broken arm, and a laceration, not to mention a lot of cuts and bruises. One poor guy will most likely lose his arm." Spencer sipped his coffee and waited. Both Detton and Steve remained silent and stone faced. Were they buying anything he was saying? Were they playing him? There was no way of knowing. The CIA must have special training on how to hold a poker face because these two guys were damn good at it.

"Do you have any suggestions on ways to improve safety and get that jerk Abdul off our backs?" Detton asked.

"I had a long meeting with Matt Garrett before leaving and he said that our options are limited. He suggested using diamond wire saws. These saws can cut narrow slices of the rock that will reduce dilution. We'll be able to use much smaller explosions, improving safety. Another method available to us is the penetrating cone fracture. This process uses a non-explosive propellant to break pre-stressed rock. It's proven safe because it generates low velocity fly rock with a controlled size distribution and minimum fines causing very little damage to the surroundings." The lies were flowing out of him so easily that he almost believed his own story.

"I see that you have really done your homework, Spencer," McPearson said. "Very impressive."

"Thanks, Bill," Spencer said. "We had a similar problem in South Africa in '92. Diamond wire saws did the job. We must have used over five thousand to get our bore completed, but never had a problem with safety.

"I agree with Spencer. I think we should proceed as he recommends." McPearson looked from Detton to Steve, "Unless one of you gentleman has a better idea."

Detton ignored McPearson's comment. "What about the time factor?" he asked Spencer. "If we proceed as you are suggesting, did you calculate how long to reach our objective?"

"We are estimating six to eight weeks, provided nothing unforeseen happens."

"What could go wrong?"

"A million things, Tom," McPearson interjected. "Those damned diamond saws tend to break easily, and the non-explosive propellant is a bitch to locate. There's only one manufacturer that I know of in Canada that handles them. What's important now is that the job gets done carefully. We've been working non-stop on this for over ten months. There's no need to start hurrying now." McPearson leaned forward. "Right, Tom?"

Detton walked across the room, refilled his coffee cup, and took a sip. Steve had moved closer to the camera so that now his face looked round and cartoonish. Spencer stifled a laugh. These two were top CIA agents, were they really so easily duped?

Detton sat down across from McPearson. "I hear what you're saying, Bill, but we have sources in Egypt concerned with the political instability of that region. The quicker we get to our objective, the less likely it is that we'll encounter additional obstacles."

Detton's eyes narrowed. He was acting evasive. Why?

"Would you care to clarify that? What's the problem with Egypt now?" McPearson leaned forward as if he had every right to demand a full explanation from the CIA.

"That's classified, but I can tell you that it involves Libya and another neighboring country that I cannot disclose."

"I am more worried about Abdul," Spencer interrupted. "If he suspects anything outside of what your people have told him, he could pull our permit." I agree with Tom. The sooner we complete this project, the better."

Detton gave McPearson a stiff smile. "You have a very capable crew here, Bill. I'm impressed with Spencer's thorough understanding of the situation." Tom turned to address the monitor. "Steve, I want you to resolve the illegal tap. I need you back here in two weeks. You can leave one of your operatives there until Spencer reaches the bottom. I'll brief you on the details later." He pushed a button on the remote and Steve's face vanished from the screen. "Thank you, Mr. Spencer. Go ahead and proceed as per your recommendations. I'll have Steve set up a new encryption program and have you linked in a few days. We'll take additional precautions with our people on site. We'll have to keep transmissions at a minimum until that tap issue is resolved." He stood up, drank the last of his coffee, and buttoned his suit coat. "Thank you, Bill, for a very well prepared and informative meeting." Detton reached over to shake Bill's hand. McPearson clasped the man's hand and led him to the door. He then turned and grinned at Spencer. "Good job, my boy," he said. "Detton seemed satisfied with your approach. I'll have the new safety specs ready by noon tomorrow." McPearson gave Spencer a big pat on the back. "Let's get together tonight and review the key points. Your hotel okay? I'll buy you dinner. You've earned it."

Why was McPearson carrying on the charade? Perhaps he was just being precautious. After all, it was possible the conference room was bugged. "Thanks, Bill, is six too early?"

"Perfect, I'll see you there." McPearson winked.

Spencer walked down the steps of Calpetro and stopped. He

needed to call Roula, but he didn't dare use his cell or call from his office phone. He walked six blocks before finding a pay phone in a dark bar.

"Hello?" Roula's voice sounded anxious.

"It's me, is everything okay?"

"Yes, fine. Are you coming back soon?" Her voice now sounded impatient.

"Not until eight tonight. McPearson is buying me dinner at the hotel. It's a decoy to get us to you. He wants to see the device in operation. Is it still charged?" It would be dark before he and McPearson could get back to the apartment.

"Yes, it's fine. I have been talking with Neflani. She documented all of the cylinders for me and explained the content. I now have a good feel on how to proceed with the viewing. Spencer, this discovery is more than both of us ever imagined. It…"

"Not now Roula, not over the phone," Spencer interrupted.

"I understand. See you tonight. Please bring me some leftovers, since I'm stuck here. I'm starving."

"Will do," he said.

Spencer made a second call. He could think of only one way to get back to the apartment with Bill and without being noticed. He needed Paul's help one more time.

Spencer slid his card key through the slot in his hotel room door and pushed the door open. Paul jumped up from the edge of the bed. His eyes were wide and glistening with anger.

"Wow, you got here fast."

"Yeah, I like a good mystery," Paul answered, his voice dripping with sarcasm. "I keep thinking you might eventually tell me what this is all about."

He had told McPearson to take a cab and go to his favorite bar where he should wait for instructions. As much as he wanted to bring Paul up to speed, he couldn't do it now. "I will Paul, really. But right now there's just no time. I need to meet someone."

"You expect me to just keep dropping everything to bail you out of secret situations? I have a right to know what's going on. This could be dangerous."

Paul's usual jovial manner was gone. The man was angry and with good reason. Should he just offer him a short version of the story? Hell, there was no short version, and telling him bits and pieces would likely cause more questions than answers. Telling Paul would just have to wait. He went to his friend and held him by his shoulders. Paul remained stiff and unyielding. "Listen." Spencer looked him in the eye. "You're my best friend and the only person in the world I trust a hundred percent. I appreciate all you've done more than you know, and I'm going to tell you everything. Just give me some time." Spencer held his gaze steady. He needed to persuade Paul to wait a little longer, not only because he needed his help, but also because he cherished their friendship. He hated putting off his best friend another time, but what else could he do? He needed to meet with McPearson right away.

Paul's shoulders relaxed and he nodded. "Okay, buddy, I trust you." He wrapped Spencer in a quick bear hug. "But I won't be put off much longer. I'm worried about you, man. Worried about all of this."

How could he reassure Paul that everything would be okay when he wasn't sure of that himself? "I'll tell you soon, I promise."

He snuck out of the hotel through the kitchen entrance, walked a couple of blocks and flagged a cab. Roula was waiting with open arms. They embraced for a long moment.

"It's so good to be in your arms, Ralph," she whispered against his ear.

"I know what you mean." He held her head in his hands and gave her a tender kiss.

She kissed him back and then laid her head on his shoulder. "This discovery is starting to scare me. Looking at the cylinders today . . . I had to constantly remind myself that what I was seeing was not some remote future, but the very distant past." She shook her head as if to dislodge the thought.

"Why are you sad?" Spencer brushed his hand against her cheek.

"I think this discovery has made me realize the importance of the present. The present is the only time that really exists. The past, whether it's five minutes or five millennia ago, is dead. The future is still to come. These people had a wonderful civilization. They were happy. They accomplished great things and yet in a very short time, it was all lost. They were erased from Earth. Everything that they worked for was destroyed except the great pyramid and the time capsule." She wiped a tear from her cheek and sighed. "I guess I'm just realizing how insignificant we are in relation to this earth and the universe. In the end, we will all perish." She look up at him, her eyes reflecting the melancholy she was feeling. She stepped back, pulled the clip from her hair, and shook her head. Soft brown curls fell to her shoulders. She squared her shoulders. "Sorry for the gloomy attitude." She forced a smile. "I spent the day with a ghost. It's got me a little freaked out." She turned away, but not fast enough to hide the tears that welled in her large brown eyes.

"You've become quite a philosopher, Roula." He smiled.

She smiled back, stifling her tears with a deep breath.

"There, now. That's better," he said. What Roula knew was that someday the fate of Phamuria would likely be repeated" He went to the kitchen table and pulled out his dinner leftovers and a bottle of wine from a vintage Napa vineyard. "Come, sit down. I'll warm this up for you. You'll feel better once you've had something to eat."

Roula didn't move. She stared at him from across the room. Her face pale and her dark eyes red rimmed. He took her hand and pulled her over to the table. He pulled out the chair for her. "Please be seated, madam," he said with a bow. He poured two glasses of wine and placed one in her hand. "This is all going to work out, I promise."

She gave him one of her radiant smiles, her perfect white teeth gleaming despite the cheap fluorescent lighting.

He piled the leftover pasta and vegetables onto a plate and

popped it in the microwave. He then called McPearson at the bar and gave him the address for their secret hideaway. "Here's what you need to do," he told McPearson. "Go home, wait thirty minutes, then sneak out your back door and pick up a cab. Make sure no one follows the cab. If you suspect anything, turn back."

"Will do," was all McPearson said.

There was no doubt McPearson would go to any extreme to protect the project and he had been around the block enough to know the risk they were all taking.

McPearson was in a cheery mood when he arrived. The combination of the beers he'd had at the bar and the adventure of the find had his eyes gleaming. "Let's get to it," he said. "We don't have much time."

They sat on the sofa with McPearson in the middle. "Start narration," Roula said.

From the moment Neflani appeared, McPearson's eyes never moved from her image. He seemed transfixed by her revelations. When Neflani spoke of her civilizations destruction, McPearson began to weep.

"Stop narration," Roula said. She rubbed McPearson's arm. "It's okay, Bill, we both reacted the same way.

"It's just . . . the magnitude of this discovery, it's beyond anything I'd dreamed of." McPearson pulled a tissue from the box Roula had placed on the coffee table. "The world might not be ready for this." McPearson sniffed. "No one will be able to watch this without becoming painfully aware of their own mortality."

"I know, but the world has the right to know. That's why we'd better make sure this never gets into the wrong hands," Spencer replied.

"I don't know if you're referring to Egypt or the CIA," McPearson said, but we need to make sure it stays out of both their hands.

Spencer walked out of the Cairo airport pulling a small suitcase behind him and with Bill McPearson at his side. It felt good to be back in Egypt. This had been his home for the last ten months and he had grown accustomed to the warm weather. He had also missed his staff. His management style had allowed for plenty of input and it had resulted in mutual trust and respect among his fellow workers. He was especially fond of Matt Garrett, his drilling superintendent.

Matt waved as Spencer and McPearson approached. "Nice to see you jet setters back in the land of kings!"

"Matt, how nice to see you! How have you been doing holding down the fort?" Spencer spoke in a lighthearted manner, but he was desperate for Matt's reassurance that no one had disturbed anything inside the main shaft.

"Everything's under control, boss. Those CIA boys wouldn't be caught dead at the bottom of a mineshaft. They've kept themselves busy trying to discover the culprit who messed with the feed access . . . and, of course, I've been giving them my full cooperation." Matt said, his voice dripping with sarcasm. "Abdul has been around a few times to make sure we're complying with his orders. He was delighted when I told him you had gone back to headquarters to resolve the new safety procedures."

"Great. We have a lot of work to do." Spencer turned to McPearson. "You remember Bill, don't you?"

"Of course," Matt said. "Good to see you, Bill."

"Matt, old boy! Looks like we'll be working together for a while." McPearson's belly shook as he chuckled.

"Bill insisted on overseeing the safety procedures himself." Spencer smiled and winked at Matt. "He'll be in charge from now on."

"No, no," McPearson said. "Not in charge. I wouldn't take that away from you. You're the boss here. I'll just help enforce the new procedures."

Bill McPearson was a wise boss. He was probably well aware of Spencer's reputation among the crew. Besides, his real purpose was the time capsule.

CHAPTER

FOURTEEN

McPearson stepped out of the jeep and walked toward the entrance to the site. He pulled a handkerchief from his back pocket and patted his brow. The damn heat had him soaked in sweat already, but for what he was here to see, suffering in the hot desert air would be well worth it. It had been months since he'd visited the site. Spencer's accomplishments in such a short time were remarkable.

Matt hopped down from the driver's side of the jeep and walked over. He clapped McPearson on the back with his typical disregard for hierarchy. "So, Bill, how the hell are you anyway? How did headquarters finally manage to get your ass in the desert?"

Before McPearson could answer, Spencer and Antonio Casenza walked over. McPearson gave his old friend a quick hug. McPearson and Antonio Casenza went back a long way. The two of them were practically an institution at Calpetro. "Antonio, old man. How nice of you to pay a visit to an old friend. How is our progress here?"

"Well, if you mean holding back that mule Abdul, we're doing just great. I have a lot less influence on our buddies from Langley though." Antonio replied with a sigh and a shake of his head.

"What's going on with them?" Spencer asked.

"They've been in everyone's face, of course," Antonio said. "Steve really wants to find the origin of the tap and he's running out of time. Last night he met with Matt and me, hoping that we would shed some light on the mystery. He has a theory involving Abdul and someone on our staff. He told us that most of the local crew doesn't have the competency to link up a satellite feed, especially doing it without detection." Antonio shook his head and frowned. "I reminded him that Abdul is very capable and would use untraceable means to infiltrate our project. I've had some dealings in the past with him and he is a conniving son of a bitch."

"Well, it looks like we have that situation diffused for now. Thank you, Antonio." Spencer looked into the faces of the small circle of men and then seemed to make up his mind. "Let's get out of this heat," Spencer led the men to the ROU. He pulled the door open and ushered them inside. "Make yourselves comfortable, gentleman. I'll turn up the air." He adjusted the thermostat then sat down at the computer. The screen flickered to life, but there was no sign of any CIA agents on the other end. "Okay," he said, looking from one man to the next, "here's our plan. We have our new approved safety procedures. Tomorrow we'll call on Abdul for his inspection, review our procedures with his staff and begin clearing the damaged shaft. Matt, I want you to assign your assistant to that project with Bill supervising the operation. We want to make sure that our procedures are in place."

Spencer spent the next several minutes going over the assignments, keeping up the ruse all the while. Perhaps he was assuming that his office was now bugged. He concluded the meeting without any mention of Phamuria or the capsule. "Bill, Matt and I would like to take you to lunch today, our treat."

McPearson nodded and gave the men a conspiratorial smile.

They arrived for a late lunch at one of Spencer's favorite cafes on the outskirts of Cairo. The restaurant resembled a desert oasis. A water fountain with a large pond filled the courtyard. Dozens of palm trees towered above them, long fronds waving in the hot desert breeze. The tables were set in a horseshoe with the fountain as the focal point. There was no better place for them to meet than in the open air where it would be almost impossible for anyone to eavesdrop. "We'll take the table on the end," Spencer said to the scantily clad Egyptian hostess.

Once the men were seated and had drinks in front of them, Spencer spoke. "We're going to use the main shaft project as a decoy. The work needs to proceed as slowly as possible without causing suspicion. Abdul thinks we've lost the main elevator and the ventilation shaft man-lift. I was able to convince the CIA of the same. Only a few of us know of the existence of the second ventilation shaft below the fifteen thousand foot level. With minimum work, we can enter the cave with less than a day's work. I want us to concentrate on this and enter the time capsule within the next twenty-four hours. Any questions?" Spencer looked around the table at each man while taking a long drink of his iced tea.

"Let's discuss our options once we have established contact with the capsule," McPearson suggested.

"According to Neflani, the fourth dimension will elapse in real time. I would like as much time as possible in Phamuria in order to understand their world," Spencer replied.

"Who the hell is Neflani? What's this fourth dimension? What in God's name are you talking about?" Matt's voice increased in volume with each question.

"Shhhh," Spencer gazed around the patio but no one seemed to have noticed Matt's outburst. "It's a very long story and I'll have to fill you in later."

Matt nodded and slumped back in his chair, but he said nothing more.

"We gave the CIA an estimate of six to eight weeks. That should be sufficient to explore the fourth dimension."

Matt heaved a sigh and rolled his eyes at the mention of the fourth dimension, but remained silent.

"I'm concerned about keeping the ventilation shaft a secret. The other problem involves our presence . . . or I should say, our absence. If we are in the capsule, we can't be available for the project. This is a situation that could cause suspicion. We'll need to address it in due time." Spencer was anxious to proceed.

McPearson leaned forward. "I understand your desire to move forward quickly, but if we overlook anything, we could pay with our lives. I think we need to resolve all issues before moving forward."

"Okay, okay, I know. I'm just getting impatient. We'll time our stay in the capsule carefully with our work schedule. In case of emergency, we'll have the guard at the capsule alert us to return. There must be a way. I'll ask Neflani."

Matt crossed his arms over his chest and let out another big sigh. Spencer would need to debrief him as soon as this meeting was over if he was going to get him on board with the project.

"All right. What about the outcome and resolution of our exploration?" McPearson asked.

"We'll need to evaluate it after we have all the facts." There was no way to make a decision on what to do with the capsule until the exploration was complete.

The waitress arrived with their lunches on a big tray. While the men ate, Spencer brought Matt up to speed on everything they had discovered so far. "The cylinders and the master computer are hidden inside one of the equipment wood crates marked," he said to Matt.

"You'll need to look for the box marked 'drilling equipment and wire saws' in all capital letters."

McPearson had come up with the idea and put the cylinders inside the crate with the wire saw boxes surrounding them. Since they were shipping twenty crates of saws, to find the right one and search inside would have been highly unlikely or exceedingly unlucky. The only question left was how to get Roula inside the time capsule with them. She'd been part of this team from the beginning and there was no way he could leave her out now. She had begun this adventure with him and he'd make sure they finished it together, regardless of the outcome.

Abdul had a full crew of inspectors standing in a circle around a makeshift table poring over the new safety procedures. Spencer had spent hours making sure he covered every detail. There was no reason Abdul shouldn't reinstate his work order.

"Mr. Spencer, it seems from these new procedures that you have done well in addressing all of my country's concerns. Of course we will want absolute compliance. Once the elevator is fully operational, I will personally inspect the main shaft." Abdul spoke in a stern manner, but that seemed to be the only way he knew how to address anyone he considered his inferior, and that was just about everyone the man encountered.

"Of course, sir," Spencer said.

As the Egyptian government vehicles pulled away, Spencer went to the FOU to get McPearson and Matt. "They're gone. Let's get started."

Spencer had assembled a small crew of loyal employees. Steve had kept a half dozen agents in the area. He had assigned three agents to the site and the other three were off with him trying to find the culprit behind the illegal feed. The agents left at the site did nothing more than stand around at the main entrance to the mine swatting at sand gnats and wiping sweat from their brows.

Spencer's first objective was to clear out the secret ventilation shaft to access the cave. Matt was in charge of the clean up operation. He had convinced Spencer to dig out a tunnel from the ventilation shaft to this new location. Access to the tunnel had been carefully concealed behind one of the main fans. Matt had a two-way electrical switch installed for the fan with the second setting inside the secret tunnel. The tunnel extended less than a hundred feet and it was large enough to fit a narrow gage rail for transporting equipment. A small open car had been installed with a pulley system and a small winch. With the fan in operation, it was impossible to hear the car's movements.

McPearson had spent his entire career in management. He had never traveled on a man-lift before. He looked panic-stricken, was sweating profusely, and let out a small whimper each time they hit a bump. There was nothing Spencer could do about McPearson's discomfort. They were on their way down and there was no going back. He turned to Matt. "If we build an additional tunnel from the main ventilation shaft to the elevator shaft, we could use it for access. This would give us precious time to join the main working crew in the elevator shaft should the situation become urgent."

The man-lift shuttered and ground to a halt. McPearson looked at Spencer, hope reflected in his eyes. "Can we get out off this contraption now?" he asked.

"Yeah," Matt said to Spencer, ignoring McPearson's words, "but we'll increase the risk of being discovered."

"I think it's worth the risk. Look at this tunnel. No one will ever find it. We can use the same approach."

"You're right," Matt said. "We can probably get away with it. Maybe we can leave a small membrane intact that could be broken in minutes if we ever have to use it."

"How long will it take you?"

"Two days max. We are only talking fifty to seventy-five feet," Matt replied with confidence.

"Great. Let's do it."

Spencer breathed a sigh of relief. The new tunnel would be extra insurance.

"For Christ's sake, Spencer! Stop with the planning and let's get moving. This rat hole is giving me the creeps," McPearson shouted.

"Fine, we can head back to the surface. Matt has things under control here."

Matt slipped off his harness and jumped off the lift. He flipped the switch and the lift jolted and then started its ascent. "Matt, call me the minute you get in the cave."

"You got it." Matt smiled.

Spencer looked to McPearson, who was busy mopping the sweat from his brow. "You need to get used to this, Bill," Spencer said. "From here on out every second will count.

Roula had done at least five-dozen laps around her apartment when the doorbell finally rang. She set down her coffee mug and ran to the door. "I thought you'd never come," she said, wrapping her arms around him and laying her cheek to his chest. She held him tight for a moment, relaxing into the steady rhythm of his heartbeat. "Thank God you're here."

"I'm here, darling. I'll always be here for you." He kissed the top of her head, and pulled her out the door. "Let's go for a walk."

She nodded and pulled the door closed behind her. They walked around to the back of the apartment complex away from prying eyes.

"Everything's in place." Spencer handed her a crumpled paper grocery bag. "Here, I brought you a some clothes for your disguise. It's the only way you can access the site without setting off the CIA's warning bells . . . or Abdul for that matter."

Roula shuttered. Abdul. She'd be happy to never lay eyes on that evil snake again. She peered into the bag and pulled out a set of miner's overalls and a hat. "I have to wear this?" she asked, incredulous.

"I'm afraid so. It's the best disguise I could come up with on short notice." Spencer's eyes glistened as he smiled.

"You're really enjoying this, aren't you?" Roula let out a boisterous laugh and then hiccupped. "I'm sorry," she said. "I'm so wound up. I get the hiccups when I get nervous."

"I know this is hard for you," he said.

She hiccupped again and tears filled her eyes. "I'm sorry," she said.

"Don't be." Spencer smiled. He reached for her hands and pulled her into a tight embrace. "There's not much we can do until we get the word from Matt," he said in a thick voice. He took her chin in his hand and tilted her head back. His lips touched hers and she melted into him. "Now that's better."

He led her back to the apartment and straight to the bedroom. Her hiccups vanished.

Roula woke the next morning and instinctively reached for Spencer. His side of the bed was empty. Metallica was blaring out of the iPod speaker stand she kept in her living room. She sat up, a wave of panic rushing through her. "Ralph?"

Spencer poked his head in the bedroom door and pointed to his ear. He was holding his cell phone and listening intently. "That's great news, Matt." He cupped his hand over his mouth. "We need to move in the next few hours. Let's make sure that we have a full crew working in the main shaft. Assemble your best men. We'll need at least two guards and two miners. I'll get McPearson and Roula to join us." He paused, listening to Matt's response. "Not to worry, I've got a disguise for her." He was silent for a moment. He smiled and winked at Roula, but then turned away. "It's a risk I'm willing to take," he said in a hushed tone, "She was instrumental in getting us inside, she deserves to be there for the rest . . ."

Roula rolled over and hugged her pillow. Would her presence really increase the danger they were all in? The answer was obvious. Of course she was an added risk, and not just because she was a woman, but because of Abdul. Her stomach turned in revulsion as the image of the fat Egyptian filled her mind, his eyes bulging and spittle flying from his lips. She despised the man . . . despised the way he had manipulated her . . . the way he had used her own ambition against her.

She sat up and tossed the pillow aside. She was tired of being afraid of Abdul. And Ralph was right; she had every right to see this discovery through to the end. She threw the covers aside and climbed out of bed. She padded to the closet and pulled out a pair of khaki slacks and a blouse. She had to wear something under the overalls.

McPearson's mouth fell open as he stepped inside the mammoth cavern. "Damn," he said. "You weren't kidding about the size of this cave, Spencer."

Spencer remained silent. He was busy setting up video cameras and giving instructions to the crew members who were carrying the cylinders. The small entourage walked another hundred yards and then turned the corner. "There it is, Bill." Spencer pointed to the time capsule. The exposed section of the capsule projected well over a hundred feet above the cave floor.

"It looks like a . . . giant spider web."

"That's what we all said." Spencer stood with his hands on his hips, staring at the complex network of wires. "According to Neflani, the webbing controls the magnetic and gravitational fields inside the capsule. This webbing is essential for the proper functioning of the fourth dimension."

Spencer approached the capsule's entrance. Roula pulled the miner's cap off her head. She stuffed it in her backpack and then pulled out her laptop. She had the entire opening sequence stored on the hard drive. Within minutes she had the door open. Spencer entered first and McPearson followed close behind. Matt carried in the cylinders and Roula followed behind with a video camera in her hand.

"This is magnificent," McPearson said. "But I can't make myself believe that this machine is over three hundred thousand years old." McPearson walked in a small circle, his mouth open and his eyes wide.

"The best is yet to come, Bill," Spencer said as he reached for the inner door.

Inside the inner chamber, Roula laid out the cylinders to be used for the fourth dimension. She had carefully marked the first four sequential cylinders as instructed by Neflani. Matt mounted two cameras on each side of the inner chamber. These were to film the actual event leading into the fourth dimension.

"We need to set our watches and synchronize our return time," Spencer said. Since the master computer has read Roula's biological input, and mine, the two of us will go in for the first experience. Matt, you and Bill stay here and observe through the cameras. The two of you will need to be outside the capsule once we start the fourth dimension or you might get sucked into the experience."

McPearson nodded, but said nothing. His face was white again, he was perspiring profusely, and he seemed to be having trouble breathing. "You okay?" Spencer asked him.

"Fine, fine," McPearson answered. "Well, maybe a little overwhelmed . . . I just never dreamed . . ." He shook himself. "I'll be okay. Go ahead, don't worry about me."

Spencer turned to Matt. "Make sure you guard the capsule at all times. Place one guard at the end of the man-lift and one at the opening of the cave. If anyone approaches, shut down the capsule's main door." Spencer paused. He had given everyone instructions the best he could, now it was up to each of them to carry out the duties he had assigned.

"Is there a way for you to signal me once you're inside the fourth dimension?" Matt asked.

Spencer looked to Roula for an answer.

"I don't know if it's possible." She frowned. "Neflani never said—"

"We'll ask Neflani," Spencer said. "It might be useful to us to find out before we embark on this new adventure."

Roula inserted the first cylinder and gave the command. The image of the lovely Neflani appeared. "I am Neflani. I am the narrator assigned by the high council of Phamuria. My duties are to tell you the history of our great country." She paused.

"Neflani, is it possible to a get signal from outside to anyone inside the fourth dimension?" asked Roula.

"Not exactly, but the way around that is to set your time alerts to coordinate with someone on the outside. In this way, on any given time alert, you have the opportunity to exit and check with your contact." Neflani's diction was impeccable. It was almost as if she'd been practicing their language over the past week.

"Holy cow!" Matt's mouth hung open.

"I know how you feel," McPearson said. "I felt the same way the first time I met . . . I mean saw her."

Neflani turned to Matt and smiled. "Cylinder numbers two, three, four, and five are the first sequences to be used. Your fourth dimensional time will be four hours."

"Is she talking to me?" Matt sounded incredulous.

"Not exactly," Roula said. "I'll explain it to you later."

Neflani nodded and continued. "The master computer shows a power up time of eleven hours forty minutes. This will be a very safe entry."

"All right then," Spencer turned to Roula. "Are we ready? Any other questions for our tour guide?" Spencer's stomach was doing flip-flops. Who would ever believe what they were about to do?

"Uh, yes," Roula said. "Neflani, can we take a camera with us? Will it work?"

"Your camera will not work in the Four-D." Neflani answered matter-of-factly.

"Will you be there, Neflani?" Roula muttered.

"Yes, I have chosen the cylinders that include my presence. I will be with you for the entire time. There is no reason to be afraid. We have created a very enjoyable experience for you." Neflani's voice was calm and reassuring. "After you place all four cylinders in the proper slots, you must stand on the platform with the master computer. Each cylinder will come to life. Once the fourth one engages, you will be immediately and virtually transported into our beautiful Phamuria. I will be there to greet you. Good luck." She looked from Spencer to Roula with a warm smile.

"Unbelievable," Matt said.

Spencer and Roula exchanged glances and smiled. McPearson and Matt stepped out of the inner chamber. They had set the alerts to coincide at two hours.

Spencer inserted the final cylinder and was instantly overtaken by a feeling of expansion, as if his body had become part of the room. Images converged before his eyes, as if he had been sucked into a multicolored tunnel. His stomach lurched and then everything turned black. Had he ever before experienced such darkness? Such stillness? A thunderous pop sounded above his head, like a sonic boom. Intense colors approached and then converged into a singular bright light. His stomach wrenched a second time, presumably from the intense gravitational pull. He shut his eyes for an instant enduring the pain and nausea. Then it appeared.

Phamuria.

He inhaled a deep breath of cold, fresh air. Never before had he breathed such unsullied air. He gulped a second breath and looked around for Roula. She was standing near him, her eyes wide and moist. Her face looked damp and was an odd shade of green, testament to the physical effects of the experience. She stood motionless, as if frozen in time. They looked around them without saying a word. Neflani stood before them, a broad smile on her exquisite face. "Welcome to Phamuria, our enchanted land," she said in greeting.

Spencer patted down his body, making certain he was all there. His eyes took in the panoramic view. He tried to move forward, but a wave of dizziness stopped him. His stomach pitched. He bent over to vomit, but then the nausea stopped just as quickly as it had come on.

"Not to worry," Neflani said. "You will quickly become accustomed to the atmosphere of our time."

He looked up at a sky so clear and so richly blue it hurt his eyes to look at it. Several objects that appeared to be large spheres floating in space hovered on the horizon. From their elevated position, he saw enormous snow-capped mountains far to his right. The peaks seemed far higher than any mountain range in the modern world. Strange sounds echoed in the distance, like the sound of rushing water in a whitewater river.

"Look." Roula pointed.

Neflani turned in the direction she was pointing and Spencer's gaze followed. A series of pyramid structures seemed to pierce the crystal blue sky. The pyramids were placed in various geometrical arrangements, which formed an eerily stunning landscape. The pyramids, of varying colors and sizes, all had smooth glassy surfaces. Some had four sides, others five or more.

Spencer looked down at his feet. The surface he stood on was gray and appeared to be artificial. To his right, about fifty feet away, stood what looked to be some type of transportation device.

"Are you all right?" Roula asked.

Spencer's awareness snapped back into his body as if he had been suddenly awakened from a dream. "Yes, I think so. Are you?"

"I'm fantastic," she exclaimed. "This is unreal!"

"Yes, it is." Spencer agreed with a smile. There was something comfortable, familiar, and inviting about Phamuria. Did Roula feel it too?

"I'll take you for a small tour of our city, and then we'll meet the high council," Neflani said.

"This will be the tour of a lifetime." Roula said.

As they walked toward the transportation craft, Spencer noticed people in the distance going about their business.

"This is a typical automobile, as you would call it," Neflani said, resting her hand against the cool metallic shell. It is powered by magnetic impulses acting in conjunction with the earth's gravitational pull."

The craft had no wheels and no steering devices. It was shaped like an egg at the base with a bubble of some kind of glowing translucent material protruding above. Neflani opened a clear panel and helped Roula to her seat. Inside, the craft had ample room for at least six passengers. Spencer sat next to Roula. The seat was dark and metallic looking, but undeniably comfortable. Immediately upon sitting down, the seat conformed to his body as if it were alive.

Neflani sat next to Roula and placed her hand on the forward control panel. "These machines are pre-programmed to travel to many destinations around Phamuria. All I need to do is instruct the computer with the sequence that I want," Neflani explained.

A jumble of questions filled Spencer's mind. Where would he begin? He looked around him. There would be time for questions later. For now he would simply enjoy the ride and take in the unprecedented view of this long extinct land.

"These travel crafts are capable of very high speeds, but we will advance at a moderate pace in order for you to view our beautiful country." Neflani said with a smile.

And beautiful it was! Had he ever seen anything like it? The freshness of the air made him breathe in big gulps. The pyramid structures lined the elliptical path that was taking them to he didn't know where. The travel craft emanated a faint gushing sound as it moved. It was a pleasant, soothing sounding. The landscape was dotted with trees and shrubs of all kinds. Some looked familiar, but there were others he had never seen before. Trees that looked like the horsetails that grew all over the marshy areas of the West Coast of the United States were in abundance. The only difference was those growing in Phamuria were about nine feet tall. The various trees outlined a web of paths that wrapped around the buildings and adorned the perimeters. It was almost too much to take in. Phamuria was clean without being stark and he again experienced a rush of warmth and a feeling of familiarity. There was nothing here to imply the future reality of the Sahara desert.

Neflani brought the craft to a smooth stop and signaled them to exit. "Here are our markets. All the merchants of Phamuria trade in this central market. Products are distributed directly to the consumers from here. Our economic system is mostly what I believe you would refer to as a barter system," Neflani continued. "We have found that this allows merchants to work toward one or two very high quality products. The Phamurian Trade Council handles any disagreements, but those are generally few."

Inside, the immense market pyramid resembled a modern day enclosed stadium. The striking difference was that the roofline converged to a single point hundreds of feet above them. Light penetrated naturally through large transparent windows. They were clearly not glass, as the material appeared to have a slight bluish glow. The light was gathered and projected towards the market floor by what looked like laser beams surrounding the entire internal perimeter of the structure. The atmosphere was that of an active bazaar with people bustling all about.

"Their clothing is so beautiful," Roula said.

Much of the clothing looked hand woven with an artistic flair. The women wore low circular platform hats decorated with patches of lined patterns. The colors were bright and the pace was elegant. Men also wore hats, but these were slightly more complex. They too had the line markings, but they also had a series of strange symbols woven into the line pattern.

"Everyone wears hats?" Roula asked.

"Yes, in public. It distinguishes each family. The symbol identifies the lineage or clan and the line marking identifies the specific family and the place within the family."

"So is it a hierarchy then? Is one clan more important than another or one person in the family more important?" Roula was curious.

"Each person in a family is treated equally, but each clan, and within each clan, each family, has earned respect depending on their specific contribution to Phamuria over the centuries," Neflani replied with a proud voice.

Spencer made his way to one of the market stalls. The table was covered with fresh vegetables and fruits. The smiling merchant offered him a slice from a piece of fruit that vaguely resembled an apple. Spencer popped it in his mouth. It was sweet and juicy. Roula also took a sample from the vendor and bit into it. "I can't believe we can even taste here," she said.

"Our hope was to give you the full Phamuria experience," Neflani said. "We would never want you to miss out on sampling our delectable cuisine.

The marketplace was the size of a small village. Each booth offered different and specialized crafts or delicious exotic foods. Every nibble of the Phamurian fare caused a tantalizing sensation in the mouth. It was as if each taste bud was being awakened for the first time.

An overall sense of harmony and coordination resonated throughout the marketplace. Everything functioned as if planned by a single entity. Could anything this harmonious and efficient ever be achieved in today's world?

Neflani proceeded to the transportation craft and Spencer and Roula followed. Neflani spoke new instructions and the craft took off so fast that all that could be seen out the window was streaks of light. Within minutes the craft slowed. They had reached their destination.

Once outside the vehicle, Spencer squinted and covered his eyes. "Here," Neflani said. "She handed him an unusual pair of sunglasses then gave Roula a similar, but smaller pair. "It's very bright, you'll need these."

The glasses did the trick. He opened his eyes and gasped. A massive wall of ice soared above them.

The glacier.

"Incredible," Roula said.

"Let me take you closer," Neflani said. They climbed back inside the craft. She pulled the lever and they moved straight up until they reached the upper edge of the ice field. Spencer craned his neck.

The glacier extended as far as the eye could see.

"This is the outer region of Phamuria," she said. "We have traveled approximately two-hundred miles from our central market location. Here lies the beginning of the ice caps. These glaciers are miles thick and surround Phamuria on all sides. The world outside is very desolate," Neflani explained.

"Do you mean to tell me that we have traveled two-hundred miles in less than three minutes?" Spencer asked, incredulous.

"Yes. These crafts are capable of very high speeds. The acceleration is achieved by manipulating the intensity of the magnetic field as it relates to the gravitational forces," she explained.

"So these machines require no fuel?" asked Spencer.

"Correct. No fuel is needed. All that's required is the electrical impulse to handle the magnetic field. Electricity is generated by the sun and captured by the unit."

"But shouldn't I have felt the gravitational forces at those speeds?" Spencer asked.

"It's all compensated for by the craft. Remember, it operates by gravity or, rather, lack of it," she reminded him.

The countryside around Phamuria, lush green fields dotted with hundreds of little streams and lakes, stretched to the edges of the ice. It was a bit like the northern Minnesota landscape, a place Spencer had visited just once on a hunting expedition with a college buddy.

Roula folded her arms and shivered. The ice that surrounded them seemed to radiate frigid air. "Does it stay this cold all year?" Roula asked Neflani.

"Yes, but the people who live here are accustomed to the cold."

The countryside houses were also shaped like pyramids, but unlike the smooth glassy material of the city, these buildings were made of some kind of tightly woven fiber. The houses, Neflani assured them, were warm, spacious, and comfortable.

"Neflani," Spencer said, "What we first observed when we arrived were not the white-capped volcanic mountains were they? Those are what we now see far off in the distance. We were seeing these glaciers, weren't we?"

"That is correct," Neflani said.

That Phamuria had a host of wildlife was evident. Birds, fish in the fresh water lakes, even deer-like mammals, appeared much like the wildlife of modern day. Other species bore no resemblance to anything Spencer had ever seen before.

In the distance there were a few more spheres hanging above the horizon. They resembled low-orbit satellites.

"What are those sphere-like objects in the sky?" Spencer asked, perplexed.

"Those are relay stations. They make communication possible for the entire region. They have many uses such as controlling traffic for every single vehicle in Phamuria. With the use of special tracking devices, we have eliminated any type of . . . I believe you call them collisions."

Spencer remained silent. A lump had formed in his throat. The beauty of Phamuria had him captivated. The countryside was like a dark, shining emerald, the foliage lush, the ice glaciers majestic, and the sky a deep blue. This world seemed so fresh and uncontaminated compared to the earth he knew. He could see in the distance for a hundred miles or more. The ubiquitous haze of pollution that now enveloped the planet did not seem to exist here.

Neflani signaled that it was time to return to the craft. She gave some verbal instructions and they were off. The trip back to the main city of Phamuria was just as quick as the trip to the countryside. The craft made a gentle stop in a circular courtyard just outside an immense building. The great edifice stood alone in the center of a large compound surrounded by abundant landscaping with vibrant flowers blooming in every hue imaginable. Neflani walked briskly around the corner. Spencer's mouth fell open as he followed her. Directly ahead was the main entrance to the palatial structure. The architecture was superb. The pyramid-shaped building stood on an octagonal base. Each side extended to its apex some three hundred feet above ground. The finishing material looked like white marble, giving the structure a cathedral like appearance.

"This is where our leaders conduct business. Its function is similar to your capitol building in Washington," explained Neflani. "I am taking you inside to meet our High Council," she concluded.

"This is breathtaking," Roula exclaimed.

"Look at the construction. I've never seen anything like it." Spencer's head was tipped back so that he could admire the converging sides.

"Really?" Neflani asked in disbelief and with a strange smile. "Never?"

The main entrance to the building protruded outward from the slanted sides. Five massive columns created the outer courtyard leading to the main door. The columns were the same solid white stone and were carved in the form of men in royal attire. Their expressions were commanding, projecting images of great strength.

"These are the first five rulers of modern Phamuria," Neflani explained. "Our high council consists of five members voted into office by the general populous from all of the regions of Phamuria, similar to your senate. Our council members serve for life or until unable to properly conduct the business and duties bestowed upon them. Our present council consists of three men and two women," Neflani continued, as if anticipating Roula's next question. She reached the main door and the huge double doors opened as if it had detected her presence. She signaled for Spencer and Roula to join her inside.

"Have you ever seen a more beautiful building?" Roula asked.

Spencer gazed around the room. Great murals of colorful scenes and paintings of what were likely past council leaders adorned the walls. The lighting was both natural and artificial. Huge triangular windows dotted the entire perimeter, bringing in the natural light. Laser-like streams of high intensity light hung above them in all variety of patterns and directions. The beams of light seemed to anticipate each person's motions and adjust themselves accordingly.

"This building is almost alive," Roula mumbled to herself. She looked to Neflani for an explanation. "The lights seem to follow my eyes and shine on the objects that I am focusing on. How is that possible?" asked Roula.

"This building is equipped with thousands of biological sensors. The main computer managing all of the building's functions picks up your electrical impulses and accomplishes your sensory requests. We call many of our sensory functions involuntary, but the computers, in this case, still pick up your optimal optical needs from the optical nerve and your brain, of course, and provides more or less light accordingly," Neflani explained. "We call this structure the truth chamber. Political arguments and decisions are debated here. Thanks to the sensors, no one is able to present positions in this room that are misleading or fictitious. The sensors would pick up the change in electrical impulses and warn the rest of the council that the words spoken are false. Arguments in here must be based on one hundred percent fact and the honest and sincere offering of opinions." She smiled.

"Washington would never get anything done in here, Neflani." Spencer said, unable to hide the contempt he held for his own government.

"That's sad," Neflani said, compassion in her voice. "Our government was once corrupt as well, but it was many years before my birth."

"Thank you, Neflani," Roula said. "Knowing that gives us hope."

They had reached the podium where the high council was seated. The podium was shaped like a horseshoe with the curve facing the audience. At the center sat a man on a large chair that contoured to his body. His attire was elaborate—that of a king. Next to him sat two men and two women. The shape of the podium gave each member a clear view of the others. Neflani stopped directly in front of the podium, brought her right arm straight out and then, with a quick movement, brought the same hand to her left shoulder. "Honor and justice to the High Council." She spoke in a solemn manner.

"Honor and justice to you, Neflani," The man at the center replied.

"I have brought visitors from the future. This is Ralph Spencer and Roula Grazulis. They have found our time capsule and were able to activate the fourth dimension."

"I see." he said. Well then, welcome to Phamuria. I am Samir, the president of the High Council." Samir extended his hand as a salutation.

"Spencer and Roula are from the distant future," Neflani said. "Apparently some three hundred thousand years in the future. The world they know is infinitely different from this one. In their world, the polar caps have receded and land is in abundance. People have populated the entire earth with their numbers in the billions," Neflani explained to the council.

"Amazing," Samir said, his bright blue eyes shining. So humans still exist . . . and in such abundance." Why was Samir surprised by the news? Had he expected the entire species to be vanquished with Phamuria's demise? Spencer shifted from on foot to the other. He had so many questions for Samir, but how did one address an official of such high rank?

"Mr. . . . uh, Samir, sir . . . our world is not as advanced technologically as this one. Roula and I are still trying to fathom your many accomplishments. I will have so much to report to my people. Thank you, sir. So many new discoveries will be made for our people because of the contributions of Phamuria."

Samir leaned forward, his blue eyes sparkling. "I assume that you discovered our time capsule then."

"Yes," Spencer said.

"I see the plan worked," Samir muttered under his breath, looking at Neflani.

"I'm sorry?" Spencer said.

"Nothing....forgive the mutterings of an old man."

Spencer cleared his throat.

"We found the time capsule deep underground—eighteen thousand feet below the surface to be exact. The capsule had been buried by an erupting volcano," Spencer added.

"Oh, yes," Samir said, a sadness in his tone, "that was the beginning of the end for our civilization. The vast movement of the earth's tectonic plates caused our immediate destruction." Samir's eyes darkened as he frowned. Then his eyes suddenly brightened and he grinned. "Some of us must have survived then," he said. "The two of you are proof of that. I'm sure Neflani has outlined our history. This council will be glad to answer any questions you might have about our civilization."

He introduced the rest of the council and explained the council's position of power. He also invited Spencer and Roula to his home for a tour.

"One of the most beautiful homes in Phamuria," he said proudly. Spencer glanced at his watch. The first alert with McPearson was only a few minutes away.

"Thank you so much for the invitation, Mr. Samir. Right now, unfortunately, we need to get back to our time. But perhaps when we next visit?"

"Of course," Samir replied with a smile.

Spencer looked to Roula and pointed to his watch. Neflani nodded and smile and the high council president chuckled. "Another time then," he said

"Return us to our time," Spencer ordered.

In an instant it was as if he had been sucked into a vacuum. The trip back to reality proved similar to the one that took them to Phamuria. They arrived back in the inner chamber exhausted, more than a little nauseous, and bubbling with excitement.

Spencer stood up and shook himself, trying to clear his head and dispel the nausea.

"Roula, are you okay?

"Yes, thanks. That was some ride." She held her head in her hands as if to steady her dizzy mind.

"Nice to have you back in one piece." Matt smiled.

"How was it?" McPearson asked, waiting impatiently at the edge of the inner chamber.

"Out of this world," Spencer replied with a laugh. "Literally."

"We have a problem developing," Matt interrupted. "Steve is becoming suspicious. He was unable to solve the link interception. He's looking for you, Spencer. This could be trouble." Matt gestured for them to come out of the chamber. "We'd better get going."

Roula looked to Spencer. Her pupils were so dilated they nearly filled the irises and her face and neck were splotched in crimson.

Spencer's mouth had gone dry and his heart was in his throat. "Don't worry," he said to Roula. "I'm sure we'll be fine." He wasn't certain of that at all, but he had to keep Roula calm. If any of them panicked, it could be devastating to the project. He turned to McPearson. "I guess we'll have to tell you all about our adventure later. For now let's get this capsule closed and head for the surface."

Roula appeared to be in some kind of daze. He touched her arm and she jumped. "Let's leave all of our equipment here for the next visit," he said, looking into her eyes. He had to keep her from going into shock. "Everything will be safe here as long as the doors are closed. No one can open them but Roula."

Roula smiled at him and a happier blush came into her cheeks. "Okay," she said. "but let's take the master computer. If we are discovered, the cylinders will be of no use without it." Her eyes searched his. "Ralph, your eyes . . ."

"I know," he said. "Yours look the same."

She swallowed hard but said only, "Let's get out of here . . . for now."

CHAPTER

FIFTEEN

Roula slipped into the workman's overhauls and tucked her hair inside the hat. Spencer could only pray that no one would stop her once they reached the top. The team hurried to the lifts and headed for the surface. They had been underground for exactly three hours. Spencer reached the surface first. He surveyed the area and then signaled for them to move. "Quickly," he whispered.

Matt had hidden the main computer inside a core sample tube, which he now handed to Spencer. He told the crew to disperse and sent Roula home. McPearson went to his hotel and Matt went to check on the main shaft.

Once inside his FOU unit, he looked for a safe place for the master computer. Eight core tubes, two for each leg, held up his drafting table. He removed the back leg and replaced it with the tube containing the computer. He would take the computer somewhere safer as soon as was humanly possible.

He picked up his cell phone and dialed Antonio's number. "Hi Antonio, it's Spencer. I'd like to get together to go over the safety procedures," he said.

"How about next week," Antonio said. "I have meetings—"

"We have complications," Spencer said, his voice sober. "Can you call me back in fifteen minutes with a meeting time?" Antonio was sure to understand that he meant for him to call back from the private telephone at the bar near his office. Spencer stepped out of the FOU and stretched, then walked fifty yards from the FOU. Within minutes his cell phone rang.

"Okay, what happened?" Antonio asked.

"It's Steve. I think he's on to us. We have reason to believe he suspects me and key members of my staff. He thinks we're hiding something."

"Well, you are," Antonio blurted.

"I know that! Can you help me formulate a plan? I need to meet with you." The pleading tone of his voice irritated him, but he had to have Antonio's help.

"Of course I'll meet with you, my boy. Both our necks are on the line here. I think we'd better meet at the old dock by the Nile. I have friends there."

"Great. When?"

"In an hour. Oh, and bring Roula."

"Why?"

"Just bring her, okay?"

"Of course." He flipped the cell phone shut, faked a yawn and a stretch, and then strolled back to the FOU with a bored air.

If anyone could beat the CIA at their own game, it was Antonio. He needed Antonio to help him buy time so he could retrieve the cylinders from the capsule. Along with the computer, they would be his only insurance. But why was Antonio so concerned with Roula? He radioed Matt, who was still at the bottom of the main shaft. "Matt, I need the rest of that equipment. This is important."

"Will do, see you in thirty minutes," Matt replied.

The pre-arranged meeting place was at a local bar near Roula's apartment. It would be best for him to head out quietly before Steve had a chance to search the shafts. Maybe Steve was there right now. Maybe Matt wouldn't make it. He shook himself. This was no time for negative speculation. He needed to be on the move.

Back in the FOU, he packed a few necessities and the main computer module. He opened a drawer and pulled out the gun Steve had provided him. Aside from target practice, he had never used it. He tucked it into one of the backpack compartments. Outside, the moon illuminated the deceptively quiet desert. He heaved the backpack over his shoulder and headed for the jeep. A few steps later he gasped as he crossed paths with one of Matt's superintendents.

"Sorry," the man said. "Matt told me to hurry. That CIA guy is inside the shaft with his goons."

"Where's Matt?" Spencer asked, frantic now to get away with the capsule's master computer.

"He left the main shaft to follow your orders. He's okay."

"Thanks." Spencer laid a reassuring hand on the man's shoulder. "Tell Matt that I'm on my way to meet with Antonio. Tell him I have the . . ." What word could he use besides computer that Matt would understand? "Tell him I have the master key. He'll know what that means. Tell him he just needs to bring the locks."

The man nodded, his eyes wide. "Yessir," he said.

Spencer sped down the desert highway at a breakneck pace, checking the rear view mirror every few seconds. He finally let out a big exhale. There was no sign of anyone following him.

The ride to the meeting location took less than fifteen minutes. He ordered a cold beer, sat down at a table with four chairs, and made a futile attempt at steadying his breathing. He checked his watch. Matt was late. Had Steve found him? Had he asked Matt to show him what was inside the core sample tubes? It wasn't yet time to panic. Matt was a smart guy. He'd figure out a way to dodge Steve and the rest of the CIA goons. Damn, he needed those cylinders. He called Roula. "I'm at the bar down the street," he said as nonchalantly as he could muster. "Care to join me for a drink?"

"Sure," she said. "I'd like that."

She came through the door a few minutes later with a smile and wave. She wore her usual khaki shorts with a low-cut white t-shirt that showed off her firm breasts and flawless skin. She looked like any woman greeting her date. Apparently she was starting to get the hang of this counter-operative thing. Her casual smile had fooled even him for a minute.

She sat in the chair directly across from him and folded her long legs. "Hey, good lookin'," she said with a wink.

"It's good to see you," he said, his voice a little too loud even to his own ears. He signaled to the waitress who came over and set a glass of red wine in front of Roula.

He leaned forward and smiled. "Drink this," he pushed the wine toward her, "then go home and pack." He stroked her hand. "I think we've been discovered. We need to leave in fifteen minutes."

Roula spent a few minutes sipping the wine and making small talk about Cairo's weather. A few minutes later she stood up and kissed him on the cheek whispering, "I'll be ready in five."

Matt arrived a few minutes later. He was twenty-five minutes late.

"You made it," Spencer said. "Did you run into trouble? Did you get them?"

"Yes, to the trouble question," he said, "and yeah, I have the . . . uh . . . locks right here." Matt patted the backpack that hung over his shoulder. "Steve found the tunnel between the main shaft and the lower man-lift. I was just coming out of the capsule when I heard voices. We were lucky, the door was already closed. The capsule actually saved my life. Once they saw it, they were too stunned to even notice me. I seized the moment to get into the lift and escape," Matt's words came out in a rush.

"So the cat's out of the bag. Shit! We needed just a couple more days." Spencer struggled to keep his frustration at bay.

"Just be glad you're here and not there . . . and that you're alive. Pure luck, you know. What's your plan now?" Matt asked.

"I'm hoping Antonio has a plan. Roula and I are meeting him in a few minutes. You need to alert McPearson. Tell him I'll make contact as soon as I can."

Matt slipped the backpack onto the chair next to Spencer but didn't make a move to leave.

"Matt." Spencer stood and looked the man in the eye. "Steve's not after you. He knows I'm the one behind this. Don't worry, you'll be fine."

"I'm worried about you . . . and Roula," he said. "Where will you go?"

"Let us worry about that, okay?"

Uncertainty flashed across Matt's young face, but then he seemed to make up his mind. "Okay," he said with a weak smile.

"Thanks, I owe you." Spencer gave Matt a bear hug and then watched him leave the bar. He waited a few minutes and then gathered up the two backpacks. When he stepped outside, Roula was approaching. She had a large duffle bag over her shoulder.

"Get in, quick!" Spencer called from his jeep. In a moment they were off to meet Antonio. A lovely full moon reflected across the Nile. It was a romantic sight, but Spencer's mind was racing, projecting them forward to a place and time where they would be safe.

At the dock, Antonio was pacing impatiently. "Steve has discovered the capsule. We're in deep shit, Antonio." Spencer said between gasps.

"I suspected as much." Antonio rubbed his arms as if he'd just had a chill. "The two of you will need to hide. I have the perfect place. Come on board." Antonio led them to a large motorboat nearby.

"Is this yours?" Spencer asked.

"No, it belongs to a friend. Come, quickly."

The main cabin of the boat was both luxurious and spacious.

Spencer dropped his luggage, which consisted of two backpacks full of cylinders and one master computer, onto the plush leather sofa. He had managed to throw some clothes in a separate suitcase, including all of his documents, his laptop, and some cash.

Roula had the duffle bag and her trusted laptop. She had also managed to bring all of her documents and cash. She looked at Spencer for the first time since he had picked her up. "What's going on?"

"Steve discovered the capsule."

Roula gasped.

He wanted to tell her they were safe, that it would all work out somehow, but how could he? Now that the CIA had uncovered his scheme and they were on to him, dire consequences were sure to follow.

"Now, now," Antonio said, "we all knew this was inevitable. Sooner or later they were going to figure it out. Later would have been much better." He shrugged, "But now we must deal with the situation at hand."

"We have all the cylinders and the master computer. Without them, the capsule is useless," Spencer reassured Antonio.

Antonio nodded. "That was a good move. It will give us bargaining power."

"I'm sure that without my help, it will be almost impossible for them to open the capsule main door," Roula said.

"Who could they bring in to decipher the hieroglyphics, Roula?" Spencer asked.

"Professor Benedict from Columbia is one of the best, but it will take time for anyone to get up to speed on this new version, it's never been seen before."

"They'll bring in someone they can trust, someone from the family. This is a classified project," Antonio reminded them.

"So we do have time on our side, and that's just what we need right now . . . time to formulate a plan." Spencer's stomach was doing flip-flops. He had put so many people's lives at risk. Maybe it would have been better to just turn the whole thing over to the CIA in the first place. He sighed. Speculating about what might have been was a waste of time. He knew that. Focusing on the future was what would keep them alive.

They headed north down the Nile. Water lapped gently against the boat and reflected the moonlight. If he hadn't been so scared, it would have been a perfectly romantic moment. Antonio pointed to a small village on the shore.

"My friend has a nice houseboat there. He's been out of the country for months. You'll be safe there. This small village can only be accessed by boat. Steve will be looking at all the airlines and ship departures. The best place to hide is right under his nose,"

Antonio's confident statements did little to reassure him, but he smiled and nodded.

"The boat is well stocked with all kinds of supplies and the latest modern conveniences. You will be very comfortable."

Spencer helped Roula with her luggage and followed Antonio onto the houseboat. Inside, an elderly Egyptian greeted him. "Spencer, Roula, this is Sukeshi, the housekeeper. She's the caretaker here. Anything you need, cooking, errands into the village, she'll take care of it." Antonio pulled the woman aside and had a quiet word with her. She smiled at him and patted his cheek.

"You are not to set foot off this boat for any reason," Antonio said to Roula. "I'll negotiate our terms with the CIA. Your job is to stay out of sight." Antonio spoke to Roula like a stern father. "No excursions, clear?"

"Loud and clear, Antonio," Roula laughed, holding up her hands in defeat.

"We'll pretend to be on vacation," Spencer laughed. "What about my jeep?"

"I'll take care of it, let me have the keys."

What would he have done without Antonio who always seemed to have everything under control? The heavy weight of exhaustion suddenly took hold. He turned to Roula. Her pallor was unusually pale and she had dark smudges under her eyes. If only they could go to sleep and wake up from this whole mess like a bad dream.

He couldn't be too surprised by how quickly Steve and the CIA had moved. It was what they were trained to do, what they dreamed of doing. No doubt Tom Detton was on his way with a small army of agents and equipment. By now the project was surely a high level covert operation with full presidential approval. The objective would be to seal the mine and take full control of the situation. The only major obstacle Steve had standing in his way was the ubiquitous Abdul. The CIA probably had only a handful of trusted employees privy to the real objective of the mission and even fewer had actually seen the time capsule. The workers at the mine were surely kept under strict surveillance and a new security procedure had been implemented before he'd even left. Abdul, however, was sure to come calling and demand an explanation for all the new security. With agents crawling everywhere, he was bound to have new suspicions.

CHAPTER

SIXTEEN

Steve tilted his head back as a thunderous noise ripped through the sky. The noise soon became deafening. He counted as many as twelve choppers approaching. Egyptian workers were running everywhere pointing skyward, fear radiating from their brown faces. The buzz was now nearly unbearable. The choppers landed swiftly along the cement plant strip. Out of them came a fully armed stream of men in camouflage.

"Great, it's the Navy Seals," Steve muttered under his breath while the whir of the huge blades pounded his eardrums.

He would be meeting with McPearson and Matt later to try to find out where Ralph Spencer and Roula Grazulis might be hiding. How a geologist and an archeology student managed to slip right out from under his nose was beyond him. He needed to find them soon or he'd have hell to pay from Detton.

The soldiers circled the perimeter and easily wrested full control from the Egyptian troops posted by Abdul's government. It was hard to say how much Abdul actually knew since he'd had unauthorized access to the satellite feed, it would seem, from the beginning. It didn't really matter. The man could be quickly silenced if necessary.

A few of the Egyptian patrolmen refused to abandon their posts at first, but were quickly persuaded by Tom that they were grossly outnumbered. Within thirty minutes, the Navy Seals had the entire complex under their control and had rounded up all the workers. Steve now stood at the center of the perimeter as Tom Detton approached to apprise him of the latest situation.

"Good morning, Tom," Steve said.

Detton ignored his greeting. "I want the name of every employee who saw whatever's down there and I want the report with full details," Tom ordered. "The rest of the workers will be removed from the site now. This project has the full backing of the President and I will tolerate no screw-ups." He took a step closer and breathed heavily into Steve's face. "Is that clear?"

"Yes sir . . . but, uh . . ."

"But, what?"

"We actually already know who was involved. I have two of the major players in Spencer's FOU."

Detton's upper lip twitched. "Good, then let's assemble the rest of the workers and get them the hell out of the way."

"What about the Egyptian Government? They're not going to sit still and take this—"

"That's under control." Detton barked the words as if it were none of Steve's business. "The Secretary of State is on his way to meet with the President of Egypt. Our President made a few phone calls and came up with an excuse," Tom replied with no attempt to hide the impatience in his voice.

"It must be some excuse."

Tom lowered his head and looked Steve in the eye. "Preliminary finds have uncovered an unknown but dangerous biological contamination precipitated by the accident. Because of the high risk involved, our government acted quickly and evacuated and sealed the entire area. Teams of highly skilled technicians were deployed and are presently working at the site. Their main objective is to take control of the situation, determine the contaminate and stop it from spreading to the surface."

This was surely the official disclosure that would be presented to the Egyptian Government by the Secretary of State. "Very impressive." Steve said with a smile. "Your idea?"

"Yes, as a matter of fact." Detton's face flushed red. He rounded his shoulders and looked away.

Was the man actually embarrassed by a simple compliment? Best to change the subject. "How will we keep the workers from circulating other rumors?"

"Let me handle the workers. Tell them that we will be meeting in about thirty minutes. I need to find out what McPearson and his supervisory staff know about this.

Let's go and find out." Tom signaled for Steve to return to the FOU.

McPearson sat at the small table in the FOU. He had a blank look on his face and was visibly shaken. Matt Garrett leaned toward the window watching all the activity outside. Two CIA agents guarded the door to the FOU unit. There'd be no chance to escape. His only hope was Spencer with the computer and cylinders.

"Bill, how the hell are you?" Detton said as he came through the door. He shook McPearson's hand and ignored Matt. "You come down here and all hell breaks loose." He sat at the table and relaxed back, folding his hands behind his head.

Relief washed over McPearson's face and he seemed to melt into his chair. My God, the man wasn't actually going to fall for Detton's act, was he?

"Bill, we need an explanation," Detton said in a friendly tone.

McPearson stared at him, his face a picture of perfect innocence.

Detton sat forward and spoke earnestly. "Bill, we need to know now . . . for our nation's security."

"I wish I could help you . . ." McPearson stammered. The loose skin of his neck jiggled as he shook his head. "I . . . I don't know what's going on."

"Well, Bill, maybe you can answer this. Why wasn't I immediately informed about the find?" Tom demanded.

"I'm in the dark as much as you are. Matt and I have spent the last few hours going over every detail, trying to figure out just when Spencer could have found that . . . that . . . thing. We think it was discovered within the last twenty-four hours. Your men stumbled on it, I think, just as Spencer's crew was on their way out to report the findings."

Ah, so McPearson was going to play dumb. Very convincing.

"With all due respect, that's bullshit, Bill," Detton said, maintaining his friendly manner. "We've already found the secret passage that led to the lower man-lift. Once we descended to the base of the lift, we had an open view to the spaceship . . . or whatever that thing is."

"What secret passage?" Bill asked, his tone incredulous. "I don't know about any secret passage."

"The one that leads to the lower man-lift, Bill" Detton said as if he were speaking to a child.

"Oh, that," McPearson said as if he had just realized what Detton was saying. "There's no secret there, Tom. My men drilled that passage to gain access to the main shaft." McPearson looked to Matt for the first time. "There was nothing secret about it, was there?"

"No, of course not. We used a ventilation fan as the access point for practical purposes and to introduce fresh air into the tunnel," Matt said.

"Well, where the hell is Spencer now? No one's seen him in the last four hours." Steve's face had turned crimson and he spoke through gritted teeth. His impatience was bubbling to the surface despite his attempt at following Detton's nice guy ploy. "We have a lot of questions—"

"Bill." Detton leaned across the table. "Look at me . . . This is serious. We haven't heard from Spencer. So if he was on his way out to report his findings, where did he go to make his report?" Detton's voice dripped with contempt. He obviously was no longer trying to keep up the good cop ruse.

"Well, I don't know the answer to that," Bill said, his voice thoughtful. "I would assume he went to see Antonio."

"I know they were both concerned about Abdul," Matt added. "He probably wanted directions from Antonio before making contact with you, sir."

"Steve, let's get Antonio on the phone. I want to get to the bottom of this and fast. I am going to speak to the workers now. McPearson, I need your support here."

"Anything I can do, Tom, you know that.

Detton described the government's official fabrication and then nodded toward McPearson. "Please come with me."

Matt looked from Detton to Steve.

"You, too," Steve added.

They proceeded to the central area where the armed CIA agents had herded the workers. The men's faces reflected fear and disgust and most of them looked like they wanted nothing more than to get out of there.

Matt let out a long breath. The good news was, the CIA was clueless as to what they'd found. They thought it was a spaceship or some alien craft. That was good. If they had no idea what the capsule was, they couldn't make the connection to the master computer and cylinders. Spencer and Roula were safe for now.

Detton turned to McPearson. "Please explain the situation to your men," he said.

When McPearson was through describing the possible contaminant, Detton added a few of his own dramatics.

"I am here on behalf of the US government."

There was a murmur of disapproval among the men. Detton's smug manner didn't seem to sit well with these men who worked so hard for their livings.

"Your safety is our main concern and for that reason we are shutting down this project."

A few of the men gathered their belongings and walked away. Others stood their ground, grumbling about lost wages.

"We are asking that you leave these premises immediately. After we have regained control of the situation, you will be contacted to return to work. I am pleased to announce that Calpetro Corp. has decided to give each one of you one-month's salary as severance pay. Mr. McPearson from Calpetro is here to help with the distribution."

"What severance pay are you talking about, Tom?" McPearson asked incredulously.

"We have arranged a cash payment for each employee. Don't worry, the US government is taking care of it. I just need you to confirm the amounts and play along." He gave McPearson a quick elbow to the ribs. "It's good for Calpetro's image."

The man actually winked at McPearson and smirked. Was there no end to Detton's arrogance?

Within the next three hours, Detton had the workers all paid and removed from the property. What was coming next was obvious. Detton would want to lay his eyes on the mysterious device at the bottom of the mine.

"It's time to go see what all this fuss is about," he said to Steve. "Matt, take us to the bottom."

Tom Detton let his eyes roam from the cave floor to the top of the strange structure. A contingency of guards stood ready at the capsule's main entrance. There was no question the damn thing was breathtaking. "What is it?" he asked.

Steve walked up from behind. "No one seems to have a good goddamn clue. Maybe it's some kind of spaceship."

"I don't think so. The thing is about as aerodynamic as a bar of lead. I don't see how it could fly." Detton moved closer to Matt and looked the young man in the eye. "Tell me honestly, do you know what this is? Did Spencer say anything to you?"

Mat held his ground. "I'm sorry, sir, we're as clueless as everyone else. As far as I know, Spencer only just found it before Steve got there. Maybe he's off somewhere trying to figure it out."

Detton looked Matt up and down. The boy seemed sincere, but that didn't mean he could trust a word of what he said. He drew a deep breath and turned back to Steve. "I want the best team we can assemble here on the double. Bring in some of the brains behind the Nevada project at hanger fifty-one and our best metallurgists. I want this thing documented. I will be personally debriefing the president and I need some answers. We won't be able to keep the Egyptians at bay for long." Detton drew in a deep breath and walked closer to the capsule. He ran his fingers along the webbing. "Outstanding find," he said to no one in particular. His excitement was bubbling to the surface, but he needed to stay in command. "Steve, I want to see Spencer the minute you find him. No one is to leave the site," He turned to McPearson. "Not even you."

McPearson gasped but said nothing.

"I don't want this leaked anywhere. All outside communication must be authorized by me."

"Are you holding us prisoner, Tom?" McPearson asked.

"Call it what you want. I've had enough of your staff disappearing on me. This operation is under my command, which means it operates under the highest secrecy. I am not about to compromise anything."

"Where will we stay?" McPearson asked.

"The Navy Seals will set up a camp. You will be provided adequate quarters. I am setting up a field command operation with full satellite support. Bill, I need you as part of the evaluating team." He turned and looked at Steve. "Apparently, we can't find the only other geologist we have on this project."

Steve's face turned crimson but he said nothing.

"You got it." McPearson said

Of course he would get what he wanted. As long as Tom Detton was in command, no one had any other choice.

McPearson stepped out into the sunshine and stopped dead in his tracks. The entire area had been transformed into a military compound in the few short hours he'd been beneath the surface. Damned if it didn't take him right back to Vietnam, a place still etched in his darkest subconscious. Like so many GIs, his time in Vietnam was filled with ugly memories that he'd worked hard to forget.

Matt stood next to him, his face etched with worry lines that he was far too young to have. "Jesus," he said under his breath. He turned to McPearson. "We've got to figure out how to contact Spencer or Antonio, but we can't get a minute away from the these goons."

Steve had taken off to God-knows-where, but not before assigning one of the Navy Seal captains and another solider to be the military escort for the two of them. "Well, Matt, isn't this quite the wild twist to our project," McPearson said loud enough for their escorts to hear.

The two men glanced up and then went back to their own conversation.

"I think we're going to have to wait for Spencer to contact us," McPearson said under his breath.

"At least they have no idea what it is," Matt looked over his shoulder at the two soldiers behind them. "Maybe Spencer will be okay. They couldn't possibly know that we've already been inside."

"That's right, but we can't take any chances right now. Our best bet is to contact Antonio . . . before they get to him."

"I'll try to sneak inside one of the offices and call his portable phone," Matt said.

As if on cue, a contingency of soldiers approached the captain with questions about the temporary housing they were setting up. While the captain was busy giving orders to the soldiers, Matt slipped out and managed to get in one of the offices.

Antonio sat in his office poring over the safety protocols he had helped Spencer draft. It would be important that they stick to the accidental explosion story they'd told the CIA and Abdul. He'd need to convince Detton that Spencer had found the capsule just before Steve did. It was the only way to keep Spencer safe.

His private cell phone vibrated. He glanced at the caller ID. It was coming from one of the office phones at the site. "Hello?"

"Antonio, it's Matt."

"Matt, my boy, where are you?"

"Soldiers are everywhere," Matt whispered. "I had to hide under a desk to call you."

"What? You're hiding under a desk? What the hell's going on there?"

"Tom Detton is here and he's taken over the project. We are under a military siege. He's looking for you and he really wants to know where Spencer's gone. As of now, they have no idea what the object is or that we've been inside . . . or, for that matter, that we took anything . . . So maybe Spencer is okay?" He paused, but when Antonio didn't answer he went on. "I told them that Spencer's looking for you and that he discovered the object just before Steve did. We told them Spencer wanted to check with you first so that you could prepare for Abdul." Matt's voice was now a frantic whisper.

"Okay, okay. Don't say anything more over the airwaves, Matt. I know this is a secure line, but the CIA can tap just about anything. I understand what you've told me. Thank you." Antonio closed his cell phone and glanced at his watch. The conversation had lasted less than fifteen seconds, not nearly enough time to trace the line.

Antonio breathed a sigh of relief. Matt and McPearson were safe for now and the lie they had told played into his plan perfectly.

A few minutes later he left his office and headed back to the docks. He pulled his Mercedes in behind Spencer's jeep. He sat in the car for several minutes, watching his rear view mirror to make sure no one had followed. The sun was setting and the Nile reflected the magenta and golden light of twilight. It was the time of evening when one's eyes could play tricks. He got out of the car, closed the door, and pushed the remote lock button. He stood watching the river for a long moment with all of his senses on high alert for any sign of trouble. The only sound he heard was water lapping against the hulls of the docked boats.

He headed down the dock until he reached a small houseboat that was clearly a permanent residence. "Giuseppe?" he called.

"Si" the man answered as he came through the door, his face lighting up when he recognized his visitor. "Antonio, amico mio, how are you?"

"I need your help," Antonio said. "See that jeep over there?" He pointed. "I need that vehicle hidden where no one will find it? Can I count on you to take care of it?"

"For you, Antonio, we'll have that little jeep so far under wraps that not even God could find it." Giuseppe grinned.

Antonio had done a lot for the dockworkers and had been instrumental in persuading the Egyptian Government to allow Giuseppe and some of his skilled co-workers to work and train the locals in this busy and strategic shipping center. He nodded at Giuseppe and smiled back. "Grazie, amico mio."

Antonio drove to his favorite restaurant for a large Italian meal and then back to his office. He intentionally took his time, going through the motions as if he didn't have a care in the world.

Maria, his blonde secretary, greeted him with a stack of papers and a smile. "Mr. Casenza, they need you at the mine. Steve Sullivan is looking for you. He also asked about Mr. Spencer. He said there's some type of emergency and he wants both of you to report there immediately."

Antonio took the stack of papers and sighed. It was exactly what he'd expected, but he still wasn't looking forward to facing the CIA or Abdul.

"Oh," Maria said, "We've also received several messages from Abdul's office requesting your immediate attention."

Antonio had worked with Maria for four years now and he had never seen her so worried. He picked up the phone and dialed Spencer's number at the mine office. As expected, Steve Sullivan answered. "Steve," he said, "this is Antonio Casenza. My secretary tells me you've been looking for me. Sorry for the delay, I was at dinner and—"

"Antonio, is Spencer with you?"

"Um, no, no he's not. He left a while ago, but we have some incredible news for you." He paused, waiting for Steve's reaction.

"I already know. We've seen it." Steve said, disappointment in his voice. He clearly was focused on getting to Spencer. "I can't discuss this over the phone," he added. Can you come in?"

"I suppose so," Antonio said. "Give me thirty minutes?"

"Sure," Steve said. He sounded resigned now.

Antonio hung up the phone. His plan was unfolding nicely. "Maria, call Abdul's office and tell him to meet me at the mine in forty five minutes."

He arrived at the mine to an unfriendly reception. Navy Seals guarded

the main entrance and the grounds looked more like a war zone than a mining project.

"Antonio, how nice to see you!" Steve attempted a smile but could only muster a smirk.

"Steve, what the hell is going on here?" Antonio said, looking around. "Where is everybody?" Antonio asked.

Steve ignored his question. "So, where's our friend Spencer?"

"Well, I'm not sure where he is right now. He came to see me today. He was damned excited about the discovery, and frankly, so am I. He's concerned about Abdul, though," Antonio added thoughtfully. "Maybe he's gone off to figure out how to deal with him."

"Why the hell would he do that?"

"He thinks Abdul is up to something."

Steve stared at him, his eyes cold and hard.

"Think about it, man," Antonio scolded the young agent. "Abdul could jeopardize this entire project." Antonio paused, letting what he'd said sink in.

"Abdul is not Spencer's concern. His first responsibility is to us."

"His first responsibility is to his employer," Antonio corrected.

Steve ignored the comment. "We need to talk to him about the . . . the . . . whatever it is. Abdul will be taken care of. The Secretary of State himself is flying here to meet with the President of Egypt to explain the, uh, situation."

"And what, precisely, is the situation Steve?" Antonio couldn't wait to hear the story CIA had come up with to sell the locals.

"Well, we did send all of the miners home. We also sent home the domestic patrol. We needed a foolproof story for that. In a nutshell," he said with defiance, "this project is now contaminated with a deadly biological agent."

"What?" Antonio laughed. "How will you pull that off?"

"We already have. The secretary will explain that the latest accident released some type of biological agent that escaped from the bottom of the mine injuring a few people and creating panic among the workers. Fortunately, the US sent a containment team to examine the area." Steve paused.

"Do you honestly think these people are that stupid? Abdul will never buy it." His words were carefully stated to plant a seed of doubt in Steve's mind.

"Whether he buys it or not is immaterial. We are not going to be disturbed by anyone as long as that thing sits at the bottom of this mine." Steve shuffled from one foot to the other. His cheeks were flushed cherry red.

"Spencer will be in some serious hot water unless he shows up today with some answers," Steve warned.

"Spencer sent me over to see Abdul and explain the situation. He is waiting for my instructions."

"Well then get him here, goddammit!" Steve shouted.

Tom Detton appeared at Steve's side. "Steve, we have company. I'm told it's that Egyptian again. Get rid of him."

"Yes sir. It will be my pleasure."

"I would be careful, sir," Antonio interrupted.

"Antonio Casenza right? I'm Tom Detton of the CIA." Detton thumped Antonio's chest with his index finger. "I'm running this project now."

Anger roiled in Antonio's gut. "I see," he said, "Just like that, huh? I was under the impression Nick Spencer was in charge here." He was playing with fire by pushing them, but he needed to get these guys off Spencer's trail.

"He has just been replaced. We do, however, need him here." Detton pointed at the ground as if he wanted Spencer in that very spot. "But for now, we need to deal with the nuisance that just showed up at our doorsteps."

"That nuisance is my responsibility. Let me handle it, sir?" Antonio said with as much graciousness as he could muster.

Detton studied Antonio's face for a moment. "That's right, you're the liaison, aren't you? Very well. Have you been briefed?"

"Yes, harmful biological contamination," Antonio reassured him.

"All right then, your presence may help to diffuse him. But Steve and I need to be there." Tom's impatience showed clearly on his face.

"Of course."

Antonio walked with purpose toward the tent where Abdul was waiting. Detton and Steve flanked him on both sides and the military captain followed behind. Upon reaching the tent, the captain came around and pulled open the tent's flap for them. Detton signaled for Antonio to go first.

Abdul all but leapt out of the folding chair upon which he'd been precariously perched. "Mr. Casenza, what is the meaning of all this? I hope it's a joke. If so, it's a very bad one." Spittle flew from Abdul's lips as he spoke. He sounded more like a wild animal than a man.

"Mr. Abdul, please sit down."

Abdul stood his ground, staring at Abdul with an obstinate frown. "I demand to know what's going on."

Antonio gestured toward Detton and Steve. "Let me introduce you to some of our distinguished colleagues. They're here to help with this unstable situation. This is Tom Detton and Steve Sullivan. They are from the Pentagon and are here to help us out."

"The Pentagon? What the hell does the Pentagon have to do with an oil drilling operation?" Abdul broke into a sweat. "What's happened to our own workers and our local patrol?" He looked at each man's face, his eyes bloodshot and bulging. "Who are these people?" Abdul demanded.

"Mr. Abdul." Antonio laid his hand on his own chest. "You and I have worked together for years. You know you can trust me. Please, just take a seat and I'll explain everything."

Abdul grunted, but he finally moved to sit down. Antonio sat across from him and Steve unfolded two additional chairs. The three men formed a semi-circle around Abdul.

Detton leaned in. "Mr. Abdul—"

Antonio raised his hand. "Please, let me."

Detton leaned back in his chair and signaled for Antonio to proceed.

Antonio looked Abdul in the eye. "Sir, the mine accident was more serious than anyone had imagined. The blast released a contaminated biological agent. We are sitting on potentially lethal biological material here. The Pentagon was our best and first resort." Antonio put heavy emphasis on his last words.

"You are joking, right?" Abdul laughed. "This is not the United States. This is an Egyptian issue."

"Let me assure you, this is no joke, "Antonio said.

"As we speak, our Secretary of State is on his way to see your President," Steve said.

Antonio flashed a warning glance at Steve.

"Is this true?" Abdul said to Antonio.

"Yes, and we need your cooperation and that of your government. This must be handled with mutual cooperation and under the strictest surveillance. None of us can afford any civilian disasters," Antonio said. "Our military experts assure us that the deadly biological contamination will soon be contained within the mine and that no danger will exist for the people of Cairo or its surroundings."

Abdul stood up and pounded his cane into the ground. "This is all bullshit!" he screamed. "What are you really hiding under there, Antonio?"

Detton rose and faced the fuming Egyptian. "Mr. Abdul, please—"

"No. First it was gold, now it's biological contamination? I demand to see the bottom of that mine right now." Abdul stood tall and pointed his cane at Steve.

"I'm afraid you must leave immediately," Detton said with authority. "Captain, see that Mr. Abdul is escorted outside. This meeting is adjourned." Tom glanced angrily at Antonio as he walked out.

Steve followed Detton out of the tent. Antonio stood up and gestured with open palms to Abdul. "I'm truly sorry about what went on here tonight."

"This is not over. I will get to the bottom of this."

Antonio moved so that his back was to the captain. "I want you to know that this was totally out of my control, " he whispered, handing him his card with a number scribbled on the back. "Please call me at this number tonight."

Abdul looked over Antonio's shoulder at the captain. He huffed, but took the card, tucked it into his palm, then wrapped his hand around the cane.

Antonio walked out of the tent and left Abdul to fume at the unfortunate captain. He hastened his steps to catch up with Detton and Steve. "That was not very diplomatic," he told them. "Abdul will not take this sitting down."

Detton stopped and turned to Antonio, his face only inches away. "You have until nine tonight to deliver Spencer to me." He turned to walk away and then looked back. "Trust me, Mr. Casenza, you don't want to disappoint me."

Spencer sat on the leather sofa with Roula curled up beside him. She breathed in the rhythm of deep sleep. Thank God she was finally getting some rest. She would need all the rest she could get for what was to come. He slowly slipped off the sofa, laid a blanket over Roula, kissed her head, and then walked into the small kitchen.

He pulled his cell phone from his hip pocket and keyed in Paul's number. He trusted Antonio, but the waiting was driving him crazy. It was time for a contingency plan.

The phone made a series of clicking noises, but didn't ring. "Come on," he muttered. "Make the connection." After six rings, Paul's voice came on the line."

"Hey, man. What's going on? I've been wondering what the hell's going on with you."

"Hi Paul. I'm sorry, but I've got something really important I need to talk to you about." Spencer sounded rushed, even to himself, and his voice was cracking.

"Okay . . . this doesn't sound good. What's up? Where are you?" Paul spoke with none of his usual nonchalance.

"I'm still in Egypt and I'm in trouble. I need your help." He desperately needed to confide in his old friend and finally tell him the truth, but now was not the time.

"Listen, man, I know you're in hot water, but you've gotta tell me what's going on if I'm gonna keep helping you?"

"I am afraid the water's boiling," Spencer said. "I need you to do something that might be quite dangerous. If you say no, I'll understand." Spencer hesitated, waiting for his friend's reply.

"Come on, buddy, what the hell is this all about?"

"I know, I know. I need to tell you the whole story, and I will, I promise . . . but not over the phone. You'll just need to trust that what I'm asking you to do is vital to all of us."

CHAPTER

SEVENTEEN

Antonio headed back to his office. He needed to talk to Spencer right away. He strolled over to the bar across from his office. From the back room pay phone, he placed a call to Spencer's mobile line.

"Spencer, my boy, we're in luck. The CIA thinks you only just discovered the capsule when they did. They need you. Detton wants you to report to him in the next ninety minutes."

"To hell with Detton. I don't trust the CIA. I'm working on a contingency plan."

"You don't want to do anything rash. Not now. I can protect you only if you listen to my advice," Antonio warned.

"If I come in, I come with nothing. They have no idea about the cylinders or the master computer. It needs to stay that way."

"Of course, I wouldn't ask you to do anything otherwise."

"I also want you to make them guarantee my safety . . . and Roula's."

"Yes, yes, I'm sure we can do all that. Just don't make any moves that could put us all in jeopardy. There may come a time when the CIA learns the true purpose of that device, and they're going to want the computer and cylinders."

Antonio spoke in a calm and reassuring tone, but Spencer didn't feel very reassured. Antonio seemed convinced that the best move was for him and Roula to continue feigning cooperation. If nothing else, it could buy them more time. There wasn't much they could accomplish as long as they were fugitives, and there was no other way they'd be able to get close to the capsule again.

"I am going to pick you up in the next sixty minutes," Antonio said.

"What about my jeep?"

"It's hidden, and that's where it should stay. Be ready in sixty minutes, okay?

"Yes, okay," Spencer said.

Spencer walked over to the sofa and sat down next to Roula. He rubbed her shoulders and kissed her cheek. "Roula, darling, wake up. We've got to go."

Roula sat up with a start. "Go where?"

"We're going back to the site. The CIA hasn't figured out what the capsule is. They're asking for our help."

Roula was fully awake now, her eyes wide with fear. "We can't go back . . . We need to protect Neflani . . . Samir . . ."

"Roula, they're not real."

"I know, but they feel real to me. Their lives . . . their story . . . look at what they went through just to make sure their culture would be remembered. We've got to protect that."

"The CIA knows nothing. They probably think it's an alien ship or something. We're safe for now." He took her chin in his hand. "There's no other way we'll get close to the capsule . . . let alone back inside. We have to go back and pretend to help them.

Roula's body trembled in his arms. "What about Abdul?"

"Antonio will take care of him."

Fat tears rolled down Roula's cheeks. "Oh, Ralph," she sobbed. "How did this turn into such a mess. "It's all my fault."

"Your fault? Roula, no." He kissed her tenderly. "None of this is your fault."

"Yes, yes it is. You don't know—"

He sat her down on the sofa and held her by the shoulders. "Listen to me." He wiped a tear from her cheek. "What I know is that I've fallen totally and irrevocably in love with you."

She looked into his eyes. "You love me? Really?" She sniffed. "Because I love you, too." She wrapped her arms around his neck. "I love you so much."

His heart soared. She loved him. That was all that mattered now. "Then we'll get through this together," he said.

She wiped the tears from her cheek and nodded. "Okay, yes, we'll do this together."

He ran his fingers through her hair and then kissed her cheeks, her nose, her lips. "Then go freshen up and get your things around. Antonio will be here in less than an hour."

Roula padded off to the bathroom and Spencer called out for Sukeshi. He whispered instructions to her. She nodded and walked away.

"Well, if it isn't our fearless leader." Steve smirked and gave Spencer an exaggerated salute. "We were beginning to wonder if you had disappeared somewhere into the desert.

"I see from the look of things that you've turned this place into a war zone," Spencer replied coolly.

"Operali is now under the direction and control of Tom Detton. The CIA has full jurisdiction and the project is highly classified. We need to identify that alien object and for that I need your help and that of your girlfriend. Tomorrow we'll meet here at seven am. Bring her." He nodded in Roula's general direction.

"Her name is Roula."

"Whatever." Steve crossed his arms. "I know she's seen the object, so don't try to send her off into the night. We need her to decipher the hieroglyphics." Steve turned to walk away as Detton approached.

"Mr. Spencer, Miss Grazulis, I'm glad to see you were wise enough to return."

"Of course," Spencer said, "Why wouldn't we come back?"

"Right," Detton said with a sneer. "So where've you been?"

Roula stepped forward. "We didn't know what to make of what we saw," she said. "Honestly? We got scared." She nodded toward Spencer. "He was worried about Mr. Abdul finding out. That man is . . ." She shuddered.

"I know what Abdul is, I've had my own experiences with him."

"Well then you understand . . ." Roula looked at Detton without blinking, her eyes round, innocent . . . beseeching.

"Tom, we came back to help," Spencer said. "We want to know what that thing is as much as you do. Antonio assured us that you'd taken care of Abdul, so we came back."

"All right, I'll take you at your word," Detton said. "Steve will see you here at seven tomorrow morning."

Spencer turned to Roula. "Let's go back to your apartment." He took her hand and started to walk away.

"By the way, Mr. Spencer, there'll be guards posted at Ms. Grazulis's apartment all night." His attempt at a chuckle came out more like a snort. "That's how I take people at their word."

Spencer swallowed hard but didn't respond. What was there to say? Detton needed to feel in charge and it would benefit them more to let him.

They drove back to Roula's apartment in silence. Spencer tried to stop himself from glancing in his rearview mirror at the dark sedan that followed a few car lengths behind, but couldn't help himself, even though every glance at the vehicle made his stomach churn.

They parked in Roula's assigned spot and walked the path to her apartment. The sedan pulled into a guest spot and the two agents followed their steps, keeping only a few paces behind.

Spencer reached for the apartment door. "Once we're inside say nothing about Neflani and Samir," he whispered to Roula. "Your apartment's probably bugged by now."

She looked into his eyes and nodded. The fear that had been reflected in her eyes earlier was gone. It was replaced by something else, something that made her eyes bright and alert and had put the color back in her cheeks. Was it the words they had spoken earlier, or was she genuinely excited to be openly included in a covert CIA operation? Either way, she looked more beautiful than ever.

Spencer arrived at the site fifteen minutes before seven with Roula at his side. Neither of them had been able to sleep so they'd gotten up early, had a quick breakfast of eggs and toast, and then headed out the door. He was nervous, to say the least, but a new excitement pumped his heart. They cylinders and master computer were safely hidden away and under the careful watch of a few Antonio's tough and loyal dockworkers. Now he, Spencer, was playing a double agent, one for the CIA and one for himself. The danger was mounting and each day would bring new challenges. He was ready.

"Good morning Spencer. Good morning Roula." Steve smiled at Roula. "I am sure Spencer briefed you on the assignment. I'll need to see you in private before we proceed." Steve's angry attitude from the night before was gone. He was in a jovial mood.

Roula looked to Spencer a question in her eyes.

"It's okay," he said "Go ahead."

Steve guided her into the office and closed the door. Spencer waited patiently along with two cameramen, Antonio, and four Navy Seal officers armed to the teeth. Within ten minutes Steve and Roula stepped out of the office. Roula smiled and Spencer winked back at her. Steve gave the order to proceed.

The inside of the cave looked so different, Spencer barely recognized it. High intensity lights had been placed around the capsule and it reflected back an eerie glow. To Spencer, though, nothing could have looked more breathtaking than the cool underground half-light in which he had first seen the capsule.

"So, Spencer, what do you make of this?" Steve was ready, and the cameras were rolling.

Spencer put his hands on his hips and looked about as if appraising the capsule. "It's the most incredible . . . thing . . . I have ever seen."

"Tom Detton has pretty much ruled out the notion that it's an alien craft. In examining the aerodynamics, he thinks this contraption could never fly," Steve said.

"The apparent dynamics may not point to an aircraft, but neither do our stealths." He held back a smile. Why not keep them guessing?

Steve looked puzzled for a moment and then turned to Roula. "We need to get inside. What do you make of the hieroglyphics?" He asked point blank.

Roula moved closer to examine the symbols. "I'll need to photograph all of this and input the data into my computer program." Her lie was as smooth as glass.

"Okay, people, let's get to work." Steve clapped his hands. "Mr.

Detton wants this device identified on the double. This project is being watched from high places in Washington." Steve moved everyone along.

In Silicon Valley, Paul answered his door. A courier stood on the front step, a package in his hand. He signed for it and closed the door without saying a word to the deliveryman. He turned the small box over in his hands. It was the latest package shipped priority mail by Spencer. It was not very large, but from what Spencer had said it was crucially important. He turned on his computer and e-mailed Spencer. They had agreed on a coded message to avoid suspicions.

Spencer, I hope to see you soon here at my place. The new coffee place has wonderful lattes. I have not heard from you in a while… when are you coming for a visit? Please take a minute to write back and let me know. See you. Paul"

Paul took the package to his bank and opened a safety deposit box in his own name. He carefully placed the package in the box. He asked for an extra signature card and, as instructed, mailed it to Antonio's office in Egypt addressed to Ralph Spencer. He hated to admit it, but he was enjoying the intrigue of this covert operation. Why hadn't he chosen a more adventurous profession such as private eye or detective as a career? If only he knew what the hell was going on. If the sound of Spencer's voice during their last call was any indication, it was monumental. But what could it be? He drove back to the Marriott and stopped to see the concierge. "I need you to hold this letter for a Mr. Ralph Spencer. He will be checking into this hotel some time next month. Please take good care of this for him." He placed the letter in the concierge's hand and with a smile handed him a hundred dollar bill.

"Yes, sir. It will be my pleasure to take care of this for Mr. Spencer. Does Mr. Spencer have reservations here?"

"No, not yet. He is presently in Africa, but he is expected here next month. He has stayed here before. You may check the hotel records."

The man nodded. Paul smiled at him and headed for the door. He stopped at the entrance and turned around. The concierge left his post and went behind the registration counter. He placed the envelope in one of the hotel's safes.

Paul arrived home late. He had stopped for a drink with a new office beauty, but she had turned down his offer for a ride home. He walked through his front door and froze. Something was very wrong. His hand trembled as he reached for the light switch. "Shit," he muttered. His place was in a shambles. All of his books and CDs were in piles on the floor. The sofa cushions had huge slits in them and half the stuffing was pulled out. It was as if the place had been turned upside down. He made his way to the kitchen. It was the same situation. All of his kitchenware was strewn across the floor. Shards of broken glass and china were everywhere. "Double shit."

Who the hell would do this? His stomach lurched and his mouth went dry. Whoever had been in his place, it had to be connected with whatever Spencer was up to, and now they knew he was involved. The police arrived within twenty minutes. He made a full report, leaving out any mention of Ralph Spencer. He explained that robbery was most likely the motive and that, fortunately, he never keeps cash at home anyway. Once the police left, fear and exhaustion set in. He looked around his place and made a decision. He grabbed his jacket and headed for the door. He needed to check Spencer's original apartment. If it wasn't demolished he'd spend the night there. If it was destroyed as his had been . . . well, he'd figure out what to do from there. No matter what happened, though, he'd stay away from the secret apartment. Chances were good he would be followed.

It was nearly two am when he arrived at Spencer's apartment. The weight of anxiety and exhaustion made the climb up the stairs seem interminable. When he entered through the front door, he had a sense of déjà vu. He flicked on the light switch. Spencer's apartment was ten times more destroyed than his had been. Whoever was behind this was looking for something and was serious about finding it. He froze for a moment, took a deep breath and turned off the light. Calling the police would only draw attention to the situation, and someone was definitely watching. He'd check into a local hotel. Hopefully after a good night's sleep he'd know what to do. He had had enough for one evening.

Paul fell into a deep, exhausted sleep. He awoke to the sound of tapping at the hotel room door. "Housekeeping," a voice called.

Damn, he'd forgotten to put out the do not disturb sign. "Not now," he called out. He waited for the sound of wheels rolling further down the hall and then swung his legs over the edge of the bed. He needed to think for a second, to regain his bearings. The memory of the two torn up apartments made his stomach do a flip-flop. Shit. What a horrible night. He scratched his head and looked around the hotel room. What now?

Probably the best thing to do was nothing. He'd get dressed in the clothing he'd worn the day before, go to work, and hope no one noticed his rumpled appearance. He'd shower, get dressed, and then grab a quick bite in the hotel's coffee shop.

At his office, he felt watched. His suit smelled musty and his two-day-old shirt was uncomfortable. He kept trying to smooth the wrinkles, but to no avail. He tried to get some work done, but couldn't concentrate. He stared at his computer screen for a moment and then brought up his email. He typed a message to Spencer.

Yesterday they closed the coffee shop for no reason. I really wanted you to see it. Maybe they are remodeling because when I peeked through the windows, everything was in shambles. I have some time off, so perhaps I could visit you. I have never been to Egypt. Please write back. Paul

It wasn't until that evening that Spencer had an opportunity to turn on his computer and check his latest e-mail. He was anxious to see if Paul had received his precious shipment. He quickly scanned the first message from Paul, relieved to see that his package was now safe in a bank vault. The second message alarmed him. He picked up his cell phone and called Antonio. "Antonio, my friend, how about an aperitivo?" Antonio had been teaching Spencer the finer things in life, particularly the Italian tradition of an after-dinner drink to settle the stomach. It was also a new code they had devised to communicate in case there were bugs around.

Fifteen minutes later the two men met at their favorite local bar. Antonio ordered two glasses of Italian grappa, a drink that was slowly growing on Spencer.

"Antonio, we have problems. If I read Paul's coded message right, his place in Palo Alto was just made over. I think my apartment was too. Paul's running scared. He wants to come to Egypt." Spencer leaned forward, took a sip of his drink, and looked Antonio in the eye. "What do we do?"

"What's Paul got to do with this? What were they looking for?"

"He's been helping me all along. I sent him a package two days ago. It contains the two critical cylinders explaining the translation process." Spencer looked around the room but no one seemed to be paying any attention to them. "He was able to store them in a safety deposit box at the local bank. Your office should already be holding mail for me that contains the signature card for me to sign." He kept his voice as calm as possible and then raised his glass. "A toast . . . to good friends," he said.

"Ah," Antonio said, "I'll drink to that." He tapped Spencer's glass and took a sip of his grappa. He looked at Spencer over his glasses. "So was that a part of your contingency plan?"

"Yes, it's our insurance policy."

"So why the search? Somebody is suspicious and I think we know who." Antonio was shaking his head in disapproval.

"None of this happened until the capsule was discovered by the CIA. Detton must have given the order to search all possible places for anything unusual." Spencer took a big gulp of his drink and sighed. "I just don't get how they made Paul. I took every precaution when Roula and I visited McPearson." Spencer was sure that no one had followed him at the time.

"We can't be sure of anything now. Your movements aroused someone's suspicion."

"Okay, but even if that is the case, they still have nothing. We'll just pretend that it never happened. I'll tell Paul to play it like a robbery. In the meantime, I'd like you, Antonio, to draft some type of document assuring our safety. Do you have any ideas?"

Antonio shook his hard. "I don't think that's a good idea. We'll only increase the suspicion that we're hiding something." Antonio swallowed the last of his drink. "All in due time. For now, we just play along." He signaled to the waitress for another round. "You look like you could use another drink," he said. "Besides," he said in a low voice. "This might give you a chance to return to Phamuria."

"I thought that too, but it would be very dangerous." Spencer couldn't hide the need he felt to return. It ate at him, like a compulsion. Roula, he was certain, had the same urge to go back. "I respect your opinion on this, Antonio. We'll do it your way."

"Good. Let's continue with the project as Steve tells us and proceed cautiously. We'll worry about your precious package in due time."

"What about Paul?"

"Tell Paul that you are extremely busy and now is not a good time to visit. Can you write him a coded e-mail, telling him to expect overnight mail, say at his office?"

"Sure. What do you want me to tell him?"

"Tell him the truth. He's stuck his neck out for you. He deserves to know what he's involved in. The way he's had your back this whole time, I feel pretty confident he can be trusted. Tell him to contact the news media if you send him a signal that things are getting out of hand here. Paul could save us if things go badly for us."

"I had a similar plan for him. My package already includes instructions for activating the cylinders. The only problem is the master computer. Without it, nothing will work," Spencer explained.

"Maybe we'll be able to ship the computer to Paul the minute you return from Phamuria." Antonio winked.

"Antonio, you make it sound as if it will be easy to make another visit to Phamuria with the CIA guarding the capsule twenty four hours a day, seven days a week." Spencer sighed.

"You leave that to me."

Spencer smiled. If anyone could pull this off, it was Antonio.

Spencer returned to his apartment. As he turned to close his door, two agents were getting out of a black sedan. He sighed, close the door, and sat down at his computer. Getting the message to Paul would be tricky. The only way he could tell the whole story would be on some type of encrypted program. He started by outlining the whole incredible story to Paul. He saved the file on an encrypted USB stick. He had sent the code for the encryption with the last package. Later that evening he handed off the USB stick to Antonio, who would have his secretary over-night it to Paul's work. When he returned home, he sat down at his computer again.

Hi Paul, I am sorry to hear about the new coffee shop being closed. I will be detained in Egypt for a while and unfortunately am not able to come home yet. I need a favor from you. Please contact my Mom in Virginia and tell her that I'm doing fine and will write very soon. I'm chicken to call her since I promised her I would be home by now By the way, she has a new phone number. It's 7739381551. Thanks Paul. Spencer.

Paul would understand his message once he tried to read the USB stick. Since the CIA was setting up camp at the mine site, this was probably his last opportunity to contact Paul without difficulties. Things would soon be different, very different. He tried to sleep, but his mind kept spinning and the constant danger had his heart pounding. He finally drifted off with the image of Roula in his mind and an odd sense of comfort that the CIA was outside her door.

CHAPTER

EIGHTEEN

"Sir?" a voice said from the entrance of the FOU. "Sir, I think you need to wake up.

"What the devil's going on?" Detton asked, still groggy with sleep. The ground beneath him seemed to be rumbling. "What's that noise?"

"Sir, we have a motorcade approaching at high speed. Patrol informs me that it's a convoy of Egyptian troops."

"Shit! What time is it?"

"Ten minutes past oh-six-hundred, sir!" The captain stood at attention but averted his eyes. "The place is secure, sir," he added.

"Thank you, Captain. Get Steve in here and get hold of Mr. Casenza immediately. Tell him I want him here on the double." Detton was wide awake now and stepping into his trousers. He was not about to let a couple of Egyptian troops uproot his precious discovery.

"Sir, Mr. Casenza's already here. He arrived at about oh-four-hundred with Mr. Spencer and Ms. Grazulis."

"What?" Detton fumed. "Why wasn't I informed of this? Who authorized their entry?"

"Sir, Mr. Sullivan did. He didn't see any reason to wake you so early."

Detton was hastily dressing while listening to the captain. He excused himself as he slammed the bathroom door and told the captain to wait a minute.

"Good morning, Tom," Steve said as Detton came out of the bathroom. "I see you have been briefed regarding our visitors." Steve handed Detton a steaming cup of coffee. He had seated himself in front of the large monitors that had recently been installed in the FOU. The captain was nowhere in sight.

Detton swung open the door and looked out across the desert. A caravan of vehicles was fast approaching the site creating a long stream of dust at least a mile long.

"What the hell is going on, Steve?" Tom blurted.

"Well, a lot's happened since last night when that little prick left in such a huff," Steve said, referring to Abdul. "Apparently our friend Abdul went right to the Egyptian prime minister after our visit and demanded to know what was going on."

"Our Secretary of State was detained for twenty four hours in the States and Abdul wouldn't wait for other diplomatic appearances. He's convinced the Egyptian prime minister to send out a military patrol. They're going to demand that we shut down the mine immediately." Steve hesitated before adding. "And word has it that Abdul has orders to go down into the mine himself to see what's going on."

"That asshole's been more trouble." Detton ran his fingers through his hair and sighed.

"I'm guessing that he thinks we are smuggling the gold out of Egypt. He is not aware of our find. At least, this is what Antonio tells me."

I think he knows the gold story is a bunch of shit," Detton said. "He wants to know what's down there, and we've got to stop him." Detton took a few sips from the hot coffee and grunted. "Send him down the mine, huh? I'll send him down the mine all right. When did all this take place?" Detton asked, irritably.

"I received an urgent call from Antonio Casenza at about three this morning. He suggested we bring in Spencer and Roula to work on the hieroglyphics immediately. Antonio said he would take care of Abdul when he got here." Steve poured himself a cup of coffee and sat back down at the computer station. "We just thought you'd want to be there, sir."

Detton stood in the center of the room staring at Steve. "What the hell was Spencer doing here at four in the morning?"

"Oh, that. Antonio actually came up with a good plan. He suggested we send Spencer and Roula down to the cave and then close off the tunnel temporarily until the situation with Abdul is diffused. We gave them plenty of oxygen, removed all the guards from the cave and blasted closed a small section of the tunnel passage leading to the man-lift."

"You did what?"

"I, uh . . . actually thought it was a pretty damned brilliant idea," Steve stammered. "We let Abdul take a look inside the mine and satisfy himself that what we have down there is exactly what we say we have down there. Once he sees that the tunnel did collapse, and once we show him the contamination zone, he won't bother us anymore. By then our prime minister will have worked out all the details with Egypt's president."

Tom paced around the small space but said nothing.

"This way we don't lose any time, either. Spencer and Roula went right to work this morning. They're being very cooperative. I think they want to know what's inside that thing as much as we do."

Detton remained silent. His mind was racing. He had been put in charge of the most important discovery in human history, and he had a bunch of assholes running around making decisions while he slept.

Steve looked at Detton with wide eyes. "Since Antonio is the expert with the locals, I felt his plan merited implementation . . ." He shrugged, obviously unsure of whether or not he'd done the right thing.

"All right, Steve, I think you made the right decision." Detton lowered his voice. "In the future, though, make sure you consult with me on these decisions. I don't care if it's three o'clock in the goddamned morning.

"Yes, sir."

"I hate to have to face that prick again, but at least we aren't losing valuable time. Hopefully Roula will tell us what the writing is all about once we open the tunnel." Detton gulped down the last of his coffee. "After that we'll figure out what to do with those two.

CHAPTER NINETEEN

Spencer and Roula entered the truth chamber. The mammoth structure towered above them. Roula was in awe of how deftly Antonio had masterminded a plan to get them back inside the capsule. Collapsing the tunnel had been a brilliant idea. It would give them valuable time inside Phamuria. She drew a deep breath of Phamuria's fresh air. It felt great to be back in the midst of the bittersweet beauty of the once superior civilization.

As they approached, Neflani turned and smiled. Neflani's appearance had changed dramatically. Her hair had streaks of gray and her face, although still lovely, was scored with deep lines.

"You have arrived at a different time in our history." Neflani said simply. She escorted them along a long hallway leading to an immense hall. Once inside, a number of figures stood in the distance. Roula watched Neflani's expressive face and sadness tugged at her heart. It was as if Neflani was someone she had known before. But that couldn't be. It was probably just that she had spent so much time with her back in Spencer's apartment. In that time, Neflani had become like a friend to her. She sighed. But that was just her mind playing tricks on her; she was befriending a ghost.

"This is our . . . prayer room," Neflani explained. Here our elders pray to the Creator and meditate."

They had reached the foot of what Roula perceived was some type of altar. An elderly man dressed in an elegant magenta and gold colored robe stood up to greet them. "Greetings."

"Oh, my God." Roula said.

"What?" Spencer asked.

We are in the presence of Samir," she said.

Samir looked as though many decades had passed since they'd last seen him. He must have been under great stress, knowing that his people were soon to be destroyed. His hair was white and his blue eyes sat deep in the sockets. His once mighty height had fallen considerably and his back was stooped. His regal attire had not changed, nor had his level of confidence and authority. He was calm and soft-spoken. "It is important that you understand certain things about our culture and our history. Now that you have become more familiar with this great land, all of our efforts will not have been in vain." Samir spoke with the same authority he had shown during their first visit. “This time I am going to take you on a journey that will detail our history’s most relevant achievements . . . and disasters,” Samir explained.

Roula had chosen the cylinders that would describe the actual catastrophe that led to the final destruction of the Phamurian civilization, a decision she was starting to regret.

Neflani motioned for them to follow Samir. The group entered one of the many transportation crafts stationed around the structure. The craft took them through the South region of Phamuria. Within minutes, they reached a volcanically active stretch of land. The immediate area was pitted with steam vents and old craters. Signs of recent eruptions were visible in the distance. Here the landscaping resembled the Sahara that this land would eventually become, very different from the lush Phamuria they had seen on their first tour.

“This region is called the Valley of Death,” Samir said. “Not long ago this area was flourishing and was one of our main agricultural resources. During the last hundred years of our existence, violent eruptions transformed this place into what you are seeing today. Accounts of our final days were recorded, with heroic effort I might add, so that you and future civilizations could witness our destruction firsthand.” Samir’s voice shook and he turned to keep them from seeing the tears in his eyes.

Roula and Spencer looked at the ground respectfully.

“Quickly,” Samir coughed. We must return to the main city before it’s too late. If we stay here, we’ll soon be covered in lava and ash and you’ll be thrown back into your own time.”

Samir took them above the city. He stopped and stood in a square that overlooked the city of Phamuria. The view was breathtaking.

“This reminds me of the view from Piazzale Michelangelo in Florence, Italy.” Roula choked back a sob. Far to the south plumes of thick black smoke filled the air. There was a low rumble and then the earth shook violently beneath their feet. Roula’s knees began to quiver and she fell to the ground.

“Are you all right?” Spencer stretched out his arm to grab her.

She managed a nod, but her eyes had filled with tears.

"It's time," Samir whispered. "You are witnessing our last hours. Soon this land will no longer exist. Hundreds of people were running through the streets. A variety of flying crafts took off from the East and dozens of other crafts rushed in every direction. The rumbling sounds became louder and louder. There were screams. Panic was spreading.

"Our citizens have been warned daily," Samir continued, "but many did not want to believe this would happen. What you see are people hoping to escape. Unfortunately, many of us know that escape is not possible. We have chosen to die with dignity." Samir was looking below and sadly shaking his head. "The force of nature is the ultimate force. Great civilizations will rise and fall, but nature moves on its own agenda and stops for no one."

There were several eruptions in the distance. The blasts were deafening. Explosion after explosion hurled molten rock into space. Huge boulders hurled into distant buildings. The city below broke into pandemonium. The sky was turning black and breathing was becoming difficult. Somebody close by was screaming frantically. Roula turned around looking for the source of the scream. It was coming from her own throat. She looked to Spencer. The horror of the situation was reflected in his eyes. "Take me back, Ralph. I want to go home . . . Please, get me out of here."

Samir rested his hand on here shoulder. She looked at the long, bony fingers in surprise. It was the first time any of the Phamurians had actually touched her. She could actually feel the warmth of his hand.

"We are witnessing the very beginning," Samir said. "The destruction will not be complete for three days. You are safe for now."

A large flaming boulder flew through the sky and hit a flying craft, disintegrating it instantly. Screams could now be heard from every direction as families scrambled to safety. Roula wept on Spencer's shoulder.

Samir pointed to the south at what appeared to be a massive lava flow. "The lava moved so violently and quickly that many people remained trapped in their homes. The flow was estimated to be several hundred feet thick and traveled at speeds well over a hundred twenty five miles per hour. Judging from the depth of our time capsule, this lava flow went on for several months, maybe years, covering everything below. Only the Great Pyramid, erected at a much higher elevation, was spared."

To the north huge steam clouds rose into the sky. Spencer tightened his hold on Roula. She looked up into his eyes. Watching the destruction was clearly as painful for him as it was for her. But neither of them could stop watching. They were transfixed. They had to remember.

"What you see there is lava hitting the outer ice glaciers and melting them," Samir explained. "Much of Phamuria was flooded by the rapidly melting glaciers around it. Fire and water; the two elements essential to our planet . . . and the same two elements that destroyed our beloved land. Come, let's proceed back to the time capsule. I think you have had enough of this and I want to make sure that the last cylinders recording this event are safely stored in the capsule's inner chamber."

Roula stared at Samir in disbelief. The placement of the cylinders was surely academic by now since they were witnessing this disaster and therefore the cylinders did make it into the capsule. It was a reminder of just how far from this disaster they really were.

The terrain leading to the capsule was shaking constantly under their feet. People were running in every direction, panic reflected in their brilliant blue eyes. The chaos was mounting to a fever pitch. Roula shut out the thought of the terrible days awaiting these gentle people.

Neflani had a faint smile full of sadness as she showed Roula and Spencer inside the capsule. Chunks of hot rock were falling all around them and the roaring of the exploding mountains could still be heard. The capsule stood, majestic, in the center of the square surrounded by workers and technicians rushing to finish documenting its contents.

They entered the capsule and turned to look at Neflani and Samir, possibly for the last time. Neflani smiled and waved. Samir looked away as if he could not endure this last moment. Neflani closed the door behind them. Roula looked at Spencer in panic as the capsule began to shake and sink underground.

"Stop narration." Spencer ordered.

Immediately they were hurled into a tunnel of light and rocketed back to reality.

"Roula," Spencer whispered, holding her tightly against him. He was shaking and compulsively brushing at his clothing as if to remove the ash that would have covered him back in Phamuria. They sat in dark silence, thinking of their long dead friends, wrapped in each other's arms, crying.

"That really happened." She hugged him as if still needing protection. "We . . . we were there."

"What we have here is an incredible tool capable of first-hand teaching about an advanced civilization that's long gone. A civilization no one on earth today knows ever existed. We have a responsibility to protect it." Spencer gasped out the words. He seemed to be having trouble breathing.

"Are you okay?" Roula asked.

"Yeah, I just can't bear to remember." He looked at his watch. We've been in the capsule just under three hours." He placed the master computer and the cylinders in the backpack and looked around the chamber.

"What're you doing?" she asked.

"Making sure not to leave any evidence behind."

They exited the capsule and Roula closed the main door. They walked toward the area where the tunnel had collapsed.

"How long did Matt tell you it would take for them to reach us?" Roula said with a quiver in her voice. She cleared her throat, not wanting Spencer to know how nervous she was.

"This is very soft, collapsed material. With the drilling equipment at Matt's disposal, we should see him in less than two hours," Spencer reassured her. She hugged him and gently kissed his lips. Her eyes searched his. They held each other, exhausted, disturbed, and baffled by what they had witnessed.

Spencer looked sadly at Roula. "I'm sure that the NSA will take over as soon as this little crisis with Egypt is resolved. They are the experts in codes and language interpretation."

"I'm sure you're right, but I doubt they've ever tackled hieroglyphics as a national security problem." Roula laughed.

"The NSA has unlimited funds and unlimited talent. Trust me, they'll take over the minute Tom gives them the word. They probably would have already if they knew what was going on here."

"You know," Spencer said, "Steve told me the NSA monitors all communications globally and decodes every transmission on every line from every country. They tap into all long distance calls and download them to special computers where research can be conducted on suspicious language and conversation."

"What do you mean?" Roula was confused. She had no idea that her own government monitored all calls and stored them in their computers. "Sounds like an invasion of privacy to me," she protested.

"Well yes, of course, but in the shadow of protecting our national security, the NSA is above all that nonsense of privacy." Spencer chucked and shook his head. He could only laugh at the irony. "Say you make a call home and in talking to your uncle or whomever, you mention this project and use the word gold in your conversation. If the NSA is doing research on conversations containing the word gold, your conversation will be flagged as will a multitude of others that have the word gold in them. The computer program translates the conversation if it's in another language, and flags the word gold in all the conversations. Then, if anything suspicious comes across, they have you."

"I'd like to see them do it with hieroglyphics." Roula laughed.

"You have a point. I imagine that's the reason Detton allowed us to be involved. In fact, that's probably the reason Detton and Steve are still involved themselves. Even the NSA might have to do a little research in order to come up with their best linguist in hieroglyphics." Spencer replied.

"Did you hear that?" Roula sat up and moved closer to the tunnel entrance.

"Matt must be getting close. We'll tell them that we were unable to gain access, but are getting very close to breaking the hieroglyphics code."

"What's going to happen next?" Roula tried to keep the panic out of her voice. She wasn't sure who would be at the other end of the tunnel once it opened and was even less sure of what that person might do or say.

"If we play our cards right, Antonio will have things under control and will know what to do next. My main concern is making this master computer and the cylinders disappear. I just hope none of the CIA agents thinks to check my backpack."

"Since they have no idea that we've opened the capsule, there shouldn't really be any strict scrutiny of our personal belongings."

Spencer sighed. "That's what I'm hoping."

The noise was getting louder. It would be only a few minutes before the workers broke through. Roula looked once more at the massive capsule in the distance and her mind was transported back to Phamuria. She could recall every detail of the fresh air and magnificent glaciers. The people of Phamuria, especially, Neflani and Samir, were her most treasured memory. Their accomplishments, their gentle souls, were irreplaceable. Why did it all feel so familiar to her? It was like going home.

Matt grinned as he emerged from the new opening. "Welcome back." He had fresh drinks and a fresh supply of oxygen for them.

Roula took long swallows of the water while Spencer gulped from the water bottle until it was empty, barely stopping for breath.

"Thirsty much?" Matt laughed.

"More than I realized, must've been all those white glaciers and fresh air that did it," Spencer replied.

"Aren't they virtual reality?" Matt asked surprised.

Spencer said nothing, but looked over Matt's shoulder. Along with Matt there were three trusted miners. They were all smiling at them. "Where's the CIA?"

Matt grinned. "I told them it would be a couple more hours before we broke through. Those goons are scared shitless to be down here in the dark. They're not about to come this deep into the earth unless they have to." He chuckled.

"Abdul?"

"He's been here and gone.

Roula let out a huge sigh.

"Good work." Spencer patted him on the back. "We're safe for now." That meant the backpack would be safe from scrutiny for now as well.

Once out of the line of sight of the CIA cameras, Spencer and Roula packed the remaining cylinders into the backpack. Once they got to the surface, the CIA would be looking very carefully at every move he made. Matt was his only chance to get the cylinders to a safe place and away from the CIA. "Matt, can you get my backpack to the surface without being noticed?"

Matt gave him another of his infamous grins. He walked to the far side of the lift and opened an oversized toolbox. "Let me have it," he said.

Spencer handed it to him gingerly. "Make sure Antonio gets it without anybody looking in it," Spencer whispered. "Tell Antonio to put it somewhere safe until I have a chance to get it back."

Matt nodded. "I'll guard it with my life." He laid the backpack in the toolbox, clipped the lock shut, and carried it to the lift.

It was true; Matt would have done anything for Spencer. Their time together on the project had made them very close friends.

"Who's waiting for us up there?" Spencer asked in a strained voice.

"Don't know," Matt answered with a shrug, "but Antonio and Mr. McPearson were working on a diversion. All we can do is hope the coast will be clear."

Five military guards and two CIA agents surrounded the lift at the surface. "I broke through faster than I thought," Matt said with his usual affable grin.

The CIA agents glared at him but said nothing. They would be in hot water if Detton knew they had been on the surface when the crew broke through.

"Where's Tom Detton?" Spencer asked one of the agents.

The man pointed to the FOU.

"Thanks."

Matt heaved the locked toolbox off the lift and headed toward the shed. Spencer took Roula's hand and led her to the FOU. "Don't be scared. Just stick to the story and we'll be fine. They have no reason not to believe us.

"Well?" Detton snapped the moment he laid on eyes on Spencer, "We are all waiting to hear your explanation. Were you able to gain access and get inside?"

The CIA had been filming their movements. They already knew that he and Roula had been inside. "Yes," Spencer replied with huge smile.

"It was incredible gentlemen," Roula said. "My computer program translated the decoding of the outer door and we were able to open it. Once inside, we found a very large, adorned hallway that led us to yet another inner-chamber—"

"The inner-chamber was locked," Spencer added.

"And I was able to film the inscriptions on the door. We didn't have enough time to de-code the second set of hieroglyphics."

Spencer nodded his head in agreement. Would the CIA buy their story? They would not have been able to film anything inside the inner chamber so they had no reason to doubt what he and Roula were telling them.

"Hot damn," Steve said.

"Incredible . . ." McPearson had a look of wonder on his face as if he was hearing all this for the first time. "Absolutely incredible."

"I promise you, sir, I'll work on the encryption program until I've cracked the code." Roula gave Tom Detton one of her irresistible smiles. "This is just so damned exciting . . . Once we have the code, I'd like a chance to get back down and open the inner-chamber door."

Detton stood up and walked to where Roula stood. "Let me be the first to congratulate you on a job well done," he said. He took her right hand and shook it with a firm grip.

Roula's eyes were wide with surprise. She accepted his compliment without so much as a blink. "Thank you, sir," she managed to blurt out.

Spencer breathed a mental sigh of relief. They had protected Phamuria for a little while longer. That was all he could hope for right now. His thoughts were reeling with images of the ancient civilization. How could such a land exist? How could those people be so harmonious and yet so advanced? Was this all real? So much was happening, how could he keep it straight in his mind? A shiver ran down his spine as he thought of the strange sensation he'd had on the day the master computer read his brain. Had the machine altered his thinking in some way? Now that they were safe, exhaustion set in. He looked at Roula and saw it in her eyes as well.

"If it's okay with all of you, I'm really exhausted and would like to get some sleep," Roula said as if reading Spencer's mind.

"I have to admit that this whole experience underground with very little oxygen has gotten to me." Spencer muttered. "I could use some rest as well.

"He's right," Detton said. "I think we've accomplished enough for today. Let's let these two rest and we'll re-group tomorrow." With that, Tom rose and proceeded to the door.

Spencer and Roula returned to her apartment with the usual CIA agents following behind. By this point Spencer didn't even care. The pair fell into bed without a word. Their claim of exhaustion was not an exaggeration. Spencer had barely fallen asleep when the ring of his cell phone woke him. He sat up in bed, still half asleep. "Hello," he said in a gruff voice.

"I'm sorry," Antonio said, "did I wake you?"

"Yeah, yeah you did," Spencer mumbled. Antonio's voice sounded far away and distorted. Spencer held the phone away from his ear for a moment and shook his head trying to clear the cobwebs of sleep. "I heard the great news from Tom, congrats!" Antonio obviously though the line was tapped. "This calls for a celebration, dinner's on me tonight. I'll pick you up at say six thirty?" Antonio insisted.

"Uh, yeah, okay," He glanced over at Roula's sleeping form. She looked so vulnerable. He didn't want to leave her side for even a minute.

"I'd like this to be just the two of us," Antonio said as if he'd understood Spencer's silence.

"Roula deserves to celebrate more than any of us."

"You're right, and we'll plan a party when we meet for dinner, okay?"

"Sure, okay."

"See you tonight then." Antonio hung up without waiting for Spencer to respond.

Spencer was waiting outside of Roula's apartment at six thirty when Antonio pulled up in an unfamiliar long black luxury car.

"Nice car," Spencer said as he opened the door.

"We need to talk," Antonio said as soon as Spencer slid into the back seat. "I have this car as a favor . . . but I only have about an hour. We can speak safely here." Antonio signaled for the driver to go. "You did very well, Spencer. I'm impressed."

"Thanks, but you didn't ask me to meet alone to tell me that."

"No, no I didn't." Antonio told the driver to turn onto a narrow residential street. The man was driving less than ten miles an hour. "You and Roula are in a serious situation here. I believe that the cylinders you snuck out of the time capsule will be the only things keeping you and Roula safe once Detton finds out what's going on."

"But they still need us." Spencer objected.

"This is true." Antonio paused to open a small bar in front of him. Two crystal glasses rose on a small platform along with several bottles of alcohol. Antonio poured himself a whiskey on the rocks and looked inquisitively at Spencer. Spencer nodded. Antonio took a drink and then continued. "They need you for now Spencer, and they need Roula especially, with her talent for deciphering hieroglyphics. However, once they're inside, they will no longer need you."

"But they will still need the cylinders," Spencer said, feigning a confidence he didn't feel.

"And that will keep you involved," Antonio said. "But think about it, you and Roula will be on the run, very likely for the rest of your lives. If they find out about those cylinders, and they will, the CIA will stop at nothing to get them."

Spencer was quiet for a moment. He trusted Antonio and he had a great deal of respect for the man. He looked out the rear window at the black car that followed them and shuddered.

"Don't worry about them," Antonio said.

"It's hard not to. They're everywhere I go now." He took a swig of the whiskey Antonio had handed him. "What should we do, Antonio?"

Antonio smiled. "My friend, there is only one answer," Antonio said as he raised his glass. "And I know just what it is." He clinked Spencer's glass and smiled.

An hour later Antonio dropped Spencer off at Roula's apartment. Roula opened the door and rushed into his arms. "I'm sorry to be such a scaredy-cat," she said into his shoulder. "It's just getting so dangerous now—"

"Let's go inside, sweetheart," he said. "Everything is going to be just fine." He looked over his shoulder at the agents who stood in the parking lot smoking cigarettes. He'd never get used to that.

He pulled her inside and closed the door. He poured them both drinks and they sat down on the couch.

Roula reached for the music player that she carried everywhere, pulled out the earphones and popped it into the small speaker system. She pushed a few buttons and the room filled with a melodic jazz tune. She reached for his hand and pulled him off the sofa. "Let's dance," she said.

He slid his arms around her small waist and she wrapped her arms around his neck. They stood in one place, swaying with the rhythm of the music. He nibbled at her ear and then whispered what he and Antonio had decided.

"I'll be so glad when all this is over," she whispered. "When we can go back to our normal lives . . . whatever that is.

"We'll have a wonderful life together . . . I promise," he said.

"I've been meaning to ask you . . . uh . . . that is, I . . ."

"What is it, Roula?"

"Well, don't you think it's strange . . . those feelings we get when we visit Phamuria? You know, how it seems kind of familiar and . . . comfortable . . . like home?"

"Yeah, I suppose so. I think you're more sensitive to that that I am . . . but I think I know what you're talking about."

She looked up at him. "What do you think it means?"

"Well, I haven't given it too much though, but in a way it makes sense. Think about it. The master computer had total access to our minds . . . all our memories, thoughts, feelings – everything."

"Right."

"And it has access to the entire history of Phamuria . . . all of the people that lived there . . . the entire history. That's an astounding amount of information. It makes sense that a computer so powerful would be capable of helping us draw connections. You know, this place looks a bit like that place from my childhood, or this person smiles a little like another person I used to know. That happens even in our own realities without an entirely different one superimposed on us. I imagine it's even possible that the master computer could interchange some of the events of Phamuria with those of our own present day lives."

"Do you really think that's it? Will it hurt us?"

"No, I don't think so. Even if we don't fully understand it, I trust the Phamurians. I don't believe they would do anything to hurt us." Spencer looked at Roula's face. She seemed to relax, tension draining from her face.

"Poor thing," he said, caressing her cheek, "This has all been really hard on you hasn't it?"

Roula smiled thinly, "Maybe that effect is only temporary" she said almost to herself.

"What effect?"

"The feeling is so strong . . . like I've actually been in Phamuria before. I even knew what places would look like before we got there. It confuses me."

He brushed his hand along her cheek. "I don't know, darling. We'll remember to ask Neflani or Samir about it . . . if we ever get back there that is. I think the stress has been really hard on both of us." He stroked her neck and back. "We should try to relax for the rest of the night. I feel like I've barely seen you, and I've been at your side practically every moment."

There was a sudden knock on the door and Roula jumped. "Who could be here at this hour?"

Spencer shrugged. "Maybe Antonio came back for some reason."

"Maybe the agents want something." Roula turned off the music while Spencer went to answer the door.

Abdul stood in the doorway with a red face and tightly clenched teeth. In an instant he was holding a gun to Spencer's head

CHAPTER

TWENTY

"Move inside," Abdul said.

Spencer held his hands in the air. He looked over Abdul's shoulder for the agents, but no one was in sight.

"Move."

Spencer took one step backwards into the apartment, and then another. Abdul gave him a shove and then kicked the door closed behind him.

"Abdul, I—"

"Shut your mouth!" Abdul waved the gun in Spencer's face.

"Where are the CIA agents? What have you done with them?

"You and your CIA. You think you can trick Abdul!" Like before, dry flecks of spittle flew from the man's mouth.

"What are you doing Abdul?" Roula shouted, taking a step toward him.

"Roula, no. Stay where you are," Spencer said. "Abdul, why don't you calm down and tell me what this is all about?"

"All about! All about! This is about you and your government stealing what is rightfully Egypt's from our own land, right under our noses. This is about you and your CIA thinking that we are too stupid to notice what you're doing and then . . . and then, telling us to . . . to . . . how did that son-of-a-bitch Detton put it? Telling us to 'cool it' and let the U.S. handle it. How dare you?"

"Abdul just calm down and tell us what you're doing here. You know perfectly well that we have no control over any of this. We're being told what to do just the same as you." Spencer tried to reason with him. The man was clearly coming unhinged. Abdul looked at him with narrowed eyes. "No one makes a fool of Abdul," he added in a low snarl that was far more frightening than the shouting.

Spencer lowered his hands slightly. "Abdul, listen to me—"

"At first," he said, "I thought I would just shoot that bastard Detton right where he stood. Then I thought I had a better answer. He needs the two of you, that much is clear. I thought I'd just kidnap you and then see what they have to say about this bullshit biological contamination. But now that I'm here, I see there is another option." He turned to Roula with sneer. "You've served me well before . . . Now I have one more task for you. Only this time, it isn't your precious Visa at stake—"

Spencer looked at Roula. Her eyes were wide and her face was as white as death. "Roula, what's he talking about?"

Abdul laughed. "So you haven't told him what a good little spy you are?" Abdul said.

"I'm sorry," Roula said to Spencer and then she was sobbing.

"I'm sorry," Abdul mimicked her. "She's not sorry," he said, "not sorry at all."

A sharp pain of realization ripped through Spencer's heart. "My God."

Abdul laughed. "She was so easy. She'd do anything to keep her Visa. She's nothing more than an ambitious little slut.

"Shut up!" Spencer yelled despite the gun Abdul held to his head. He needed to think. The woman he had fallen in love with was a spy. She'd been spying on him. She had set him up and then had lied to his face. Anger rushed to his head. How could he have been so stupid . . . so naïve? Roula had betrayed him and he'd fallen for her anyway like a boulder falls over a cliff.

Roula brushed back her tears and moved toward him.

"No," Spencer said. "Just stay where you are. And to think I thought you loved me." Spencer said bitterly. "What a fool I am."

"I do love you, Ralph," she whispered. "Please, just let me explain . . . Abdul wanted to know why you had a satellite up-link." She sobbed. "I did it . . . I'm the one who tapped your feed. I did it just like he ordered me to. He said the transmission was from Washington and not Calpetro. He said he thought the American CIA was trying to steal from Egypt."

"How much do they know, Roula?" Spencer asked again calmly.

Abdul grunted. "We know enough."

"He could only get audio and it wasn't of very good quality. I knew that most of the time the transmission would be garbled." Roula started sobbing again. "Please, Ralph, you have to understand . . . I needed to keep my Visa . . . I had to stay in Egypt.

"Why didn't you tell me the truth?"

"I thought you'd hate me . . . that you wouldn't trust me. And besides, you had already found the feed and disconnected it. I couldn't see the point—"

"The point," Spencer said through gritted teeth, "Would have been telling me the truth."

"Enough of this," Abdul said. "You can sort out your silly lover's spat later. As to my option . . ."

"What option is that?" Spencer asked, bracing himself for the worst.

"You are going to take me down into the mine. Now. Tonight. You're going to show me what all this is about once and for all. And then we will decide what happens next and who is in control here." Abdul began to chuckle to himself. "Come on," he yelled. "Get moving!"

Spencer moved slowly and reached for Roula's hand. Not matter what she'd done, he had gotten her into this and it was his responsibility to protect her. "It's okay," he said. We had better do what the man says."

"That's right." Abdul laughed. "Do what the man with the gun says, Roula."

Spencer considered his own options. Abdul was at least thirty years older than he was and in poor health. Wrestling the gun from him would probably be rather easy. But then what would they do with him? No, he had to get past his own anger. There was a better way to handle this. "Wait," he said, "I need to get something."

"You need nothing," Abdul warned.

"If you want to see what's down there, you'll let me get what I need."

Abdul grabbed Roula's arm and pulled her to him. He put his fat arm around her throat and held the gun to her head. "Go."

Spencer walked backwards toward the bedroom, his hands in the air, and then slipped into the bedroom.

"If you're not back in ten seconds, she's dead."

Spencer reappeared a moment later with his backpack slung over his back. Roula's eyes, wild and glassy, stared at the backpack. She looked as though she might faint.

Abdul gave Roula a shove toward Spencer. "Let's go," he said.

They walked from the apartment to the car with Abdul holding the gun behind them, Roula stole a glance in Spencer's direction. "Please . . ." she said.

Spencer, who was facing away from Abdul, nodded. "Just do as he says and it'll be fine."

Roula looked from Spencer to the backpack, blinked twice, but said nothing more. They all piled into the cab that was waiting outside the apartment. There was no sign of the CIA agents. What had Abdul done with them?

The drive to the dig was in silence. The air was as thick with tension as it was with humidity. Spencer and Roula led Abdul to the secret lift and helped him make his way down into the depths to the time capsule. Abdul sweated profusely, his breathing was labored, and his eyes bulged with fear, but he said nothing. They stopped at the edge of the tunnel. Two guards were standing outside the main entry doors chatting amiably.

Abdul gasped as he caught a glimpse of the outer shell of the time capsule. His jaw dropped and the gun hung slack in his hand.

"What . . . what the hell is that?"

"That is a time capsule. It holds the entire recorded history of an ancient civilization," Spencer said calmly.

Roula stared at Spencer with her own jaw slack. She surely thought he was crazy.

Abdul took a deep breath and put his hand up against his chest as if to slow down his heartbeat.

"Follow behind me closely," Abdul said. He reached into his jacket pocket and took out a silencer. In a few deft movements, he attached it to his gun, reached around the corner, and shot first one guard and then the other. Roula seemed to struggle for breath. Spencer remained silence. He needed to stay calm for the both of them. It was clear now what Abdul had done with the agents outside of Roula's apartment. The CIA wouldn't let that one go. They didn't take the death of their agents lightly. It would only be a matter of minutes before they showed up.

"You're insane," Roula said to Abdul. She went to the fallen men and felt for pulses. "They're both dead."

"Who cares," Abdul pointed the gun at the capsule entry. "Open it."

Roula moved past the dead agents and laid her hand on the door. She looked at Spencer with a question in her eyes. Should she open it?

Spencer nodded.

Roula entered the code to the inner chamber and the door slid away. Abdul pushed her aside and charged inside. Spencer and Roula followed him in.

"What the hell is this thing?" Abdul asked, brandishing the gun at Spencer.

"I've told you what it is, Abdul. Now let me show you how it works." Spencer zipped open a pocket inside the backpack and pulled out four cylinders. He then opened another pocket and brought out the small pyramid.

Roula looked up at him, disbelief reflected in her eyes. "Where did you get that?" she asked.

"I got it back from Matt just in case—"

"In case what? In case you wanted to let a madman into Phamuria?"

"Shut your mouth, bitch," Abdul said.

"Roula, please . . ." Spencer turned back to Abdul. "I will place these four cylinders into this small pyramid. This is a master computer. Once the cylinders are spinning at the correct speed, you will be transported to a virtual representation of Phamuria, the ancient civilization that built this place.

"You mean it's a time machine?" Abdul asked.

"No. It's more like virtual reality. You won't be able to change anything. Just remember to say return me to my time," Spencer said. "Are you ready, sir?"

Abdul nodded, "Do it."

Spencer inserted the cylinders and waited to make certain Abdul had been transported. In an instant, Roula turned on him. "Are you crazy? Why would you send him to Phamuria?"

"Roula, the man would have killed us. He knew something was here and he would have found out what at all costs. We have to think only of our survival now."

Roula grabbed Spencer's hand. Her eyes searched his. "What are you talking about?"

Spencer glanced at the four spinning cylinders and then back at Roula.

"Oh, my God." She held her hand to her mouth. "Do we have to?"

"I don't think there's any other way."

A strange tugging sensation pulled at Abdul's insides. He was suddenly nauseous. He looked around and the blood drained from his face. Strange pyramidal buildings surrounded him. People were milling about all around him. Strange, oddly dressed people. They all wore hats . . . hats like he had never seen before. He appeared to be in some kind of marketplace. A small boy wandered past him. He was eating what looked to be some kind of fruit . . . small, dark purple, strange fruit. Abdul grabbed the child by the arms and shook him.

"Where am I boy? What is this place?"

The boy's eyes lit up in alarm. He shook his head and struggled to free himself.

"Are you deaf, little brat? I said where the hell am I?" The boy still said nothing, but looked up at Abdul with wide eyes.

Abdul, furious and frightened, smacked the boy across the face, sending him reeling. At this, the boy sat up and hollered loudly in a language Abdul could not understand. Abdul walked away from the boy, leaving him in the street like a piece of forgotten trash. He gazed around the marketplace as if he had just become aware of his surroundings. A vehicle whooshed by and then hovered in the air. Abdul looked around, realizing for the first time, what this discovery really meant. Those cars! Those cars alone could make him a billionaire!

A long dark shadow fell across Abdul. He looked up at a small, black hovercraft. It was oblong, but only about two feet long. The craft unfolded mechanical arms from under a black glassy surface. It dropped lower and grabbed Abdul under the arms.

"Let me down," he screamed.

The craft rose above the ground and then sped away. Abdul cried out and kicked his legs fruitlessly as he was carried off. Then, without warning, the tugging sensation in his mid-section came back, only this time it was agonizing. Oh God, he was going to vomit . . . and then there was only darkness.

Inside the inner chamber of the time capsule, Spencer yanked one cylinder out of the master computer, tossed it in the air, and then caught it again square in his palm. He smiled. "So sorry, Abdul, but you had to go." he said.

"My God, Ralph, we just killed a man." Roula said.

"Not a man . . . a maniac." He took her by the shoulders. "And we didn't kill him, he's just lost."

Roula stared at him. Her face was so pale, like a china doll.

"We had no choice."

She swallowed hard and nodded. "I know." She looked up into his eyes. "We have to go back."

"What? Where?"

"This is our last chance to return to Phamuria before the CIA takes over the time capsule. There are still so many unanswered questions. I mean, we can ask Neflani with just the master computer, of course . . . but this is the last chance for us to see for ourselves....to talk to Samir. I need to go, Ralph. Everything in my heart and soul is telling me that this last trip is vital. I know you're angry with me and probably never want to speak to me again . . . but please, do this one last thing for me."

"Of course." he nodded. "We'll go back."

Spencer replaced the cylinder and surrendered himself to being sucked through the tunnel. The trip into Phamuria was much easier when he was relaxed and didn't fight the sensations.

Roula's face had a slight green tint as they arrived on the square, but she still smiled weakly. "Thank you," she said.

"You have returned. Welcome." Neflani stated serenely. "Your friend is lost. He attempted to interact violently with the system. His desire to cause harm made him unwelcome here. We intended to hold him in the halls of justice until he understood the failing, but one of the cylinders was removed while he was here. He will not return."

"We understand," Spencer said.

Neflani turned to face Roula. "Now it is time, Roula. There is a reason your desire to return to Phamuria is so strong. It is time for you to know the truth. Please come with me. Samir wishes to speak with you."

Spencer and Roula exchanged glances. They traveled with Neflani to the truth chamber within a few minutes and were greeted by Samir. He looked much healthier and happier than the last time they had seen him—when he had been in Phamuria's future, at the brink of its destruction.

"Roula," Samir said. "I know why you are here. There is a lot to tell you and I'm afraid that it will not be easy for you."

Roula swallowed and held Spencer's hand with an iron grip. Her eyes stayed on Samir as she waited to find out what he had to say.

"You have felt sensations of familiarity. You have felt a tugging at your heartstrings here in Phamuria that did not, somehow, feel . . . correct. Am I right?"

Roula nodded.

"There is no easy way to tell you this." Samir sighed. "Your instincts are not leading you astray. You are, in fact, a Phamurian my dear. You are the last Phamurian."

Spencer and Roula gasped in unison.

"But how?" Spencer asked

"That's impossible." Roula said, her voice quavering.

Samir held up his hand and sighed. "Just wait. I will explain. When we built the time capsule and the master computer, we quickly realized that our expectations might be too high. We had no guarantee that the people who found the capsule would be able to get in, much less run the master computer or understand the cylinders."

"But it read our minds," Spencer objected.

"Yes it read your mind, once you got in and activated it." Samir sighed again. "I must ask that you not interrupt until I have told you everything. Time is short, and I gather from your thoughts, that you do not believe that you will be able to return." Spencer and Roula nodded.

"Now," Samir continued, "we needed some kind of guarantee. My daughter volunteered for this ultimate of sacrifices. We stored the contents of her mind . . . her memories, her feelings, and, perhaps most important of all, her language and knowledge of Phamurian culture in each of the sensors."

"Sensors?" Spencer interrupted, unable to help himself.

"Yes. That's what you found in the desert that day, and then again in your core sample."

Roula turned to Spencer. "What did you find in the desert?"

"It was a sensor," Samir answered. "There were many placed all around the time capsule and on the outer walls themselves. They were set to detach on contact. When you touched it, it transferred my daughter's essence to you.

"Yes . . . I felt something."

The transfer to you was only temporary. You were not an . . . appropriate . . . host. So her essence traveled with you until a permanent host could be found. Then, by chance, you rescued that young woman at the bottom of the pool?"

"But…" Roula said, and Samir held up his hand once again.

"That young Greek girl was traveling in Egypt and was, very conveniently I might add, a student of hieroglyphics. Fortunately, she died that day."

Roula put her hand to her throat. Her face had gone pale and her eyes were wide with fear. "What do you mean—"

Samir ignored the interruption. "The moment she died, Mr. Spencer, you were touching her, and my daughter's essence was received by the girl's body."

"That's right, I felt something then too—"

Samir nodded. "The master computer had specific instructions to find a suitable host that could accept her mind. The only possibility was a dying brain. This kept not only my daughter's mind alive, but merged it with the mind of the dead girl, keeping her life and memories alive as well." He turned to Roula. "You are a child born in two senses, my dear," he said. "Your body was born of a man and a woman like all people, but your mind is also the combination of two people. This was the only way that we could be sure that your home . . . Phamuria . . . would live on even after its destruction. We knew that you would be able to lead the people who found our capsule into its depths. We were confident that you would be able to decipher the mystery for them, my daughter."

Roula burst into tears and threw her arms around Samir's neck. At the same moment a glow emanated from the pair.

Spencer stood by silent, pale, and worried. "But Samir," he said. "Phamuria is a virtual reality now. Your daughter is virtual reality. If she is a Phamurian, how can she survive with me . . . in our time?"

"Never fear, Mr. Spencer," Samir reassured him. "You are hearing this now and that means that everything is settled."

Roula clung to Samir as if she was afraid to let him go, afraid to lose him for a second time.

"You see, if my daughter had not led you here within a certain period of time, her existence would have . . . how should I put this? Her existence would have—timed out. But each journey that you made to Phamuria allowed the system to incorporate my daughter's electrical impulses more tangibly with Roula's physical being. She is, by and large, the same woman that drowned in the pool."

Roula turned to look at Spencer for the first time since getting the news, and then her eyes quickly went back to Samir. "Your daughter saved my life."

"Yes, I suppose that's true," Samir said. Roula is now also a Phamurian. She is my daughter, perfectly integrated by this final visit, perfectly alive and well in your time. It is all that we hoped for."

"Roula, look at me," Spencer said.

She hesitated, but then turned toward Spencer.

"My God," Spencer gasped. Roula's eyes had turned the same brilliant blue as the other Phamurians. "Her eyes—" Spencer muttered.

Samir ignored him and looked down at Roula who was still clinging to his cloak.

"There is no going back, my dearest. Phamuria is gone. There is only the present and the future. Ours is the perfect union. We have preserved your life, and you have preserved ours." Roula clung to her father and wept.

"What was her name?" she managed.

"I was called Nala," Roula said.

"That is correct." Samir smiled and patted her head just the way any father would show affection for his child.

Roula wept in a way Spencer had never seen before. Was she weeping because of the familiarity of Phamuria or because of her own near death? It was impossible to tell. Perhaps it was both. Or perhaps it was the Nala part of her who knew the touch and voice of the master computer's version of Samir would never be the same as being comforted by the true weight of her father's arms.

Roula and Samir sat down together on the steps. They spoke in low whispers with Roula clinging to Samir's arm as if she was afraid to let him go. Her bright blue eyes never left Samir's face.

Neflani approached the pair with quiet steps. "I'm sorry, Nala, but it is time for you to go.

One look at Roula's face and a lump rose in Spencer's throat. She seemed both panicked and heartbroken.

Roula put on a brave smile as she said goodbye to her father and to her home world for the last time. "I will not forget, father," she said, hugging him in a long embrace.

"Good." He chuckled and tears came into his eyes. "I am so proud of you Nala . . . and Roula. While you are busy not forgetting, remember that you are loved, now and forever."

"I love you too, Father."

"Wait," Spencer said, "Her eyes . . .how will we explain . . ."

Samir gave him an anemic smile. "Her eyes will return to normal as soon as you leave Phamuria."

When Spencer and Roula returned to the inner chamber of the time capsule, Spencer held her tightly.

"What's wrong with my eyes?" Roula asked.

Spencer laid his hands on her shoulders. "Nothing, they're beautiful, like you." He pulled her into a tight embrace. God, if only he could keep her here, safe in his arms. "I can't believe how close I came to losing you," he whispered into her hair. "Thank God. Thank God, we went back."

She brushed the tears from her cheeks and looked up into his eyes. "Then you don't hate me?"

He looked into her large eyes that were once again the rich chocolate brown he had come to love. "I could never hate you, darling. It's no wonder you were willing to do just about anything to stay in Egypt. It was Nala, she needed to see her father . . . her homeland."

"Yes," Roula nodded. "I didn't understand it then, but now I know her thoughts, I feel her pain . . . and her love."

"You've been given an incredible gift."

They held each other for a few minutes, preparing themselves for what they knew would, by now, be waiting above ground. Spencer wiped Roula's tear stained face and kissed the tip of her nose.

She smoothed back her hair and gave him a weak smile. "I must look a mess."

"You look beautiful."

She gave him her best attempt at a smile, but the shadow in the wells of her eyes gave her away. "Ralph, we've got to protect Phamuria for future generations. Do you think Antonio's plan will work?"

Spencer pulled out the cylinders and stuffed them and the master computer into the backpack. "I'm going to leave this here."

"What . . . are you crazy?"

"If Antonio's plan works, it won't matter. If it doesn't work, well, I guess it won't matter at that point, either. We can only hope that he had enough time."

They came through the entrance hand-in-hand. Detton stood with a contingency of armed men. "You two are going to have to come with me now. We have a lot of questions that need answering, not the least of which is who killed our agents!" Detton's face turned beat red at the mention of his dead men.

Two officers flanked Spencer and then two more stepped between him and Roula, forcing their hands apart.

"Let's go," Detton said.

The group walked to a black sedan. Matt and McPearson stood helplessly outside of the FOU. Two agents Spencer had never seen before drove them to a small deserted building in the center of Cairo. The place stunk of motor oil and urine. Chunks of crumbled plaster covered the floor. The men led them to a small room with a beat-up table and two faded wooden chairs. A few moments later, Detton stepped into the room and closed the door behind him.

"What is this?" Spencer demanded.

"You." Detton pointed to Roula. "Sit here." He gestured to a chair then nodded to one of the agents who nodded back and went over to Roula. He tied her wrists and ankles.

"That's not necessary," Spencer protested. "We haven't done anything wrong."

The man ignored him and stuffed a dirty rag in Roula's mouth. Fear filled her eyes along with fat tears. She gagged on the rag and started to squirm, fighting against the restraints.

"Just breath through your nose," Spencer said.

Her screams came out like a distant rumble. Her face was now a deep crimson and her fear was palpable. She struggled against the ropes at her wrists but only succeeded in rubbing her tender skin raw.

"Roula, listen to me . . . You've got to stop struggling. Breathe through your nose and try to relax." Spencer breathed in and out slowly. "Come on, Baby, take my lead. "Just breathe . . . like this . . ."

"She'll be fine," Detton said as stepped between them. "Now, Mr. Spencer, please have a seat. His voice all but dripped with sarcasm as he gestured toward the second broken-down chair. "You are going to answer some questions. How well you answer these questions will determine how many questions Roula here will have to answer." He gave Spencer a meaningful look. "I think we understand each other."

Spencer nodded. His only choice now was to follow Antonio's plan to the letter and pray. How he hated watching Roula go through this. He had to protect her at all costs. "I don't know what you want from me," Spencer said, "You know as much as I do."

Detton pulled out his gun and backhanded him, ramming the butt of the gun into Spencer's nose.

Spencer's fingers went to his face. Blood gushed into his mouth, down his chin and collected into his hands. "What the fu—"

"Talk," Detton said.

He had to pretend that he wasn't going to talk for as long as possible. Antonio would need all the time he could get to set things in motion. "I've already told you—"

"You're lying . . . Tell me what's in that monstrosity."

"I don't know—"

Detton rammed a fist into his gut. "Stop lying to me."

Spencer doubled over. In an instant his lungs were void of oxygen. He tried to take a breath, but his throat was so constricted no air could get through. His stomach roiled and his mouth filled with bile. He spat blood and vomit at Detton's feet and then finally caught his breath. "You have no right—"

"We have every right," Detton snarled. "We're the CIA. Our job is to protect the good old US of A." He spoke through gritted teeth. "It's your duty, as a United States Citizen, to tell us what we want to know."

Spencer sat forward and rested his arms on his thighs. He held his head in his hands and spat another glob of blood onto the floor. His head lolled to the left and his eyes rolled into the back of his head.

"Jesus, what a mother-fucking pansy," Detton said, "You're not going to pass out on us." He grabbed Spencer by the hair and yanked his head back. "Wake up, you bastard."

Spencer kept his eyes rolled back and left his eyelids at half-mast. Let them think he was a pansy. If it bought him more time, it was worth it.

"Dammit," Detton shouted. "He's not going to tell us anything. Load up the serum into a hypodermic and we'll make her talk."

Shit!

Spencer rolled his head up. He had to speak up now, before they touched Roula.

"That won't be necessary, Tom," he mumbled. "It's a time capsule."

"What?"

"It's a time capsule from an ancient civilization. I'll tell you everything . . . just please take that gag out of Roula's mouth.

Spencer and Roula spent the next half hour telling Detton about the time capsule. He explained what it was and how it worked. The only part he left out was the master computer's ability to read their minds and convert their language and he made no mention of Nala or Roula's connection to her.

"So where are these cylinders now?" Detton asked.

"They are in a secret location . . . safe." He rubbed at the dried blood on his fingers. "I'll need twenty-four hours to retrieve them."

"No, what you'll need to do is tell me where they are."

"You can send one of your agents with me."

Detton scratched at his day-old beard but said nothing. "Just tell me where they're at, Spencer."

"Sir, even if you found them, you wouldn't know what to do with them. They're all encoded in hieroglyphics. Roula and I will have them ready for you in twenty-four hours. Without us, you'll spend years trying to figure them out . . . Send ten agents with us . . . I don't care."

Detton paced the floor. He gave the stubble on his beard another indecisive scratch.

"You can check with Antonio and he will confirm everything I've told you." Twenty-four hours was how much time he and Roula needed to re-number the cylinders. The tag-along agents could be dealt with.

"All right." He turned to the two agents on his left. "Take him wherever he needs to go to get cleaned up. Then get those cylinders."

"Yes, sir," one of the men said.

"And don't let these two out of your sight for a minute."

He and Roula would hang on to the cylinder that explained the workings of the master computer, the mind reading, and language conversion. If he were lucky, he would also get enough time to secretly contact Paul.

"Very well, Spencer," Detton said. "You have twenty-four hours, but if you even try to escape or trick us in any way, we will kill you on sight. These men and at least a dozen others will be watching your every move."

Spencer swallowed and nodded.

"Let these two out." Detton shouted, "And get me Antonio Casenza."

Spencer had the agents drive them back to the FOU. Ironically, it was the only place he'd be able to get a secure phone line, at least for now. It wouldn't take the CIA long to cover that base. He swung open the door and Roula went inside. The two agents went to follow her. "Gentleman," Spencer said. "Are you going to watch the lady shower and dress?" He looked into the eyes of one agent and then the other. "How much trouble can we get into in a CIA vehicle?"

One of the agents nodded to the other. "Okay," he said. "We'll be right here."

Spencer made a quick call to Paul's cell phone.

"I've got great news," Paul said. "The coffee shop has reopened,"

"That's all I needed to know," Spencer said. "Sorry, buddy, but I can't say anything more right now."

"Not a problem," Paul said. "See you soon?"

"Yep, soon."

He called McPearson's cell phone. "Bill," he said. "Don't say anything. You need to fly back to San Francisco right away."

"But—"

"Listen to me. The CIA's forgotten about you for the moment, but the situation could change in the blink of an eye." There was no sense in compromising Bill's safety any further. "Please . . ."

"Okay, I'll be on the next flight."

"Good, I'll see you back in San Francisco soon. He hung up and made his final call.

By three the next afternoon Spencer and Roula had all the cylinders renumbered and lined up in two suitcases provided by the CIA. They had done it all right under the noses of the agents, who only knew that Roula needed to translate the hieroglyphics.

"Gentleman," Spencer said. "We're ready."

The two men lifted the cases gingerly, carried them out to the sedan, and laid them in the trunk. Spencer and Roula slid into the back seats. They drove in silence to the Cairo Marriott where Antonio had arranged for them all to meet up so Spencer could turn over the master computer and cylinders to the CIA.

They pulled up in front of the hotel and the one of the agents flashed his badge at the bellman. "We'll handle our own luggage," he said.

The bellman nodded and backed away.

Spencer and Roula walked through large double doors with the two agents behind them. Detton, Antonio, Steve, and a handful of agents stood in a semi-circle in the lobby.

"Ah," Antonio said, "Here we are." He reached out and shook Spencer's hand then kissed Roula on one cheek and then the other. "I've got a nice private room for us," he said with a wink at Spencer. "This way . . ."

They walked down a short hallway, then down an escalator to the convention center. "Here we are," Antonio said.

Detton reached for the door.

"Ladies first, don't you think?" Antonio said to him.

Detton nodded and gestured for Roula to step forward. Spencer fell in behind her. Detton pulled the door open and Spencer and Roula stepped into a firestorm of flashing light. Questions were shouted at them from every corner of the room and dozens of microphones came at them.

"What the hell is this," Detton sputtered.

"Oh, Tom, I'm sorry," Antonio said with a slap to Detton's back. "Did I forget to tell you that I had invited a few of my friends from the press to our little meeting?"

"This is an outrage . . . You'll all be sorry . . ."

Detton's voice was soon drowned out by the cacophony of questions.

"Please, everyone, be seated. Mr. Spencer and Ms. Grazulis will be happy to answer your questions." Paul stood on the podium and smiled at the audience. He held his hands up and gestured for people to settle down.

Spencer took the suitcases from the two mute agents and together he and Roula made their way to the podium.

"I've never seen so many reporters in my life" Roula laughed.

"No kidding . . . they seem to multiply like rabbits. I know this is the biggest news in all of human history, but how will we ever get any work done now?"

They walked hand-in-hand onto the platform. "I know you have a lot of questions," Spencer said. "But I think I know someone who can answer them better than we can." He opened one of the cases and placed it on a table. He loaded one of the cylinders into the master computer. When Neflani appeared the reporters gasped in unison. Spencer turned to Roula. She was beaming. Phamuria would never be forgotten.

CHAPTER

TWENTY-ONE

Later in the day Spencer and Roula met in quiet quarters with reporters from CNN and the BBC along with a panel of renowned scientists that Paul had contacted for him in case there was any question as to authenticity. By that evening the footage of Neflani's appearance had been broadcast all over the world.

Early the next morning Tom Detton was waiting for them in the hotel lobby.

The CIA had taken the master computer and the cylinders the moment the last press conference ended. They would have no choice but to deal with the press now. It would be just another hassle for them. And the CIA knew how to deal with hassles.

"Well played, Spencer," Detton said in a failed attempt to be gracious. "But you're not out of the woods yet. Do you realize how many American institutions you've turned upside down yesterday? Religion . . . science . . . the theory of evolution . . . God only knows what'll happen now."

"Whatever it is, it's the right thing," Roula said, "because it's the truth. And everyone deserves to know the truth."

"Well, I guess you've won for now." Detton cleared his throat and shuffled his feet. "I've been instructed to bring the two of you on as . . . uh . . . consultants," Detton said.

"Instructed by whom," Antonio asked.

"The . . . uh . . . president."

"The president of the United States?" Spencer asked.

"Um . . . yeah." Detton tugged at his collar. "I suppose you could be of use to us anyway."

Antonio slapped Spencer on the back. "Good work, my boy."

"Of course," Detton said with his first genuine smile, "After seeing the way you handled Abdul, I could probably even make an agent out of you."

Spencer's face flushed. "You saw that?"

We recorded everything." Detton shrugged. "It took us a while to figure out where Abdul went . . ." he leaned in, "and why he didn't come back." He looked from Antonio to Roula and then back to Spencer. "Don't worry," he said with a laugh. "We'll leave it to the Egyptian government to find Abdul. They'll just be looking for a really, really long time."

"Thank you, we appreciate that," Roula said, her face brightening.

"Welcome to the CIA, Spencer. You too, Roula." He shook both their hands. "Now, we're going to fly everything back to Langley where it belongs."

Detton walked away with an entourage of agents trailing behind him. Spencer breathed a sigh of relief. He turned to Roula and smiled. He would spend the rest of his life with the woman he loved working on the greatest archeological find of all time. He was the luckiest man in the world. "Will you excuse me a moment?" he said.

Antonio and Roula nodded. He stepped into a quiet alcove and phoned Paul. "So what do you think?" he asked.

"This has been the greatest adventure of my life," Paul answered. "Thanks, man."

"You saved my life, Paul, I'll always be grateful for everything you've done for me." He lowered his voice. "What I'd like to know, though, is whether or not you found the encoded plans for building the master computer that I put on that memory stick.

"What?"

"You'll be rich, Paul."

"Well, hot damn. I don't know how to thank you, Spencer. I can hardly believe everything we've been through, and now I'm somehow going to profit from this futuristic . . . I mean ancient computer technology? Thanks, man."

"Forget it! I owe you."

Spencer patted his jacket pocket, reassuring himself that cylinder number thirty-four was still there. After Paul had a chance to build a new master computer, they would be able to view it free from the probing eyes of the CIA. Then they would work on the map and instructions for finding whatever was hidden under the Great Pyramid. In the meantime, as consultants for the CIA, they could have input on the project, and, if everything worked in their favor, Roula might even get to see Samir again.

By morning the time capsule had been removed without a trace and Calpetro's Egyptian project was closed down for good. Spencer and Roula flew back to San Francisco together and met with McPearson. They filled him in on everything that had happened. McPearson smiled over his steaming mug of hot coffee.

"I knew it was the only way to assure all of our continued safety. I think the people of our time deserve to know about the people of Phamuria. We can learn a lot from them. I don't believe it's right to hide this discovery. And . . ." He paused, smiling at McPearson, "if we all eventually become incredibly rich and famous because of it, well, we'll just have to try to hold up under the burden."

Bill laced his fingers across his belly and laughed. "Spencer, you really are one of a kind."

"Don't be offended, Bill. But Roula and I are going to leave you now. I've barely had the woman alone for a moment in weeks and I have every intention of taking her out on the town tonight."

Bill winked at Spencer. "You bet."

Spencer took Roula to one of San Francisco's most famous restaurants. There was a string quartet playing near their table and they could smell the sea air through an open window. Spencer took a small box out of his pocket and held Roula's hand.

"Roula, you know I'm not very good with words. I, that is . . . you . . ." Spencer gave up and simply opened the box in the candlelight. Roula looked a little confused, but as the box opened and the candlelight danced off the beautiful Egyptian diamond ring, her eyes sparkled with tears.

"Yes, Ralph," she whispered.

"What do you think, sweetheart? After we're on The Tonight Show and Today this week, should we say yes to those teaching jobs at Columbia?"

"What? And quit archeology? Never! Just tell them that we'll show up and give lectures from time to time. Honestly, I think we have enough talk shows and university lectures booked right now to keep us busy for a lifetime." She wrapped her arms around his neck and the people at the surrounding tables applauded. Roula flashed the ring around the room.

"Congratulations, honey," a woman at the next table said.

Spencer reached into an inside pocket of his jacket and pulled out another box. "I have one more gift for you," he said.

"What could be better than this," she said, fingering the glittering diamond on her finger.

He handed her a small, blue unwrapped box. "Open it."

She lifted the lid and sitting inside, on a black velvet bed, sat a shimmering green-gold orb. "Oh my God," she said. "It's Nala's sensor."

"Yes it is. I've been waiting for the right time to give it to you. This seemed like the right time."

"It's beautiful," she uttered. "I'll cherish it."

"I knew you would."

Her eyes shimmered with tears of happiness. "This is the best night of my life."

"Mine, too."

The waiter arrived with a huge platter of steaming Dungeness crab legs, prawns, and mussels. Roula forked a prawn, blew on it a few times, and then popped it in her mouth. "Ralph, do you think the CIA will ever find out that we have those other cylinders?"

"I doubt it." He cracked open a crab leg. "I suppose it's possible that someone may suspect something. But they're going to have their hands full just trying to catch up with Phamurian science and technology, not to mention dealing with the press and the world's thirst for answers. That's enough to keep even the CIA busy."

She followed his lead and cracked a crab leg. "Darling, I know that we have a lot to do, what with all this publicity. Not to mention that we have a wedding to plan, but do you think . . . that is . . ."

"What is it, Roula?"

"Do you think that we might have our honeymoon in Egypt?"

Spencer laughed hard and long.

"It's just that I was remembering what Neflani said about cylinder thirty-four and the tunnel that's under the Great Pyramid."

"Nothing would please me more than going to Egypt for our honeymoon." He looked into Roula's brown eyes and smiled. She smiled back and, for the briefest moment, her eyes flashed a twinkle of blue. Roula was his perfect partner. There was no one who understood his love of archeology better than Roula. She was probably intellectually far superior to him, what with her own knowledge combined with Nala's. He gazed across the table at her and smiled. Had this amazing woman really just agreed to spend the rest of her life with him?

Over the weeks that followed, Spencer and Roula planned their wedding, opened a Swiss bank account, bought an apartment in Cairo and, it seemed to them, spoke on every talk show and at every university under the sun. Before they flew to Egypt for their honeymoon, Bill McPearson had insisted on meeting them for lunch.

"How's the happy couple?" he asked, looking at them and not needing an answer. "Listen Spencer . . . I have some news. I can't tell you what a boon you've been to Calpetro. I understand you want to move on in life and continue with archeology, of course. I feel like I, well, I feel like I kind of owe you . . . so I took the liberty of having a word with the Egyptian government.

"What on earth are you talking about, Bill?" Spencer asked. "You don't owe me a thing. You helped me follow my dream."

"Nonetheless, Calpetro is better off because of your efforts, and so is Egypt. They're so thrilled with their tourism numbers, they can hardly see straight. And, I guess I have to admit that I've never been better off myself." He said all this with a gleam in his eye. "You're a great friend. It was the least I could do."

"What is it exactly that you did, Bill?" Roula laughed.

"Well you've got two weeks to live it up, love birds, then it's back to the grindstone."

"What do you mean?" Spencer asked.

"You're expected at a new dig." Bill smiled. "You're expected at the Great Pyramid."

THE END

www.ingramcontent.com/pod-product-compliance
Lightning Source LLC
LaVergne TN
LVHW091034080826
845145LV00002B/488

9780578033310